The Bonding

By: Tamara Ely

iUniverse, Inc.
New York Bloomington

This is a work of fiction. All of the characters, names, incidents, organizations, and dialogue in this novel are either the products of the author's imagination or are used fictitiously.

iUniverse books may be ordered through booksellers or by contacting:
iUniverse
1663 Liberty Drive
Bloomington, IN 47403
www.iuniverse.com
1-800-Authors (1-800-288-4677)

ISBN: 978-1-4401-4568-1 (sc)
ISBN: 978-1-4401-4569-8 (ebook)

Printed in the United States of America

iUniverse rev. date: 6/10/2009

1

Sam was in her bedroom working on her final art project for the semester. She knew she had the whole week of Thanksgiving break to do it in, but liked getting work done first even though she still had two more years of college left. It was about six thirty at night when she heard a knock on the door.

"Come in." She said.

It was Devin, the guy she met at The Lighthouse dance club in White Cove a few weeks ago. Although she was taken by how cute he was. Tall and skinny with soft brown eyes, nice smile, and shoulder length reddish-brown hair, which he wore in a ponytail. Had she known what was to follow that evening she would never have said yes to the date.

He waited until she was done with her project before they left. Even though she was nerves she just blew it off. First they went to some of her friend's house. By the time they got to Christine and Maria's house she was so upset cause she had asked Devin several times to stop touching her, but he didn't.

Pulling Christine aside. "I don't know what to do. I've asked him to leave me alone, but he won't. He's making me uneasy and scared. Could you talk to him?"

"Sure, don't worry about it. If your not comfortable then just have him take you home, but I'll talk to him."

"Thanks Christine, I owe you." Heading back to the living room.

Christine took Devin to the kitchen to talk to him. When they came back everything was fine for awhile. They left around nine and headed to his friend's house in Bloomfield.

The neighborhood was nice. Filled with $300,000.00 houses. They pulled up to a stone two story. The landscape was beautiful. Flowers along the drive, shrubs by the door, and a white archway at the sidewalk leading to the door. As they entered, the house looked bigger inside than the outside. All Hardwood floors and white walls with little lights that looked like candles everywhere to give the house a soft, warm feel.

Devin introduced Sam to three other couples who seemed nice. They watched some movies for a few hours. As the night went on Sam grew tired and asked Devin to take her home, so they said their good-byes and left.

The car ride was quiet. Sam and Devin didn't talk much they just listened to music. As they rounded the corner to go into the sub Sam noticed that her parents weren't home yet. Devin didn't know that though, because they shared their space with four other houses and her mom left the lights on. She was still nerves because of earlier, so she just wanted to go to sleep. Devin parked the car, turned down the radio and asked if she had a good time.

"Yes, I had a good time tonight, but I'm tired, sick, and just want to go to bed."

"Well I'm glad you had a good time and hope you feel better."

He leaned over to kiss her, but she told him she didn't want him to get sick. He said he had a great immune system. Then locked the doors.

"What are you doing? Let me out!"

"All I want is a kiss."

"Well you're not getting one!" Sam said as she struggled with the handle. He grabbed her arms, pulling her away from the door. She tried to move away, but he was too strong. Closer and closer he dragged her to him. Sam was so frightened inside and angry that she turned herself so she could knee him, but was to slow. He put one leg over hers. She heard the sound of shattering glass. It was Mike from across the street. He unlocked the door and got Sam out, but before he could do anything else Devin sped off. Mike helped her in the house and stayed until her parents got home.

The next week was a blur until her birthday came that Saturday. Sam picked up her friends Nichole and Sam in Heart Court so they could celebrate Sam's twenty-first birthday. First at the movies and then at The Lighthouse.

Shit, Devin was coming up the stairs. She didn't think he would be here tonight. Sam hurried to the snacks and lucky for her he didn't see her yet, but he was looking. Everyone kept her hidden and Christine told him to leave Sam alone and that she didn't want to see him again.

The guys Christine invited, from her graphics class, showed up next. One reminded her of a big teddy bear his name was John. He was about 6'3" with short brown hair and was intimidating. Next to him were two other guys, Daniel who was the shortest with short dark brown hair and eyes and Christian who was of medium height and build with reddish-brown hair and brown eyes. They were both cute, but Sam was instantly attracted to Christian so she kept her eye on him. The group was all over in the game room talking when Devin came stalking over from the dance floor. He grabbed Sam's arm, and pulled her over to one of the dark corners on the dance floor.

"What the hell is going on?" He snapped.

"What are you talking about?" Sam squirmed.

"Who are those guys and why have you been hiding from me?"

"They are friend's of Christine and I haven't been hiding I'm ignoring you. And for your info we are not a couple, we had one date and it didn't work. You scare me and I can't deal with that so leave me alone." Sam turned to walk away, but Devin shackled her wrist and pulled her back. Her heart started to accelerate. Then Mike came up to them.

"Is there a problem Sam?"

"Yes, he doesn't know the meaning of the word NO. And won't leave me alone."

Mike grabbed her wrist from Devin and pulled her away from him. "Go sit with Christine. Devin and I will have a little talk." She was scared, but went over to Christine who told her that Mike saw the whole thing and would take care of it. A few minutes later Mike came back saying Devin will not bother anyone again. She hoped he was right, but had a feeling that she hadn't seen the last of him. Devin's not the type of guy to just leave something once he sees what he wants.

Sam told Christine she would be right back because she had forgotten her camera. Devin had left hours ago so she thought it would be safe to go to her car for the camera, she was wrong. *You won't get away from me so easily,* she heard in her head. Sam looked around the parking lot, but didn't see anything wishing she'd parked closer. As she rounded the back of the building someone grabbed her and pushed her to the wall.

"You think you are too good to be with me? Soon you will learn respect." Devin spat as he pulled her towards his van.

"What are you doing? I never said that. Let me go Devin!" She said as she fought. She was about to yell when he put his hand over her mouth. She bit down hard, which just angered him more. He slapped her so hard she saw stars. *Do it again and I'll knock you out.* She stopped fighting. "What do you want with me?"

"Your special, you have certain gifts I could use." He said with a wicked smile.

"What are you talking about. I don't have any special gifts."

"Your aura says otherwise. Now get in the van we are going for a ride." He loosened his grip on her arms enough for her to turn and kick him between the legs. She brought up her knee and hit him in the head. He fell to the ground. She turned to run, but his left hand snaked out and grabbed her leg, causing her to fall to the ground hard hitting her head on a rock. Everything went black. *What is wrong? I feel your pain and fear,* the mental path was different from the one Devin used. She didn't know who this was, but figured maybe he could help. As she came to she sent her message. *I need help. I'm outside The Lighthouse and someone is trying to abduct me.*

I'll be there in a minute Sam. Don't worry I'm almost to the door.

Thank you. Who is this?

This is Christian. We just met in the Lighthouse. I'm almost there, relief swept through her. She just laid there waiting for her head to stop spinning. Glancing to her left she saw Devin getting back on his feet advancing towards her. Sam tried to move, but started to get sick. Devin grabbed a hand full of hair pulling hard enough to bring tears to her eyes.

"Get up!" He said in a low tone. She did her best to move as he was pulling her to stand. "You will pay for that."

"Screw you!" She said not caring anymore how much he hurt her, she wasn't going with him. *I'm here. Try to move to the right. I will be at his left.*

"Is there a problem here." Christian stood tall in front of Devin. "Let her go."

"This is none of your business, leave us." Devin stated angrily as he let go of her hair, but retained her arm.

"It is if your hurting her. Let her go." He stated again, seeing Daniel and John come out from the other side of the building.

I'll let you go for now, but I'll be back, she heard Devin say as he pushed her towards Christian, then hopped in his van and took off.

"Are you O.K.?" Christian asked with concern as he looked at her head. "We need to get you to a hospital you could have a concussion."

"I'll be fine, just take me back inside. I just need to sit down and get some ice." She said wearily. He helped her back inside and got her some ice. Christine and Shelby came running over to her.

"What the hell happened?" Shelby asked.

"Devin's what happened. He was waiting for me when I went to get the camera." She told them as Christian came over with ice.

"You need to call Lisa to you." Christine whispered.

"I'll be fine. Besides she's out having fun too and I don't want to ruin it for her."

"If you don't and your mother finds out."

"Okay you have a point." Sam confirmed. *Lisa are you close I have need of your healing.*

I'm almost home. What did you do now?

Just get here and I'll explain. "She's on her way. Happy now?'

"Yes, stubborn. I'll get you some juice." Christine replied smiling before walking away.

Lisa showed up five minutes later with Sam's juice. "What happened?" Asking as she handed Sam her juice.

"Devin wouldn't take no for a answer so he thought he'd force me instead. He knows about me Lisa." Sam said as she took a sip.

"We'll get through this like we always do." She asked Christian. "Who are you?"

"Lisa this is Christian. He and his friend's Daniel and John helped me." Sam told her. *Its okay he is telepathic and I believe they can be trusted.*

"Well in that case does Christine have the room ready?" Inquiring as she carefully helped Sam to stand.

"If you want to help me with her that would be great." Looking at Christian.

"Sure, What should I do?"

"Just help her to the room over there and make sure she stays awake." Going to get candles and incense.

"OK." He helped Sam walk to the room, then let her lie down on the couch. *Are you alright.? What is she going to do to you?*

I'll be fine soon. Lisa is my sister and is able to heal.

And what is it that you can do that Devin wants so badly?

She sat up slowly taking another sip of juice, *I have several abilities. I can see the past and future through premonitions and touching objects. I'm telepathic like you and can also move things, but that's it and only my friends know.*

I won't tell. Can your sister heal you completely? She's telepathic too isn't she?

"Yes, but just talks to me. We get it from our mother." Sam stated as she laid back down.

Lisa came in with candles and incense and started to light them, "You can go now. I will heal her, then call you back in." Lisa said.

"I would prefer to stay with her if its okay with both of you."

"Fine, but I need complete silence." Lisa went to the job of healing as the heat from her hand went into Sam's head to stop the swelling and fix the crack in her skull. It took her forty-five minutes before she was done.

"She will be fine and I'm going home." Telling Christian. "Will you be alright?" She asked Sam.

"I'll be fine. Go get some rest and thank you." She kissed Sam on the cheek then left. Sam closed her eyes to rested for awhile.

Sam awoke alone, deciding to go look for everyone she went to the dance floor. It was really loud in the club, but she spotted Shelby by the drink station talking to Daniel. As she approached them, she heard Devin again, *They can't protect you. I will get you by any means necessary. You will be mine soon,* she went to her knees from the pain in her head. Devin's way of showing her he meant what he said. Sam felt warmth as the pain receded and strong arms came around her to help her up. Turning she saw Christian there with a grim look on his face. She was so relieved she laid her head on his chest trying to relax.

"He was talking to you again wasn't he?"

"Yes. He said I was his and none of you could protect me. Then he sent the pain as a warning."

"Don't worry I'll protect you. He will never have you, I promise." Walking her to the drink station.

Christine came running up to them. "Hey Sam, Tony wants to see you up in the DJ booth. Said he needs to ask you a question."

"I'll be right back." Walking cautiously to the DJ booth. All the sudden she felt danger in the air. She looked for Devin, but didn't see him. *Do you feel that?* She asked Christian.

It is nothing just feeling an emotion I haven't felt before. I will try to control it.

What emotion? Jealousy? We just met why would you have it? She asked heading up stairs.

"Hey Tony, what's up?"

"Hey girl. What was going on down there? You okay?"

"Yeah, just a guy who doesn't like NO. I'm fine."

"Who's the group down there?"

"Friend's of Christine from school."

"Well the one seems a little more than friendly towards you. Hon, just be careful and if you need me I'm here."

"Thanks Tony. I can handle it." Hugging him then headed back down stairs. Sam danced the night away with her friends, having a great time. Closing time came to fast, but she was tired and needed rest.

Christian walked her to her car. "I'm glad I met you. Can I see you again?"

"Sure, here's my number." Handing him a piece of paper. He took it, then leaned in for a kiss. As their lips touched a jolt went right through her. She'd never felt like that before and wished for it to never end. When he pulled away she felt the lose. He closed the door to her car and waved as she drove off.

"So what are you thinking? Another conquest?" John asked from behind.

"No, not this time." And with that got in John's van. This time would change everything for him. She was the one and he would do anything to keep her.

2

The next week seemed to fly by. Sam did her usual things like going to school, working, and babysitting for the lady down the street. Her and Christian talked on the phone almost every day and passed notes through Christine. They agreed to see each other at the Lighthouse on Friday and Saturday night.

When the weekend came Sam was so excited. She went and picked up her best friend Shelby and they headed to Christine and Maria's house before they all went to the Lighthouse that night. They still had two hours before the club opened so Christine and Sam made a fast food run.

The night was cool and crisp as fresh snow coated the ground. The sky was so clear you could see all the stars and the full moon. As they entered the restaurant Sam felt a feeling of dread come over her. Her chest got tight and she was having problems getting air into her lungs. She looked around to assure herself that there was no one causing this. She sat down at a table, closed her eyes, and focused on relaxing her chest and letting air into her lungs. It took ten minutes for the feeling to go away, then she was fine. That was her lovely warning system. It was letting her know something bad was going to happen tonight. She told

Christine to just be prepared for possible trouble. They got the food and went back to Christine's house.

When they pulled into the drive Sam noticed Lisa's car was there. Walking in her and Lisa's eyes met. "Don't say it. I already know. Is that why you're here?"

"No, Mike asked if I wanted to go with him to the Lighthouse and I thought why not. So here I am. He's in the living room."

"Well I'm glad you came. Are you hungry? I'll split my dinner with you."

"Sure, I haven't ate since lunch. Oh mom said her and dad had a party to go to and not to wait up. I told her ok, but wasn't when we'd be home anyway. She said to just be careful and have fun."

"She's in a good mood, cool!" Sam add as she handed Lisa fries and nuggets to split. Everyone started coming to the dinning room for their food. Christine and Maris's family was always welcoming and fun. They lived in a old farm white house with three bedrooms, one bath, and had several friendly ghosts. A old man they called Monty and his cat boots. He liked to play jokes on you, but never caused any harm. Sam always felt comfy there, even when she spent the night.

After they all ate they started getting ready to go to the Lighthouse. Doing their hair and touching up their makeup. Shelby and Christine climbed into Sam's car while Maria and Mike rode with Lisa. As they pulled into the parking lot they noticed how unusually busy it was, but it was the weekend before Christmas. They parked close to the front door.

It was nice and warm inside with the music blasting. They went up the stairs to the dance club. It was crowded, dark, and smoke filled as usual. They headed to the game room to see who all was there. That's where they all started out and then went their own way.

"Hey I'll be right back. I want to say hi to Tony or he'll get mad at me." Sam said walking away. She squeezed her way through the crowd to the other side of the room. Headed up the stairs and stopped abruptly.

"Hello Sam and where are you going in such a hurry?" Mark asked

"Away from you. I'm going to say hi to Tony."

"Well don't let me stop you."

"Move than. I don't feel like fighting with you."

"Promise me a dance and I'll move."

"Why?" Getting ticked.

"Cause that was one thing I enjoyed with you. Come on. I'm asking nicely and I'll try not to be an ass to you tonight." Mark pleaded.

"Oh one night of you being nice, what a shock. Okay one dance, that's it."

"OK, you may go." Moving out of her way.

"Thank you." Sam headed to the booth and gave Tony a big hug as she watched Mark go down stairs.

"Hey honey, glad to see you. What's the plan for tonight?"

"Nothing much, just hanging out here. Anything special for tonight?" Sam asked

"Nothing big. CJ's just going to pass out Santa hats later, but all the big stuff will be next week."

"Cool, I'll be here next week with Lisa. She's here tonight. Spur of the moment."

"Tell her to come say hi later."

"I will Tony, I should get back. See ya later." She waved as she headed down stairs.

Everyone was in good spirits. The girls pushed there way to the stage to dance. The next song Tony played was *Da'butt*, which was one of their favorites. They formed a line as the music started. Swaying their hips, doing all the dance steps required. Sam was finally enjoying herself.

❧

Outside a van pulled into the parking lot. "I don't have a good feeling about tonight so just keep alert. Something is coming." Christian told them as he closed the van door. They walked into the club and had to turn down the volume because of the blaring music. Reaching the entrance to the second floor Christian's breath caught in his lungs as he watched Sam dancing on stage. Her blond hair moving around her as she turned in a circle. The white tank, with short black jacket and tight black jeans formed to her figure perfectly. He couldn't take his eye's off her as Daniel and John pushed him over towards the game room.

"Calm your emotions or she'll run." John said. Christian gave him a death look that said fuck off. John just shrugged and started watching the girls.

As the music changed to a slow song, the girls started walking off the stage. Sam reached the bottom step in time to have Mark take her hand. "Dance with me. You promised, to our song." His eyes made promises he never kept.

"Fine. One dance that's it."

"I promise, let's go over towards the window since there's more room there." He led her over there. Putting his hands on her hips he pulled her against his body. She put her arms around his neck and made the mistake of looking in his eyes. She was lost.

Passing Christian to go into the game room. Lisa felt the air vibrate with menace. She turned to look at him, then followed his gaze to see Sam dancing with Mark. Lisa tried telepathy, but received pain in response. John came to her add.

"Damn it." She said holding her head.

"What's wrong?" John asked with concern.

"Nothing. Mark's just pulling his shit again. Shelby, Sam doesn't have her amulet on again. Is it in the car?"

"It might be. Why?"

"Its Mark again. Look." Lisa pointed to the corner where they were dancing.

"Shit and he put a shield around them didn't he?"

"Yes, I'll go get her amulet and you try to figure out how to get it on her." Heading to the car.

"What is going on?" Christian bit out to Shelby.

"Mark has put a shield over them so he can have her for himself. Sam is his ex and this is one reason she broke up with him." She stole a glance before continuing. "Sam wears a amulet that stops him from this, but sometimes forgets to put it on. Now we have to figure out how to get it on her though the shield."

"I will get it on her."

"No, the spell is specified especially for males. To keep them away. We will take care of it like we have before." Shelby stood at the stairs waiting for Lisa to return.

Christian continued to watch Mark and Sam as his blood boiled.

Mark turned his head and smiled, then turned back to Sam and leaned closer towards her mouth. That was it he'd reached his limit of patients. He started to walk over there, but John stopped him. "You have to let them do this. They know what they're doing."

"You don't understand I can't allow this. My soul won't allow this. She is not like the rest. I need her, to survive the darkness in me."

"Alright. Give Lisa a chance, then we'll intervene."

"Fine!" This was killing him. She was his. His heart, mind, and soul called to her. He draw back into the shadows, watching.

Mark leaned closer to her mouth. Sam felt the electricity as their lips met. His tongue dueled with hers. The only thing was that Mark would soon have a very shocking surprise. The heat increased rapidly, he watched as her eyes go from brownish-green to dark green. He didn't have time to react, he knew he was in trouble. Pulling away he felt his skin burning. She looked at him and smiled.

"I may not be well versed in magic, but because of you I'm learning fast. Last warning. LEAVE ME ALONE." Sam said in a low voice. "Or you will wish you'd never touched me." She walked away as Lisa came up the stairs with her amulet. Mark decided to leave, for now.

"Are you alright?" Lisa questioned handing her the amulet. "What happened?"

"Remember how mom was yelling at me for burning candles? Well I found a protection spell and used it against him, but I had to make him think he was in control."

"Well it worked. He left and I guess you don't need the amulet anymore."

"Oh I'll still wear it, better safe then sorry." She put it on. It was a silver dragon with emerald eyes and a tiger eye in its claws and she loved it. Sitting down on one of the couches next to Christian, he put his arm around her and pulled her close. She felt a sense of security.

"Your eyes are dark green. I thought they were brown." As he stared at them a minute longer before they changed back. Sam laid her head on his chest and closed her eyes.

"Sam's eyes are a mix of both, but go to green when she gets mad or her emotions run high." Lisa explained. *Are you sure your alright? Do you want some juice?*

Yes, I'm fine just drained and yes juice would help. Thank you sis, Lisa left to get her juice.

Eric Clapton's *Wonderful Tonight* came on and Daniel grabbed Shelby while John grabbed Lisa and headed for the stage to dance. Christian stood looking down at Sam with his chocolate colored eyes.

"May I have this dance?" Holding out his hand.

"I would love too." Taking his hand to walk to the dance floor. Sam actually took a good look at him for the first time since they met. He was tall and masculine with reddish brown hair that hung around his shoulders. He had the nicest brown eyes that had gold flax in them. Mysterious and powerful, yet sincere and gentle towards her.

He held her close as she let the music take her away. She felt protected, cherished like she was meant to be with him. Never experiencing this before it was a little frightening, but exciting also.

Christian's voice invaded her thoughts, *Are you okay? You've gone quiet again.*

Opening her eyes she answered, *I'm just having happy thoughts. I'm glad you came tonight.*

I'm glad too. You are so beautiful and your skin is so soft. I was really worried about you earlier.

Oh my god how long had you been there?

During the whole thing and I don't want you to ever do anything like that again. Promise me.

I'm sorry I didn't mean to worry you, but if I hadn't done that he would have kept trying to get me.

What do you mean by trying to get you?

See, the one thing Mark wants from me more then anything else is sex. Every girl he's been with has given it to him but me. I'm saving myself for that special someone, if you know what I mean. Anyway he sees me as a challenge.

I understand and I'm glad to hear that.

Oh, you think your that special someone.

I know I am, he answered with confidents.

We will see, as she laid her head on his chest while they finished the dance.

The night was beautiful. Everyone was having a good time. At eleven CJ started passing out the Santa hats. Sam grabbed one put it on and ran over to Christian. "Do you want a hat?"

"No. I'm not wearing one of those things."

"Party pooper." She headed back to the stage to dance some more. Sam was so happy that everyone was together with new friends and the most impressive guy she'd ever met was with her.

"Well, what do you think? Is she worth your struggle?" Daniel asked Christian as they headed to play Mortal Kombat.

"You know she is. She's the one I've been looking for for so long." He answered putting two quarters in the machine and started playing.

"You can't wait too long to claim her."

"Don't you think I know that I won't push her though. She has to come to me of her own free will."

"Fine, don't say I didn't warning you if you loose your soul."

"Screw you Daniel. Go dance with Shelby or something and leave me alone." He said grimly as he continued to play his game.

Sam came running up to him "Hey are you busy tomorrow around four?"

"No, why?"

"Well Lisa, Shelby, and I were going to go to a movie then dinner before coming here tomorrow night. We were just wondering if you guys wanted to join us."

"Sure, where should we meet?"

"Everyone's meeting at mine and Lisa's house. Do you need directions. We live in the sub. off eight mile beyond the tracks. 1512 Armstrong is the address. It's a white colonial. You can't miss it my dad over did the Christmas lights."

"I think we'll find it. Are you having fun?"

"Yes, this has turned out to be a wonderful night. Are you?"

"As long as you're here I will." Kissing her cheek. The rest of the night was very uneventful, which was fine with everyone.

Saturday Sam worked at Ziti's until three, then went home to wash off the smell of pizza from her hair and skin. Lisa burst into the bathroom. "Hey have you seen my white angora sweater? I can't find it."

"I think its in the laundry room. Mom just picked up the dry cleaning and hung it all there."

"Thanks. Its almost four you'd better hurry. Shelby is already here."

"I will. Can you pull out my blue silk shirt, black tank, and jeans and put them on my bed." Sam asked as she stepped out of the shower.

"Sure, but hurry the guys should be here soon." Lisa said quickly shut the door. Since she was running late Sam used her telekinesis to help with makeup and hair. Shelby knocked on the door. "Come in."

As she came in she almost ran into the floating brush while trying to get to the mirror. "I don't think I'll ever get use to you doing that." She said checking her eyeliner and lip stick.

"To bad It's natural to me to use it when necessary, you know that."

"I know. You'd better hurry the guys will be here any minute."

We are already here, beautiful. Are you ready? Sam heard Christian in her mind. Her heart skipped a beat then accelerated with excitement, *I just have to get dressed then I'll be out.*

Just like a woman to be late. I'll be waiting.

Sam smiled, "They're already here. Move so I can get dressed." Pushing Shelby out of her way. Shelby just shook her head as she finished her touchups.

Dressing fast Sam stopped Shelby outside her door. "Hey tonight I need all of the girls to meet in the back room at the Lighthouse. Since we are now dealing with both Devin and Mark I want to teach you some spells just in case. None of us are safe anymore and we need to protect ourselves. CJ said its alright don't worry."

"Okay I'll spread the word, now let's go. We've left them with your parents long enough."

When they entered the living room Sam's eyes lit up. Christian was standing by the couch all in black, Lisa was talking to John in the kitchen, and Shelby sat down on the couch next to Daniel. Sam started to walk over to him when her mother intervened *Sam I need to talk with you in my bedroom,* so Sam told him she'd be right back and followed her mother to the bedroom.

"What is it mom?"

"Lisa told me you had some trouble with Mark last week. Now I know you handled it, but I think its time to give you this." Handing Sam a gold cross with tiny crystals in it. "This was your grandmothers. She said to give it to you when the time was right, which it is. Your grandma was a white sorceress. They go back to the beginning of time. You have the natural ability of a sorceress just like your grandmother and she knew it. That's why she wanted you to have this and her spell book, which for now I have hid. I will give it to you and explain when you get back tonight. Now go and have fun." Her mother hugged her. Then they walked back to the living room.

Before her mother let her go she put the necklace on her. When the cross touched her chest she felt a jolt as her grandmother's essence go through her. Tears came to her eyes. She missed her so much, but now she felt closer then ever to her. *She will always be with you and can help if you have great need, even from beyond,* she heard her mother say.

"You guys should get going or you'll miss the movie." Their mom said.

They saw *Wolf* and ate dinner at Bennie's out in Ford city. Now they were at Christine's house to pick up everyone else before going to the Lighthouse since John's van was big enough.

The guys, including Mike, were in the living room. While the girls were in the dining room talking. All the sudden Sam got a pain in her head like someone was trying to invade her mind. She ran to the bathroom to be sick. Feeling warmth as the pain receded, strong arms helped her up. "I'm here beautiful, tell me what is wrong." As he held her to him taking the pain away.

"I don't know. I just got a pain in my head like someone was probing my mind."

"You need to learn how to put up barriers so no one can enter. I will teach you. Do you think you can face everyone now?"

"Yes, but I need to go outside for a minute. I'll be ok, just stay here. You can remain in my mind if you wish, but I have to do this alone." She told him feeling the strong need even though he was fighting his protective nature.

"I will remain a shadow in your mind and watch from the door." He stated grimly. watching her walk outside towards the woods.

She let her senses flare out trying to find any information that would give her the cause of her pain. The wind howled through the trees, the ground was snow covered, but when she looked out into the woods she saw foot prints. Sniffing the air brought a smell of Axe Phoenix colon. She knew of only one who wore it, Devin.

Turning to run back to the house she heard a lone wolf cry. She looked back towards the woods to see its eyes glowing eerily in the darkness. *Christian Help!* is all she got out before darkness took her.

Christian bolted out the door reaching her before she hit the ground. He carried her back inside and Christine had him lay her on her own bed. Lisa came upstairs to examine her. "She is in a dream state. We have to let her ride it out before she will come to."

"How long will this take?" He calmly asked. "Why is it happening?"

"It could take up to an hour. Its our bodies defense system against strong psychic attacks like this. I don't know what happened, but maybe we can get the answers when she awakes."

"I'll stay with her."

"Alright, if you need us we'll be down stairs." Lisa and Christine left.

Christian sat on the bed next to Sam. He just watched her dream. She was so precious to his race, a miracle to him. His soul mate. He'd searched for centuries for her and now she's here with him, but she's in danger. He must find a way to protect her and remove the danger.

In her dream state Sam saw a lot of white fog. Out of the fog came her grandmother. She ran to her and gave her a hug. "Oh grandma I'm so glad to see you. I've missed you and I don't understand what is happening right now."

"Don't worry, everything will be fine. You are of age to become a sorceress, but you will have to learn on your own."

"How?" Sam looked at her with tears in her eyes.

"With the things your mother will give you later and Christian's help."

"What do you mean with Christian's help? What does he have to do with all this?"

"Christian is part of a ancient race of people who were allies with the white sorcerers and sorceress a long time ago. We had to separate to keep both races safe, but we must ban together again to save the human race. Christian and his friends aren't here by coincidence, it was already written in the stars. He is also your soul mate. It will be hard to bring both races together again, but I know you two can do it."

"How long have you known all this?"

"Always, but you weren't ready to hear it, you are now. I must go. Call if you need me. I love you Sam."

"I love you too grandmother." She said in a tearful voice as she watched her walk back into the fog. Then Sam started to wake up.

Christian helped her sit up. "Are you alright? What happened?" Looking at her with worry in his big brown eyes.

"I'm ok now. Everything is so clear now and I know who you guys are, but you don't know me."

He looked at her with shock and puzzlement. "And what is it you think you know?"

"You are of an ancient race, yet I know not which one. You are my soul mate and our two races are suppose to unite again. Oh and your suppose to help me with my magic."

"Who told you all this?" He asked suspiciously.

"My grandmother told me in my dream." Trying to clear her head.

"What race are you?"

"White Sorceress. What race are you?" Still rubbing her head, "What are soul mates and why am I yours?"

For a minute he couldn't breath. Happiness flooded him. He hadn't heard that name for centuries, believing the sorceress where all dead and all the sorcerers believed to have turned evil. Of all the soul mates his was a white sorceress. Her voice brought him back to his senses.

"Christian what's wrong?"

"I'm fine. Your grandmother was right we are soul mates. I knew it when I first saw you. The powers that be put together souls before birth. I'm learning this as I go, but I have some friends and family who found their soul mates and are very happy. Especially since the darkness is gone. I am from a ancient race from Pyrenees mountains that run a border between Frances and Spain. "

"What darkness?" She asked looking up at him.

"The males have darkness in them. They fight to stay on the side of good, but as we get older its harder to fight. We use the elements of the earth, but power corrupts. So we have to find our soul mates to balance it or lose our souls. If we lose our souls we will use our powers for evil, then we are hunted down and destroyed to protect the human race."

"How awful, but I still don't get it. I still feel the darkness in you. How can I be yours than?"

"I haven't spoke the ritual words to bring our souls together. That is truly the only way we become one heart, mind, and soul."

"What if I'm not your salvation?"

"Only true soul mates recognizes each other. I knew you were in trouble, if I wasn't meant for you I won't have felt your fear and pain as if it were my own."

"This is all too confusing and I have a splitting headache. Can we talk about this later?" Sam inquired as she laid back on the bed. "When I'm thinking straight."

"Yes sweetheart, we will wait until later." He leaned down kissing her on the her head. *Lisa, Sam is awake and in pain please come and help,* hearing Lisa and Shelby running up the stairs.

Lisa sat down on the bed looking at her sister with fear in her eyes. "How were you able to talk to me telepathically?" Not looking at him.

"I used the path I saw in your sisters mind." He stated truthfully. "Can you take her headache away? I hate to see her in pain."

"Yes, Shelby get the candles and incense, Christian lay her head on you lap, Sam is there anything else that hurts or just your head?" Lisa made sure the window was cracked for fresh air. Shelby came running in with the candles as Christine stood in the door watching.

"My right hip hurts too, like I burned it."

"Let me look at it. Pull down your jeans." Sam revealed a crescent moon with three stars on the right of the moon. "What is that?" Lisa looked closer.

Christian glanced down at her hip and saw the symbol. "That's the mark of the White Sorceress."

"What is the White Sorceress?"

Christian did his best to explain so Sam didn't have to while her sister healed her.

"How are you feeling now? Better?" Lisa asked helping Sam sit up.

"Yes, thank you yet again."

"You owe me big time, sis. You keep this up and I'll start charging." She said with a smile as she helped Christine clean up while Shelby closed the window.

It was already ten at night when Sam went into the living room where everyone else was. "I'm sorry about all this. I hope I didn't ruin your night."

"There's no reason to apologize. You are fine and that's all we care about right now." John said moving from the chair so she could sit.

"Well since we are all here I need to tell you that we are not safe anymore and you will need protection from Mark and Devin. I will teach those of you who need to learn the spells. The others will consult with Christian on what to do. Tonight though since I'm not up to par I ask that Christian, John, and Daniel help to protect us for now. Now Mike before you get pissed I'll explain later, when we're at the Lighthouse, what is happening."

"You aren't going anywhere beautiful. You need to rest." Christian said in a low voice.

"Oh yes I am. I can't let them think they scared me. We do everything we always do just stay alert. Now let's get going."

Christian let out a low growl as Sam sashayed passed him. She turned and smiled. *Don't you growl at me you big grouch. Remember this before you say your ritual words, I do what I want when I want.*

We will see little one. Your safety will always come first, but we will find a middle ground if you wish.

I would like that, but let's get going I want to dance.

What am I going to do with you?

Just enjoy me the way I am, she laughed heading to John's van with the others.

Christian remained in the living room with Daniel and John, knowing what they were about to ask, he just answered first. "Yes, she knows and no I didn't tell her. She is from the White Sorceress. Her Grandmother came to her in her dream state and told her. She also knows I'm her soul mate."

"Well, I guess that answers our questions. Let's go to The Lighthouse." Daniel headed to the van with John and Christian.

By the time they reached the Lighthouse Sam had changed her mind about the spells and briefly went over them with everyone. They climbed out of the van and headed inside the club. As usual it was crowded, loud, and dark. They pushed their way to the game room. The smoke in there was burning Sam's lungs. Christian merged with her and cleared the smoke. "Thank you. I wish I could do that." Smiling up at him.

"When we are one you will be able to, but for now I will help you." He whispered kissing her gently on the cheek. She went on stage with the girls to dance, while the guys remained in the shadows, alert. No one would attack tonight, not if they wanted to live.

He kept scanning the crowd, but found nothing. So he went into the game room to play his favorite game with John while Daniel took over scanning.

Sam, Shelby, and Christine were on stage dancing while Maria, Mike, and Lisa were at the drink station. CJ had opened both balconies since they were running out of room on the dance floor and stage. The balconies were dark, but you had a clear view of everything below.

"Hey, let's go up on the balcony. It won't be crowded and we can see everyone who comes in." Shelby suggested. They all agreed and headed up there. Sam walked to the window to take a look outside. Not seeing any signs of Mark or Devin she relaxed and started dancing with the others.

The night went off without a hitch and everyone was having fun. When a slow song came on. Sam walked back to the window to look at the stars and think about all that had happened. Strong arms circled her waist, knowing who it was she leaned back into his chest to take his masculine sent into her lungs.

Christian leaned down whispering in her ear, "Hi beautiful." As he lightly kissed her cheek again.

The sound of his voice always sent an unexpected sensation through her. She loved the way he felt to her. The way he looked at her like she was the only woman on earth. He made her feel wanted and loved more than words could express. He held her so tenderly not letting his strength crush her. They just moved slowly back and forth to the music as they looked out the window.

When the music stopped for a brief announcement, Christine came over and pulled Sam to the far corner. "Hey I called my parents and they said there's a bad snow storm heading this way. They said if you all want to stay at our house it was ok."

"Just the girls or guys too? Christian and them live a half hour away." Sam asked.

"Mom said all of you. We have enough room and she'd call your parents and explain the situation."

"Well that's fine with me. I know my mom won't have a problem with it so Lisa and I will stay."

"Great, I'll talk to the others, then call my mom back." Christine went to everyone else and they all said yes. Sam was so excited she would have Christian all night.

Sam made the mistake of letting her guard and the barriers that Christian taught her in her mind down. She heard someone whisper her name, but she couldn't tell where it was coming from. Looking across the balcony floor and down on the dance floor, she didn't see anything different.

She felt a compulsion to go over to the other balcony across the way. Her symbol on her hip started to tingle, but the compulsion was so strong she headed down the stairs and across the crowded dance floor to the other side. Stopping at the bottom of the stairs to the other balcony, fear welled up out of nowhere. She knew something wasn't right.

She automatically merged with Christian, *Christian I need you,* is all she got out before something blocked her off from him and Lisa. She bit her bottom lip hard so the pain would help her focus.

Taking a deep breath she lifted her head up and continued up the stairs. Sam was tired of being afraid. If this was her destiny so be it. Embrace the sorceress in her she reached the landing looking for anything odd. She saw darkness on the far left corner, knowing that's were she was suppose to go.

Focusing her mind she looked closer at the darkness as she moved forward. In a low whisper she said "Show yourself to me."

She was five feet from it when Devin appeared. Her heart skipped a beat, lungs fought for air. She focused on calming herself. "What do you want Devin?" Giving him a pissed off look.

"I want you, my dear and no one will stop me." He went to grab her arm, but received a shock instead. "What the hell." Rubbing his hand looking at her.

"I've come into my own powers and you'll never have me. Leave now." She was pissed.

"You've just got them. Your not strong enough to fight me. Come with me and no one will get hurt." Holding out his hand.

"I'll never go with you" She bit out trying to turn to leave, but he froze her movements.

Pulling her into the shadows he whispered, "I'd hate to see your pretty little sister get hurt. I know you are not bonded with Christian yet and even if you were I would still have you." As Devin looked up he saw Christian, Daniel, John, and Lisa standing at the top of the stairs. All the sudden Lisa grabbed her throat problems breathing,

"Stop it!" She focused on Lisa and was able to counter act his magic. Lisa started breathing normally again.

Sam found her inner strength, broke out of his grasp, and pushed him into a wall. She felt Christians strength pour into her. Walking over to him, her eyes going dark green. "I may not be bonded yet, but I can still fight. Leave my sister alone."

Devin threw his hands around her throat. "Don't tempt me I could kill you right now before Christian could reach you." All the sudden smoke started coming from his hands. Devin pulled away with a curse. "You bitch, what did you do."

"It's a protection spell, now leave us alone. You'll never have me without a fight." Sam stood her ground, then she watched as he faded into nothing.

As she let out a sigh Lisa came running over. "Are you OK?"

"I'm better now that he's gone. Are you alright?"

"I'm fine. How did you stop him from choking me?"

"I thought of how I would choke someone then reversed it."

Christian pulled Sam to him. She wrapped her arms around him savoring the feeling. Looking up into his eyes she saw swirling anger mixed with fear. He looked calm to everyone else, but she was beginning to see the many sides of emotions he had. She figured it best to just hold him quietly then anger him more. Since he was upset that she went up here alone.

They all headed down stairs to get drinks. Christine told all them that everyone's parents said it was okay to stay at her house, so they decided to run to the video store on the way back to Christine's house to get some movies to watch.

When they got back to Christine's house everyone picked out there sleeping spots and got settled for the night. Christine and Maria would sleep in their own rooms, Lisa, John, Daniel, Shelby, and Mike would stay in the living room, and Christine didn't see a problem with Sam and Christian staying in the bedroom by the dining room. She really didn't care anyway cause she was just happy that Sam finally found someone.

Their parents had gone to bed early, so Christine decided to pop some popcorn and get drinks before the movie started. They all agreed on horror movies so first up was *The Exorcist.*

Sam came in the kitchen in a light orange tank and shorts she borrowed from Maria since they were close in size. Her hair was up in a ponytail with bare feet. "Hey can I help you with something?"

"Sure, if you could get the cups down." Christine turned around to show her where they were. "You know that fits you better than it does Maria."

"Yeah, she said the same thing. So which cupboard is it?"

"The one on your upper left. Just put them on the table, everyone can get their own drinks." She said as she placed four bowls of popcorn on the table.

The buttery aroma was making Sam's stomach growl. As if sensing her hunger Christian came walking into the kitchen, filled two glasses with pop, grabbed a bowl of popcorn, and handed Sam a glass. Taking her hand he lead her to one of the couches in the living room. She snuggled up as close as possible to him with the popcorn in his lap she took a handful and started eating it.

"Better?"

"Yes." She smiled at him. Soon everyone was in the living room getting settled for the movie. Maria turned out the lights as she walked in and sat on the floor.

By the time they got done with the second movie half of them were asleep including Sam, who had laid in Christian's lap earlier. He sent a soft metal awake so he wouldn't scare her. Sam sat up slowly so he could lifted her gently into his arms like a child and take her to the bedroom.

He moved the bedspread and sheets without lifting a finger.Putting her soft, limber body on the bed. He took her hair out of the ponytail holder, combing through it with his fingers he preferred her hair down. It was like golden stands of silk in his hands. She had the softest skin, always smelling of raspberries he loved touching her.

She was petite and short, but she made up for it with her strength and stubbornness. He loved everything about her, even her temper which caused her eyes to turn the color of dark emeralds and got him so hot and hard he could hardly wait to bury himself in her. It was always hard to leave her at night, but not tonight, he had her all to himself all night long.

Sam watched as he closed the door and lit some candles to provide some soft light to the room. He moved silently like a tiger hunting its prey, fluid and graceful. The light played with the angles of his face, reminding her of a warrior of days long past. His eyes were that of an old soul with intelligence and wisdom beyond her time. Pulling off his shirt her breath caught in her throat. Looking at him in the candle light she ached to touch him, to feel the warmth of his body against hers.

He sat down on the edge of the bed. Time stood still as he lightly caressed her cheek, sliding his hand down to her neck he noticed her pulse beating slightly fast, "Sam are you afraid of me?"

His question startled her. "No, never that. Its just… I've never been with anyone and that's what I'm afraid of."

"I would never do anything to hurt you. Do you trust me?"

"Yes." She closed her eyes for a second. This was happening so fast yet she wanted this, wanted him, but what if she wasn't what he wanted. What if she did something wrong or didn't please him. Doubt filler her mind.

The softness of her name on his lips got her attention. "Samantha, I know your scared, but I promise you that you will feel pleasure above everything else. I will be as gentle as possible, trust in me." His words warmed her making her forget everything but him.

He pulled her tank top over her head, tossing it carelessly on the floor. She took off the shorts, but left on the pale blue thong she wore. The light gleamed over her body, emphasizing the fullness of her breasts, her narrow ribcage, and petite waist. His body raged at him for release. His jeans were to tight, he pulled them off quickly. Still sensing her uneasiness, he gently lifted her chin, looked into her worried eyes, and whispered, "Trust in me," against her soft lips before kissing her breathlessly. She succumbed to his kiss, hungered for more want to feel his hands on her.

He didn't disappoint her as he trailed kisses down her throat to her breasts, leaving liquid fire in their wake. He fed on her, flicking her nipples with his tongue savoring the feel of them. He continued down her flat stomach, feeling her convulse with pleasure he stopped when he got to her thong, wanting to ripe the offending material from her body. Looking up at her, he slowly removed them, tossing them on the floor with the rest of their clothes.

Watching her he slightly pushed her legs apart, sliding one finger into her core. She was so hot and wet swelling him even more, he slide another finger into her. Moving in and out of her slowly, showing her he wouldn't hurt her, he kissed her swollen lips as his fingers brought her a unbelievable sensation.

Fire was building inside, her whole body ultra sensitive to his touch. She moved her hands up and down his back raking her nails lightly as she went. Feeling his response to her every move, his hard length pressed against her.

He moved from her lips to her stomach kissing softly down to her inner thighs and back to the junction of dark curls between her legs. Her scent was exotic and intoxicating. He brought his fingers to his lips, her taste of liquid honey. Thirsting for more he lowered his head using his tongue to taste and probe her insisting on bringing her to the ultimate climax.

Her hips moving of their own accord. Driving any thoughts of doubt and fear from her mind. She was floating on a sea of intense emotions. Losing control of her inhibitions. His need so intense she would give him anything to sate it.

He raised above her with intense hunger in his eyes. Using his knee, he spread her legs apart, like a pagan sacrifice he looked down at her. Passion, desire coursed through his veins. Continuing to look at her he slowly inserted himself yet stopped when he reached her barrier, then with one hard thrust he was through. Closing his mouth over hers he took in her screams as pleasure over took the pain of her first time. He merged with her, letting her feel what he was feeling, increasing the sensations.

Surging faster he felt her ripple with pleasure, her soft cries enhancing his own. She was the most attractive woman he'd ever seen. So giving of herself for others and she was his other half, making him feel for the first time in centuries. He knew it would be like this for all time.

The ritual words beating at him. He could no longer hold them back, "I bind you to me heart, mind, and soul. Your safety and happiness will come before my own. I offer you my life and love. Soul mates for all eternity as was written by the powers above. So mote it be." Feeling them as one now, his incisors lengthened as he leaned down sinking his teeth deep into her soft breast. Still in her mind, he made sure she felt no pain. Taking just enough to complete the ritual, he closed the small wound. Then put her in a trance so not to scare her. A small line of blood appeared on his chest. Gently he moved her closer so her lips touched the blood. Lapping at it she took just enough to complete the ritual.

She was his and he hers, for all time. Kissing her he released her from the trance as he swept the inside of her mouth with his tongue, making sure no blood remained. He watched her eyes flutter open as she looked at him with a puzzled expression. "Why do I have the feeling you did something I'm not going to like?" She asked as she traced his lower lip sending a jolt through his body, while he continued to build the friction between them. "What did you do?"

She forgot her question as wave after wave of extreme pleasure hit her. Her cries music to his ears as his own pleasure consumed him. Their release explosive. Collapsing to the bed he rolled on his side so not to hurt her with his weight. She was everything he could never imagine, thinking how fortunate he was. She moved around him to get to her clothes, her skin glistened from their lovemaking enhancing her looks even more.

She peaked out the door to make sure everyone was asleep before heading to the bathroom to clean up. Peering in the mirror she didn't recognize the person looking back. She looked different, but not sure why. Lord knows she felt different. She washed her face and brushed her teeth before heading into the kitchen. It was dark in there when she was looking out the backdoor leading to the wood, then she felt a cat rub her leg so she bent down to pet it, but nothing was there. For a minute her heart accelerated as she calmed down realizing it must be boots. She was so sensitive lately especially to the spirit world. Everything was so intense lately that she didn't know if it was the white sorceress in her or Christian. On that note she asked him for an answer knowing he was hoping she forgot *Answer my question. What did you do?* Waiting, a little afraid of the answer.

Are you sure you want it now? I feel your fear.

I maybe afraid, but I won't break.

I said the ritual words. It is complete. We are one heart, mind, and soul.

She let his answer wash over her. At first she was furious that he did it without her knowledge, but something slipped into her mind defusing her anger. *Are you alright now? No chance of you losing your soul or turning evil?* she asked holding her breath.

No little one. My soul is now safe and yours for all time.

She let out her breath slowly, relief washed over her at the sound of that. She continued to look out into the woods, even when they looked evil. She had a sense of calmness. Feeling a hand on her shoulder she turned to see a old man in a dark blue shirt and overalls staring back at her. "Don't let the woods give you a false sense of security. There is evil lurking in there. I wouldn't want you hurt Sam. Please heed my warning." He said with a sad look in his dark eyes.

"I'll be careful Monty I promise." With that he faded away. She decided to sit in one of the chairs on the back porch and within a minute she was asleep.

Knowing she was a strong person he gave her the time he knew she needed to get use to this, he left her alone, but remained a shadow in her mind. When he knew her mind was peacefully blank, a nice rest from the chaos of earlier, he walked out to the back porch and carried her back to bed.

Going outside he found John and Daniel out by the barn. The air cool and crisp while the wind howled through the trees singing its nightly haunting melody.

"Is she asleep?" John asked as Christian approached them.

"Yes, peacefully." Looking back at the house, thinking how small she looked laying in bed.

"Now how will we stop the danger to her or the others? If they can't get to her you know they will try through them." John asked a little worried yet determined to fight for their safety.

"She is bonded to me now. I will remove the danger to her." Christian stated a challenging tone to his voice.

In the distance they watched fog moved towards them slowly rolling across the yard to the barn. Out of it came a woman in a white flowing dress her gray hair in a bun, a sparkle in her light blue eyes. Walking up to Christian she said, "You may be bonded to my granddaughter, but until she receives her full powers and completes our half of the bond mate ritual, she is still in danger."

"What do you mean?" Christian questioned knowing this must be Sam's grandmother in spirit form.

"She must complete the White Sorceress ritual before she is completely safe from Devin and Mark. She is yours for all time, but they can still try to get her and her powers and believe me they will. She will be fine until mid-May when she must get ready for the Blue Moon ritual, then everything will be complete and our two races will be one." Looking at him with love in her eyes, "I am putting my trust in you to take care of her and help her to prepare for the ritual. She will be very stubborn, but I see in her heart, even if she doesn't yet, that she loves you unconditionally. I also know you feel the same. Nicholas can vouch for me if you need to contact him. Your leader knows all about this. Tell him Sarina is your soul mates grandmother. I must go now, but I will come if there is need. Blessed be." She turned disappearing into the fog.

"Well if that wasn't the weirdest shit, I don't know what is." Daniel said with humor in his voice.

"I know she's right. All we can do is prepare, but we'll lay low for now. Let's go back in the house and rest. We'll talk to everyone later." Christian said.

3

The months went by without any problems. Winter turned into spring and Christian helped Sam with learning her magic. John and Lisa, along with Daniel and Shelby, had become a couple. Most of the time you'd see all three couples together. They kept with their usual routines of school and Sam still worked and babysat, against Christians wishes of course. The guys had to keep up the appearance of being human, which took its toil on them, but they only had less than a month. They preferred the night when their powers were at their highest, which meant they slept from dawn until early evening.

It had been unusually warm this May. Sam took the weekend off work and babysitting so she could go to the beach with everyone. She loved the water and couldn't wait to be in it.

"Hurry up Sam, its time to go and we're going to be late." Lisa yelled down the hallway.

"Keep your pants on I'm just getting our towels." Going to their mom's room to let her know they were leaving.

Looking up from the laundry her mom caught her eye. "You know it's almost time to complete the ritual and then you'll be living with Christian." The tears in her voice were breaking Sam's heart.

"Mom don't cry I'll come if you need me. I love him so much, but I hate to see you cry." Handing her a tissue.

"I'll be fine I'll just miss having you around the house, but you'll understand when you have kids and they leave the nest. You will have kids right? I'd like some grandchildren."

"Mom slow down we just got together we have plenty of time for kids if we choose to have them, but not right away."

"Alright, but don't wait to long we won't live as long as you will now and would like to enjoy them a little."

Sam changed the subject, not wanting to argue with her. "Lisa and I are leaving for the beach. We'll probably be home late."

"Have fun and think about what I said about kids." She said with a hopeful note.

"Sure mom, see you later." Sam yelled hurrying down the hall and out the door.

The beach was about twenty minutes from their house, back in the woods. The lake was pretty big, a popular spot for the local teens. It was already getting crowded when they pulled in and parked. Sam grabbed her beach bag and followed Lisa down the gravel path that lead through a small bit of woods to the sandy beach ahead.

The sun was hot as it shown through the sky, while the breeze off the lake felt good on her skin. Little ones were building castles in the sand as their parents looked on. You could hear others in the water splashing, laughing, and having fun. She loved this time of the year everything seemed so light and free. No cares in the world just having fun.

Lisa picked a spot in the shade by the woods and put her stuff down. She made sure there was a grill so they could grill the hamburgers and hot dogs later, then she grabbed her and Sam's towels to find a spot in the sand to lay.

"I'll stay here and wait for the others before joining you OK?" Sam said sitting on the table with her back to the woods.

"OK, I'll just run to the bathroom real quick then I'll be on the sand sunning." Lisa smiled heading to the restrooms.

Sam looked out over the water watching the waves hit the shore. It was a peaceful rhythm, the waves moving around. She leaned back on the table, closing her eyes for a moment, trying to soak in the sounds of nature. The soft whisper of the wind through the trees, the birds calling to one another, while the bees gathered nectar and the water lightly crashing to the shore.

Out of the serene of the moment came the cry of an injured animal in the woods. Sam got up and headed for the forest. Running fast through the brush and tall oaks she came to a clearing where she saw a black cat with the strangest yellow eyes laying on the far side of the clearing. Sam approached him slowly watching its tail twitching. He let out a hiss as she tried to mentally show him she was going to help him. For a moment she didn't think it worked, but then the cat calmed and let her get close enough to pick him up.

As soon as she had him in her arms she had a strange feeling she some how knew this cat. She looked at his paw, which had a wicked looking splinter of wood sticking out of it. Sending him a calming, soothing images of making his paw feeling better Sam started to heal as she pulled out the sliver, but the cat scratched her with his other paw in retaliation for causing him more pain. She pulled back knowing it was just a reaction sitting down on the soft grass with the cat in her lap Sam slowly began to pet him to calm the cat while she continued to pull out the wood. Using her injured hand she began to pull it again and the cat moved his head towards her hand lapping at the small amount of blood left form the scratch.

His tongue felt like sandpaper, but she left it, not wanting to frighten him anymore. When he was done she finished pulling out the sliver which started to bleed a little. The cat put his bloody paw over the cut on her hand and as soon as his blood reached the cut she felt a strange dizziness over come her. Everything started spinning and she ended up on her back. Turning her head to see where the cat went she watched as the cat transformed into Mark.

Sam was very lethargic her whole body felt like lead. Her voice frozen, her heart was beating so fast she thought it would come through her chest. Her eye lids were so heavy that the last thing she saw before they closed was Mark's smile as he bent down to pick her up in his strong arms.

"Sam, I'm sorry about this, but I need to make sure your safe. Now that our blood is mixed I can find you anywhere, anytime. I know you hear me and you can still talk to me mentally, but no one else." Mark stated as he continued to walk through the woods to the far side of the beach.

As they reached the clearing to the beach the hot sun stared to warm and relax Sam a little. *Why are you doing this Mark? There is nothing between us and I have plenty of protection,* Sam wearily questioned. She was so tired she just wanted to sleep, but fought it hoping Lisa would realize she was gone and send help.

"I don't believe your soul mate knows who he's dealing with. Devin is extremely powerful and he wants you so badly that he will kill anyone that interferes. I won't say I don't want you, cause I do, more than you know, but your safety will always come first. I've always had feelings for you, but it wasn't about the sex. I was just confused over how strong my feelings for you were." Baring his soul out to her made her want to weep for him. "I know its too late now. If I can't have you I'll at least try to protect you and I knew you won't exchange blood with me any other way. That's why I chose an injured black cat. I knew you'd help it, its in your nature."

Mark, your right I won't have voluntarily exchanged with you, but why drug your blood?

"Because first off I didn't feel like having a painful retaliation from you. Second I didn't need you calling your soul mate right away for help. I needed to talk to you alone." The sadness in his eyes warmed her.

Christian will be here soon. When Lisa discovers I'm missing she will call him to her. Mark if you are telling the truth about just doing this to protect me than you should go before he gets here. I don't want a fight, but if your lying he will kill you.

"Sam, I am telling the truth I will not run from him. I am not afraid of him or his wrath. Right now I will leave you here on the beach, the effects of the drug will wear off very soon. I will come to you tonight." Laying her in his lap he leaned down and kissed her sealing his promise with a kiss and hating himself for all he'd done to her. Although if he could he would find away to bring her back to him. He put her down on the warm white sand knowing the effects should be gone in an hour. Giving her a strong mental push to sleep he left her until tonight when he would face her and eventually Christian. He would be ready.

As Mark laid her on the sand she felt the strong push unable to fight it as darkness claimed her. "Enjoy your dream"' Mark whispered as he left.

In her dream she saw herself in a dark room with white candles all around. The smell of ylang-ylang, cloves, and jasmine in the air. Sam was in a white satin nightgown lying on a four poster bed, rose petals all around her, she sat up slightly confused as to where she was. She heard the door open but didn't see who entered before the light of the hall disappeared.

Out of the darkness came Mark. His muscles rippled as he walked towards her. Sam found herself was quite attracted to him, so much so that she couldn't wait to touch him or feel his hands all over her.

He reached the bed in three long strides. Pulling her into his arms he kissed her passionately, devouring her. She wrapped her arms around his neck. Excepting his hunger for her he reached under her gown to cup her full breast. Rubbing her nipples until they were in hard peeks, while he moved from her mouth and down her neck. She let out a soft cry as he found the sensitive spot on her neck few knew about. Then she felt his teeth scrape exotically back and forth, sending shivers down to her core. Wanting him in her so badly, as his teeth sank deep into her.

Out of the darkness of this exotic dream she heard Christian calling to her. *Sam come back to me. You need to wake up. Your in a dream. Its not real. Wake up now!* His voice was so commanding that everything she saw and felt disappeared.

She awoke to Christian cradling her in his arms strained lines around his mouth and worry in his eyes. He bent down and used his tongue to stop the blood that was running down her neck from the two tiny holes in her neck. He licked off the rest of the blood sending heat coiling through her body. Calming her body she focused on Christian's eyes as they watched her.

"What the hell happened? Why weren't you over with Lisa?" He asked calmly trying to keep a leash on his anger over the situation not Sam.

Sam explained about the cat she saw and Mark as she watched Christian's eye turned cold at what happened. Even though his outer expression was calm. She knew his inner turmoil over keeping her safe and was happy over his restraint.

"Christian, he seemed sincere enough." Sam told him.

"I doubt it." Christian stated.

"Well I want to hear him out. He's coming over tonight." She said defiantly.

"Sam, I forbid you to see him tonight." His voice as cold as death.

Her eyes turned dark green in an instant. She jumped out of his lap and turned to face him as he casually stood up to tower over her. "Screw you, I will do what I want. Don't you *dare* tell me what to do." Fuming at him she turned and ran down the beach. Boiling over with anger she needed to find a safe place to calm down were she could be alone.

Go to the other end of the beach there's a small wooded area that's semi secluded and safe. The woods will calm you, Lisa told her thoughtfully.

Thank you. Give me at least fifteen minutes and keep him away. I don't want to see him right now.

Will do sis. I'll see you shortly, sending her a metal hug before leaving.

Sam slowed to a jog then a walk as she entered the woods she found a nice grassy spot to sit and calm down. Sitting cross legged, she closed her eyes and just let the sun envelop her with its warmth.

Back at the beach Lisa was trying to convince Christian to leave Sam for now while they both cooled down. "Christian, she'll be with us shortly. You need to back off or she'll leave. This has all happened so fast and she's doing her best to accept it in her own way." She tried telling him.

"She is my soul mate and I am responsible for her safety, yet she finds trouble everywhere. I just want to lock her up somewhere to keep her safe." He said wearily.

"You can't keep her caged she's a free spirit."

"I know Lisa. Its just hard for me to accept I will really try to fix that flaw." He smiled at her then turned to go into the lake to cool off.

Sam opened her eyes to find some bunnies, squirrels, and birds around her. She loved nature and accepted everything it had to offer as a gift. A bunny hopped over and sat in her lap. She began to pet its gray fur, loving the silky feel of it. Sitting quietly she thought over what just happened. She understood why Christian didn't want her to see Mark, but maybe he'd change his mind if he came with her tonight. It was worth a shot. She didn't want to fight with him and knew he'd get worse the closer to the ceremony they got until the ritual was completed. She'd really try to be patient, but she hated being told what to do.

She decided to go back to the group, not wanting to ruin everyone's fun. So she gently lifted the bunny and put him back on the grass. Saying her good-byes she headed back to the beach feeling at peace now that she had her alone time.

Shelby and Daniel were over at the play ground entertaining some little girls and by the looks of things Daniel was getting the bad end of it. Sam laughed to herself over it. She saw John at the grill starting on the burgers and dogs while Lisa and Maria started getting the table ready. She didn't see Christian or Christine, so she headed over to the table to find out where they were.

"Hey Sam, Better?" Lisa asked as she got the plates out of the bag.

"Yes, where is Christian and Christine? I didn't see them anywhere."

"Last I saw Christian he was going for a swim and Christine was going to call Mike to see where he was at."

"Oh, do you need help?" Sam asked as she took off her tee shirt cause she was hot, to reveal her yellow bikini top with Hawaiian flowers on it.

"Yeah, could you go to John's van and get the pop?"

"Sure." Sam went down the gravel path to the parking lot. After a minute of looking she found the van. While she had the back door's open she felt someone watching her so she turned to find… nothing unusual. Grabbing the pop, shut and locked the van, and went back down the gravel path to the beach.

Did you enjoy your freedom these last couple of months? I hope you did cause I'll have you soon. Good bye for now my love, hearing Devin right before shards of glass type pain overtook her mind.

Dropping the pop Sam leaned towards the bushes to get sick. Lisa ran to her to help, but John got there first. Holding her hair as she became violently sick. The pain subsided and she finally quit getting sick. John helped her back to the table while Lisa grabbed the pop.

"Where is Christian? Why didn't he come for me?" Hurt in her voice.

"Sam, he had his own battle going on. Something was trying to drown him in the lake. That's why he sent me for you." He said handing her a drink.

"Is he okay?" Concern in her voice.

Before John could answer she saw Christine coming up to them from the beach. Water dripping from his masculine body. His face that of a stone statue. He walked right to her engulfing her in his powerful arms burying his face in her golden hair. "I am fine Mi Amour. Are you?"

"Now that you're here and safe, I am."

He just held her not caring who saw. Knowing Daniel was secretly laughing, but not for long. *We must remove this danger from her Now. I can't let this go on,* Christian informed John.

You know she won't be truly safe until her part of the ritual is completed at the end of the month, John clearly stated.

Christian raised his head meeting John's eye with a glare. Getting up from the table, "I'll be right back I need to talk to John for a minute." Planting a light kiss on Sam's head he headed to the beach with John.

She watched them walk down the shore talking. Sam continued setting up the table wanting as much normalcy as possible for now. Her struggle was getting worse her fear over took her more and more each day. She was worried about everything, her future with Christian, being taken by Devin. Her life was so upside down now she needed peace.

Telling Maria she would be at the play ground, she sat on one of the swings. Closing herself off from everything she just swung through the air, feeling the warm wind on her face. Smelling the perfume of her grandmother in the air she stopped swinging and took a look around. *Samantha, you have more strength than you know. You have to learn to let go of you fears. Trust in yourself and your abilities. Once you do that everything will be better. Remember love is the strongest of all. Trust in your soul mate, he will always be there for you. I love you Sam,* then she was gone. Feeling better she went back to the table to wait for John, Christian, Christine, and Mike to get back so they could eat.

As she talked to Lisa and Maria she saw everyone else heading back. Although she did noticed Christine had her hand on Christian while she was talking to him which caused something ugly rise out of nowhere. Jealousy. All the sudden the wind picked up, blowing Sam's hair from her face her eye's turned into dark emerald and everything seemed ten degrees hotter all the sudden, watching them approach.

Christian stopped abruptly feeling the tension over towards Sam. Seeing her eye's he had an idea of the problem. "Christine very slowly remove your hand from my arm. John take her way from me another direction to the table. No sudden moves just do it slowly." He instructed.

Christine did what was asked and went with John around the trees to the other side of the table, while Christian moved slowly but efficiently towards her.

Christian, Maria and I are going to pull her into the woods so we don't cause anymore attention, Lisa instructed moving Sam slowly into the woods. As he reached them unseen force pulled Sam through the air, putting her gently on a huge rock, encasing her in a bubble. He heard Mark's voice as he appeared out of nowhere. "Christian Stop! Don't touch her yet."

Christian turned to face him. "What have you done to her." He bit out between clenched teeth.

"I'm protecting her and everyone else from her wrath." Mark clearly stated. "Haven't you paid attention when she gets angry? Everything gets hot. Her power lies in heat from any source. The sun, the moon, a body, any source big or small. She has extreme power, but can't control it yet. See how the bubble is yellow through red and green. Her emotions are very high. I can contain her power, but you must calm her, now!"

Sam honey, I'm here. You must calm down before something happens, Christian kept his voice calm and steady.

Why was she touching you? Sending small flames in his mind

It was a reaction nothing more. I love only you, saying with a calming compulsion.

Slowly the colors disappeared, the tension dissipated, and Mark released Sam from the bubble. She sat down on the rock, tears flowing down her face. "I'm such a terrible person. How could I want to hurt her?"

Christian sat on the rock next to her wrapping his arms around her. Mark came over. "Your not a terrible person. Everyone goes through this when they receive their powers. Its hard to control at first, but with practice you'll be fine."

She looked up at him, "How did you know?"

"The same way Christian does. Your blood is also in my veins as mine is in yours. I also went through a similar experience. I'm a lot older than you think Sam. I've had my powers for a long time. If you both would allow me, I could teach Sam how to control them." Mark asked sincerely.

"Let us discuss it later." Christian answered. "I thank you for helping her. Come join us for dinner. Nothing special just hot dogs and hamburgers."

"Yes, I think I will. I appreciate the invite." Mark smiled and followed Maria back to the table.

"Thank you for being civil with Mark. I would like him to help since he knows all about it, with you there of course, just in case." She added thoughtfully.

With a heavy sigh he agreed. Knowing it would make her happy and not feel alone. Since Mark went through it. Although keeping his emotions under control when the time came would be another question. He wouldn't think about it now.

They all sat down and ate enjoying the rest of the early evening. They went swimming as the girls laid out a little bit before going back to Maria and Christine's house to rinse off and change. After they got to the house the girls were fighting for the bathroom and this went on for an hour before everyone got cleaned up and changed.

There was a small carnival being held outside The Lighthouse. The air smelled of cotton candy and funnel cake. The night was warm, hearing the crickets and frogs in the distance. As they walked towards the carnival you could hear the screams from the rollercoaster's and fun houses, the little kids with stuffed animals and balloons asking their parent's for one more game or ride. The guys showing off for their dates trying their hand at various games to win a big prize. This was the normalcy Sam was looking for just out with friends, having fun, enjoying the beauty of the evening.

They went on various rides like the star, the tilt-a-whirl, the fun house, and played some games winning stuffed animals and stuff for the girls. Christian won Sam two pictures with two white kittens on both of them. One with a neon blue background and the other was red faded to black and she loved them more than any stuffed animal.

John and Lisa took everyone's stuff to John's van, while the rest of them went into the club. The strobe lights were going along with the disco balls. The music was blaring as usual and it was extremely crowded. Between the smoke and all the other smells it was hard to get any clean air in your lungs. Squeezing through the crowd they made it to the game room to wait for John and Lisa.CJ came up to them with some drinks. "Hey, I saw you guys come in. Here's some smoothies there pretty good." Handing them out to everyone.

"Thanks CJ. Could we get two more Lisa and John are on their way up. They just dropped our some stuff to the van." Christine asked.

"Sure, I'll be right back." Heading down stairs to get two more smoothies.

Christian and Daniel went over to the Mortal Kombat to play a couple of games. The girls just drank their smoothies watching everyone dance, occasionally commenting on how people danced or what they were wearing. CJ came up just before John and Lisa did and waited to hand them their drinks. Mark and Mike stayed near Maria and the rest of the girls just in case of any trouble, but so far everything was going smoothly.

Tony put on *"Da 'Butt"* at Christine's request so all the girls headed on stage as the guys, including Christian and Daniel, who ended their game early, watched them dance.Through the loud music Sam heard a cat. She continued dancing, but kept looking around. She made Christian and Mark aware of it so they could also look. When the music stopped she went back to Christian while Mark stayed close by.

What is up with the cats? Christian asked.

Before Sam could answer Mark did, *Sam loves anything feline, especially if its black like panthers.*

So that's why you used an injured cat. You knew she won't hesitate to help it, eyeing Mark.

Yes, but few knew that about her. I think some how Devin found out and is trying to get her away from everyone.

I agree. I will tell the other's to keep a look out for him, Christian made sure that Sam didn't leave his side. She was quite annoyed, but understood the precaution. He let her dance with the girls a couple of times, but remained by the stairs of the stage.

As the night whined down everyone decided to go home a little early. Since tomorrow was the dance of the year and the girls had so much to do they wanted to get their rest. John dropped Maria, Christine, and Mark off first, then dropped off Shelby, which Daniel said he'd be home later, and finally Lisa, Sam, and Mike.

Mike said his good byes and headed to his home across the street while Lisa took John inside for a minute so Sam and Christian could be alone.

"Thank you for taking me to the dance. It probably seems silly to you, since we're in college." She said shyly.

"No. I can't wait to see how beautiful you look. It will give me a glimpse of how you will look on our wedding day." He said coyly.

Her eyes lit up. "Do you really mean it. We can have a wedding."

"I know its what you'll want, even though we'll already be together. I would like to have it as close to the ritual as possible, but I need to ask you something else." Looking her in the eyes, "I would like you to stay the night with me at my house."

"I don't see a problem with that, but why now? We've been together for six months and now you want me to see your home?" Sam questioned.

"Because I want you to see where you will be living soon and if you need me to change or add anything. This is killing me, you know, having to let you go every night."

"I hate seeing you go too. I dream of you every night."

"Me too, but tomorrow night no dreaming it will be real and very special and before I leave you," Handing her a black velvet box. She opened it to revel a petite silver ring with a emerald in the center and diamonds circling it. "So everyone will know you are mine."

"Oh Christian, it's the most beautiful ring I've ever seen." Sam tearfully answered throwing her arms around him kissing him with so much passion. "When can we let everyone know and plan the wedding?"

"Whenever you wish sweetheart. I'm just glad your happy and that's all that matters." He said with a grin.

"Hey now! Get a room you two." John said as him and Lisa came down the walk laughing.

"Lisa look!" Sam exclaimed running to show her the ring.

"It's beautiful Sam." Lisa stated looking at it.

"We're going to have a wedding and I need you to be my maid of honor. I'm so excited. So much to plan in such a short time." Sam's excitement spilled over onto everyone else.

"Slow down honey." Christian laughed, "First you have to get through the dance tomorrow, then we'll start on the wedding." He held her feeling her happiness warmed him.

"I'm just so excited, but now you have to go don't you?" She said with a pout.

"Yes, but I'll see you tomorrow and we'll be together all night." Lovingly kissing her on the lips before getting in John's van.

Sam and Lisa went inside to tell their mom about the wedding and showing her the ring as they all cried with happiness. Least to say their dad left the room not believing their display of affection, but still excited for his daughter.

4

Mean while on the way home Christian asked John to be his best man, which he excepted of course. "I'll talk to Daniel later when he comes home." He told John.

"So your bring her to our house tomorrow night?"

"Yes why? We live in a huge mansion. There is enough room for several families."

"Hey I just asked. So where will you two live after all this?" John curiously questioned.

"The west wing. Its big enough so when we decide on children they have enough room to run and play."

"Thinking a little far ahead aren't you. You know Sam won't be ready for kids yet."

"Yes, but at least we'll be a little prepared just in case."

"Alright, see you in the morning." John headed for his room in the north wing. "I'm going to call Lisa."

"You just saw her." Christian yelled after him as he waved and turned the corner.

❧

Back at Sam's they were still admiring the ring. "We should try and get some sleep. We have a big day tomorrow." Lisa stated as she yawned.

"I know, I know. I'm just so excited. I'll see you in the morning." Sam headed for her room just as her phone rang.

"Hello?"

"Hey, What's you doing?" John asked.

"Nothing John, but you got the wrong sister. Hold on I'll get her."

"Sorry, I have a hard time telling you two apart on the phone." He said a little embarrassed.

"Hey, Lisa its John." Handing her the phone."Didn't you just see him?" Sam questioned with a grin.

"Go away." Shutting her door.

Sam went to her room, shutting the door she opened the window and lit some candles. She enjoyed sleeping to the music of the night. As she laid on her pillow Sam began to read a book about vampires trying to find love. Soon she was asleep dreaming of her life with Christian.

The howl of a coyote brought Sam out of her dream. Now wide awake, she peered out the window trying to see if she could spot the animal. Trotting into view she stared at it astonished that it was in plain sight. It watched her with its glowing yellow eyes, then turned back toward the woods running to the tree line and stopped, glanced over its shoulder and disappeared into the woods.

Sam went down stairs to making some hot cocoa to help her go back to sleep. Sitting on the back porch she looked at the trees wondering if she would see the coyote again. As if reading her thoughts he approached. Putting down her cup, Sam left the protection of the back porch, and headed towards the animal like an unbreakable compulsion. She felt her legs moving forward, unable to stop them and when she reached the creature it changed into Devin.

"How lovely you look tonight Sam. I told you I'd see you soon." He said gently. "Are you surprised to see me?"

"Not really, I knew you'd come sooner or later." She said calmly even though her heart was beating a mile a minute.

Sam, calm down and make sure Devin doesn't know your talking to me. He doesn't know of our blood bond just of yours and Christians. Mark calmly remarked.

I can't contact Christian, why? she was so scared.

Devin has blocked you from Christian and Lisa. Listen I'll take the form of the cat. I'll come to you and we'll combine our powers. Stall him for a few minutes I'm still to far away.

OK Mark, but please hurry, Sam stated anxiously.

I will, then he was gone.

Sam felt very vulnerable out there by herself with Devin. As he took a step forward she caught a glimpse of something shiny in his hand. She tried to move, but was unable to. Devin grabbed her right arm, holding it palm up, he reveled a ceremonial knife. It looked old the handle was white with some kind of words in an ancients language on it.

He started a spell which required both their blood to be combined. She yelled a denial trying to pull her arm away, as Devin brought the knife down. Making a two inch slash in her skin Sam watched as her blood ran slowly down her arm.

Next she heard the meow of a cat. Thinking quick she called out a name " Jaz, come here." Holding out her other arm out the cat jumped into her arm, combining their powers, Mark told her what to do next, *Build your anger, embrace the heat. That is where your power lies. Don't worry I will help you control and focus it, but do it now!* Mark urged immediately.

She followed his directions to the tee and was able to build a fireball, sending it Devin's way before he knew what happened. He was thrown back, the knife fell to the ground, the cat ran to the knife picking it up in his mouth and running back to Sam. There he encased them both in a protective bubble.

Devin got to his feet sending a shock of power her way, but the bubble stopped in from hitting her and dissipating shortly after it hit. "Well I see you've learned a thing or two with the time you've had to practice." He said with a sneer. "I just want to let you know the knife I used was poisoned, just in case something went wrong. Enjoy your last hours cause your soul mate will suffer. I will be back for you later."

"I thought you said I was going to die?" A quiver in her voice.

"Yes and no, see the poison in you will slow your heart so much they'll think your dead. Your soul mate will become either evil or decide to join you in the after life. Meanwhile I'll collect your body, finish the ritual, and you will be mine."

"Why am I so important to you?"

"Haven't you figured it out yet? I am one of the oldest of the sorcerers left. With you and your powers we can make this our playground, be the king and you my queen. Of course we will have to destroy all the Pyreneans first. Can't have Christian or the other's trying to stop us."

"I will..." Sam doubled over in pain.

"Oh, its very painful too. Sorry forgot to tell you. Well gotta go love. I'll be back later." Disappearing into the woods.

The bubble disappeared, Mark changed back gathering Sam in his arms as he merged with her and contacted Christian to come immediately. Carrying her into the house he took her to her room laying her on the bed.

"I'll be right back I need Lisa's help too." Distressed as he covered her.

He opened Lisa's door gently shaking her, "Lisa, Wake up Sam's hurt."

Her eye's flew open, "What did you do?" Anger building as she rose.

"Nothing, Devin cut Sam's arm with a poisoned knife trying to combine their blood. I stopped him, but now we need to save her." He ran back to Sam's room. As he entered he was shocked to see how pale she was, almost gray while sweat poured off her.

Fear in Sam's eyes, "I don't want to die Mark." Tears in her voice.

"I know Sam. Lisa is here now and Christian's on his way." He held her hand feeling the pain ravaging her. Lisa looked at the wound on her arm using a wet towel she cleaned off the blood.

"Mark, wake mom up and tell her we need the healing herbs. All of them, along with the candles and incense." She asked calmly. "Is Christian on his way?"

"Yes, I contacted him first. They are all coming to help. We will need it I'll go get your mom." Leaving Lisa alone with Sam.

Lisa held her hand as she wiped her forehead. "Honey, you know you'll have to go with Christian tonight your no longer safe here. You will make it through this I won't let you die, Sam do you hear me!" Tears falling like a rain now.

"I love you Lisa." Sam whispered.

"I love you too." Lisa kissed her cheek.

"Lisa merge with me and contact grandmother." Closing her eyes to rest between the waves of pain.

But before she could she heard a gasp. Turning Lisa saw Christian in the door frame. She moved to let him sit. Their mom and Mark came in the room and started setting up for the healing ritual.

"I'm here baby." Christian softly whispered as he looked her over. "Can you heal her and remove the poison.?" Looking at Lisa.

"Yes, but I need a lot of power. Did John and Daniel come?"

"They are here, on their way up now. She will need my blood also since we are bonded. Will help a lot to speed the healing."

"Ok, she said to summon my grandmother also."

"Sarina will be of great help as will your mother. Let me give her my blood first." He whispered in Sam's ear a command to drink as he held her to the cut on his chest that just appeared.

As soon as his rich blood touched her lips her teeth lengthened and pierced his skin. She heard his soft groan as she took the ancient liquid into her starving body. Next she felt the pain again and quickly closed the wound, *Christian please take away the pain. I hurt so bad.*

I know honey, just hold on. We'll get through this. I love you, his compassion helped give her the strength to make it through the next couple of hours.

Lisa, Mark, and Sarina were able to neutralize the poison and help heal Sam while the others lent there strength and power. It took three hours to complete even though it seemed like forever.

Sleeping peacefully at Sarina's command, everyone left Sam in her room and went into the living room to discuss their next course of action.

"Sam is in too much danger here. Now Anne before you protest you know she would be much safer and well protected with Christian. I suggest she be moved there immediately." Giving Anne a stern look knowing her daughter wouldn't argue over Sam's safety, especially being so close to the blue moon ritual.

"Yes mother, as you wish." She said with a heavy sigh.

Watching Christian go back up stairs Anne felt his need to be with her daughter, she turned to Lisa, suggesting breakfast for everyone since they were all drained and would need fuel to go on with the rest of the day. John and Daniel helped in the kitchen, Sarina took her leave, and Mark left also.

Up in Sam's room Christian sat on the edge of the bed stroking her hair. "Soon you'll be home with me safe from Devin." He whispered softly vowing to kill Devin the next time he saw him. No one will ever threaten his soul mate's life again without grave consequences. He laid down next to her and just held her as she slept.

Not sure how long he'd laid there with her, but he must have fallen asleep because he heard a soft rapping on the door. "Come in." Answering in a slightly groggy voice.

"It's just me." Lisa whispered looking in. "She's still asleep huh?"

"Yeah, I fell asleep too. Is everything alright?" He yawned.

"Everything's fine. Breakfast is ready and mom said Sam should get up now. Let me check her first then you can awake her to eat. She'll need her strength for the dance tonight and don't think to deny her this. Its very important to her." Lisa slowly looked her over visually, then sent herself inside Sam to check everything else. "She is healed and all poison is gone. Awaken her and come down to eat."

Lisa got up to leave and Christian gently put his hand on her arm, "Thank you for everything you all have done and I would never deny her her the dance. We will be down in a minute." He smiled at her.

"You are part of our family now and we always take care of our own. I'll help with her things later." Smiling she left them alone.

Honey, Its time to wake up and eat, softly kissing her luscious lips taking in her soft sigh as she awoke.

"Mmmm... Did I sleep to long?" Sam asked while she stretched reminding him of a cat.

"No honey, Lisa just came to let us know that breakfast is done. How do you feel?" Helping her to sit.

"Just a little groggy, but I am starving."

"Well let's see what they cooked up." Grabbing her hand they headed down stairs.

The smell of bacon, sausage, pancakes, and eggs overwhelmed them. Sam's stomach growled. Looking at Christian a little embarrassed, she walked faster to get to the kitchen.

"How are you feeling honey?" Sam's mom asked giving her a big hug.

"I feel better, but I'm starving."

"That's my girl. Always hungry."

"Mom!"

"Go eat, you and Lisa have your hair and nail appointment at eleven. Oh and while your there might as well set up one for the wedding and make one for me too.

They got their food and sat down at the table with Lisa and John. Shelby had shown up half an hour ago and was just finishing up the toast. Soon it was time for everyone to split up and get ready for the dance. Agreeing to start at Shelby's house for pictures and ending at Christine and Maria's before dinner.

5

Lisa and Sam got their hair and nails done, but Sam wanted to wait on setting the appointment so she could discuss it with Christian first. She did gave the hairdresser a tentative date of two in a half weeks though. Next they met the other girls at Christine's so her older sister could do all their makeup. By the time they got done it was three and the guys would start picking them up around four, so Sam and Lisa headed home to get dressed.

Sam's dress was a floor length satin midnight blue strapless with a V front to emphasize her breasts with little rhinestones along the lower half and a slit from her hip down showing off her shapely legs. Dark blue satin heels, dark blue lace choker with a heart shaped sapphire in the center and sapphire earrings and bracelet to match. Her hair was up in a French twist with a few strands in loose curls around her face.

Lisa's dress was also floor length. It was a light satin peach off the shoulder with sequences through out. Very simple. She wore a pearl choker with earrings and bracelet to match. Her hair was in a classic chiffon at the nape of her neck and peach colored heels.

Their mother took so many pictures before the guys got there that

Sam kept seeing flashes of light for five minutes. "Mom stop with the pictures I'm blind."

"Fine! I'll wait for the guys. Its just you two look so beautiful and this is one of your last dances." Putting down the digital camera.

There was a knock on the door, "They're here." Lisa said answering the door.

First Christian walked in wearing a classic black tux with a dark blue vest to match Sam's dress. He took her breath away as usual. Next came John in the same tux with a black vest, he wasn't wearing any other color, and finally Daniel with a wine colored vest to match Shelby's dress.

"Oh don't you guys look handsome. Come I need pictures." Grabbing the camera again.

"Mom!" Sam and Lisa said in unison.

"Don't mom me get over there." She issued in a stern voice.

They gathered for the pictures. Christian stood next to Sam and leaned down to whisper that she looked beautiful. Sam beamed with happiness as John and Lisa stood next to them while Daniel kneeled in front After what seemed like several hundred pictures, their mom finally let them sit down.

"Ok, now tell me who each couple will be so all of you could go." Asked their mom.

"Well, Christian and I, Lisa and John, Daniel and Shelby, Mike and Christine, and finally Mark and Maria." Sam answered as John handed her a drink, "Where is Mike by the way?"

"I just called him he's on his way over now." Daniel said.

As if on cue, Mike walked in the door. "Sorry, had trouble with my tie." Smiling sheepishly. He had on a black tux with a black cumber bun. He always had to be different. Sam smiled at that thought.

"Sorry to cut this short, but we should get going." Daniel suggested anxious to see Shelby. As they got up to leave Sam's mom requested one more picture. Next they picked up Shelby and headed to Christine and Maria's house.

The sunset made a perfect background for their group picture, but they first took couple pictures. Christine had on a turquoise strapless satin dress, straight form fitting and it looked pretty on her with her hair in a french braid, and babies breath intertwined in it. Maria had on a similar dress in dark red with her hair was in a bun. They both had on black lace chokers and heels. Shelby had on a wine colored off the shoulder dress that went to her ankles, tapered at the waist with rhinestones through out, black choker and heels and her hair in a french twist. Mark's vest matched the color of Maria's dress. They all looked great and were very excited about the evening.

After all the pictures were done, the girls were heading for John's van when a long black limo pulled into the drive way. The girls stopped and stared as Christian walked over to the drive. "Running a little late Armond?"

"Sorry Christian, got stuck in traffic. Are you ready to go to dinner now?" Armond questioned.

"I believe so. Oh can you put Sam's things in the trunk she's moving in a little earlier than expected." Christian turned and smiled at Sam lovingly.

"Yes, Christian." He got Sam's stuff and loaded it into the trunk as everyone got in the limo.

"How did you afford this?" Sam asked in awe as she looked at the lights above and the leather seats. There was also a fridge with liquor and soda in it.

"Armond had been with us for years." Scooting towards the front to let everyone else in. "And living so long you acquire quite a bit of money if you invest wisely, which I have." Hugging her to him before putting on her corsage, then handing the guys the rest of them as they all got settled.

"I must stop for gas before we get on the road." Armond informed them.

"Ok just stop up here than." Pointing to the gas station. "Does anyone need anything before we go? If so go now."

The girls got out with Mark and Mike to get waters while Daniel, Christian, and John remained in the limo.

"Hey since it is a special night and we have all night, why not just invite them all to stay at our place. There's more than enough room." Daniel suggested.

"I have no problems as long as you stay away from my wing. I have something special planned for Sam." Christian stated.

"Sounds like a plan to me." John smiled.

"We should at least let their parents know where they'll be. John start calling them." Christian suggested as John started dialing.

In the store the girls were arguing over which water was best. Sam grabbed her raspberry Canadian water and headed outside. She went to the limo to wait for the others. Within less than five minutes they were back on the road. All their parents said fine for them to stay at the guys place tonight, but it would be a surprise. So the guys would tell them later.

As they drove to dinner at Carinos, Sam stared out the window watching the scenery go by. Blocking out all the conversations going on around her she tried a mini meditation to calm her nerves. Closing her eyes she envisioning a white room with nothing in it. Next she built a white sandy beach, with waves softly hitting the shore as the warm sun hit her face. Hearing the seagulls over head she could smell the salty air. Sam always pictured Gulf Shores where her grandmother use to live, because it was her favorite place.

As she looked out over the ocean the scene began to change. The water turned blood red, the sky turned black, she heard Devin's laughter. Turning she ran down the shore to Christian on the sand. She knelt down to wake him, but he didn't move. His skin was so cold and he had several cuts on his body, dark puddles of blood under him. When she leaned down to lift him she noticed two thin red lines formed on her arms, then they began to bleed. She screamed.

Her screams and fear brought her back to the present. Everyone was looking at her in silence as Christian tried to calm her, but her tears wouldn't stop falling. He just held her rocking gently until she finally calmed enough to tell them what she saw.

"The one thing about premonitions is that they can be changed. Don't worry, now we have an idea of what to look for." He whispered softly.

Come to me. Let me calm your fears my love, she heard Devin ever so softly request.

Sam threw up her barriers fast as her eyes went green and locked her gaze with Lisa. Merging with her, she replayed the commanding words to her. The temperature continued to increase in the limo.

"Mark and Christian merge with us. Sam is fighting a strong compulsion to go to Devin. He knows she's ok." Lisa told them.

"No! I want to do this myself." Sam bit out.

"Christian her arm, the slash is back." Lisa cried out.

"Honey your not strong enough yet. You need more healing. Let us help or he may win this." He calmly used a stronger command to get her to listen to him as Mark added his strength to Christian's command to fight Devin's compulsion. Within minutes everything cooled. Sam gave in to their power, and Devin let go of her. Hearing thunder in the distance conformed Devin's defeat this time.

Lisa sat by Sam so she could heal the slash again while Christian provided his warmth to her mind and body to let her know he's always with her. Mark gave her some cold water.

Dinner was good. Sam loved Italian food. John told everyone about staying at their place tonight to lighten the mood. Everyone was excited about the rest of the evening.

They arrived at Elizabeth Manor around eight. As they came through the lobby, there were black and silver balloons going up the staircase on their left. Colors of white and gold all around the lobby, giving it a soft, romantic look. They went up stairs to were the dance was being held.

Entering the huge room the balloons continued through out with streamers of the same colors. Tables were set up around the DJ booth and dance floor, while food and drinks were along the back wall. White linen covered all the tables with confetti on them and a champagne flute at every setting. The flutes were engraved with the year and the theme *"Forever in Your Eyes"*.

They picked a table near the back corner. The music was going, people were dancing, eating, laughing. Sam forgot the earlier incident, grabbed Shelby and Christine, and went to the dance floor. Christian just shook his head grinning at her delightfulness for the night as he set at the table watching her. The rest of the girls went to dance with Sam, leaving the guys at the table.

"This night has turned out great so far." Christian told them.

"Yes and hopefully it stays that way." John responded.

"*Wonderful Tonight*" came on. Sam ran over to the table pulling Christian to the dance floor. She put her arms around his neck as he pulled her closer encircling her waist. "Have I told you how beautiful you look tonight?" Telling her as they danced.

"Yes and I think you look extremely handsome tonight." Smiling at him.

She loved being with him and couldn't wait to see his house. He always made her feel safe. Just two more weeks until everything was complete and she would be his for all time. With that thought she laid her head on his shoulder until the end of the song. After that song they played another slow song. Christian and Sam continued to dance until Mark and Maria came over.

"Would you mind if I cut in?" Mark asked sincerely. "Maria would dance with you Christian, if its ok."

"I don't care." Sam stated.

"Alright." Christian handed Sam to Mark while he took Maria's hand to dance.

Sam put her arms around his neck as he circled her waist. "I'm glad everything is working out between you and Maria. You two make a cute couple."

"I'm glad too. She makes me happy and I love her smile." He said twirling her around the dance floor. "Sam, I have something I want to give you when we get done with this dance."

"Mark you didn't need to get me anything. You should be getting Maria a gift."

"I know and I have. I just haven't given it to her yet, but what I have for you is a protection bracelet. I'll give it to you when the song is done and Christian is with us. I don't want to alarm you when I put it on you."

"Why would you alarm me?" Sam asked with a puzzled look.

Spinning her around again he answered "The way the bracelet is fashioned, once it comes in contact with your skin it will embed itself until you decide to take it off."

"Will it hurt? What's it made of?"

"No, it won't hurt. I made sure of that personally. You will feel a warming sensation as it penetrates your skin. The bracelet has three crystals, with your name engraved on each one, and one Amethyst, Chalcedony, Malachite, and Peridot in between each crystal inlaid in gold. Its an ancient amulet spell I found and thought it would help. The bonus is that with your name engraved on the crystals you are the only one it will work with." The song ended. Mark took Sam's hand leading her back to Christian.

"Maria will you get me the bracelet." Mark smiled at her as she handed it to him. "Let's do this over there where its darker so no one sees." Maria remained by his side as all four of them walked to the dark corner. Mark explained it to Christian before he opened the box for Sam.

Sam picked it up. It was as he described it. "It's amazing. I just put it on my wrist?" When she put it on she felt the sensation of warmth as the bracelet penetrated her skin. Taking on the look of a beautiful tattoo.

"Now all she has to do to take it off is what, envision it first, then reach for it as it solidifies?" questioned Christian.

"Yes, but its safer to leave it on at all times and just say it's a tattoo." Mark commented.

"Mark, thank you for such a precious gift." Sam hugged him.

"You are welcome. I was just thinking of your safety and since magic is my forte' I thought this would help."

They headed back to the table to show Lisa and then just the two of them decided to step outside for some fresh air. "Do you trust him enough to trust his intentions for the bracelet?" Lisa inquired looking at the night sky.

"I think he's more than proved himself trustworthy. Anyway grandma would have known if he wasn't." Sam confidently stated. "So are you having fun so far?"

"Yes, this has been a wonderful night and I can't wait to see their house so I'll know where you'll be living."

"I know I can't either. I'm still a little scared, this is a big step. I'm glad you'll be near tonight if I need you." She smiled.

"I'll always be there for you if not physically than mentally you should know that." Handing Sam some small rocks to spin around, feeling her need to expel some magic to relax.

"Thanks." Taking the stones and spinning them slowly. "I know you'll always be with me I just feel better when your physically with me." Spinning them faster now as she relaxed. Looking around to make sure no one was around, she sent one stone over the balcony into the small fountain below.

"Sam! We're going to get in trouble. Stop it." Lisa was shocked at her boldness, even though her eyes were filled with laughter as a slow smile creped in. "Do it again. No ones here."

Sam propelled the rest into the water right before she was reprimanded. *Samantha!* She heard laughter in his voice causing her to laugh, "Come on Lisa before the big bad wolf comes after us."

As they turned to walk in Sam felt really dizzy and nauseated. "Lisa,

I'm not feeling good. I think my sugar level's low I need to sit down and get something to speed it up fast."

But it was to late her hearing went, then her vision, and she passed out. Luckily Lisa caught her before she hit the floor and eased her down, *Christian, Sam passed out. I need your help to bring her in and have Shelby get a coke with extra sugar in it,* Lisa waited for Christian.

He stalked through the door, bent down to pick Sam up in his arms, and headed in with Lisa following. Shelby put the coke on the table as Christian sat with Sam cradled in his lap. "How did this happen?" Trying to control his emotions of not being able to prevent this.

"I don't know, maybe because of everything going on. I'm not sure though I just want her conscious." Worry in Lisa's voice showed how upset she was. John pulled her into his embrace to comfort her.

"I'm sorry, I didn't mean to be so harsh. We'll bring her level up and then she'll be fine." He said supportively to calm Lisa.

"Sam? She's coming to, give her some coke now!" She instructed, pulling out of John's embrace to get closer to Sam.

"Sweetheart, drink slowly." He helped her with the coke making sure she drank it all. Trying to calm his rapidly beating heart.

He held her for awhile as they listened to the music. Life with her would be an adventure he was looking forward to.

"And why is that?" Sam startled him with her question not realizing she would voluntarily slip into his mind. He never once told her about that.

"Because you are always keeping my heart rate up and I love you for it, even though it scares me to death sometimes." Kissing the top of her head, "And I never thought you'd read my mind."

"I think I should. You have some interesting thoughts." Turning to smile up at him, before gently kissing his cheek. "I'm feeling much better now. I'm sorry I didn't tell you about my low sugar."

Christine came up and pulled Sam out on the dance floor. It was the last song before they played *"In Your Eyes"* and closed down for the night.

Christian got up and went to the corner where the rest of the guys were. He was finding it hard to control his sexual reaction to Sam as he watched her seductive moves that he was sure she was unaware of making, *I'm reading your mind,* she wickedly whispered in his head.

Smiling, he walked over to the dance floor. Sam turned her head in time to see him grab her in his arms and twirl her around. She let out a squeal before laughing out loud at his actions.

He lowered her to the floor. "Just remember beautiful, that you are with me for all time now." Pointing out with smug male amusement.

"For which I am grateful." Kissing him before he left her to the rest of the dance.

After they finished the last dance and said their good-byes, they got in the limo to go to the guys house for the night. They had a long night so the girls just laid on the guys and closed their eyes until they arrived at the mansion. Christian stared out the window, watching the scenery go by, thinking how lucky he was to have such a treasure as Sam.

"Of course you are. As am I." She said. The limo pulled up to the house. Armond opened the door to let everyone out. The girls got out first, their mouths gapped open at what they saw as the guys got out.

"You said you lived in a house." Sam exclaimed.

"And I do. Now let's go inside." Christian ushered them on.

"This is not a house. It's a huge mansion."

"Does that bother you?"

"I just didn't realize. This may take awhile to get use to." Going up the steps, the mansion was at least two football fields wide and no telling how long. There were two huge stone lions at either side of the stairs as you went up to the front door. The place looked ominous. It was all in dark gray stone, reminding her of a gothic style castle in Europe, at least what she could see since it was so dark out. It still made her feel safe despite the look. The door was a beautifully carved oak with a dark cherry finish and various animals on both sides of it.

As they entered the main hall, there were candles everywhere. The walls were done in a warm red with hardwood floors, and oriental rugs through out. Several big vases were on either side of the entry ways to the library, sitting room, and music room.

The library was quite big. Books floor to ceiling with a fireplace on the far wall. Two desks on either side of the room with computers, which she assumed were used for various work. A lot of the books were old, no doubt some were first edition.

The sitting room was a cross the hall. Done in creams and gold's. Several chairs, couches, and tables through out. A radio in the corner for soft background music. Plants and flowers in the corners and on some tables.

The music room had various instruments. Drums, guitars, keyboard, grand piano, and a few wind instruments. The room was sound proof. A small sound room in the corner to make recordings if they wish.

As they continued down the hall there stood a huge Ming vase in the center as the hall split into four directions. "To your left the hall leads to the TV room, kitchen, and exercise and pool area. The two split halls ahead of you are John and Daniel's wings and to your right is my wing. The cook is asleep, but I'm sure we have some snacks in the kitchen. You are all welcome to look around." Christian said as he moved Sam down the hall that lead to his wing.

"This is the most exquisite house I've ever seen." Sam stated as she looked at the paintings on the walls while following him down the hall.

"Thank you. We also have a garden and a lake behind the house. I'll show you later." Stopping at a wood door at the end of the hall.

He opened it to reveal a big master bedroom. The whole room was done in black's, red's, and gold's. Including furniture and bedding. There was a four poster Mahogany bed on one wall, a fireplace with a quant little sitting area on another wall. There was also a specious master bath with a whirlpool tub and separate shower, a walk-in closet, and dressing room at the end of the bathroom.

Sam was speechless as she gazed around at everything. She sat down on the bed, it was so comfortable she wanted to go to sleep, but she also wanted to explore some more. "You have a nice bedroom. Its very spacious."

"This is also your room now too. If you wish to change anything just let me know."

"Oh no, I love all of it. Although I like candles in the room, but other than that I'm fine." All the sudden a black cat ran into the room and jumped into Sam's lap. "And who is this?" She asked automatically petting the cat.

"A pain in the ass. Gabriel get down." The cat hissed at Christian then laid his head on Sam's lap.

"Christian! That wasn't nice. Is he yours?"

"Yes and no. He showed up one day and never left and for some reason loves to pester me by following me around, sleeping on my bed, and trying to get my food." He growls at the cat.

"Stop it! He obviously has picked you as his owner or he wouldn't be here. Will Armond be bring my stuff up or should I go get it?"

"He will bring it. I have picked up some clothes for you if you want to change. They're in the closet."

Sam walked to the closet with Gabriel in her arms. There were gowns, dresses, jeans, shirts, and skirts. In the dresser were undergarments, sweats, socks, and shorts. She pulled out a pink tank and pink sweat pants to wear. He also had picked out various shoes for her including slippers which she put on before she followed him to the kitchen to get a snack.

The kitchen looked like one of those chief kitchens you'd see in a fancy restaurant they show on TV. Stainless steel appliances, granite counter tops, the whole nine yards. Everyone was gathered around one of the main island trying to decide what to snack on as they watched some movies.

"He has a cat?" Lisa asked walking over to pet Gabriel.

"Isn't he cute?" Sam tried to hand him to Lisa, but the cat dug its claws into her and meowed. "Well I'd let you hold him, but he's literally attached to me for now. Maybe later when he gets use to us ok?"

"That's fine. I'll just pet him for now. What's his name?"

"Gabriel and he's more of a pain than anything." Christian answered trying to take the cat from Sam.

The cat hissed Sam pulled away from Christian with Gabriel. "I'm fine holding him for now Christian."

"Fine! Has everyone decided on snacks?"

"Popcorn, chips, and sodas. You guys go to the TV room and we'll bring it out." Shelby said.

Sam looked around for a bowl and put some milk in. Putting the bowl on the counter, Gabriel sat in front of it and drank while Sam helped Shelby with the popcorn. Maria and Lisa took out the soda. Sam, Christine, and Shelby brought out the popcorn and chips.

They watched several movies from horror to comedy. No one started going to bed until around four in the morning. Christian and Sam went to their room. As the door opened and to her surprise candles sprang up out of nowhere. Illuminating the room in a soft glow. The smell of lilac's filled her lungs as Beethoven's *Moonlight Sonata* started playing.

"Go sit on the bed I have a gift for you." Christian softly whispered.

So Sam sat down on the bed, while she watched Christian pulled out a small black box from a drawer. He looked extremely sexy in his black jeans without a shirt. The light played over his well defined chest and flat stomach. He had put his hair in a leather thong, at the base of his neck, to keep it out of his face.

He handed her the box, "I thought you would like this."

Sam opened the box to reveal a gold necklace in the shape of a heart with the words *I Love You* in the center of it. "Its beautiful Christian, Thank you." Kissing him.

"Let me put it on you."

"I'm glad I'm here with you. I feel so relaxed and at peace here. Like a weight has been lifted off my shoulders."

"I am too. I know you've gone through so much in such a short time. I just wanted to say how amazed and proud of how you've accepted everything."

"I'm actually surprised I didn't have a breakdown. Some days I thought I was going crazy, but not when I'm with you. You help me to see everything clearly and then I know I can handle it."

"Well I'm glad you feel that way. You are everything to me. God help everyone if something ever happened to you."

"I'm sure we will be just fine." Smiling at him.

He couldn't help but kiss her sensual lips. Heat coiled through both their bodies. The flames from the candles rose as everything in the room grew hotter. He striped off both their clothes.

Laying her down on the bed, coolness of the silk sheets felt good against her raging body. The feel of his lips on her neck sent a jolt through her. She groaned while he continued his sensual assault of her senses while his hands traveled slowly down her body. Stopping to caress her sumptuous breasts, then moving down her stomach to the triangle of dark curls. Feeling her heat he inserted his fingers, her muscles tightened around them causing him to become even harder, heightening her sensations. Bending his head he feasted on her breast. Licking once, twice, then sinking his teeth deep. Hearing her cry out with pleasure she tasted so sweet.

Merged as he was with her, he continued to build the fire within her as he closed the pin pricks. Withdrawing his fingers he brought them to his mouth to taste the spicy honey that was her. Looking in her now dark green eyes, he thrust into her unable to control himself.

I want you to loose control. Just be free. Show me the predatory lover you can be, her sultry voice sent flames through him as he moved faster, building the friction.

Sam raked her nails along his back. Feeling him grow even more in her. She kissed his roped muscles on his chest finding his pulse beating franticly in anticipation for her. Sam pierced his skin, feeding her own sexual frenzy as she heard his hoarse groans. He tasted of hot spice as the ancients blood flowed through her veins. She closed the wound right before they both exploded into what felt like a million pieces.

They laid locked together for a long while. Not wanting to separate. "Do you think we could make it to the tub like this?" Sam asked.

"We could always try." Christian smiled wickedly.

Sam just loved that smile. She kissed him before she separated them. As she got up she heard the water in the whirlpool start along with the jets. She turned to look at him.

"I do have my own powers Mi Amour." He smugly stated.

Sam walked into the bathroom, putting two towels on the corner of the tub and stepped into the hot bubbling water. It felt so good as she slipped beneath the water. When she emerged Christian was next to her.

He washed her hair and body with raspberry smelling shampoo, conditioner, and body wash. Then he started giving her the most incredible massage. They made love several times that morning before they were both over come with exhaustion sleeping peacefully through the afternoon.

6

Christian woke around three opening his eyes he now knew this was all real. She was with him forever. Smiling he got up, stretched, put on his jeans, and went to the kitchen. He didn't want to wake her. After everything she'd been through last night she'd need her rest.

He opened the door and Gabriel ran into the room and jumped on the bed. "You better not wake her or you'll be dog food." He harshly whispered. The cat just glared at him a minute before settling down next to Sam and closed his eyes.

Christian entered the kitchen, scaring Maggie, his cook and house keeper. "My god Christian why don't you give an old woman a heart attack?" She teasingly accused him.

"Sorry. Is everyone still here?"

"I believe so. Will they be staying for dinner? Armond said he'd BBQ if they were."

"I'm sure they will. They may stay another night too if it won't be to much trouble."

"You know you or your friends are never too much trouble. How is Sam doing? Are all her things here?"

"Sam is fine. She's still asleep. Gabriel is in with her. Everything she needs, right now is here. We can get the rest later."

"I will let Armond know everyone is staying. Is chicken and ribs ok or do you want surf and turf?"

"Ribs and chicken will be fine Maggie and could you make your famous peach cobbler?"

"Anything for you Christian. Oh and tell Daniel to stay out of the kitchen or he'll eat all the cobbler, then you two will get into another argument and I don't think you want Sam to witness that her first full night here."

"Thank you and I'll tell Daniel." Kissing her cheek, he headed to the pool for a quick swim.

The water was refreshing like cool fingers lightly massaging him as he did several laps. Swimming back towards the shallow end of the pool he sensed someone watching him. Looking around he saw Christine watching from the door.

"You okay?" He asked as he emerged from the pool. Water dripping from his sculpted body.

"Yes, just watching. Is the water as warm as it looks?" Christine asked heading towards Christian with a towel.

"It's between eighty-five and ninety degrees." He answered suspiciously. "Where is everyone else?"

"I don't know maybe still asleep. I just thought I'd go for a swim. Care to get back in with me?" She asked as she took off her shorts and t-shirt to revel a string bikini. "Come on Christian one swim won't hurt.

Sam's still asleep I assume since she's not with you." Sliding her hands down his wet chest.

She looked up into his eyes and he noticed that there was something not quite right with her. Next thing he knew she was pulled away and thrown into the wall, then her body moved towards the door where Sam was standing. Christine was stunned, her eyes out of focus, like she was in trance. Sam had her a few feet from the floor when a wave of water splashed over Christine. Bring her out of whatever trance she was in.

"Christine go change and meet me in the kitchen." Sam calmly said allowing Christine to get her clothes and leave.

Behind Christian lightening struck across the sky as the wind picked up and dark clouds formed over head. "Sam, what's wrong?" Knowing she was fighting her emotions.

"She was in a trance and you let your defenses down. She had a knife, intended for you." As a small switchblade flew through the door into Sam's hand. Christine yelled in frustration over it being taken, but she continued down the hall to change.

"Shit! I'm sorry honey, but how could this happened.? There's no way Devin could have gotten in here."

"He could have done it at the dance or before. Programmed her for whenever you two were alone. Probably hoping I'd fly off the handle and hurt her, which would have destroyed me mentally, but I'm learning fast to control both my emotions and my powers." Handing him the knife, "Don't worry Christian, everything will be fine." Standing on her tippy toes she kissed his cheek, then headed for the doors to the outside, but Christian seized her wrist. Pulling her back for one of the most passionate kisses she'd ever had.

He always took her breath away when he did that. Letting go Sam went out into the small storm she created to cool off and collect herself. The wind and rain was refreshing and helped to clear her head. She walked down to the lake and sat at the end of the dock. Watching the rain fall into the water it created a beautiful melody as the wind whistled through the trees.

Back in the house Christian showered, then went to look for Daniel to make sure he didn't bother Maggie or touch the cobbler. He ran into Mark in Daniel's wing. "Have you seen Daniel?"

"He's in the TV room with the girls. Where's Sam? I thought she was with you?"

"She's on the dock. She wanted to be alone for awhile."

"Is she safe here?"

"Of course she is. Devin can't be near here without me knowing and I would protect her with my life." A challenge to Christian's tone.

"As would I, just wanted to make sure." Mark calmly replied walking past him towards the TV room.

Do you need me? Hearing Sam's sweet voice drained all the tension out of him.

No sweetheart, you come in when you are ready. I'll wait for you in the TV room with the others, sending her waves of warmth to show his support knowing she was smiling, he turned to go back to the TV room to make sure Daniel stayed out of the kitchen.

Outside the wind calmed down, the rain stopped, and the clouds cleared. Sam had everything under control now and was about to head in when she heard the cry of a bird. She looked up, turning in a circle to try and see the bird. Backing up as she watched it fly over head her foot went off the dock and she was falling towards the water when an invisible platform stopped her from going in. Next she was lifted by unseen hands and placed gently back on the dock.

When Sam looked up she saw Mark with his hand extended to help her up. "Thank you. Guess I was too distracted to see where I was going. Why are you out here anyway? Shouldn't you be with Maria?" Sam asked a little nerves because she still didn't feel comfortable being a lone with him.

"I was looking for you. Good thing too or you'd be soaked right now." Smiling down at her with that smile that always caused her to melt. Even now and he knew it.

"Why?" Trying to not feel anything for him.

"I could feel your emotions and struggle for control. Are you OK? " Putting his arm around her to make sure she got off the dock safely. While trying to control his desire.

Relaxing, she walked with him back. "Christine was in a trance and tried to kill Christian while trying to push my emotions over the edge. All programmed by Devin I assume." She swayed a little, loosing her footing.

Mark held her close, then decided to carry her the rest of the way. "Have you ate today?" With general concern in his voice.

Sam just laid her head against his chest "No, I just got up and went looking for Christian when everything else happened. I guess I should I'm drained again I really appreciate everything you've done to help and would like you to help me with my control and focus of my magic."

"What about Christian? Is it ok with him?" Continuing up the stairs to the house.

"He will have to be. You know more than he does in this and its almost time for the ritual. I need all the help I can get to prepare."

"You know I'll help you with anything you ask of me."

"Thanks Mark." Kissing him on the cheek.

Meanwhile Christian found Daniel and threatened him if he went in the kitchen to bother Maggie. After a brief, but not unusual argument, Christian looked out the window to see if Sam was on her way since the storm stopped. To his surprise he saw Mark carrying her up the stairs.

He headed for the outside door in the pool area. As he opened it he saw Sam kiss Mark. He couldn't tell if it was on his cheek or lips because her hair had fallen in the way. Lightening arched across the sky before he realized it. He caught Sam's eyes as he continued to watch them.

Stopping at the top of the stairs leading down to the dock, he waited for them. "What is going on?" Venom in his voice.

Mark put Sam on the porch. "Nothing, she almost fell in the water. I stopped her, then she almost fainted. She needs food her levels are low and she's drained. I figured I'd carry her back to save her energy." Mark plainly stated not one bit intimidated by Christian.

"Go inside Mark I'll be in shortly." Sam defiantly stated, lifting her chin.

Mark left them alone, *If you need me call,* his voice a whisper.

"What the hell was that kiss all about? And don't deny it I saw you." His voice an octave lower.

"It was nothing. I thanked him for his help and asked him to help me with my focus and control. He said sure *after* he asked your reaction. I just said you'd have to live with it I need all the help I can get right now. Whether you get pissed or not. Then I thanked him again and kissed him on the cheek." Her eye's turning green as the temperature rising.

Christian took a breath calming himself first. Laying a hand on her hot skin he looked in her eyes, took possession of her mouth, and thoroughly kissing her to calm and bring the passion that was Sam back.

Sam blinked up at him, her eye's back to normal and temperature back to normal. Catching her breath she asked, "Are we crazy?"

"Yes, but we'll make it through. We both have a lot to still overcome and we'll do it together. I think control should be our first priority though." Smiling down at her.

"Yes, but not when we make love. I like when we are both out of control and free." Smiling wickedly at him sending a very detailed picture to him.

"You are so bad sometimes Mi Amour. Come let's go in and see when dinner will be done. Armond is barbequing and Maggie is making her delicious peach cobbler." Putting his arm around her as they walked inside.

They headed in the kitchen in time to see a glass bowl fall off the counter. It was caught in midair and put lightly back on the counter. Maggie looked up to see Christian standing there with who must be Sam his soul mate.

"Oh Christian thanks. I didn't feel like cleaning that up." Maggie smiled.

"That wasn't me Maggie. Sam did it. I wasn't that focused.

"Oh! How nice to know." Wiping her hands on her apron. "Hi, I'm Maggie. I'm Christian's housekeeper and cook." Extending her hand.

"Hi, I hope we aren't to much trouble for you." Smiling and shaking her hand.

"Oh no dear, I don't mind. I'm just glad to see the boys all happy."

"Well how nice to hear Maggie and you are family to all of us." Christian said. "The cobbler smells good." Walking towards the oven.

"You stay out of there." Maggie threw a towel at him that would have missed, but Sam gave it a little push and it hit him in the back.

"Hey! Don't be ganging up on me." He teased walking towards Sam.

"You leave her alone." Maggie stepped in his path. "I think you need someone to gang up on you." Winking at Sam.

Sam just laughed as Christian ran around Maggie and caught Sam before she could get away. Lifting her in the air laughing also. He was finally happy after all these centuries.

"Ok you two out so I can finish dinner." Maggie laughed.

"When will it be done? Sam's sugar is low."

"In twenty minutes, but get her some orange juice and a cookie. That should help until than."

Grabbing the OJ and cookies, they left the kitchen going into the TV room. "Cookies!" Daniel walked towards Christian.

"Back off, these are for Sam her sugar is low. Maggie said dinner will be ready in twenty minutes." Putting the juice and cookies on the coffee table.

Sam sat on the couch next to Christian taking a drink of juice. *Are you ok now?* Mark asked while holding Maria next to him.

Yes, everything is fine and I'll start feeling better in a minute. Thank you for your concern, smiling at Mark as he nodded.

"What were you two talking about?" Feeling the jealousy rising.

Sam felt his reaction and tried to calm him. "He was just checking on me that's all." Trying to sooth him.

They all watched some TV until Maggie called them to the dinning room for dinner. Entering they saw a long oak table in the center of the room that could fit at least eighteen people, a stone fireplace to the left with a huge picture window to the right showing you a great view of the lake. There was a huge chandelier in the center of the room over the table, several candelabra's throughout, and the walls were a dark red with wood trim.

They sat down to a huge feast of BBQ chicken and ribs, potato and macaroni salad, coleslaw, baked beans, chips, a relish tray, a couple other salads, and for dessert there was peach cobbler and watermelon.

"This looks delicious Maggie." John said helping Lisa with her seat.

"You always say that John." Smiling as she waited for everyone to sit before leaving to make sure they didn't need anything else.

"Oh Maggie, I'll introduce everyone to you. That's Lisa, Sam's sister next to John, Shelby over by Daniel, then Mark and Maria, and finally Christine and Mike." Christian said.

"Well, its very nice to meet all of you. If your all set I need to clean the kitchen." She left them to their dinner.

"I was thinking if you guys wanted to stay another night or so you can. Your welcome anytime." Christian stated as he started eating.

They all agreed to one more night for now. Everyone enjoyed there dinner with light conversation and some laughs. Next everyone decided to go swimming in the pool, because the mosquito's were out by now. Armond turned on the lights in the pool, some music, and made sure the Jacuzzi was ready.

Sam was getting ready when she had a bad feeling come over her. She walked over to the window and peered out into the woods. Christian came striding through the door straight to her enveloping her in his enormous strength. "What is it? I feel your uneasiness, but don't detect anything?" At that point Lisa came running in with John right behind her and Mark and Maria followed.

"Someone's near I feel evil lurking in the woods. Hatred. Venomous eye's watching us all." Next thing Sam was completely still, her eye's glazed over. By now Mike, Christine, Shelby, and Daniel had joined them.

"Sam! Baby!" Christian tried bring her back.

"NO! Let her do this. She is trying to find the source and maybe seeing through their eyes." Lisa expressed strongly.

"He's in the woods looking at us through the trees. Running in the form of a coyote along a stream testing your security to see if you notice. He's cloaked himself knowing you can't find him." A soft cry escaped her.

"She's in trouble he knows she's tracking him. Hurry link with me so we can keep her grounded. Christian you must hold her soul to you or he will attempted to take it." Lisa held out her hands. They all formed a circle around Sam.

"Who is it Lisa? Is it Devin?" Christian calmly asked while holding Sam's soul to him.

Lisa concentrated, "I'm not sure could be, but who ever it is is very strong. Possibly an ancient well versed in magic, but not a sorcerer." She swayed, feeling drained and sick, but determined to get her sister back. "Alright Mark, can you connect with her?"

"Yes"

"Good. Do it now and help her focus to bring her back to her body."

Sam, listen to me. We are going to build power together.

I'm so scared Mark. Where's Christian? her tearful voice broke his heart.

Its ok he's here. Right now he's holding tight to your soul. Who ever it is is very strong and determined according to your sis.

His name is Victor. His hatred is directed at Christian. He thinks he stole me from him and he says Christian will pay dearly for it.

Ok Sam, let's focus on getting back in your body first. Build the heat into a huge fireball. Imagine it attacking his insides. I'll make sure you feel nothing.

She did it. In the distance they heard a painful cry, then Sam went flying through the air, as Victor through her back into her body. Christian brought her to him with little thought. "Oh sweetheart, are you ok?" Checking to make sure she was physically alright.

"Do you know a Victor? Cause he's extremely pissed at you." She ask quit shaken.

"Oh Shit!" Daniel exclaimed looking from John to Christian.

Christian went to the window scanning the woods. He saw movement towards the lake a coyote appeared. Next a lightning bolt shot through the sky and it in the leg as it ran. The coyote transformed into a tall, elegant man with blond hair. "He use to be a friend., but didn't want to wait to find his soul mate." His voice calm, but Sam felt the cauldron of anger boiling within at the threat of his soul mate.

Sam watched as Victor gave a salute before disappearing. The wind picked up in gusts, as lightning arched across the sky and the rain poured down. She knew Christian was upset and pissed. She ushered everyone out and told them to meet at the pool. Closing the door softly, she lit some candles and incense, then gently put a hand on his back. She flooded his mind with warmth, mentally hugging him.

Christian closed his eyes letting the mental and physical feel of her surround him. He turned around taking possession of her mouth tears came to his eyes yet didn't fall. If he lost her the world was in trouble. He would take his anger out on everything at the lose of her. All the sudden he smelled vanilla and raspberries. It reminded him of her. "I don't have that scent in anything. How did you do that?"

"That's my little secret." Sam eyes danced with mischief.

She lightly ran her finger's down the back of his neck and back causing the most amazing sensations. He was instantly hard and ready for her. "Beautiful, you can't do that and expect me to face everyone down at the pool." Walking into the bathroom to splash some water on his face. He heard her laughter echo after him. "Come here, I want to show you something before we join the others." Taking her hand and leading her out the door.

"Where are we going?"

"That's *my* secret." He softly whispered sending shivers down her spine.

Christian stopped at the third door from their room. Opening it Sam saw a dark wooded staircase with a red carpeted runner leading to the second floor. "What's up there?" A little hesitant to proceed.

"Its ok sweetheart. There's nothing up there yet, but we can turn it into whatever we want I just want you to see it. Each wing has its own entrance to the upstairs." Pulling her up the stairs to show her there was nothing to be afraid of.

When they reached the top of the stairs candles sprang to life illuminating the main room in soft light. The carpet was a dark green, wood paneling halfway up the walls while the rest was a warm tan. There were two rooms on either side that could be used as bedrooms or offices. The interior was similar in all the rooms.

"Not much for change are you?" Peering into each room.

"I had no reason to come up here before now." Following her.

"Why now?" She asked a little distracted.

"Because of you." Pulling her into his embrace.

"Me? Why would I make the difference?" Looking into his soft brown eyes.

"You are my world now and this is your home. Now we can create this living space together. Making it ours and if and when your ready for children, we can turn the rooms into nurseries."

"I love you Christian." Kissing him lightly on the lips. "I don't need to decide all this now do I? It's a lot to absorb all at once."

"No honey you take as long as you want. We have our room downstairs for now and if you just wish to remain there than that's fine with me. I just want you to feel comfortable here and happy." Kissing the top of her head.

"I'm always happy when I'm with you."

"I'm glad. Come we need to head to the pool or someone will come looking for us thinking something happened."

They went back down stairs to the pool it was nice and steamy in there. Daniel and Shelby were in the Jacuzzi, while everyone else was in the pool. Music was playing. Sam set their towels down on the chair and sat down for a minute. She was so happy and everyone else seemed to be also this had been a great weekend.

I'm glad your happy, because that makes me happy too beautiful, Christian sent to her while she watched his grin reach his eyes. She stood up and gave him a hug. "I love you forever and always." He said then kissed her.

He jumped in the pool right after, splashing water on her. "That was cute!" She playfully yelled at him. He tried to look innocent, but she saw his intent in his eyes.

Sam waited for Shelby. Her and Daniel were heading her way to get in the pool. As her and Shelby were walking along the edge of the pool Daniel managed to push them both in. As Sam surfaced, she levitated Daniel over the deep end of the pool, but didn't drop him immediately.

"Come on Sam! I was only playing you know I can't swim. Christian, come on man tell her to put me back on the floor."

"Sorry, I don't control her and you should have known she'd retaliate." He laughed.

"Shelby, tell her to put me down."

"Hey, you pushed me in too honey, but I'm sure she'd put you down. Right Sam?"

"Oh sure, if that's what he wants." Sam lowered him to about a inch above the water. Everyone was just laughing.

"Come on! I promise to never push either of you in again ok." Now he was getting a little desperate.

Sam got out of the water, walked over to the edge of the pool where Daniel was, then brought him back on to solid ground. His expression of relief was priceless. "Give me a hug and I'll accept that as your promise."

Daniel hugged her, but whispered in her ear, "This isn't over. You haven't seen my power's yet." He pulled back and Sam saw the mischief dancing in his eyes.

"I won't expect anything less. This should be an exciting experience." Smiling at him.

Water hit Daniel. He turned to see Christian "Are you threatening my soul mate?" He jokingly asked.

"Now why would I do that? It's not like she tried to dunk me in the pool. Oh wait! She did. No threats, just some friendly pranks." He smiled walking to the shallow end.

Shelby swam over to Daniel and splashed him. "Hey! What was that for?"

"For pushing me in and your lucky I don't have her power's cause I would have dunked your ass. She's just too nice for that."

So far everything was going fine. They all swam for awhile eventually sitting in the Jacuzzi to relax. By than it was dark, the stars were out, and there was a three quarter moon out.

"Christian the night is so beautiful out can we have a bonfire?" Sam asked hopefully itching to be outside in nature.

"Of course honey, anything you want. John and I will go start it while we all meet out there in ten minutes. Let's go get changed." Grabbing her hand.

"Thank you. All the girls meet me in the kitchen to get snacks in five." Sam told then as she went out the door.

As they reached the bedroom door Christian swung Sam up into his arms and carried her through the entrance kicking it closed behind them. With a soft meow Gabriel let them know of his presents.

Christian glared at him, "Sometimes I just want to throw him out." Gabriel hissed at him.

"Well as long as I'm here you won't. And since I'll be with you for all time he will remain with us too." Smiling at the cat.

"Fine, but later tonight I want you all to myself." Lowering Sam to the floor.

"Yes, later I'm all yours, but we both need to change. I think I may need help with my suite. Do you mind?" Looking sexy and innocent all at once.

"Of course Mi Amour." Following her into the bathroom.

Christian closed the door so they had privacy from prying eyes. He slowly untied her bikini top and hung it over the shower door. Next he slowly pulled down her bottoms. First over her thighs, revealing the dark triangle of curls between her legs, beckoning him to feel the wetness he was sure was there. Moving the bikini the rest of the way down her shapely legs to her petite feet. She stepped out of them.

As he stood back up he took off his swimming trunks, revealing to Sam just how much such a simple request could make him want her.

She reveled in the sexual power she had over him at that moment. Kneeling in front of him she wrapped her hands around him and began to stroke. Christian looked down at her, a groan to escape him as she took him into the warmth of her mouth. Sam added suction while she flicked his tip with her tongue feeling his pleasure as shivers went through him. She looked up and caught his gaze the fire in his eyes was intense and increased the passion she was feeling.

Christian couldn't take it anymore. He pulled Sam up and sat her on the counter. Spreading her legs, like a sacrifice for only him, and impaled her as she wrapped her legs around his waist. The friction was a delicious sensation of sexual hunger thrusting harder, faster. He wanted to be so deep in her he would never be able to leave.

Sam was consumed with so much ecstasy she was drowning in it. Floating on wave after wave of passion she never wanted it to end. Christian took them so high that she felt beyond everything sensible and real. The fire kept building that she thought they'd both be engulfed. When they came, it was so intense she heard them both and wasn't sure if it was out loud or in her head, but she didn't care anymore.

Christian had to sit Sam on the counter again and steady himself before his legs gave out from such pleasure and they both ended up on the floor. "Are there any burn marks because I swear I thought we'd caught something on fire. Is it always going to be like this?" Sam asked a little breathless.

"No burn marks and yes its always like this. I've been told our sexual desires for each other will increase as time goes on, but for now my beautiful lover, we should get dressed and get back down stairs. I'm sure they are already talking about us and what they think we are doing. Which would be right, but I won't give them the satisfaction of knowing that." Grinning at her, he dressed quickly to distract himself so he wouldn't be temped to pull her to the floor and screw her brains out again. He kissed her saying he'd let her have some privacy to get dressed and meet her outside in a little bit.

Quit fucking around and get your ass down here. I need help with the snacks and I can't find the marshmallows, Lisa lovingly told her.

First, I can fuck around with my soul mate whenever I want and second I don't think they have marshmallows. So make a list and send Mark and Maria to the store. I'll be down in a minute, Sam envisioned Lisa rolling her eyes, but did what was asked.

Lisa handed Maria the list. Her, Mark, and Mike had Armond drive them to the store quickly. Luckily it wasn't to late and everything was still opened as they entered the store Mark had a bad feeling they were being watched. He scanned, but couldn't detected anything unusual. They split up so they could get everything on the list faster. Mark went to the back of the store to get some Ready Whip for the strawberry shortcake for later. While he was back there he was drawn to one of the doors leading to the storage room. Entering the room he saw the same man he saw earlier at the house that Christian referred to as Victor. "What do you want?" He asked cautiously.

"Just to talk. I feel your need to be with Christian's soul mate. Did he take her from you?" Victor questioned casually.

"No, they were meant to be together. Stay away from Sam she is under my protection along with Christian's." Mark challenged.

"I see. You can't deny you crave her, you long to feel her inside you. That's a challenge you never achieved I can help you, if you'd like."

"I'm fine." Mark eyed him cautiously.

Victor grabbed his forearm, more as a gesture of understanding, as he walked past him. When he removed his hand he scratched Mark. There was a thin line of blood about a inch long on his arm. Mark just found some paper towel to stop the bleeding. Not thinking much about the incident he met up with Maria and Mike at the car and they headed back to the houses.

Mean while Sam was in the kitchen helping Lisa with the snacks. "So what do we have?" Sam asked.

"Well I sent Mark to get the stuff for s`mores and strawberry shortcake. We still have some cobbler, ice cream, and watermelon left."

"That should be enough. Christine can you get the bowls and plates and take then out to Shelby. She's helping Daniel outside by the fire."

"Sure." Getting everything out of the cabinet, then going outside.

"So are you still getting ready for the ritual? You have less than a week and a half, then the wedding after that." Concern in Lisa's voice.

"What do you think? Of course I'm not ready. I still have a lot to learn. Mark is going to help me tomorrow morning. Mom is helping with making out the wedding list."

"Mom's helping with the list? When are you going shopping for your wedding dress? You have a lot to do for this wedding too. Let me know what I can do to help."

"I will, but let's just leave it for one more night. Then I'll get serious about everything tomorrow. I promise."

Handing Sam the cobbler and ice cream, they went outside to the picnic table surprisingly there were no mosquito's. She heard one owl call to another, *How beautiful. I love nature at night or during the day.*

I know honey, I want you to feel at home here. Either inside with me or out here in nature.

Sam went up to Christian and gave him a hug as Mark, Maria, and Mike joined them with the rest of the food.

"If that is all Christian, I'm going to retire for the evening." Armond stated.

"Thank you Armond see you tomorrow." Christian answered. Armond turned with a nod and went back inside.

"Sam would you mind a magic lesson tonight? The moon is just right for one. We would remain by the dock so you could see us Christian." Mark politely questioned both of them.

Sam looked at Christian, who nodded his approval. Sam took Marks hand and went down to the dock. "So what is the lesson?"

"It's a simple one. Face me and place your hands in mine, now I'm thinking of several objects. What I want you to do is figure out what they are, find them, and bring them here. All with the power of your mind."

"I can't that's to much." Sam tried to pull away, but Mark increased his grip.

"Sam you can and you have done so unconsciously already. Look at me!" Bring her focus back to him only. "Release your fears and doubts. I believe in you now believe in yourself and your powers."

Sam took a deep breath and let it out slowly, then began her focus. Eyes going green, heat increasing. She saw the white handled knife, a purple candle, and a pewter cat.

"Good you've done the first one. Now locating them will require more energy. Keep focus." Mark encouraged her.

She found the candle in the dinning room, the pewter cat in the library, and the knife in Mark's bag.

"Keep going. Bring them to you, call for them to you."

The heat increased more. Sam was sweating now. The back door to the house opened and out came the candle, cat, and knife past the table, down to the dock, and finally into Sam's hands. Her eye's lit up as she realized she'd done it. "I did it, Mark. Christian did you see? I did it!" She yelled excitedly.

"Yes honey I saw it. I'm proud of you." Christian yelled back.

"Alright Sam we'll stop for tonight and really get to work on it tomorrow. Let's headed back up." Turning her towards the stairs.

She put her hand on his forearm for a minute and felt his wince slightly. "What happened?" Seeing his scratch.

Mark told her about his encounter with Victor while they walked back to the table, at least some of it, he wasn't about to let Sam know how he still felt about her. "Lisa come here and heal Mark's arm please."

"What happened?" Lisa asked as she headed towards them with Maria in tow.

Sam told them everything Mark had told her. Lisa put her hand over the wound and Mark could feel the heat coming from her into him as his body started to heal. He was amazed at her healing abilities. He was glad to be their friend and not their enemy. Especially Sam's, cause once she had a good understanding and hold on her magic she'll be quite powerful.

Lisa's voice pulled him away from his thoughts, "Your all healed now lets have some fun. Does anyone have a radio for out here?"

"I'll get mine honey be right back." As John headed back inside.

"Sam? Lisa?" The wind whispered to them. They looked at each other, then looked at everyone else. No one seemed to hear it but them two.

What should we do Sam? It sounds like grandma, but wouldn't she show herself?

Yes. I don't think its her. Take my hand and keep your mind open to mine. I'm going to try and find out who it is.

I'm afraid Sam.

Lisa I'm right here with you and so are the guys. If we need help they will know immediately. Now its going to get a little hot, she told Lisa. The wind began to increase, temperature went up, and a faint glow began to form around them.

Sensing the change Christian looked over at Sam. He watched as a white light engulfed them. *John where the hell are you?*

I'm on my way out of the house. Lisa wanted a radio. Why? What's wrong?

Get out here now! Something is happening to Lisa and Sam.

John ran out the door to where the girls were. Daniel, Mark, and Christian surrounded them. The heat from the light was so intense he thought they'd all get burned.

Lisa I only kept my link with you opened. I'm going to transfer some of my power to you for a bit. The guys are getting to close and I'm afraid they'll get hurt. Just focus and move them back. Like a little push, then envision a bubble around us. After all that the power will be sent back to me ok?

I think I have it, Taking a breath, *I'm ready. Go ahead.*

"Christian what is happening to them?" John calmly asked.

"I'm not sure, but I'm going to get…" Christian, along with the others, was thrown back about twenty feet from Lisa and Sam with the wave of Lisa's hand. Then a barrier formed around the girls and the heat disappeared. It was contained a long with them, in the barrier.

"What the hell was that?" Daniel asked dusting himself off.

"They were trying to protect us from the heat." Mark stated standing up.

"But I didn't think Lisa had any powers like that." John stared at Lisa.

"She doesn't." Mark told him.

"Then how the hell was she able to throw us all back like that?" Now John was getting pissed.

"Calm down, Sam must have transferred some of her power to Lisa temporarily. She was trying to protect us from her power. I just wish I knew what she was doing." Looking a little lost Christian just watched her.

Its done Sam. That was kind of fun.

Thank you sis. It may seem like fun, but its hard to control at first. Now I can't find the exact location, but it was carried from the woods across the lake. So no it wasn't our grandmother. Who ever it is had a mental path to us. Use you barrier I taught you and I'll make the guys aware of this.

Ok, Lisa closed her eyes as the barrier disappeared along with the heat. When she opened them Sam was smiling at her.

The white handled knife flew into Sam's hand and she placed her other hand on the blade. "Listen, with whoever is out there after us, if you need me I want to be able to help you anytime. What we will do is mix our blood so we can help each other, but I won't force you."

"I understand and I'm willing to do it, but hurry before they stop us." Watching the guys head their way.

Sam sliced her palm, then Lisa's and joined together, interlocking their fingers. "Bound by blood. Sister to sister. Once put together let nothing take apart. Through miles or death. When in need, let us unite to help the other. So mote it be." Sam finished just in time.

"Samantha, What have you done?" Christian asked with concern.

"She bound them together and made their sister connection stronger. Its been done on and off through out the centuries among sorceress families." Then Sam saw recognition in Mark's eyes. "Especially if someone is after them."

"Who's after you two Sam?" Christian pulled her hand from Lisa's seeing their wounds were healed.

"I don't know, but whoever it is knows our family. The winds carried the voice from across the lake in the woods. They're gone now."

"What did it say?"

"Just our names in grandmother's voice, but I know for sure it wasn't her."

"Everyone stay on alert until we figure all this out." Ushering Sam towards the door.

"No! I will not hide." Sam sternly said.

"Neither will I." Lisa agreed pulling out of John's embrace to stand by her sister.

"OH MY GOD! You two are going to drive me crazy. Fine! We will continue with our plans, but no one goes anywhere alone." Holding his temper down he pulled Sam to him and kissed her feverishly.

"Thank god Shelby's not like that. You two have your hands full." But as Daniel turned Shelby was right there.

"And what do you mean by that?" Fire in her eyes.

"Shit!" He ran, but didn't make it far. He ran into a invisible wall.

Glaring back at Sam, "You just wait missy. I'll get you back."

Sam smiled at Daniel as she walked over to the table. Then she blew him a kiss. Shelby hit the back of his head over the threat and was playfully yelling at him. Christine and Mike sat down in front of Sam.

"So when are you going to plan the wedding? It's almost time and you haven't done anything yet." Christine asked.

"Probably tomorrow night. I want all my bridesmaids to meet me at the bridal shop at three tomorrow to help me with picking out your dresses and mine. Don't worry, it will all get done." She smiled at Christine. "Mike I'll need you to come with us too, Since someone thinks we can't take care of ourselves."

"Sure, I'll be there."

The rest of the girls joined them and really got into talking about the wedding, while the guys stayed by the fire. Later they all took a walk along the lake front the water felt cool as they walked. Sam occasionally sent some water Daniel's way, but eventually quit when he deflected it and sent it her way. Showing Sam he did have powers.

"Smart ass." Glaring at him.

"Right back at ya' babe."

"Okay you two grow up." Christian laughed right before water covered him. Sam went one way and Daniel went the other. Soon everyone was soaked. Splashing each other and laughing. They all just decided to swim in the lake. Water going everywhere, with and without the use of their powers, everyone was having fun.

Water logged they headed for the bonfire to dry out. John and Lisa got everyone towels to dry off with. They sat by the fire awhile, talking about a little of everything. They eventually all turned in for the night.

7

Sam dreamt of cheetahs on and off all night. Sometimes the dreams turned dark. Blood, screams, and death all around her. She awoke sweating and scared, but Christian was there calming her and surrounding her with his warmth.

"I'll let nothing happen to you." Turning her head so he could look in her frightened eyes. "I promise." He whispered confident, yet lovingly.

Soon Sam was asleep again and Christian reinforced her sleep with a sharp command. He met John and Daniel in the library. Daniel was standing by the fireplace drinking a beer and John was pacing the floor like a caged lion. "What's wrong with him?" Christian asked Daniel taking the beer he handed him.

"What the hell do you think is wrong with me? Lisa has been threatened twice now." Christian saw the fire in John's eyes and noticed his nails lengthening.

"John you need to calm down first. Before someone comes down and see's you. I understand your frustration. We will all get through this." Christian calmly told him.

John's anger was coming at him in waves. The wind had increased and a storm moved in Christian couldn't blame him for how he felt. He wished he could figure out what was happening himself. "Here, this may help for now." Handing John a beer. "Right now we know Devin is after Sam for her powers, Victor has shown up for some reason and wants her to save his soul, and something else is after her and Lisa so what options do we have?"

"We could just keep them here. Then we know they'll be safe." Daniel answered.

"Yeah, then we'd hear them bitch that they can't go anywhere." John bitterly stated.

"John's right. We can't keep them caged. I hate to do this, but we need to keep track of everyone around them and if need be scan their mind. It's the only way for now." Christian plainly said.

"Fine." John grumbled.

"Alright." Daniel shrugged.

"Let's go play some video games and calm down." They all moved to the TV room.

Sam was having a strange dream. She was in a candle lit room. The walls were a dark mustard color, the floor a tan, and a four poster bed with royal red sheets on it. She heard faint music playing, but couldn't locate it or figure out what exactly was playing. There were no windows in the room and one door. Opening the door to a dark hallway she walked down it towards the music. She saw light flickering from a room on her left. As she entered the room it looked just like Christian's library. A fire was going in the fireplace and she noticed someone sitting in front of the fire. "Hello?"

"Sam? What are you doing here?" Mark turned to her.

"I don't know. I just woke up in a strange room and followed the music here."

"Well come and sit down by the fire. Its nice and warm and you look cold."

She was a little cold. She had no idea why she was wearing such a skimpy nightgown. As she sat down she got a kink in her neck, so she was trying to rub it out with no relief.

"You ok?" Mark asked sincerely.

"Yeah, I just have a kink in my neck. I must have just slept on it wrong." Sam answered trying to stretch.

"Here let me help you."

Sam sat between his legs so he could massage her neck he was gentle, yet firm and she seemed to relax immediately. She didn't want him to stop it felt so good. She didn't move away when he moved to her shoulders, then he kissed her neck in the spot he knew would drive her crazy.

"Sam you always smell so good and always look beautiful no matter what you've been doing." Mark whispered in her ear.

"Thank you Mark, I think that's one of the nicest things you've ever said to me. And I always thought you looked good." She smiled up at him.

Mark looked down at Sam and couldn't resist her luscious lips. He took possession of her mouth before either one of them could think about it. She didn't pull away, but deepened the kiss. Mark knew she would cause she never could resist his kisses. Pulling her to the floor he cupped her full breast underneath her nightgown. He was so hot and hard right now that he wanted to rip off her clothes and fuck her right here and now.

Sam was getting so hot and wet that the feel of his hands on her was driving her crazy her skin was becoming to sensitive for her clothes. As if reading her mind, which he probably was, Mark took off both their clothes. He started kissing down her chest, stopping to suckle on her breasts he then continued down her flat stomach to spread her legs and view what he'd been waited all this time to have.

Mark watched Sam close her eyes moaning softly as he inserted two fingers into her wet core. Moving in and out slowly, he knew he was increasing her pleasure wanting to taste her sweetness. As soon as his tongue touched her, her hips bucked of their own accord causing more moans to be torn from her throat. Her cries were increasing the searing fire building in his body. He moved to insert himself into her tight sheath. The feeling was the most incredible thing he'd ever experience. He moved faster, in and out, building the friction taking them higher and higher.

Back in reality Maria came running into the TV room. "Christian I need you. Hurry something's wrong with Mark." Grabbing his hand and pulling him of the room. John and Daniel followed.

"Ok I'm coming. Calm down Maria and tell me what's wrong."

"Its Mark. There's blood on his arm and I can't wake him. Its like he's stuck in some kind of dream, but he's bleeding a lot." Tears streaming her face.

They opened the bedroom door to see Mark lying on the bed groaning, his arm was covered in blood, then he called out for Sam.

Reality hit Christian hard as he realized what was happening and who was doing it. "No!" He ran to his room to find Sam in the same state. "John!" He yelled as lightening crashed to the ground.

John came running in and was speechless as he saw Sam. Lisa came in and paled visibly as she saw her sister like that and all the blood. "My god." She whispered.

"Its Victor. I won't let him have her." Venom in his voice.

"Christian, we must get them out of there now or we'll lose them both." John tried to calm him. Now understanding his feelings. "I'll have Daniel get the herbs and candles for both of them while I go wakeup everyone. We'll need their help." Heading out, the door bell rang. "Who the hell is that at this time of night?" Talking to no one special as he waked out.

Lisa walked over to Sam's bloody arm to start cleaning it when Christian stopped her. "You mustn't touch the blood or it could infect you too. Then I'd have to deal with John and I'm just not in the mood right now. Wait for him to return with the herbs and candles first."

Lisa shook her head and just sat on a chair by the bed, feeling helpless for now. She felt a strange vibration and liked up to see one of the most dangerous and frightening man she'd ever saw. Power clung to him like a second skin. His long black hair pulled back and tired in a leather thong, his piercing gray eye's looked from Lisa to Sam.

"Nicholas, welcome brother." Christian stood up and hugged him briefly. "Your timing is excellent as I could use all the help I can get."

"I sensed danger around you and thought I'd come check it out. So who are these lovely women and what is wrong with her?" Eyeing Sam.

"This is Lisa, my soul mate's sister and my soul mate Sam, of the White Sorceress, who lays there stuck in one of Victor's death dreams." Christian introduced grimly.

"I see and where is Daniel?" Nicholas questioned.

"With Mark. He is also caught in the dream. They are ex's and must be why Victor picked him."

"I sense your distress Lisa. Do you have a way to get to Sam in her dream?" Nicholas calmly asked.

"I've never tried, but Sam increased our connection earlier tonight. I'm a healer and no of nothing else." Worry crossed her face.

"If you'd allow me I can help, but we are running out of time."

Lisa looked from Nicholas to Sam to Christain. "Lisa its ok, Nicholas is my older brother. He has great power and can help, but he needs your connection to Sam to do it and I will be with you all the way." Christian sent warmth to her.

I will too sweetheart, Lisa looked at the door to see John enter with herbs and candles.

"Okay what do I need to do?" Determined to save them both with John encouragement.

"First if you can find a connection to her."

Lisa closed her eyes, she followed the link, but it was blocked. "Dammit its blocked. I'm sorry John. Save me too." Touching Sam's bloody arm before anyone knew of her intentions.

"Lisa!" John cried out, lunging to pull her back, but Nicholas was there first.

"John, we will save her, but this may be the only way to save them all." He said holding John back with little effort.

Then they heard Lisa "They are in… wait, looks like your library

Christian. A fire is going and I hear music. Beethovan's *Moonlight Sonata.* One of Sam's favorites. I'm sorry I can't stop them, but I can report what they're doing… or not. I don't think you want to know Christian."

More lightening struck along with the raging storm outside. "Why would she do this?"

"Christian if you'd think she can't help it she's trapped there, but we need to stop them now." Nicholas informed him again.

"Wait, something else is happening." Lisa had their attention.

❧

In the dream, Sam's vision cleared long enough to see two feline's in the far corner. One cheetah and one black panther. "Mark"

"Yes, Sam?" A little out of breathless.

"Why are there two big cats over there?"

"I'll tell you later." Mark took possession of her mouth, filling her mind with passion and desire. Bringing her to the breaking point.

Sam, a far off voice called, *Come back.*

"Lisa?" Recognizing her voice. "Mark something is wrong." Trying to fight the friction building between them.

"What do you mean?" Feeling not quite himself, but unable to stop the desire.

"We are making love." Out of breathe. "But not really." Unable to stop what they were doing they were going higher and higher floating above everything.

Sam your caught in a death dream. You must fight it. Both of you have to stop. Your bleeding to death in reality.

The reality of the situation hit her like a rock. "Oh my god, Mark we have to stop. This isn't real." Now getting control of herself, but he was to heavy. "Mark!" She yelled then hit him with all her might.

The impact disoriented him enough to think on his own. "Owe! No don't hit me again. I'm myself." Rubbing his jaw.

"Good now how do we awake?" Sam asked looking for her gown.

"I'm not sure, but I think they have to wake us up some how."

The cats were still in the corner just watching them now. "So since we have time, explain about the cats." Sam itched to go pet one.

Mark understood her need to touch the cats, to be with them. It was normal for them as they were associated with the feline side. "Fine, each of us, when we receive our magic, also receive a natural life so to say. Some get animals, like we do, some get the elements, and some get trees, plants, flowers. Its all part of our coming of age. You are of the cheetah, fast, cunning, strong. I'm of the black panther same as the cheetah and if we ever need to, we can shape shift into these animals, but it takes lots of practice to shift and control the animal. I'll teach you that later."

"Can I go pet them?" Sam asked.

"I think you should be careful. I'll go over there with you." Following her over to the corner.

Sam was in awe at being so close to something so wild in nature. She slowly moved her hand towards the cheetah. Stopping to let her sniff it before allowing Sam to pet her. Touching the animal's fur was like feeling silk it was so soft and lush. Sam turned to Mark with a smile. She moved closer and the cheetah rubbed her head on Sam's arms and back, probably to show others Sam was hers.

The black panther eyed Mark deciding he was still no threat, he knocked Mark over playfully. Mark played with the big cat for awhile, while Sam and her cheetah just laid in the corner watching.

Lisa seemed a little more focused, now that Sam and Mark understood what was going on and had a handle on their desire. "Ok, now that they know what's happening. How do we get them out of there?"

"First, we'll clean their wounds and heal them, then we should hopefully be able to just wake them up." Nicholas answered as he brought Lisa the towel and water. With his help Lisa wasn't infected. They cleaned Sam's arm, while Maria did the same for Mark, as Christian held Sam's other hand. Needing the physical contact.

Lisa and Nicholas started healing both of them. It was a long processes, as there bodies were shutting down. They were both given blood to help with healing. Mark awoke first a little confused as to where he was. "Where's Sam? Is she ok?" Looking around he saw Maria tears in her eyes, "Oh honey, I'm so sorry. I had no idea this was going to happen. Please stop crying." Pulling her to him to comfort her.

"I'm just glad your ok." Snuggling closer to him.

Mark looked at the man at his side and then Daniel, "Mark this is Nicholas. He is Christian's older brother and the one who healed you."

"I am in your debt, thank you." Nicholas just nodded. "Is Sam awake yet?" Mark asked Daniel.

"John said she is still out and if you are ok, to bring you to Sam's room." Daniel led the way.

As Mark entered, he was taken back at what he saw. Sam was so pale her skin looked transparent her lips were almost white. Christian looked up with a glare.

"Now brother, we will settle this later. For now we must focus on Sam." Nicholas sat next to Lisa. Lightening struck again in retaliation.

❧

Figuring she had fallen asleep. Sam raised her head to find herself in the woods. "Mark? Where are you?" Silence answered her. The cats were gone too.

Rising she could tell it had just rained and it must still be before three in the morning. She started walking, growing more afraid by the second. Not of the woods, but of the situation and wondering who was doing it.

As if on cue Victor appeared before her. "Hello Sam, beautiful evening isn't it?"

"What do you want? Why are you doing this to me?" Moving back as he came towards her.

"Why? Well I guess because I want Christian to suffer, to know how I feel. To see him fall from that high pedestal he's on."

"Why? What did he do to you?" Sam felt warmth surround her. Relief filled her at the knowledge that Christian was finally with her.

"He took you from me and now I will take you back. He and his brothers have always thought they were better than the rest of us cause leadership has been handed down their bloodline through the centuries." Pinning Sam up against a tree. Victor smiled wicked as one of his nails lengthened into a sharp talon. "Now since he isn't here physically, you'll pay for what he did." Running his nail down the soft flesh of her chest shredding her gown, exposing her body to him.

Tears ran down her face, but she refused to make a sound. Her eyes changing the winds increasing as he continued to slash her. Shallow cuts so she'd bleed slowly. Raising her hand, with great effort, she attempted to bring a bolder towards her, in hopes of knocking him out or at least enough so he'd let her go.

Bringing both her hands above her head he spat, "Nice try, now its my turn and I intend to have fun with you." He draw closer, inhaling her sent, then surprised Sam by sinking his teeth into her neck.

She tried to move to throw him off, but his powers were a lot stronger than hers. She cried out for Christian in desperation sending a thought to all of them, *I'm sorry I failed you,* then all went black.

The storm outside the house increased ten fold as Christian shook with fury. His brother laid a hand on his shoulder, *Raphael and Lucian are on their way. We will not lose her. Do you feel her spirit? It is strong she's a fighter and you must be too,* the calm voice helped to stable the fury within him. He no longer saw shades of red.

Taking a deep breathe then exhaling, he looked at Sam again. Every slash of Victor talon appered on her, along with the pin pricks from his teeth. She looked almost dead her heart was irregular, her breathing labored. "Lisa can you contact Sarina?" Calming his tone.

"Yes I'll have her here in a minute." And right after she said it Sarina appeared.

"What is happening to her?" Concern in her eyes as she walked over to the bed.

"Victor has Sam in a death dream. Mark was there too, but we were able to get him out." Nicholas answered.

Straightening Sarina looked at Nicholas, "You know what we must do."

"Yes and my brothers have just arrived to help, but I don't know of Christian's reaction to this situation.

"I will deal with his wrath later we must act fast. I see candles and incense are laid out. Daniel get more herbs please. Mark where is the knife Devin had?"

"I think Sam had it last."

"Call it to you we need it. When everyone is here form a mental link. Draw on all your powers. Christian I need you to hold her soul to you no matter what don't let her go to summerland. Its not a place for her. Her place is with you always."

Everyone formed a circle as Daniel and Christian's other two brother's entered the room. Mark handed Sarina the knife.

"I need now Mark, Christian, and Lisa at Sam's sides." Christian stayed where he was, Lisa stood next to him and Mark across form them.

"Good, now I need blood from each of you."

"No! She's not strong enough yet." Mark implied.

"You will do as I asked Mark. Now!" Fire in Sarina's eyes matched Marks as he lifted his hand towards Sarina. She slashed his palm, then Sam's and placed them together. Next was Lisa's and Sam's other hand. "Now Christian you must drain her to almost the point of death."

"I will not take her life and neither will you." He tried to grab for Sam, but his brother's restrained him. "I swear if you kill her…" Seathing even more.

Laying a gentle hand on him, "My child, I would never hurt one of my own, but this is the only way to save her now. Victor has taken her blood. She will live have faith in me. Now please do as a I say."

Christian calmed enough to get a little control leaning over Sam he whispered his love for her, then his teeth pierced her.

"Ok, Nicholas I need you at her head and your other brothers at her feet." The boys took there position. "Good hold her down tight, cause once this starts her change will happen fast. Mark and Lisa link your finger's with hers." Checking on Christian she noticed he was done. "Now you must replenish her with your blood. She will go through a painful change, but its necessary. At some point her animal will fight to save her and may take shape. Still hold tight. Sam's very powerful at such a young age." Sarina smiled at the thought.

Sam became aware of something happening to her. Pain sliced through her like a knife it took her breath away as her eyes flew open to see Christian. A faint coppery taste filled her mouth, but she continued to gulp down the spicy liquid, then the pain hit again. She couldn't even cry out. Sam knew than, she was dying, *Christian I don't want to die. I haven't really lived. I need you. I love you. Please save me.*

Her weak voice crying out to him, made him want to destroy everything due to the state she was in, *I will never let you go. Sarina says you are going through a change that will save you. I'm sorry your in pain and I'd take it myself if I could. Please hold on. For me. It's almost over.*

"Good Christian. Keep up her confidents she's almost through it. Let her know her animal will always be a part of her."

Sam your grandmother say's your animal will always be a part of you. Whatever that means, Christian heard a soft laugh in his head. Then felt her relax enough to just float above the pain.

"Hold tight, Sam is letting it all happen now and I sense her animal wanting out." Sarina stated. Next thing they see is fur start appearing on her. The brothers and Lisa could feel her bones reshaping and within a minute a cheetah laid where Sam was. "It is done you can release her." Sarina watched the cat roll onto her stomach and lay her head on Christian's lap.

"Will she change back soon?" Christian asked automatically petting her head.

"Yes while she sleeps. I will send her to sleep now so her body can adjust and heal." And with that Sarina sent a strong command to Sam to sleep. Everyone, but Christian, left. He laid on the bed with her and also went to sleep to heal, mentally anyway.

8

Several hours had past by the time Christian awoke. Turning his head he saw Sam in human form again. He leaned over and kissed her cheek, then slowly got out of bed trying not to disturb her. He heard a soft rapping on their door.

"Yes?" Opening it to find Mark standing there.

"Is she awake yet?"Mark questioned.

"No, but she's back in human form. Why?" Glaring at him

"Because I wanted to know. Even if you don't like it, I will always be apart of her life."

"That maybe, but I still don't completely trust you. Especially with what just happened."

"That I didn't do purposely I had no control."

"She should remain asleep for another hour or so." Closing the door as he entered the hall. "I trust you will leave her alone." Christian challenged.

"Of course." He replied following Christian back down the hall.

Christian walked by the TV room on his way to the kitchen. "Hey Christian?" John called.

"Yeah John, What's up?" Walking into the TV room.

"How's Sam? Is she up yet?" Concern in John's eyes as he held Lisa.

"She's still asleep, but back in human form. She should awake in a couple of hours." Chrstian said right before they heard Sam scream.

He was at her side in a instant. "Mi Amour, Its ok I'm here. Your home again." Holding her shaking body while trying to calm her.

John and Lisa came in the room and sat on the other side of her. "Sam what is it?" Lisa asked calmy as she touched her arm.

"Its nothing I just thought I was still stuck in the dream. Everything came rushing back as I awoke I didn't mean to scare you." Smiling a little at Christian.

"Never apologizes for something you couldn't help. Come let's lay you back down you still need rest." Christian tried fixing the pillows for her.

"Christian, I don't want to sleep anymore." Hearing the desperation in her voice her helped her out of bed.

"Are you hungry? I was just going to have Maggie fix me something."

"That would be fine." Taking a step, but her legs gave out and he caught her.

"Maybe I'll carry you to the kitchen, then we'll change and go in the pool to work on strengthening your legs again. I can't very well carry you down the aisle for our wedding now can I?" Teasing her to lighten the mood.

Sam just laughed a little, "I guess not that would probably look a little funny."

"Carrying you wouldn't be funny to me." A hint of mischief in his brown eyes. Sam really laughed as he took her to the kitchen Lisa and John joined them.

"What can I get you guys?" Maggie asked.

"Let's see, eggs, bacon, steak, yes a nice juicey steak if you have it and OJ." Sam told her.

"Are we a little hungry Sam?" John asked playfully.

"She needs lots of protein to build her strength especially after what she's been through. I'll have the same Maggie, if you don't mind." Christian said.

"Us too." John added.

"Sure, its no problem. It will be ready in twenty minutes." Handing Sam her OJ. "Drink this so no one worries about you passing out." Smiling at her.

"Thank you Maggie." Taking a sip.

"So any plans today or are you going to wait until tomorrow?" Maggie asked as she scrambled the eggs.

"I think I'll just stay here and rest, but maybe someone could get me some wedding books and a planner so I could start a little today." Sam looked at Christian lovingly.

"Yes my dear I'll have someone go get that stuff for you." Kissing her cheek.

In came Daniel, "I smell food. What's cooking?"

"Steak and eggs. I suppose you want some too." Daniel said yes. "I swear no one can eat around here without you knowing about it." Maggie laughed.

"Nope and that smells delicious."

"Well go find out if anyone else wants some."

"Alright be right back."

"I'm sure you will"

Well just as Maggie thought, everyone wanted some so she had it all ready in twenty minutes and they all sat in the dinning room for breakfast. Conversation was light most of it was about the wedding. They only had two weeks left even though Sam had gone through the change early, she still had to complete the rest of the ritual next Saturday evening.

After breakfast everyone split off and did their own thing. Sam and Christian went to the pool to work her legs, John and Lisa went to find books for Sam, and the rest of them decided to go play vollyball on the beach in back.

The water was nice and warm. Christian had Sam just sit on the edge with her legs in the water. He helped her exercise them and when he thought she was warmed up enough he had her do some laps. He enjoyed watching her in the pool she seemed like a dolphin the way she swam so easily.

"Alright my little mermaid, time to go soak in the jacuzz." Laughing as he diverted her splashes. Watching her, as she got out of the pool, he grew hard instantly as the water ran off her body. He pulled her to him letting her feel his hard length press against her stomach.

"Do we have a problem?" Sam smiled as she rubbed him through his swimming trucks.

"Nothing we can't take care of." Smiling wickedly back. He pulled her towards the sauna kissing her feverishly.

"Christian! We can't do this here, during the day. There's to many people right outside." Shocked at his boldness.

"Woman, you drive me crazy. I will find a way to calm down for now, but tonight your mine." A challenge in his voice.

Mike came running through the door with Christine following. She was dripping wet. "Mike get back here." She yelled.

"No, I told you not to tickle me." Laughing as her ran around the pool to get away from her.

"Christine what did he do?" Sam questioned.

"He threw me off the dock." Angerly answering.

"I told her not to tickle me, but she wouldn't listen." Trying to defend himself.

Mark and Maria came in laughing. They walked over towards Christine and Sam to watch the show. Daniel and Shelby joined them shortly after.

"Do you need help Christine?" Maria asked.

"Hey now! That's not fare." Mike yelled.

"Neither was throwing me in the lake. Sam can you just put him in the pool?"

"Hey!"

"Sorry, Christine. I must use my powers only for good." Sam tried to keep a straight face, but couldn't help laughing at it all.

"Thanks Sam." Mike smiled, "See she likes me better."

"Just for that." Sam sent him in the pool with a loud splash. Everyone was laughing over it.

Are you ok Sam? Mark inquired, not looking at her, but at Mike smiling so Christian wouldn't know he was talking to her. Figuring Sam couldn't handle a fight right now.

I'm fine, thank you, interlocking her fingers with Christian.

"Oh Christian, I have to call work and let them know I'm sick today." Sam tried walking away.

He pulled her back. "I already took care of it. They said they'd see you tomorrow and you can give your notice then.

"You always take care of me don't you?"

"Of course, it is my duty as your soul mate, to put your health and happiness first." Grinning at Sam as he helping her into the Jacuzzi.

Shelby and Maria went to put on their suits along with Mark while Christine and Mike put on some dry clothes. Daniel just lounged in one of the pool chairs and Christian held Sam in the Jacuzzi massaging her shoulders.

Maggie came in, "Christian I'm sorry to interupt, but you have a phone call."

"Do you know who it is?"

"No, they just asked for you."

"Okay I'll get it. Are my brother's up yet?" He asked as he got out of the Jacuzzi. "I'll be right back."

Sam watched as he left, then leaned her head back and closed her eyes. The hot water felt good on her legs. She was moving them a lot better now.

"Hey Sam, do you mind if I turn on the radio? It's to quiet in here."

"Go head Daniel. I don't care." She answered with her eyes still closed.

"Do you want a coke? I'm going to get one."

"Diet please. Thanks." She heard him leave.

Not sure how long she'd laid there alone, but she became aware of someone watching her. She opened her eyes to see Mark staring down at her. "Yes? Do you need something?"

"No, just looking at how beautiful you are. Can I join you? I'll sit on the opposite side. I promise." Holding out his hands in surrender.

"I guess, just stay on your side." Sam was a little uneasy around him since what happened. *The Boys of Summer* started playing on the radio. She focused on that hoping Daniel would hurry up and get back here.

"Sam, listen we need to talk about what happened."

"No we don't. Its over and we both survived it. End of story." Sam was getting more nerves.

"Yes we do. I feel responsible for it because I let Victor get into my head and I didn't block it. You know I can't deny my feelings for you, but I accept your with Christian and I respect it. I'm also trying to start a new relationship with Maria. Everything is so tense with everyone right now because of this. I just wanted you to know that I will protect you at all costs and use my barriers. I'm sorry for all of this." His stark honesty was heart wrenching.

"Mark, it wasn't all you fault. Victor found out all of our weaknesses and used them against us trying to break us all up, but instead we pulled together like friends do in a time of need. As a sorcerer you should know that good always wins, you must have faith cause that's what gives us the most power." Touching his arm sympathetically.

The air grew thick around them vibrating with mence. Sam and Mark looked towards the door to see Christian watching them. His face expressionless. Nicholas came up behind him. "Sam please remove your hand from him and get out of the Jacuzzi." Nicholas calmy said. "Mark stay there. Sam you must reach for him mentally."

As she touched his mind she found a cauldren of fury, confusion, and guilt. He didn't understand his emotion hoping Nicholas would help. Sam was determined to bring him back to her. *Christian its ok, nothing happened. I'm here with you. Always. Please come to me feel me around you, in your mind. Feel my love for you above all else. I love you,* she sent warmth to him as she moved steadily to him.

As she reached him he brutally pulled her to him wanting to punish her for her betrail. How dare she touch Mark after what happened. He gave his everything to save her and she repaid him by touching and being sympathetic towards Mark. His anger grew as he merged with Sam and saw what had conspired between them.

The rain fell in sheets, thunder and lightening was everywhere. The wind howled through the trees. "Please help." Sam pleaded with him softly. Raphael and Lucian came up behind him.

"You must take her and put him to sleep until his emotions under control." Lucian stated.

"Touch her and I'll kill you. She's mine. MINE!" Christian threatened.

Sam, you must find a way to get away. I can't control this beast in me, my emotions are too raw, A calmer Christian pleaded with her from afar.

No! I will not leave you in your time of need, "Please, everyone leave. It's the only safe way right now." Sam continued to relax against his brutal strength.

Everyone left, leaving her with this beast that was her soul mate. She was a strong woman determined to see this through to bring back the man she loved and leash the beast inside. She tried to move, but Christian tightened his hold almost breaking bones.

Looking down at her, he said, "Mine forever no one will ever attempt to take you from me and live." Then he did something totally unexpected. He threw her down on the concrete and ripped her suit to shreds while ripping his off too. Smelling her fear, he pulled her benethe him, spreading her legs and thrusting hard into her soft core.

Pain shot through her, taking her breath away. She tried to relax, but it was hard with each scratch each bite brought pain and blood. She floated above it. Disconnecting and focused on trying to calm Christian. She wrapped her arms around his neck, bring warmth, showing him how tender and loving he was in her eyes.

Slowly Christian was able to leash the beast. His focuse came back. "Oh my god what have I done?" Jumping to his feet. Sam's body full of scratched, bites, and bruises. Tears ran down his face. "Why Sam? Why did you allow me to do this horrible act?" Shock over took him.

Pushing herself to a sitting position. "Because is wasn't really you, but the beast inside. It is and always will be apart of you and I did it cause had I fought we would both be dead. Love gives us strength to make it through the toughest of situations. I knew you'd find your way back to me and its no crime if I allowed it to happen. We are tested all the time, but its not a pass or fail. Its how best to handle the situation. I love you with everything and would follow where you lead. Through this life and the next." Sam tried to stand even though her legs felt like jelly. Christain came over to help even though he was afraid to touch her. "I won't break just help me to bed." Smiling at him.

After he helped clean and cloth her he tucked her in while Gabriel laid next to her. She decided to read for awhile. He took a long, hot shower trying to go over everything. How could this have happened? He had commited the ultimate crime and she should have killed him. He want to the library to do some research.

Lucian joined him. "How are you?" Sitting in a leather wing back across from the desk.

"How do you think I am? I feel like shit I just brutally attacked my mate and she calmly let me. Why? She should have killed me." Fury flowed in his eyes.

"She let you cause she knew it was the only way. She is very strong for one so young. Her love for you beyond measure and she'd do anything to save you. You know our males are predators first and she has excepted that and I'm proud to call her my sister-in-law. You must sleep the sleep of our people to rejuvenate your body and mind."

"I can't, she may need me and if I sleep I wouldn't know of danger to her." Looking lost.

"We will watch over Sam while you sleep. Nothing will happen to her. She is part of this family now too." Stating matter of fact.

"You know he is right you must get the rejuvenating sleep." Nicholas implied as he and Raphael sat down. "Do you wish me to help you sleep?"

"No! Just give me a little time. I must explain to her why I must be away for awhile." Running his hands through his hair in frustration.

"You have two hours, then you will sleep until tomorrow night." Nicholas pulled a book off the desk. "What is it your looking for Christian?"

"I don't know, anything to help explain why I did that to her I thought I was fine once we were bonded."

"Normally that would be true, but this is different. You have bonded to a White Sorceress and it, obviously, isn't complete until she says her words. We'll have to talk to Sarina she may know more."

"Sam or Lisa are the only two who ever summon her."

"She will come I'll summon her." Nicholas went to the center of the room. "Sarina of the White Sorceress please grace us with your presents. We are in need of your assistants." Formally calling her.

Mist formed in the center of the room right next to Nicholas and out of that came Sarina. "Nicholas, how nice to see you again." Smiling at him then turning to Christian. "What is the problem Christian? I feel your pain and guilt."

"Sarina, Christian has fulfilled his part of the ritual and we understand that Sam still has to do hers, but there have been reprecutions."

"What do you mean reprecutions?" She waited calmly for the answer she already knew, but knew Christian would want to tell her anyway.

Christian got up and walked over the Sarina. "I have done something beyond explanation I let the beast take over and Sam paid the price for it. I asked her to kill me, but she excepted the beast. I can't face her right now after what happened and I'm trying to understand what happened. I'm sorry for ever hurting her Sarina and I also know I don't deserve to be forgiven for it."

"Sam did what she knew was expected of her. Being with one of your race is hard, but being a White Sorceress we are very strong and are always up for a challenge. She excepted the beast because its apart of you and she loves all of you. She understands you more than you think, so go to her with no guilt. Love always rules never forget that and the powers that be knew what they were doing when they put your souls together. Be at peace Christian." Kissing his cheek.

"Thank you Sarina. I will go talk to her now." Leaving the room.

"Sarina do you know why his emotions are still out of control and why the beast came out?" Nicholas asked.

"All I can say is it must have something to do with the ritual not being complete. Obviously he will have to keep a tight leash on the beast until it is. Don't worry about Sam she's a strong soul and can handle him. I must go, but call again Nicholas if there is anything you need." She disappeared into the fog again.

"Well what do you think, Nicholas? You think she is right?" Raphael questioned.

"I'm not sure right now this is all new. What I do know is that Christian needs sleep. I'll go get him in a minute."

Christian slowly opened the door. "Sam are you awake?" Whispering softly so not to scare her.

"I'm awake Christian." Rolling over to watch him walk over to her. The way he moved, so confident and fluid, silent as a ghost, amazed her. He sat down on the bed and took her hand.

Looking in her eyes he explained the best he could, as to why he reacted the way he did. "And I'm not asking for forgiveness..."

Sam put her finger over his lips to hush him. "There is no need to apologizes for something that is part of you. I still love you and always will. Come lay with me you look tired."

"I would love to, but..." Christian was interrupted.

"Christian its time." Nicholas appered in the door.

"I must go sweetheart. I'll see you tomorrow night."

"Wait!" Retaining his arm. "Where are you going and why so long?"

"Christian you must go now I will explain to her."

"Damn it Nicholas go! I'll be there in a minute. I will explain to her, not you." His eyes hard and cold as he regarded his older brother.

Nicholas just turned and walked down the hall, *Someone is having a temper tamtrum.*

Christian waved his hand and the door slammed shut. He took a calming breath, then looked at Sam. Laughter was dancing in her eyes. "I must sleep the rejuvenating sleep of my people it will help to revive and heal me. I have neglected it for so long and I'm getting weaker. If I don't go now, of my own free will, Nicholas will command it and I will not know how long I'll be gone." Kissing her knuckles.

"I don't like being here without you, but I'll manage. I still have the ritual to practice for even though I've gone through some of it, work, and the wedding to plan." She gave him a smile that didn't quite reach her eyes.

"I know you'll keep busy. If you need anything Maggie and Armond are here and my brothers too. You won't be able to touch my mind while I sleep, but if your in danger I will know and come at once."

"I understand. You'd better go before he comes back. I love you." She kissed him feverishly, hoping it would last until she saw him tomorrow night. But she knew deep in her heart it wouldn't.

She tried to be brave at least until the door closed. Then her tears were like a river flowing down her face as her heart already ached over his absence. How would she survive the days and nights. She just laid down and curled in a ball. Gabriel moved closer to her trying to previde comfort. She soon fell asleep exhausted from crying.

Nicholas followed Christian through the basement to a secret staircase that spiraled even farther down into the earth. It was dark, but they saw as if it was daylight. After they reach the bottom, they went through a narrow hall made of rock eventually reaching a chamber with nothing but rich earth in it. Christian waved a hand and the earth opened up, welcoming him into its healing arms.

As he floated in, he looked at Nicholas, "Take good care of her. And just to let you know she's notorious for getting into trouble, so keep an eye on her also.

"I will. Nothing will happen to your soul mate. Sleep well my brother and awake strong and refreshed." Nicholas watched as the soil closed over Christian.

9

Going into the TV room he noticed a tall blond sitting on the couch. She was of average weight with light blond hair and hazel eyes. To him she was stunning. "Hello." Walking over to her. "I don't think we've been properly introduced. I'm Nicholas, Christian's older brother."

"Hi, I'm Christine, Sam's friend. Nice to meet you Nicholas." A little shy at this man.

"May I?" Indicating towards the couch.

"Sure, I'm just channel surfing." Scooting over. "So where are you from? I can't quite place your accent."

"I'm originally from the Pyrenees mountains, but I live in Venice, Italy now. Do you live around here?" Casually questioning her.

"Yes, not to far away. Venice huh? That sounds like a cool place to live." Smiling at him.

"I like it there. Its like a different world where people are very laid back and easy going. They don't seem to be here though at least from what I've seen so far."

"You'll get use to it. I'd like to go to Venice someday."

They sat and talked for awhile, then Mark and Maria joined them. Eventually the other's showed up too all but Sam, who stayed in her room most of the day.

"I'll be right back I'm going to check on Sam." Nicholas left Christine.

Walking silently down the hall he could hear her crying. He knocked on the door, "Sam are you alright? Can I come in?" Waiting for her invite.

"Hold on a minute." Trying to clean up the tissues and her tear stained face before opening the door for him. "Come in." Allowing him enterance.

He casually walked through the room noting the trash can full of tissues and Sam's red rimed eyes. "I know you miss him, but he is well and close by. He wouldn't want you crying over him. Is there something you need to do that would help distract you? I could help you with your magic if you'd like. I'm well versed in it." Trying to calm her.

Sighing she looked at him a minute. Studying his face he looked a lot like Christian. "How may years a part are you and Christian? You two look more a like than your other two brothers."

"I'm ten minutes older than him, Lucian is fifty years younger, and Raphael is seventy five years, but we are the closest brother's of our race. Usually siblings are one hundred to two hundred years a part."

"So you two are twins that explains a lot. Let me change and then would you mind going with me to my parent's? I still have a few things left I need to bring here."

"Of course. I'll wait for you in the library."

Sam threw on a black tank and jean shorts, put her hair in a ponytail and put on some tennis shoes. Kissing Gabriel on the head she went out the door. Lisa was at the end of the hall.

"Hey Sam. Are you doing any better?" Putting her arm around her as they walked.

"Just a little I miss Christian." Her voice so sad.

"He'll be back tomorrow night. John explained it to me. Where are you off to?"

"I'm going over to mom and dad's. I still have some things to bring over here. Nicholas is coming with me."

"Do you mind if I come. I need to go home and get some stuff done."

"Sure, I just need to get Nicholas he's in the library."

"Do you know anything about him? He looks dangerous to me."

"He is Christian's twin. Older by only ten minutes. Lucian is fifty years younger and Raphael is seventy five years younger. They come from the Pyrenees mountains."

"Their twins? They don't look alike their hair and eye color is different. Where are those mountains? I've never heard of them." Lisa asked as they turned into the library.

"They border Spain and France. Christian and I are identical, unlike you and Sam, but I chose to change the colors so others could tell us a part." Nicholas answered as his hair and eye color changed back to his original reddish brown hair and brown eyes.

Lisa gapped at him as she watched the transformation, then held her sister as she started crying again. "I believe you, now change back so Sam will stop crying please." glaring at him.

"I am sorry chere." Changing back. "Now you understand why I change. Lisa I would never do anything to hurt your sister. You can ask me anything."

"How did you know we were twins? We don't look exactly a like and have only told our friends."

"Because most sisters are close, but you two are closer and only twins are like that."

"Where do all of you live?"

"I live in Venice, Raphael and Lucian live in Paris, but we all pretty much live together since usually there is two of us together. It helps us to fight the darkness until we find our soul mates."

"Alright, for now let's go than." Lisa headed out the door.

"Is she always like that? Which one of you is older?"

"Yes she is and I am by three minutes. Let's go before I change my mind."

They walked into their mom's house and she stopped them immediately. "Who is this and where is Christian?" Eyeing Nicholas suspiciously.

"Mom this is Nicholas, Chistian's older brother. Christian is busy and sent Nicholas to protect us."

"Sam you never were good at lying. Where's Christian?" Sternly speaking.

"He's ill and is healing right now he will be with us tomorrow night.

I just came to get the rest of my stuff and drop Lisa off." Heading to her room.

Before she could walk in, the door slammed shut. Sam turned to see her mother gliding down the hall. "My room now!" Quietly whispering as she passed Sam.

Entering her mom's room her mother turned to her, "Samantha Lynn what the hell is wrong with you? I know I taught you better than to disrespect me." Papers blew around the room.

"I am sorry, but you came at me like I did something wrong, which I didn't"

"Well what do you expect when you show up without him and another in his place while a sorcerer is after you? Damn it Sam I hate that your not here for me to watch and you took your sister with you." Papers started blowing down the hall.

As her anger increased so did the heat. "First off no one will ever replace Christian mother and secondly Lisa went of her own free will with your approval.

"Don't you raise your voice or the heat young lady."

"What is happening?" Nicholas tried to help Lisa pick up the papers flying down the stairs.

"They're having a fight which is worse now that Sam has her powers. Can you open a window. I don't know how my father puts up with her sometimes." Putting a stack of papers on the table. "Would you like something to drink? We have water, soda, and tea."

"Water would be fine. So your mother and Sam have powers, do you?" Sitting at the table.

Lisa poured them some water and sat across from him. "I am telepathic and a healer, my mother has telepathy and telekinesis. We just thought Sam had the same as mom along with premonitions of the past and future, but she obviously has more. According to my grandmother, once Sam completes the rest of the ritual she will be quite powerful, just like my grandma was."

Next thing Lisa saw was a ball of fire coming down the stairs. "Shit!" Running for the fire extinguisher, but Nicholas stopped it before it hit the carpet.

"Do temper's run high in your family."

"Usually just between them two. Thanks for stopping that I didn't want to have them replace the carpet I really like it." Sitting back down. "So is Christian really going to be ok? I've never seen Sam so upset over a guy like this before."

"Yes, he's been neglecting his health and its finally taken a toll. When he awakes tomorrow night he'll be refreshed and healed." Nicholas watched a vase hit the wall.

"Damn it Samantha that was crystal." Their mom yelled.

"Don't get up we'll wait until their done." Sipping her water.

"Where did the temper come from? I mean who's side."

"I think my mom's side, but Sam didn't have a temper until she met her ex-boyfriend Mark. He always had a knack for bringing it out in her."

"You mean the same Mark who was stuck in the dream with Sam?" Watching Lisa nod her head. "No wonder Christian acted the way he did. We are very possessive if we feel a threat."

The front door opened. In walked a man a little over six foot with gray hair and a mustache. He must be their father. He sat his briefcase on the couch and hugged Lisa. As they walked to the kitchen another glass flew toward them.

Lisa watched as it stopped a foot from them, then flew to Nicholas. "Thank you again."

"Yes, thank you that would have hurt. I'm Lisa and Sam's dad Rich." Shacking Nicholas's hand.

"I'm Nicholas, Christian's older brother."

"Nice to meet you. Lisa what are they fighting about now?"

"I'm not sure, but its getting worse." Down flew some shoes.

"That's it! I will not have them destroy the house. Lisa get Sam out of here, while I take care of your mother." Heading upstairs.

"Can you take her to the mall. She can walk off her frustrations. I still have some stuff to do." Cleaning up the glass.

"Of course." As Sam came down the stairs.

"Good, tell John I'll see him for dinner." As they walked out the door.

"Damn her." Sam muttered as she got in the car. "I'm so sick of this. She's always trying to control me and now that I'm out she's worse." Looking out the window.

"She must love you very much or she wouldn't care so much.' Nicholas implied as he drove towards the mall.

"I guess so, but she just drives me crazy sometimes. Where are we going?"

"Lisa said to take you to the mall to walk. She said it might help"

"She would. I guess it might help."

They spent a couple of hours at the mall. Sam went to the pet store to get Gabriel a bed and some toys, then bought some shirts for Christian. They got back to the house around seven. Everyone had gone home except Shelby and Lisa pulled in right behind them.

"You just getting home?" Lisa inquired as she followed them inside.

"Yeah, I bought some stuff for Gabriel and Christian. Want to see?"

"Sure."

"Has your mother calmed down?" Nicholas sincerely asked as he put the bags on the bed.

"Yes. My dad is always able to calm her as long as her and Sam are a part. I see my suggestion worked." Smiling at Sam.

"Yes, but I had to avoid work since Christian called me in sick."

"Sorry, I forgot about that. Oh well, hurry up and show me the gifts so we can eat. Shelby and I have a surprise and its getting late."

"What is it?" Pulling the bed and cat toys out of the bag. Gabriel jumped on the bed, sniffed everything, then took off with the toy mouse in his mouth. "Well now I know which one he really likes." Putting the rest by the chair and the bed at the end of theirs.

"I'm not telling, you'll have to wait. Are these silk?"

"Yes I thought he'd look good in them. Luckily I had Nicholas with me."

"Did you make him try them on?" Holding them up to Nicholas smiling.

"Yes and I think she enjoyed it." Grimly answering.

Sam felt more power flow through the room looking up to she saw two men outside her door. "Come in. I don't remember you that well. Your Christian's other brothers"

"Yes I'm Lucian and this is Raphael." Introducing them as they entered. Lucian was tall, but stalky with long brown hair and hazel eyes. Reminding Sam of a lumberjack. Raphael had shoulder length jet black hair, dark brown eyes, and tall masculine build like a bodybuilder. Both wore their hair back in a leather thong. They resembled Christian, but not as much as Nicholas of course.

"I'm glad to meet you. This is my sister Lisa and I'm Sam, but I'm sure you already knew that." Sam smiled at them.

"Yes, we helped with the dream problem. I see your feeling better and giving my brother some grief." Lucian grinned at Nicholas, "He needs it."

I'd watch it if I were you Lucian, Nicholas warned him. Lucian just smirked.

Stepping between the two, Raphael bowed slightly. "I'm glad your better. Is there anything we can do for you? I hear you have a ritual to complete soon and still need to practice. We can help you with that if you wish."

"Thank you Raphael, maybe tomorrow. Let's go eat and we can all get to know each other and you can tell me stories about Christian." Walking towards the door.

Nicholas grabbed her wrist to stop her. "Are you sure that's a good idea? You don't need to get upset again chere."

Placing her other hand on his and gently removing it from her arm, she softly said, "I appreciate you concern, but I'll be fine." Walking out he door with Lisa following.

"Do you think that was wise? Stopping her physically like that? If Christian had seen you he'd have ripped your head off." Raphael questioned.

"I'm sure he would have, but we wouldn't be in this situation if he had taken better care of himself. I am her watcher now until tomorrow night and I'll be damned if I let anything upset or happen to her." Striding out the door.

"Do you think we should watch him?" Looking at Lucian.

"Maybe, he's too connected to Christian to not feel his emotions and need to protect her like a soul mate. I don't even think he realizes what he's doing when it comes to Sam. If he was watching from a distance, I think it would be different. Watch, but try to make it subtle." Going into the hall, *Make John and Daniel a where of this too and tell them to be careful around Nicholas until Christian rises.*

I will Lucian. As soon as I can get them alone. It will be top priority after dinner, Gliding with Lucian down the hallway to the dinning room.

The dinning room was filled with laughter as Sam, Nicholas, Lucian, and Raphael entered. Daniel had managed to knock the chair over with him in it. Shelby was telling him that's what he gets for tipping it back too far. John said nothing, but laughter danced in his eyes, while Lisa just laughed at him.

"Are you having a problem Daniel?" Sam grinned as Nicholas pushed her chair in for her.

"Ha, Ha." Picking up the chair and sitting in it again. "How was I to know it would knock over?"

"Well I would have thought after the first three times you did it." John smiled. "Guess not."

Daniel just glared at him. "Ok children its dinnertime." Maggie stated as she sat two big plates of fried chicken on the table. Armond came in behind her with a serving cart full of vegetables, mashed potatoes, gravy, and biscuit, then Maggie came out with a big salad bowl filled to the top with salad. "Now everyone eat before it get's cold."

"So where are you taking Sam tonight?" Lucian casually asked ignoring Nicholas's glare.

"Somewhere fun, but I'm not saying cause it's a surprise. Don't give me that look Sam you've fought enough for one day." Lisa responded.

"Who all is going with you?" Nicholas questioned not liking Sam out of the house.

"Christine and Maria will be meeting Shelby, Sam, and me at the surprise. It's a girls night out. No guys." Lisa knew Nicholas hated this idea, *She needs a distraction,* mentally telling him.

Not looking up from his food he answered, *She will be vulnerable and unsafe. I don't like this. Tell me where you are taking her.*

We are taking her to Tiger eye. It's a club with a bar and pool hall in it. It's twenty minutes away in Whitecove. It's on the pier and the ocean is the second place that will calm her.

That doesn't make me feel better.

Looking at Nicholas "Can I speak to you in the hall please." Getting up Lisa went into the hall followed by Nicholas. "What the hell. I understand you don't like it, but I know what she needs and she needs this."

"And I promised Christian I would watch out for her."

"If it makes you feel better you can follow, but don't let her see you. Stay in the shadow's" Taking a breath, "Nicholas she needs to enjoy herself tonight please allow this. She's my sister and she's hurting right now. You know better than most how twin's are tuned into each other." Lisa pleaded respectfully.

Seeing the sympathy in her eyes, "Very well, but if anything happens to her its both our asses cause Christian will know." Grimly agreeing.

"I know and thank you for being so understanding." She walked back to the dinning room with a smile.

As she sat back down. "I guess everything went well." John whispered.

"As well as Nicholas would allow. What a tyrant." Lisa whispered. Nicholas just looked at her. She grinned.

"Now that the tension is somewhat gone from the room can I wear what I have on or should I change?"

"Sam, I'll help you find something." Shelby replied receiving a stern look from Nicholas.

"Ok I've decided on the color's for the wedding." Sam announced.

"Let's hear, then we can look at the books I bought and figure out a design." Lisa perked up.

"Dark red and black. Don't look at me like that Lisa I like those color's and its my wedding."

"I think the dresses will look fine if we can find a nice design." Expressed Shelby.

"How is everyone doing?" Maggie popped her head into check in them.

"We're almost done Maggie. It's delicious." John answered as everyone agreed.

"Oh mom said the invitations already went out."

"Really? How many?"

"You don't want to know. I hope you have a big place picked out for the wedding and reception." Lisa inquired.

"I haven't talked to Christian yet, but I wanted to have it here. The ceremony in the garden cause its so beautiful back there and reception in the backyard by the lake. It would make pretty pictures with the sun going down for the background." Sam's eyes changed as she thought about it.

"I think that would be a great idea we haven't had a part here yet." Daniel chimed in.

"I don't see a problem, but you should talk to Maggie and Armond first. They will need help if they say its ok. Hey wait a minute. Didn't you just say your mom already sent out the invitations?" John looked at Sam suspiciously. "You already talked to them didn't you?"

"Of course I did, I just wanted to make sure you two were ok with it." Mischief danced in Sam's eyes.

"Did you know?" Looking at Lisa. She just smiled.

"It's settled than the wedding will be held here in two weeks. The color's are dark red and black. How many brides maids?" Lucian asked.

"Five, Lisa, Shelby, Christine, Maria, and Nichole. My friend Sam will be reading something I wrote for Christian also. We will need usher's though. I thought I could ask if the kid's I baby-sit for could be the ring barer and flower girl."

"Well you have this all planned out don't you" Raphael ginned at her

"Of course."

"Now its time to go get you changed. Let's go Sam." Shelby ushered her out the door to her bedroom.

Lisa decided to go help Shelby with Sam. Nicholas took a walk outside, while his brother's , Daniel, and John went to the library.

"I'm not sure if you've noticed how Nicholas is acting towards Sam without Christian here?" Lucian stated.

"We've noticed, but didn't want to say anything." John answered.

"Well just watch him. We don't think he realizes just how strongly connected to Christian he is. Just be cautious until Christian rises. Hopefully everything will be fine tomorrow night." Lucian informed them.

"We'll keep an eye on him Lucian." Daniel stated.

Meanwhile Sam was in the bathroom, radio going, water running. Sam was leaning over the toilet to get sick again.

"Sam are you almost ready?" Shelby called out.

"Be there in a minute." Sam had her own secret. She'd been having problems holding down food for a couple of weeks, but after today it didn't matter. She would deal with the lose herself, until she told Christian later. It had been a week since she lost their baby, but still couldn't stomach food and she secretly cried everyday. Too much was happening to give him more bad news.

"Sam open the door now." Lisa yelled, pounding on the door.

Next thing she knew the door flew opened and Nicholas glided in with Lisa behind him. Sam looked up from the sink, "What? I said I'd be right out." Giving Nicholas a pissed off look as she walked past him into the bedroom.

He watched her hip's sway as she headed into the bedroom. She wore a pair of tight black jeans, a red spaghetti strapped tank top and black heels. Her hair was in a french twist with some curly wisps around her face she looked hauntingly beautiful, " Leave us please." His feelings foreign to him yet very strong. Not his own, but Christian's. It was hard to distinguish the two and harder to control. He looked out the window.

"What is it Nicholas?" Sam watched Shelby and Lisa leave at her approval.

"I wish for you to stay here tonight."

"That won't happen."

"I didn't think so. Please be careful tonight." Turning to look at her.

"I will." Sam grabbed her black jacket. Nicholas grabbed her arm.

"Why black tonight Sam?"

"It fits my mood Nicholas." Pulling her arm away as she walked out the door.

"Let's go." Walking out to the car.

The Tiger eye was packed, but they were able to get a pool table. The interior was dark except for the strobe lights on the dance floor and lights over the pool tables, wood floors and walls gave it that rustic look. The bar was in front, pool tables in the back, and dance floor in the middle. The music was loud, smoke filled the air.

"I forgot my camera in the car I'll be right back." Shelby left.

"Do you want a drink?"

"Yes you know what I like." Sam let the music flow through her.

"Ok I'll hurry." Lisa rushed to the bar.

Sam grabbed a pool stick and started racking the balls when she felt someone watching her.

"Need help?" The voice was low and sexy.

Sam looked up to see a dark blond staring at her. "I'm fine thanks." Going back to the balls.

"I'm Paul."

"Sam." Moving to the other end of the table to wait for Shelby and Lisa.

"So is this your first time here?" Following her.

"Yes girls night out." Getting a little nerves until she saw Shelby.

"Sorry couldn't find the car at first. Hi I'm Shelby."

"I'm Paul, would you guys mind if we play with you." A hopeful note in his voice.

"Sure." Shelby smiled.

"Great I'll go get my friends." Leaving.

"What the hell! Are you crazy? We don't know them." Softly yelling at Shelby.

"Know who?" Lisa handed them their drinks.

"The guys Shelby just invited to play a game of pool with us."

"Shelby!"

"What! This is girls night out. We aren't going to sleep with them. Just play a game or two." Answering as the guys walked over.

"Hey, this is my friends Rich and Adam. Guys this is Sam, Shelby, and..."

"I'm Lisa nice to meet you." Smiling politely at them.

"So, guys against girls or partner up?" Paul asked.

"Guys against girls." Sam answered.

"You go first than."

Sam broke getting two solids in first, but missed the next move. Paul went next sinking in three stripes yet missed the one. Smiling he stood next to Sam trying to carry on a conversation as the others took their turns. The game was tight, but eventually the girls won with Shelby getting the eight ball in the corner pocket without scratching.

"One more game we'll even by the drinks." Paul flirted.

Sam looked at Lisa and Shelby, "Why not, its your money. I'll rack again."

"Cool let's make it a little interesting. If we win you dance one dance with us. If you win we'll buy you another round."

"Ok it's a deal." Lisa agreed.

"What are you girl's drinking?" Rich asked.

"Screwdrivers." Shelby told him. She watched him as he got their drinks. Just to make sure he didn't slip anything in them.

"Here you go." Handing them their drinks while the guys drank beer.

Playing another game left the guys zero to two. "Guess we're lucky tonight." Sam smiled a little calmer and relaxed now.

"Well I guess we owe you another drink. I'll get it."

"Do you mind if I go with you?" Wanting to watch him. Sam had a weird feeling, but just couldn't put her finger on it.

"Come on." Paul grabbed her hand.

"We'll meet you in a booth by the dance floor." Lisa yelled.

"Ok." Watching the four of them head towards the dance floor as they walked to the bar.

"So are you enjoying your night out?" Paul questioned, while they waited for their drinks.

"Yes, I'm having a good time." Smiling to hide the lie.

"Good. Here's our drinks." Handing her the girls drinks. They walked over to the booth, putting the drinks on the table. They talked for awhile, then Christine and Maria found them.

"Hey, sorry we're late. Did you make new friends?" Christine probed.

"Yes, this is Paul, Rich, and Adam. These are our friend's Christine and Maria." Sam introduced them. "Oh my god, do you hear that? They're playing *Da'Butt* come on lets dance. Do you mind." Being polite hoping they'd leave.

"No, go ahead we'll save your seats." Paul said. The guys watched as they danced.

Sam laughed as she relaxed more with all her friends there. They danced to several more fast songs until a slow one came on. Then they went back to the table. The guys were still there. They sat down and sipped on their drinks until the next slow song came on. "Will you allow me this one dance?" Paul stepped out of the booth.

They were playing *End of the Road* " Sure." Taking his hand. As they reached the dance floor, Sam felt dangerous eyes on her. Paul pulled her so close to him she felt his sexual reaction to her. As they slowly turned in a circle she saw glowing eyes in a dark corner.

Towards the end of the song she started feeling strange. Disoriented. Her vision and hearing was a little blurry. Paul was leading her to one of the dark corners when a hand grabbed her wrist.

"Hey man! She's with me." Paul protested.

"Not ever." That voice was familiar.

Sam tried to focus, but Paul let go and left her with this man. "Who are you? What is happening?"

"Your watcher Sam. That man has slipped you a disorienting drug I don't sense anything in the others."

"Nicholas?" As recognition came about, but when he came into focus he was in his natural form. "Why?"

"Because your pain radiates and I want to bring you some relief. I know I'm not Christian, but I can help you imagine he's with you." Pulling her closer as he changed his voice to sound like his brother's. "Dance with me to your song." Asking nicely as *Wonderful tonight* came on.

"Did you request it?" Laying her head on his shoulder.

"Yes." Replying in that low sexy voice that drove her crazy. She fought to remind herself it was Nicholas not Christian closing her eyes letting the music take her away as Nicholas neutralized the drug in her system so it no longer effected her.

Lisa watched the whole thing, secretly smiling as she had an idea of what happened. Paul came over to the table utterly pissed off. "Who the hell does he think he is? Sam was with me." Sitting in the booth.

"He is her watcher." Lisa replied with a somber face.

"Her watcher? Watcher for what?"

"Watcher for her fiancé. He asked his twin to watch her while he was gone and I'd stay away if I were you." Lisa warned.

"You are all a bunch of teases, but I'll take you if not her." Grabbing Lisa and pulling her out of the booth.

The air thickened as Paul turned to see Sam and her watcher approach. "You will take your hands off my sister now." Her eye's changed.

"And why would I do that?" Holding Lisa as she struggled.

"Because if you don't she will hurt you and if she doesn't I will. So take your hands off her sister." Nicholas instructed calmly.

"Fine!" Pushing Lisa towards Sam. "Its getting to hot in here anyway let's go." Heading for the door, but not before Sam sent a little shock his way. He yelped and turned to glace at her. He watched her eye's begin to glow and that sent him flying out the door, while his friends followed laughing at his actions.

"Come sit down Sam I'll get you some orange juice." Helping her sit in the booth next to Christine.

"Thank you Nicholas. For everything." Sincerely smiling at him.

"So what happened and why is he in his normal form?" Lisa asked sitting across from her.

"Paul put a drug in my drink while we were all dancing." Everyone pushed their drinks to the center of the table. "Its ok none of you have the drug in your system Nicholas scanned all of you after me."

"Thank God." Maria pulled her drink back and took a sip.

"Do you need my help?" Lisa looked at her with concern.

"No Nicholas got it out of my system."

"So why the change?"

"Because her pain and sorrow was too much and I had to help relieve it. Here drink this." Handing Sam the juice.

"Thanks." Taking a sip.

"Are you two twins?" Christine questioned.

"Yes identical, but I chose a different form so others could tell us apart.

"You do know this is a girls night out, right?" Shelby stated.

"Shelby!" Lisa exclaimed.

"I was just kidding. Thank you for watching her. That could have been bad."

"In deed." Regarding her with a nod.

"So do you want to stay here or do something else?" Maris asked Sam.

"It doesn't matter I'm feeling better, so if you want to stay we can."

Everyone agreed to stay one more hour to dance and played pool. They also found out how good Nicholas was at pool. Christine, Shelby, and Maria danced with a couple of different guy, but that was it. Lisa sat out the last twenty minutes due to fatigue. Sam allowed Nicholas to drag her out on the dance floor for the last couple of dances. Slow songs, of course.

Lisa, Shelby, Maria, and Christine drove home, agreeing to meet at Lily's Bridal tomorrow at two so they could pick out dresses. Sam rode home with Nicholas. He did change back to his other form.

"So did you enjoy your evening?"

"I guess, but I miss Christian terribly."

"I know Sam. When we get home, you go to sleep and tomorrow will go fast. What all do you have to do tomorrow anyway?"

"I have to work eight to noon, meet the girls at the bridal store at two, run to the big party store in White cove for some wedding supplies, plus try and head to Debbie's to see if she'll let Johnny and Steph be in the wedding as ring barer and flower girl."

"Do you want me to do anything? I could come help pick out your dress I have an idea of what Christian likes."

"Are you sure? I won't want to bother you if you had something else to do."

"I'm sure. I'll drive you to work tomorrow." Pulling in the drive. "You should head to bed though. You need your rest."

"I know, but I think I'll do a couple of laps in the pool first, just to relax, then go to bed. Heading in the front door, Sam turned and kissed

Nicholas on the cheek. "Thank you again for everything you did tonight. Good night Nicholas. See you in the morning."

"Your welcome Sam. See you in the morning." Watching her go down the hall. He went out to the dock to sit and watch the stars. It brought him a measure of peace.

Sam changed into her suit and went to the pool. The water was nice and cool against her soft, warm skin. She stayed in the shallow end for a little bit enjoying the water lapping at her body. It felt like soft fingers gently pulling on her inviting her to swim in it. She did several laps, then sat in the Jacuzzi and watched Nicholas on the dock. She knew he was also worried about Christian. Hopefully he would be better tomorrow night when they were all back together again.

Sam laid in her bed for a couple of hours wide awake. So she decided to go to the kitchen for some hot cocoa. Going down the hall the house was hauntingly quiet. Gabriel followed her into the kitchen. She put a bowl of milk on the floor for him. Using her magic she called everything to her.

Carrying her hot cocoa, with Gabriel following, she went to the library. She started a fire and sat down in one of the leather chairs. Gabriel jumped in her lap and fell asleep as she pet him. She was fascinated by the fire as it flickered. She too fell asleep. Her dreams were happy for once dreaming of a sunset by the lake as her and Christian danced to their song.

Walking by the library he noticed there was a fire going. At first he didn't see anyone, but as he moved around the chair Raphael found Sam and her cat asleep. He looked at his future sister-in-law with amazement. How lucky Christian was to find her. Even though she was young and small, her strength and love for his brother was great. This gave him hope that someday he would find his soul mate.

He put the fire out and was about to pick her up to carry her to bed when a letter opener came right at him straight for his heart. He moved fast, but it skinned his arm. Looking towards the door he saw nothing, but heard a low growl. Turning back to Sam a Cheetah stood in her place, twitching its tail and growling low.

"Sam, It's me Raphael. I didn't mean to scare you I was only going to take you back to your bed." Cautiously taking a slow step back. Warmth surrounded him as he watched her change back.

"Sorry, let me see your arm." Taking his arm and putting her hand over the wound.

He felt heat go into him. White light shown around and under her hand. "It was my fault I didn't think about your defenses. I thought you couldn't heal?"

"I can for minor injuries and I'm getting better at it anyway." Moving her hand she double checked. "There its all healed. No scars."

"Sam, are your alright?" Nicholas entered the room with Lucian behind him.

"Yes, Raphael was just going to take me to bed cause I fell asleep, but he didn't wake me first and I retaliated by throwing a letter opener at him and my cheetah took over. But I gained control, switched back, and healed his wound."

Lucian hung back by the door, secretly laughing at his brother's stupidity. Nicholas just shook his head. "Come on chere I'll walk you to your room."

"Gabriel." She called and the cat jumped into her arms as she followed Nicholas out the door.

"Are you an idiot? She could have seriously hurt you." Lucian questioned.

"No, and she didn't. I just didn't think I keep forgetting she's not fully human."

"She's not human anymore. Her blood is a mix of ours and white sorceress. You must remember that. She will be very powerful soon and I know you have your own powers. Just be careful."

"I will. Let's go see what movies, if any, good one's our brother has."

10

Sam's day went by pretty fast. She went to work and gave her notice. Her boss was ok with it saying he had an idea that she would quit soon, but he would definitely be at the wedding. Which made Sam happy since she'd worked there through high school so her was like a friend.

Nicholas picked her up and went to the bridal shop with her and the other girls. Lisa brought Mike too so Nicholas wouldn't feel to out of place. The girls fussed for hours over the dresses, but finally agreed on a dark red satin strapless with black sash around the waist that went to the floor with black lace at the bottom. They'd wear black satin shoes with a black beaded choker and their hair in a french twist with red rose combs in it. Nicholas thought Christine looked beautiful in the dress.

Sam was so glad that everyone finally agreed on a dress. "Thank god we're done with that it only took two hours. Mike would you go asked the sales girls what kind of smoothies they'd like, it's the least I can do since we've been here so long and I still haven't found a wedding dress yet." Sitting in a chair after signing the order slip for the dresses.

Nicholas went with Mike since the girls also wanted some smoothies too. The guys came through the door, hands full with trays of smoothies and Nicholas almost dropped his as he saw Sam in a lovely wedding dress.

"Nicholas, are you ok?" Sam came over.

"I'm fine chere. I think you've found the dress you look absolutely beautiful in it and I know Christian would agree." Smiling at her.

"Do you really think so? I really do love this dress." Turning around so he saw it from all sides.

She wore a classic off white strapless dress made of satin with little pearl beads around the bottom. The dress was form fitted from chest to waist and flowed out from there to the floor. Pearl buttons down the back with a satin train at least four feet long with pearls through out. Sam decided on a comb half veil with off white silk roses in it and would have her hair in a classic chiffon.

"Don't worry he'll love you in anything. Don't buy any jewelry let my brother's and I get it for you as part of our gift to you."

"Nicholas you don't have to do that."

"I insist." Happiness in his eyes, *Are you causing problems for my soul mate?* Laughter followed. "You'd better change now." Smiling.

"Why?" Sam looked puzzled until she felt feather light finger's caressing her face. She closed her eyes. "Christian." She whispered as a tear ran down her face. She quickly changed, setting up a time for the alterations for all of them and paid for it all.

Everyone left to go to the mansion for dinner, but before Nicholas pulled out Sam stopped him. "Could we make a couple of stops on the way home?"

"Sure, where?" Heading down town.

"Let's stop at Berman's Jewelry first, then Marv's bakery."

"What are you getting him? And don't deny it." Nicholas smirked.

"I'm looking for a necklace with something special on it, but not sure what and I wanted to get him a ice cream cake."

Pulling into the plaza, the jewelers and bakery were three door's apart. "Listen I'll go to the bakers and get a simple ice cream cake while you go to the jeweler's. It will save time and Christian is anxious to see you. He's telling me to hurry up." Nicholas smiles.

Sam laughed. "Alright we'll meet back here in fifteen minutes." Going into the store.

The store was brightly lit, marble floors, off white walls, and tables with everything from costume to custom jewelry. She was amazed at it all, but she wanted to find the perfect piece for Christian.

"Can I help you?" A familiar voice said.

As she looked up she saw Paul standing on the other side of the counter. "Hi Paul. You work here?" Sam asked.

"When I have to my dad owns it. Are you looking for something?" Getting down to business.

"Yes I'm looking for something special for my fiancé.

"Ok do you have an idea of what you'd like?"

"Something like a dagger on a chain maybe with a stone in the handle?"

"Well I don't have anything like that out here, but we do have some unique necklaces in the back." Looking over at the other sales person.

"Julie could you watch the counter I'm taking her back to the unique jewelry in the back."

"Sure Paul." She answered.

"Come on Sam follow me." Leading her to the back room.

Paul showed her an exquisite collection of custom jewelry. "These are beautiful Paul." Then she saw it, the perfect necklace on a gold chain was a dagger. The blade silver, handle gold and black with three small rubies in it. "That's it, that's the one. I'll take it." Anxious to get home.

Paul began to wrap it up. "I'm sorry about last night I shouldn't have done that."

"Nothing happened so let's just forget it." Taking the box he handed her.

"Wait Sam I have one more thing to show you." Walking to the back of the room her opened the back door to reveal Devin standing there.

"Good evening Sam." He stepped into the room.

The shock on Sam's face prompted Paul to explain. "Devin is my uncle and when I told him what happened he said he knew exactly who you were. I don't know how he knew you'd be here today, but he was right."

"Paul could you give us a minute?"

"Sure." Stepping out and closing the door.

Sam was terrified on the inside, but tried to look calm. She made sure her barriers and protection spell was in order and working. Sending a word to Christian too.

"Come sit down we need to talk." Sitting at the small table in the center of the room.

"I will stand and we have nothing to talk about." She walked to the door and found it locked. "Let me out Devin." The temperature increased.

"Now, now Sam." Cooling the room immediately. "I wouldn't want to have any problems."

The coolness left her feeling a little weak. "What are you going to say?"

"That no matter what you do." Getting up and backing her into the wall. "And whoever tries to help protect you I will get you. You are mine, my love."

It was getting quite cold in there really fast and her strength was draining. She felt her legs give way, but Devin caught her. There was a pounding on the door.

"Devin open up the door." Authority in Christian's voice.

"Let me go, they'll break down the door to get to me. You know that." Sam whispered.

"I'm sure they will, but not before I take a piece of you with me." He took possession of her mouth. Swiping the inside with his tongue. Then she felt it a strange pulling like he was taking her breath, but taking more. Blue light streaked all around them. Sam tried to fight him, but was too weak.

When Devin pulled away he wickedly smiled at her. "It is done and soon I will have your body and powers also." Feeling her shiver, "Do you sense her weakness Christian? Her power is decreasing the colder I make it."

Sam babe listen, you need to focus. Use Devin's body heat to regain your power. Nicholas and I will help you.

Sam felt warmth flow around her, through her. She lifted her head to look at Devin raising her arms she embraced him taking his heat into her raising her core temperature and giving her just enough power to break the spell in the room and release the door.

Christian stalked towards Devin pushing the table out of the way. With a wave of his hand, Devin was thrown against the far wall. Nicholas caught Sam as she fell towards the floor.

Temporarily stunned, Devin stood as Christian reached him. Throwing up a barrier he stated. "Now Christian do you think destroying me is wise? You do and you destroy a part of her also."

Christian turned to see Sam agree with Devin. "What have you done to her?" Venom in his words.

"Just a little insurance until I have her."

Christian, fight another day. I need you now. Please, Sam pleaded.

Christian stood staring at him gathering power. Then without warning, he went right through the barrier and sliced a wicked line across Devin's chest with his sharp talon. Blood formed down the line.

Devin hissed. "You will pay for that." Then he disappeared.

Sam cried out in pain. Christian was at her side taking her out of Nicholas's arms. A line of blood formed across her chest, but the shards of pain in her head were almost more than he could bare.

"Come let's get her home." Opening the back door of the car so Christian could slide in with Sam in his arms.

Maggie rushed to the door as Nicholas opened it. "Hurry get her to the bedroom. Lisa is waiting for her."

"Mark." Sam whispered.

"Why?" Carrying her to the bed.

"Because I'll need his help along with yours Christian." Lisa answered for Sam. *Mark, Sam is requesting your help.*

Mark materialized at the end of the bed. "I am here mia sorella." Ignoring Christian's glare.

"Alright Christian try to keep her calm while Mark and I take away her headache and figure out what Devin did."

Christian whispered his love and gave her encouragement to get through this. Lisa helped with the pain eventually taking it away and going on to help Mark figure out what Devin did. As Lisa checked her abdomen and reproductive organs, she found out what Sam had been hiding. Lisa continued to help Mark, planning on talking to Sam later.

I'm not quite sure, but I need to talk to Sarina. I believe Devin has taken part of her soul. Just enough so he can be a where of what she's doing.

Does he know what is happening? Concern in Lisa's tone.

No, I don't sense him. Christian and I would be a were of him. Which is good at least.

Pulling out of Sam's body, Lisa and Mark swayed a little. John gave Lisa some juice as did Maria to Mark. "Sarina we request your assistance." Formally calling her.

"Okay children. I love you guys, but calling me almost everyday?" Appearing by Lisa.

"Grandma, Mark has a question. I'm sure this will stop after the ritual." Smiling at her.

"Oh I was just kidding. What can I answer for you Mark?"

"Devin got a hold of Sam earlier and has done something to her. Is it possible for him to take a very small piece of her soul?" Mark felt the air thicken, knowing it was Christian.

"Yes it is, let me check her." Sarina took Lisa's spot and sent herself into Sam's body finding what Mark did, but also found what Lisa didn't tell her. "He has taken a part, but as long as she's with one of you to help with protection and barrier's she should be fine until I can find away to get it back." Looking at Sam with sympathy in her eyes, she read what Sam hadn't told anyone. "I'm so sorry Sam." She whispered disappearing.

"I need to talk to my sister alone please." Everyone got up and started going out the door Lisa stopped Christian. "Do you have raspberry or blackberry Canadian water?" He nodded his head. "Good, can you get her one and bring it back. After I get done I'm sure she'll want to talk to you." Looking suspiciously at Lisa, Christian left.

Sam sat up with a pillow behind her. "What is it sis?"

Lisa sat down and looked her in the eyes. "Sam when I was examining you I noticed something in your reproductive region."

"Lisa..."

"Sam let me finish. Why didn't you tell me? Does Christian even know?" She saw Sam's tears.

Tears running down her face. "No Christian doesn't know. He was already under stress with other problem's that I didn't want to add to it and you were finally happy with John and I didn't want to ruin that."

Lisa just hugged her and cried too. "How far?"

"Several weeks."

The door opened and Christian saw the two embraced crying. "Are you two ok?"

"Yes." Lisa wiped her eyes, *You must tell him now. I'll be around if you need me,* Lisa closed the door behind her.

"Honey what's wrong?" Setting the water on the nightstand.

"Umm.. Well.. I can't do this." Sam leaned over the side, grabbed the trash can, and got sick. Her sister's warmth surrounded her to show her support.

"Samantha?"

"No! I have to tell you. I was pregnant, but lost our baby a week ago. That's why I've been a little distant. I didn't tell you cause you had other problems to deal with and Lisa just found out also. Please don't be upset with me over this I know I should have told you I am sorry Christian." Sam's tears just flowed.

Christian just held her rocking back and forth as he too mourned the lose. "There will be plenty of time to try for another child beautiful. I love you no matter what. I am not upset I just wish you'd told me when it happened. Promise me you'll tell me next time?" She nodded. "Let's clean those tear's up. "He helped her clean up and then headed to the dinning room for dinner.

Entering the dinning room Lisa and Nicholas looked at Sam and Christian at the same time, *Does Nicholas know?* Sam mentally asked.

You know he does, He answered.

Silently Lisa and Nicholas got up and followed Sam and Christian into the hall way, closing the dinning room door. Nicholas hugged Sam, probably a little longer than he should, but Christian didn't mind. Sam cried on his shoulder as she felt relieved over not having to hide such a tragedy anymore. "Little sister I am sorry for the lose. It also effects Lisa and myself as we are so close to both of you. We are family now and will always stay close. As a gift for your wedding and maybe something special will happen while you are there, I have taken care of your honeymoon in Venice."

Sam's eyes sparkled with happiness. "Oh Nicholas thank you. That must have cost a fortune."

"Not at all. I own the Grand Royal there and you are my guests for two weeks. I've also invited John and Lisa, just in case you needed her, but you are in the penthouse. They will be on a lower level." He winked at Lisa.

"I love you Sam and you too Christian. You two will have plenty of time for babies later. Let's just have fun now and you two should enjoy each other, cause after a baby you won't have much alone time." Lisa hugged them both.

"Okay enough of this. Let's go eat before we get questioned." Christian laughed as he put his hand on Sam's back as she walked back into the dinning room.

Sitting down Christian asked what else had to be done for the wedding. "Well we still need to figure out flowers, decoration, food, and the cake. Everything else is done." Sam informed him.

"Dare I ask the color's?"

"They are dark red and black."

"Where are we having it?"

"Here, I already talked to everyone and Maggie and I will go over the food tomorrow. You and I have a appointment with the florist and baker the next day and yes your going. Don't give me that look Christian." Sam's eyes changed briefly just as a warning.

Daniel laughed, but had water all over him as Christian pretended to talk to Nicholas. Then a glass flew at Christian which Sam sent back towards Daniel.

"Children! This is dinner time not recess. Stop that this instant and eat." As Maggie brought out bread.

Raphael started laughing and shaking his head. "What a family we have." Catching something shiny out of the corner of his eye, "Sam don't even think about it."

"What? I didn't do anything." As the glass set down before he looked at her.

"I'm so glad you get a long with my brothers. They really like you and are happy for me." Christian whispered softly in her ear.

"I love your brothers. They are funny and make me feel like a part of them and my sister adores you, but don't tell her I told you or she'll deny it." Kissing him.

"Hey, we are trying to eat." As John threw bread at them.

Sam loved when they were all together like one big family. Everyone laughing and joking, including Maggie and Armond. They all went out back to watch the sunset. The guy's played volleyball, while the girls watched.

Sam noticed Christine paying a lot of attention to Nicholas, but not acting on it. "He's cute don't you think Christine?"

"What?" A little dazed. "Who?"

"Nicholas."

"Oh yes, I guess." Feeling uncomfortable around the other's. "I think I'll sit on the dock for awhile." Leaving them.

"What's wrong with her Maria?" Sam asked.

"I think she really like's Nicholas, but has a hard time expressing it. She's like that when she really likes someone.

"But I've never seen her that way."

"It's been a long time."

"Sam your mom's on the phone." Maggie yelled.

"Ok." Getting up. "I'll be right back." Going inside.

Picking up the phone, "Hello?"

"Hi Sam. Are you enjoying the lake?" A strange voice asked.

"Who is this?" Sam's tone stern.

"Come outside alone and you'll find out."

"Where?"

"The garden. Two minutes."

Sam hung up. Maggie asked if everything was ok and Sam assured her it was. Sam entered the garden sensing a change. Reaching the center she saw Victor. "Yes?"

"You look better."

"No thanks to you. What do you want Victor? I tire of these games."

"Just you, come now." Reaching for her.

"Never." Kicking at his hand as she flipped back.

Victor came up behind her putting his arm around her throat. She bent forward as she grabbed around his neck. He got up. "Very impressive."

"Leave Victor, you'll not take me without a fight." Waiting for his next move.

Christian and his brother's stood in the shadows. "Don't intervene yet she needs this fight It will help relieve her aggression." Nicholas whispered sensing his uneasiness.

"I love physical contact, especially with you Sam." Disappearing.

Sam looked around, sensing air movement at the last moment. Victor swept her leg causing her to fall. The wind knocked out of her for a moment, but just enough time for Victor to straddle her and hold her hands above her head.

"You smell so sweet and I think I'll have another taste." As he leaned towards her neck.

Nicholas and Lucian restrained Christian. *Wait my brother. Look, the air is subtle yet warm. Her hands are clenched close enough, for the fireball she is preparing, to be used,* Christian relaxed and they let him go.

The fireball seared his back as Victor sat up, Sam's legs caught him around the throat, laying him back so she could twist him onto his stomach. He grabbed her legs, releasing himself and putting her on her stomach again.

"That wasn't nice and you will pay." Using a long talon he sliced through the straps on her tank top, exposing her back. As he raked her back an unseen force threw him away from her.

Rolling over she held her shirt as Christian helped her stand he pushed Sam behind him. "Victor you have committed a crime against our people and me. You must be punished." The wind picked up as Christians hair flew around him, his eyes going black as night.

"You have no jurisdiction in this country Christian."

"But their laws are for humans not our race." Nicholas came up next to his brother.

"Two against one? Now is that really fare Christian? Can't fight alone?"

"If you wish Victor. Nicholas take Sam back inside."

"No!" Sam protested. The wind increased as Victor and Christian came together in a clash of teeth and claws. She watched in horror every bite, every scratched deeper than the last, clothes and tissue shredded on both as blood ran down their bodies. Sam felt Christian's pain briefly as he pushed it aside to continue the fight.

Victor disappeared at the last second to appear behind Christian with a knife. He made a quick slash across his throat. Christian clamped the wound with his hand as he too attempted to vanish, but his blood loss was to much. His form faded slightly then solidified again.

Nicholas was already pushing Sam towards the house when the heat increased around him and his fingers felt on fire as he released her. "Sam, what are you doing? You must remain safe."

"And what of Christian? Who will help him? I will not allow him to die." Moving out of Nicholas's reach she ran for Christian calling on her cheetah for help.

Feeling the cat in her, her skin started to itch, fur appeared along her arms as she heard popping of her bones, contorting into the cheetah was a frightening and exhilarating experience. Sensing the cat taking over she let go of herself as her vision changed to pick up the yellow, orange, and red of body heat.

Christian watched as his soul mate transformed into her cheetah in mid-air, then slammed into Victor. Her rage enormous, the heat sweltering as the wind provided no coolness. Nicholas and Lucian came to Christian's aid, pulling him back to the house.

A second cat emerged from the woods at great speed. A black panther. Christian stood up quickly fighting to stay conscious, bound to help Sam with this new threat. *Sam if you can hear me, god I hope you can, there is a panther heading your way. I will try to distract it,* he felt her smile.

Yes I can hear you and the panther is Mark. He came to help please allow him. I will be with you soon. I love you.

Feeling her hug him, *As I do you. Stay safe beautiful,* he allow Nicholas to take him as far as the door. They started healing him while he attempted to keep an eye on Sam.

"You must rest while they heal you I will watch and help Sam, Christian." Raphael stated going through the door going through door before he could protest.

Victor went for the panther scratching the face and front legs. Next going for the throat he sank his teeth tearing out a big chunk of flesh. Out of the corner of his eye he saw Raphael approach. Victor went for the kill shoving his hand through the panther's heart, but before he could rip it out Sam knocked him off the panther.

Raphael take Mark inside he must be healed.

No! Your safety comes first.

Damn it Raphael! Stop all this protective shit and get his ass inside so Lisa can heal him. If you all wanted to help stay out of my way and lend me some of your strength.

Taken back for a moment Raphael collected the panther and went back to the house muttering under his breath, over how she talked to him. No one had ever talked to him that way, then he heard Christian's laughter in his head. Glancing at him on the floor, he was as still as death. "Good luck with that one she is so disrespectful. My soul mate will never attempt to talk to me like that." Raphael saw the laughter in Christian's eyes when he opened them.

This is the twenty first century little brother. If your soul mate is in this century she will act the same as mine does, laughing, *Maybe it would do you some good.*

"If you weren't hurt so bad I'd kick your ass."

Maybe another day.

Emerging into his body Nicholas regarding Raphael with irritation in his eyes. "Enough! If your not here to help leave. You two haven't grown up at all have you? He is using unnecessary energy with you."

"Ok, I'll be quiet and help." Sitting next to Christian.

Outside a storm formed. Rain, lightning, thunder, and vicious winds. Sam was back in her natural form again. "You have no one to protect you now. What will you do?" Victor advanced.

"I will take care of myself."

"Yes, I can see that. Why fight Sam? I will win in the end."

"I don't think so, but try if you must." Moving back as Victor approached.

"Oh, but I have a secret weapon."

Christian shot up, *Someone else is out there with her get Daniel and John fast.*

Sam backed into something solid arms like a vise closed around her. She struggled. "Sam aren't you happy to see me?" The struggles stopped.

"Anthony." She whispered as flashes of her encounter with him in Florida came into view. His sexy charming manner in which he got her, his southern hospitality, and the ugly ending. The attempted rape, the beatings for not sleeping with him, and finally leaving the state to stay safe from him.

"This is my younger brother. I see your already acquainted with him. I'm sorry for his ill use of you he has a bad temper."

"How did you find me?" Shaking in his arms.

Anthony turned her to face him. At arms length she was gorgeous she had grown up and filled out in all the right places. Maybe he'll have his way with her now. "When my brother described you I though maybe, so I had to came check it out." Running the pad of his finger over her soft skin. Leaning close to her neck he sniffed. "Mmm... You always smelled so good and you look so gorgeous now. Do you remember how we were?" Flooding her mind with memories of them. At the beach at night, waves hitting the shore, the moon's reflection in the water, making out on the sand. Their relationship was just physical, but his manner of getting her was lethal. He was worse then Mark ever was about getting and keeping her.

"I'd be careful Anthony her soul mate is inside watching." Knowing that would set his brother off he decided to leave. He'd have more fun at a later time.

Anthony turned to see Christian looking at him unable to do much, but watch due to his injuries.

"Your soul mate? You gave him what should have been mine?" Looking back he saw that fear in her eyes he saw all those years ago which made him smiled, "Its ok darling." Kissing her throat. "I'll make sure you never get me out of your head." Injecting her with a hallucinogen.

Sam felt the prick of the needle in her arm gazing at Anthony she was back at the beach her pulse was pounding in her head. Where was everyone? "What have you done to me?"

"Just helping you remember the beach, Florida, Us." He whispered.

"I don't love you Anthony."

He back handed her splitting her lip. Pulling her hair back to expose her neck, he sank his teeth deep drinking her sweet blood.

Christian threw his brother's away from him. Breaking the door he flew at Anthony, but hit a invisible wall. Sarina appeared. "You must stop. She has to do this on her own. She has to face him alone and win."

Christian growled at her, *She needs my help.*

"You are of little help to her right now. Believe in her she will win."

Merging with Sam, he saw the atrocity of what Anthony had done to her. The physical and mental abuse he put her through. He felt her fear of the past coming into the present. Christian flooded her with his love.

Anthony was weakening her with each gulp of precious blood he took. Closing the pin pricks, he covered her mouth with his brutally kissing her, grouping her breasts, sliding his hand into her pants controlling her sexual reaction to him. Rubbing her until she was so wet and hot she thought she'd go up in flames.

"That's good. Want only me, like this. Wet, hot, slick with need. Take off your clothes." Watching her get naked her body wet for him, her nipples hard, shaking with need. "Unzip my pants and put my hard dick in that warm mouth of yours."

"Grandma what are you doing? Stop them." Lisa franticly cried.

"Call on your mother's strength. Tell her Anthony found Sam and we are going to put an end to this."

"Okay, mom's with me now. What should we do?"

"Send your energy and strength to Sam. Talk to her. I'll help."

Sam staggered, fighting the compulsion. "I won't do this." Her mind back in the present. Bending over she picked up her clothes. Next thing she knows she's on the ground. Her jaw hurting.

"You bitch, you think to defy me." He kicked her repeatedly in the ribs.

While she suffered his blows, she felt enormous strength and energy to go into her. *Sam you must end this now. Stop him before he hurts anyone else or destroys you. Don't let him,* Tear's in Lisa's voice as she witnessed it all over again.

Sam tried to sit up, but he punched her in the face again. "You little slut. Giving yourself to the highest bidder."

"At least he doesn't beat me. Do you get off on beating woman Anthony?" Spitting blood on his boot while her eyes changes.

He pulled her up by her arm and watched as clothes appeared on her. "What the fuck" Throwing her into a tree he knocked the wind out of her. "I only get off beating you Sam."

Walking over to her, he noticed the heat. He watched her push her battered and bruised body up the tree. Stepping away from the tree, he noticed her green eyes, saw her hair blowing in the hot wind, then she started to glow. "I'm so glad to hear you say that. I won't want you taking your anger out on anyone else." With a wave of her hand Sam threw him into a statue.

Dazed he shook his head trying to get his bearings. Puzzled by her powers, he watched her as she approached him. Little white and blue orbs flowed around her.

"Your time of abusing me is over and your life is done." Sending lightening his way.

Swiftly moving out of the way it scorched his arm. He grabbed Sam in a choke hold. "I don't know what has happened to you, but you will pay for that." Anthony hissed in her ear.

He pushed her towards the garden table, bending her forward over it. He looked back at Christian. "Enjoying the show Christian? I'll show you how to treat a disrespectful slut like Sam." Enjoying the fury he was creating in Christian knowing it was driving him crazy not being able to help.

Sam struggled increasing the heat, but it didn't seem to effect Anthony as he tore her skirt and thong from her body. Holding her down with his upper body weight he continued to undo his pants in another rape attempt.

Christian saw the tear's running down Sam's face knowing she didn't have the mental strength to stop him. He broke through the wall and flew at Anthony with unnatural speed pulling him off Sam with one hand. He ripped out his throat with the other, while Lisa sent another bolt of lightening towards Anthony incinerating him instantly.

11

Christian picked Sam up and carried her inside providing pants to keep her covered. He stalked past everyone to their bedroom with John and Lisa following. Laying her on the bed, "Honey do you know where you are?" Concerned for her mental state.

She gave him that deer in the headlights look. "Lisa can you run a bath with lavender in it as hot as you think she can stand. John get the candles we need to heal her." He asked his voice gravity.

"Yes Christian, but save your voice it must heal. Use your mind we can all hear you." John answered going to get the candles.

Sarina appeared next to the bed. Coming out of the bathroom. "The bath is ready Christian." Looking up she saw her. "How could you let this happen to her?" Walking towards her grandmother her anger radiating in the room.

Christian restrained Lisa, *Lisa save this for later when you are calmer. I would like you to help me heal her wounds.*

"Fine! Until later, but he nearly destroyed her this time." Focusing on Sam now.

"I am sorry child I didn't know." Grief in Sarina's voice.

"Why do you think we left the one place she loved. He physically and mentally abused and raped her mind and body. He was sick. He came across as the perfect guy, but I saw it all through Sam. By the time I convinced mom, it was almost too late. I must heal her and check on Mark."

Sam I love you. Please come back I need you. Who will referee when your sister and I get into it, he kissed her temple.

He felt her than, the warmth, her laughter, *If you let her have her way than there wouldn't be any fight.*

He hugged her pulling her into his arms, afraid to let her go, *That about killed me.*

"It about killed me too. Thank you for coming to my rescue." Sam attempted a smile, but winced at the cut on her lip.

Christian leaned down covering his lips over hers. Kissing then licking her wound to help heal it and take the sting away, *Better?*

"Yes." Mentally smiling at him closing her eyes and let Christian and Lisa heal her. When they were done, Lisa and John left to check on Mark

Christian took her in his arms and went into the bathroom. Sitting her on the counter he undressed. "What are you doing?" Amusement in her tone.

Getting undressed, mischief in his eyes.

"I can see that, why?"

So I can help relax your muscles.

"Oh really? I'm not sure how much help you'll be, but I'm glad your joining me. I can see one of your muscles isn't relaxed." She was use to his casualness of his body.

He lifted her up, stepped into the hot water, and descended into its warmth. Sam wiggled her butt around to get comfy, but this caused him some discomfort as more desire shot through him. *If you keep that up you may be sore in other places as well before you heal fully.*

Turning her head Sam looked at him with her emerald eyes. Her tongue darted out to moisten her dry lips. "I love when you make me deliciously sore." Running her fingers over his chest causing his nipples to get hard.

Holding her hand against him to stop the movement, *Please Mi Amour I'm trying to be good and not arouse you any further. Let me take care of you first.*

"Ok Christian, but later..."

I so promise, kissing her head. He massaged her neck, shoulders, and back washing her hair, and body. Even allowing her to wash his hair and do a little more healing on his throat and voice box.

"How is that?"

"Better beautiful. Should we dress and check on Mark? I owe him a lot for helping you."

"Yes, lets hurry and see how he's doing."

Walking into the guest room in John's wing Sam was shocked at the state of Mark. He was ashen, lips white, breath labored. "Lisa?'

"Victor inflicted mortal wounds trying to extract his heart. I'm doing my best, but its not enough."

"Let me see what I can do."

"Merge with me and I'll tell you what to do."

Lisa instructed Sam how to let go of her physical body and use her energy to enter Mark's. She saw where Lisa had repaired the muscle, but the bone's of the ribs were shattered. Sam went there first. Meticulously piecing them back together, then using heat she seared them closed. Moving through his body repairing the bones as Lisa followed behind her cauterizing and repairing muscle. Sam had no idea how long they'd been in there, but they were both wary when they emerged. Lucian gave Mark blood to speed the healing while Nicholas gave a sharp command to sleep for the next couple of hours.

John gave Lisa some juice to help replenish her, even though the need to give her his blood beat at him. He fought it, refusing to bond her yet it wasn't the right time yet.

Christian gave Sam blood which was his right and Sam excepted it now like it was natural. She communicated with him through minds also. Their bond was growing stronger the more they connected. He would do whatever he had to keep her safe. Loving her was an unexpected gift he would always cherish and she was an amazing woman who did great things with the gifts she was given as if she'd always had them.

"Don't look at me like that or Daniel will make fun of you." Sam teased.

"Like what? Like I'm in love? Cause I am and don't care who knows it." Grinning.

"Yes you nut. I'll be right back and I'll take Nicholas with me. I have something for you."

"What?" Calling after her.

"You'll see." Yelling back.

Pulling Nicholas by the arm, they entered the bedroom. She went to the closet and got the necklace showing him, "Do you think he'll like it?"

"Yes chere, I'm sure he'll love it. Now let's go before he comes looking for us." Going out the door Sam followed.

"*Samantha*" She heard her name ever so softly.

"Yes?"

"Yes what?" Nicholas stopped.

"Hush! Yes I'm here." Trying to listen for the voice again.

"*You must be careful evil is about.*" The voice whispered.

"What evil?"

A woman all in white with white hair appeared before her. "*Evil that's been hunting you since December.*"

"Do you mean Devin? I already..."

"*No! He's just a pawn. All that has happened is connected.*"

"Sam?" When she hushed him a second time. *Christian come, Sam won't answer me. Its like she's listening to something only she can hear.*

Sam is sensitive to the spirit world and she could be receiving something. I'm on my way.

"How is it connected?" Sam questioned as she saw Christian approach entering her mind.

"*You will see soon. Stay close to your soul mate and finish the ritual early. You will be tested and must pass to save them all. I must go.*" Fading away.

"Wait! How will I know what to do? Who are you?" Sam questioned anxiously.

"I will tell you more later. I'm a part of you." Answering in a far off whisper.

Sam looked at Christian a little sad. "I don't understand?" Confusion in her eyes.

"I'm sure she'll contact you again." Pulling her into his warm embrace.

"What just happened? I didn't see, hear, or sense anything." Nicholas asked.

"A spirit has contacted Sam to warn her of danger coming." Christian answered.

"How could you hear it and not me?"

"Through Sam, I can tap into what she hears when she let's me." Grinning at her.

They continued to walk down the hall to the library. She sat him down in the chair by the fireplace. "Now I know I didn't need to get you anything."

"No you didn't. All I want is you."

"But I wanted to, for everything you've done for me, so here." Handing him the box. "I hope you like it." Holding her breathe as she watched him open it.

He tried to hide his excitement, but she saw before he lowered his head. "Sam." Is all he could say. No one had ever gave him anything like this and he loved it.

"Christian? You don't like it?" Worry in her tone.

"No Mi amour, I love it." Taking it out to put on, but Sam snatched it from him.

"Wait!" Holding it up to the light she could see a hair like needle in the stone. Holding it over the fire the needle turned green, then shattered. Sam examined it and put a protection spell on it just in case. "I should have checked it. Especially after what happened when I got it. Sorry." Handing it back to him.

Putting it on. "Never say sorry, but thank you." Kissing her.

Sam gave him that sexy little innocent smile that reached her eyes. Causing them to change to green briefly. His heart flipped at her shy emotion. He loved her so much at that moment that words couldn't express so he just kissed her passionately. Savoring her delicious taste, the raspberry scent of her hair, the softness of her skin. Making love to her was an experience in its self.

Nicholas made noise as he approached the door so they knew he was coming. "Christian? We should gather everyone and make them a were of the changes in plans."

"Yes your right, tell them to meet here in five minutes."

Everyone moved the furniture to form a big half circle by the fire place. "Sam has received a warning from, I assume, her spirit guide. We have to move the ritual up to tomorrow night. The spirit said she will be tested and must pass it, so we must do it now."

"What is coming Christian?" Daniel asked

"I'm not sure, but we all need to be prepared. Sarina what do we need to do for this ritual?"

"Well the ritual is similar to a party, but everyone wears costumes. It is held in Sam's honor and there must be at least twenty or more people attending."

"Lisa, Daniel, Shelby, and I can invite everyone." John said.

"Good, a dinner and party are held after the ritual and don't worry no one will know of the ritual because everyone who is not of magic will be put in a trance to supply energy, then released with no memory of what happened."

"Christine, Maria, and I will help Armond and Maggie with the food." Mike told her.

"That leaves the rest of us to decorate and get Sam ready. Sam what two color's would you like to use in the ritual?"

"Royal blue and emerald green. What should I do now?"

"Well I will bring your costume with me later this afternoon. Now Nicholas let everyone know they must wear a mask its for the ritual and it makes it more fun to guess who everyone is. Its like Carnival, so I'm sure you'll know how to handle it. I'll be back later to help you Sam. For now just practice your magic."

"Alright Sarina I know exactly what to do. See you soon." Watching her disappear.

"Carnival! I always wanted to go to Venice during Carnival. I heard it's a fun and exciting time of the year." Sam exclaimed.

"Yes its one of my favorite times of the year. We have a lot to do and very little time to do it in. John just tell everyone it's a masquerade. Mike tell Maggie to make light dishes like chicken, fish, vegetables, and fruit." Watching everyone take off.

"I'm going to check on Mark again, then I'll join you on decorating."

Seeing the worry in Christian's eyes. "Don't worry I'll stay merged and be fine." Kissing his cheek she walked down the hall.

Sam knocked softly, then opened the door. "Mark? Are you awake?"

"Yes, come in." Answering in a gravely voice trying to push up to a sitting position.

"Here," Putting pillows behind him, "Let me help you."

Her touch was soft and warm. He closed his eyes to savor the feeling. "Why isn't anyone with you?"

"I can take care of myself, anyway everyone is busy getting ready for the ritual tomorrow night." Pouring him some water.

"Why is the ritual being rushed?" Anxiety in his voice.

"A spirit came to me earlier." Sam told him everything. "Don't stress it will all be fine. Now let me check you out."

Mark watched as Sam took his hands in hers, close her eyes she entered his body. He felt her warm energy checking everything to make sure he was healing and helped to speed up the healing with more energy. She swaying a little as she reentered her body. "You need juice you shouldn't have expelled so much energy Sam. I'll heal soon." Trying to steady her.

"I need you at the ritual. I want you there, healed and healthy. You need more blood to speed it up." She slit her wrist with her nail. "Here take what I offer, drink so you can heal." Raising it to his mouth. "Please Mark."

Looking in her eyes he was lost, recognizing the hidden command, but unable to fight it, he brought her wrist to his lips drinking viciously. Feeling the blood flow through him. Healing his damaged cells and bones he felt a little more like himself as he closed the wound. "Sam you need juice to replenish your lose."

"I'll be fine just let me rest here for a minute." Closing her eyes she laid her head on the bed.

"Honey you need to get Christian to help you I'm still to weak." Stroking her blond hair, "Sam? Sam! Damn it." *Christian come to my room Sam passed out again trying to heal me.*

Christian came through the door, "I told her not to waste her energy on me, but she's so damn stubborn." Mark explained.

"Yes I know." Placing her in his lap, he slashed his wrist coaxing her to drink. "Sometimes she drives me absolutely crazy."

"Thank you for saving me."

"I owe you for helping Sam. Will you be attending the ritual tomorrow night? We had to move it up."

"I know Sam told me and yes I'll be there."

Sam opened her eyes as she closed the slash, *I'm sorry I passed out again I just wanted to help heal him.*

I know Sam. You did fine and seem better.

"I am." Smiling with sparkles in her eyes. "Are you feeling better Mark?" Turning towards him.

"Yes, but you shouldn't have taken the risk. I would have healed and I still would have been at the ritual." Reprimanding her.

Sam put her palm on Christian's chest as she heard a growl. "Give us a minute."

"No!"

Turning she looked in his eyes, matching the fire she saw with her own. "Please."

"Fine! One minute." Abruptly leaving with a slam of the door.

"How dare you reprimand me in front of him." The heat increasing.

"Don't take that tone with me Sam." Catching her hand before it hit him.

"Let go of me Mark." As flames raced from her arms to his.

He cooled everything before he got burned. Flipping her so she laid next to him.

"You fucken liar. You healed very fast and didn't need my help." Breathing heavy due to her rage.

"Yes and no. I did need a little more of the energy and blood, but I still enjoy the attention once in awhile."

Sam stopped struggling and Mark released her. She got off the bed, straightening her clothes. "You would."

Looking at him she stretched her arms out casually, but Mark suddenly felt his air cut off. Sam raised her hands as his body was lifted out of the bed and up the wall.

"Sam!" Christian yelled as he entered.

She slammed the door shut and pushed Christian into a chair with a wave of her other hand. Focusing back on Mark, "If you ever deceive me again the consequences will be worse." Letting Mark fall back to the bed with a thud as she left the room.

"What the hell did you do to her?" Getting up from the chair.

"Played sick a little to well." Getting off the bed holding his throat.

"You're a dumb ass, She could have killed you."

"No she couldn't she has too much compassion, but she needs to try or she'll never survive and who best to teach her than the one person that has always brought out her anger." Walking out of the room.

Heading down the hall the walls bulged inward from the heat Sam was giving off. She ignored everyone as she went outside. The winds wiped through her hair.

Oh *Sam, what's wrong? Are we in a pissy mood?* Mark sarcastically asked.

Sam threw a fireball into the lake, then created another one just to watch the way the fire walked around her hand. Closing her hand it disappeared.

Sam, this time feeling the whisper against her neck. She turned, but he wasn't there. Walking towards the dock she heard him again. "Show yourself Mark I'm not in the mood for your games."

Coming up behind her Mark wrapped his arms around her like a steel band. "Oh come on Sam." Kissing her neck. "I thought you liked games."

"Not with you." She bit out as flames started up Marks arm.

"Especially with me." Putting out the flames, *Christian stay where you are she needs this sparring match. It will help prepare her for tomorrow night,* sensing his approach.

You harm her, I'll kill you, watching from the pool.

"Fuck you, Mark." Gathering energy to break out of his embrace.

"That's all I've ever wanted." Releasing her quickly.

Sam faced him, "You are a complete dick."

"And you are weak." His eyes going cold.

Fury boiled in her veins, the winds increased, sheets of rain came down along with the lightening and thunder. Her hair crackled around her as her eyes changed. White light formed around her as she charged at him. She engulfed him with her heat as they came together. He used her momentum to continue them into the lake soaking them both, causing steam while Sam calmed down.

Holding her to his chest. "That fury and fight is what you need to win your battles with people like Devin." He held her while her body quit shaking from the fury.

"Why must you be so hurtful?"

"Because that's the only way to bring out all your fury to help you survive." Turning her to face him. "Sam, look at me. When you fight, do it with everything in you. If you must, even though I'd hate it, pretend its me if it will help. The ritual is very important and I'm sure we'll see Victor and Devin, if not by tomorrow night before the wedding for sure. I just wanted you prepared, cause whatever is coming will use all your weaknesses to destroy you." He held her while her tears fell. "Oh honey, I didn't mean to upset you, but it would also destroy me if anything happened to you. Call Christian to help calm you."

"No." Sniffling, "I want him to see me as strong." Wiping her eyes.

"You have more strength than anyone I've ever met beautiful." Pulling her to him.

His voice invaded her body, causing it to go pliant in his arms. She closed her eyes, resting her head on his chest. "Thank you for trying to help Mark."

"Your welcome. Now I think I'll go change into some drier clothes and find Maria." Walking back to shore.

Sam felt wind around her, then it all stopped. Opening her eyes, she found them in their room. "How did you do that?"

Christian nuzzled the crock of her neck. Dragging the sweet scent of her skin into his lungs. His body raged at him to take her, but he refused to give in yet. "It all has to do with time and space, but that is for another time. Now I want to strip off those wet clothes." Pulling her top over her head and tossing it in the bathroom.

He ran his fingers lightly down her back, causing her nipples to harden as he unhooked her pink lace bra. They beckoned him to taste them so he closed his warm mouth over one, causing a soft moan to escape her lips. His erection was on the border of pain. He rubbed the other one softly with his thumb.

Unable to stand his shirt on Sam pulled it off wanting to feel the warmth of his skin with her fingers. She pulled him to her kissing him softly at first, but one tug on her lower lip with his teeth increased her desire allowing him full range to explore her mouth. His tongue stroked hers, while his hands found every sensual spot on her body. He tugged at her shorts until they fell to the floor. He undid his pants with one hand unable to wait much longer.

Sam pulled away looking at his sculpted body. Broad shoulders, masculine chest, flat stomach, tapered waist. She moved around him, twitching her hips walking to the bed hearing his deep intake of breath she loved the power she had over him as she turned and bid him to come to her with a crock of her finger. His movement always got her heart racing with anticipation so silent and fluid.

Christian stopped in front of her, "My little temptress, I could eat you alive right now. Having you begging for mercy lying on the bed spread for me, my own personal sacrifice to do with as I wish." His low sexy voice a sorcerer's spell.

Sam sat down on the bed, then looked into his molten eyes. "Today I am yours, but tonight you are mine." Scooting back on the bed to lay down.

He opened the curtains to bath her in sunlight her body taking on a pale glow. She was his and he intended to indulge in her. He trailed kisses from her neck to stomach and back leaving liquid fire in their wake as softly tracing each rid with a kiss after carelessly removing and tossing her lace thong on the floor, he began to run his hands down her slender hips and thighs going back to her hot, wet core of sweet liquid he couldn't wait to taste. Covering her with his mouth her gasps only enticed him more as he plunged his tongue deeper to get her succulent honey.

Fire raced through her, her stomach clenched as she dug her hands into the sheet. Then she shattered into a million pieces, while Christian continued his sweet assault, never giving her a break. Bring her again and again to the brink, until the last time he stopped to make her wait, want, need him to release her.

He towered over her, his hair around his face the sun giving it a fiery look. Holding her wrists against the bed he inserted himself ever so slowly knowing it was killing her as it was him, but he wanted to hold out just a little longer.

"Christian please I can't take this." Her pleas giving him the satisfaction of knowing how she felt.

"Yes you can just a little longer."

"Your killing me." Gasping out as he slowly stroked in and out.

"This is my time Mi Amour. This is how I love seeing you on the edge yet not able to let go." Nipping her neck causing her body to shake with need.

Sam did the one thing he didn't expect. She clamped on to him milking him until he couldn't hold out any longer. He surged into her harder, faster building the ecstasy until they were both screaming out with release so high on the adrenaline that they kept it up a little longer until they were both spent.

Christian laid on her, his breathe coming out fast sweat glistened both their bodies. Kissing her he rolled off her bring her on top of him still connected not wanting the separation, they soon both fell asleep from exhaustion.

12

When Sam awoke she was alone sitting up in the dark room she figured it was early evening. Cleaning up in the bathroom she smiled shyly as she remembered their love making earlier. She was startled to see a man standing behind her in the mirror. His eyes were a mesmerizing, iridescent blue.

"Don't turn around Sam. I won't hurt you."

"Who are you?" Continuing to stare at him he was taller than her. Six foot one or two with short dark blond hair, strong jaw line, and tan skin.

"You'll find out soon enough. I'm here for only you."

"What do you mean?" Almost feeling the heat from his body.

Then he leaned down and kissed the sensitive spot on her neck, causing her to close her eyes. "Only you will know." He whispered softly and when she opened her eyes he was gone.

As realization hit she blushed seeing her naked body. She ran to the closet to put on some clothes. Emerging she felt better. There was a knock on the door. "Sam can I come in?" Her grandmother asked.

"Yes."

"I have your gown for tomorrow night would you like to see it?" Pulling off the plastic before she could respond.

"Its beautiful." It was cream colored, long and flowing, off the shoulders with lace and satin on the lower half and satin on the upper.

"Here's your mask. Don't show anyone, not even Christian."

"Why?" Looking at the lace and beads on the mask and feathers on the outside corners.

"Because no one is to know who anyone is until that night." Smiling at Sam. "Your going to steal the show tomorrow night."

"Oh grandma."

"Now have you been practicing your magic?"

"Yes a little. Mark was kind of helping."

"You mean he pissed you off enough to use them to your full potential."

"Yes." Mischief in her eyes.

"The young ones always do that now and we do have bad tempers, but he's right. You must use all your strength and power even if its through your fury. You have to pass these tests Sam."

"I understand and have an idea on how to bring it all to the surface for me."

"Well just practice a little more with Mark or Nicholas tonight and tomorrow. Now let's go get some dinner I hear we're having Italian."

Walking out the door her grandmother linked arms with her and told her a little more of the ritual, but it was mostly about the party after it. By the time they got to the dinning room they were both in tears from laughing at everything that had happened at her grandma's ritual. Everyone made room for Sarina, who sat between her granddaughters. They enjoyed their meal as Sarina told of what would happen tomorrow night and that the attire was to be kept to themselves until the ritual.

After dinner they all started to decorate the inside and outside of the house. White lights were streamed everywhere. Sarina had fall leaves inside and out to represent Sam's favorite season. Royal blue and emerald green streamers and balloons were in the garden, backyard, dinning and living room. Lilac scented candles were placed on all the tables inside. They would set up the outside tables and alter tomorrow.

Sam went down to the dock to help stream the lights. "Hey I need another extension cord I'll be right back." Lisa yelled at Sam who just waved.

Sam looked across the lake briefly for no reason. As her gaze swept back she saw him on the shore, the man in the mirror. Surprisingly she wasn't frightened, but intrigued. Who was he? Why was he here, now? What did he want?

Only you Samantha, a caress in her mind, then he was gone.

She felt an overwhelming emptiness, like he took part of her when he left it enveloped her. Her breathe caught as she felt finger's lightly touch her cheek, *Where are you?*

I'm near, his voice black magic caressing her body.

Who are you and why are you here? Searching the tree line and shore for this mystery man.

You will find out tomorrow night at the ritual. Be strong Sam I know you will pass. I'll see you in your dreams, feeling his lips on her neck again.

"Um… chere could you get back on the dock." Nicholas suggested to her.

"What?" Looking around she noticed she was floating over the water. "How did I do that? Nicholas help me I don't know how to get back." A little worried.

"Its easy just focus on floating back to the dock." Coaxing her through it.

Sam envisioned herself floating back and that's exactly how she got back. Taking Nicholas's hand. "Wow! That was different although I have no idea how I got out there."

"Where is Lisa?"

"She went for more cords. Do you have any candy on you?" She swayed a little.

"No, but I'll have her bring you some juice. Here sit." Helping her down. Her body was shaking. "Are you cold?"

"No, that's part of the reaction to low sugar." She smiled at him, then her eyes changed as did her body posture. Sam straightened, searching the grounds for something, *Lisa stay merged I feel your fear.*

What is it? I can't move.

Its ok I'll find out, Sam cautiously got up. "Nicholas please stay away I don't want to hurt you. Go help Lisa."

"John is with her now, I won't leave you." Determination in his voice. Scanning the area.

"Call the rest to me." Her voice low and husky.

Sam moved off the dock stopping ten feet from it, over the water. Eyes dark, hair crackling, a glow appeared around her. "Show yourself." Her voice a sorceresses caress, a command.

Come to me of your own free will and I'll release your sister.

Release her and I will come, Sam knew the instant Lisa was released.

Come to the woods across the lake. There is a clearing about a hundred yards in.

Sam moved over the water as if on an invisible raft. Once on shore she headed for the woods, *Sam don't go in there its dangerous,* Christian calmly warned her.

I must I gave my word, severing the connection.

Christian watched as Sam disappeared into the trees. "Damn it! What is she trying to prove. I will not sit here." He moved. One minute on the dock, the next across the lake. Nicholas, Lucian, and Raphael followed.

Sam ventured into the woods her fear increasing, but she tried to remain calm. She caught glimpses of shadows everywhere moving through the trees as she approached the clearing. In the center was a man. He was tall, a little on the staulky side, but power clung to him. Moving closer she could see his piercing black eyes Cold, ruthless, looking straight into her soul. His silver hair blowing around him in the wind and he was dressed in jeans and a black shirt, reminding her of a Greek god in present time.

"I'm here."

"Come closer Sam."

"No!" Then she felt Lisa's pain. "Stop! I'm coming." Moving to stand in front of him she felt it than, the shift of power and air encasing them in a glass ball. The air was cool, reducing her powers.

"Who are you?" Sam inquired.

"Gregory! Leave her alone. You have no quarrel with her your fight is with me." Sarina appeared outside the ball.

"You chose not to be with me, so I'll be with her." Shackling Sam's wrists as he spun her around to pin her back against his chest.

"Over my dead body." Ethan appeared next to Sarina.

"That can be arranged Ethan." Sending power towards him, but Ethan deflected it.

"You must leave Ethan. If anything happens to you, you sentence her to a half magical life. Go, I will handle this." Seeing his eyes glow with anger.

"If anything happens to her..."

"Nothing will. Now go!" Sarina watched as he reluctantly vanished.

Remember his body heat, Sam heard a far off voice say. Relaxing into Gregory she slowly absorbed his heat while Sarina kept his attention on her.

Christian and his brothers came out of the woods like legendary warriors. Power pouring off them. "What is going on?" Christian voiced.

"A power struggle between that man and Sarina over Sam. I sense another power here not long ago, but I can't figure out who it is." Nicholas informed them.

They spread out around the clearing like guards, silent yet ready to strike at any minute to help Sam and Sarina.

Mark materialized by Christian. "What is happening? I felt Sam's distress."

"I'm not sure. Nicholas said it was a power struggle for Sam. Just be ready." Watching the scene unfold.

Sam waited patiently for the right moment to break free. She looked at her grandmother, reveling in her eyes, her power she would soon set free. Sarina kept her face expressionless. "You never took the time to get to know me, teach me, help me understand my powers. It was your right to do that."

"I tired of the old ways. You were mine, yet you rejected me. Do you know how humiliating that was to have your partner do that?"

"You never respected me. I needed you, but you acted like you were above it all. I hurt too. So much so that I hid, for years, from you hoping you'd fine someone to make you happy. I was way too young."

"I never meant to hurt you Sarina. I just wanted to impress you. My heart shattered that night." Seeing the hurt in his eyes broke Sarina's heart.

Sam took the opportunity to breakout of his embrace and strike. The ball was engulfed in flames. The colors so vivid and bright, the heat so intense that the glass exploded, sending shards everywhere.

"No!" An anguish cry as Sarina ran to them. Sam and Gregory both lay as if dead on the forest floor. Gregory's chest started to rise and fall steadily, but Sam never moved. "Sam, honey wake up. Please wake up." Holding her hand trying to keep it together.

Gregory turned his head to see Sam motionless. Sitting up he laid a hand on Sarina. "May I check her?"

"No! You stay the hell away from her." Gregory turned to see five men approach him and one had fury pouring off him.

"Sarina, who are they?"

"Sam's soul mate, his three brothers, and a friend. You shouldn't have done this to Sam." Holding Sam in her lap she felt Ethan near, *Ethan stop! You can't reveal yourself, not yet.*

She needs me. You know I'm the only one to help revive her.

Christian will kill you if you touch her.

She is my partner, fury in his voice.

He is her soul mate. Ethan stop!

"No!" Appearing next to Sam he took her out of Sarina's arms.

He held her gently like a child to his chest. Blurring them he began a chant to awaken her.

"What is he doing to her Sarina?" Trying to be calm about seeing another man holding his woman like that. So lovingly and gentle.

Sarina just watched Ethan with Sam. How tender he was being, risking his life to save hers. Wishing Gregory had done the same.

"Sarina!" Christian's patients extreme thin.

Christian's stern voice brought her attention to him. Dreading this moment. "He is trying to revive her through magic."

"Why?" He bit out.

"Because he is the only one who can." Tears streamed down her face. "Please leave him to his duty. I will explain it all to you later Christian I promise." She felt a strange warmth surround her. Turning her head she saw Gregory watching her, *I am so sorry my love*, he began to disappear, but she grabbed his hand.

"Please stay."

"As you wish." Holding her hand.

❧

Sam heard a far off chanting, felt a strange heat surround her. Sam felt calm as she looked down to see the scene below. The stranger from the mirror holding her softly while he chanted as a pale yellow light formed around her body. Her grandmother holding Gregory's hand. Christian seething with menace, and Mark staying alert to see what their next move would be.

Feeling her spirit being pulled back to her body, she went willingly. The stranger giving her her first breath she took in. Her eyes fluttered open to see those iridescent blue eyes. They held her for a moment, looking at more than her eyes.

"Are you ok Sam?" He asked in a low compelling voice.

"Who are you?" Question's in her eyes.

"I can't tell you yet. Tomorrow night you'll know. Are you fine?" Asking again.

"Yes, thank you."

"I must go than."

"What? Why? I have so many questions."

"Which I will gladly answer tomorrow night, but I feel the need of your soul mate to get to you and he's pissed I'm holding you. Until later." He kissed her hand and vanished.

"Sam!" Sarina pulled her into her loving arms. "Are you alright?"

"Yes, grandma I'm fine." Watching Christian come towards them, *Who was that that helped me?*

I can't say yet, but you will see a lot of him from now on.

Sam left it at that, for now. "Christian." Reaching for him.

He pulled her up holding her against his chest so she could feel his rapid heart beat at the idea of losing her.

"You didn't though." Kissing him.

His brothers stood in front of them to protect them against this new comer. "Sarina would you like to introduce us?" Nicholas questioned.

"Yes, this is Gregory my partner." Hearing Sam gasp. "Its ok child we will all be fine. Gregory and I must get reacquainted first." Looking at him with hope nothing more.

"Yes my love, we will start out slow." Smiling.

"Grandma?"

"Oh yes, Gregory this is Sam's soul mate Christian." Nicholas moved to reveal him. "And his brother's Nicholas, Raphael, and Lucian. Where is Mark."

"He went back to check on Maria." Lucian answered.

"Well, Mark is a close friend of Sam's." Sarina turned as Christian growled. "And a sorcerer." Ignoring him.

"Sam needs to eat. Before you started all this." Nicholas said to Gregory. "She was having the shakes."

"Yes get her food. I'll take Gregory with me and see you all tomorrow." Smiling as fog surrounded them.

Entering the door Lisa pulled Sam away from Christian. "Are you ok? Your not hurt are you?" Checking her for injuries.

Sam got her attention by grabbing her hand's. Looking at her she held her gaze. "I'm fine. Are you?"

"Yes. You need to eat I feel your weakness. Come on I'll fix you something." Putting her arm around Sam as they walked to the kitchen.

Passing the guy's Sam looked over her shoulder at Christian. Giving him a luscious, mystical smile. Her eyes sparkled, showing a hint of mischief before turning back. Swaying her hips just for him. Knowing he loved her ass.

My little seductress you are playing with fire, showing her vivid pictures of what he would do if she kept it up. Her laughter danced through him in response.

"What control you have of her." Raphael joked.

"Keep it up and I'll show you control." He teased.

Are you fine? Nicholas casually whispered.

I'm not sure. My emotion's are trying to get the best of me although I seemed to stay in control a little longer. I want to know who that man was that was holding Sam. She was as confused about it as I am, but Sarina seemed to know who he was.

"I will find out who he is. You'd better keep an eye on Sam I think she has something up her sleeve." Staring down the hall where she was.

"Yes, I believe your right. Come let's see if there's anything more we can help with." Walking down the hall. "After, movies."

In the kitchen "So who was that guy? He's hot." Lisa inquired looking in the fridge for food.

"I don't know, but I feel connected to him somehow." Still puzzled.

Closing the door Lisa studied her sister. Noticing she was trying to remember. "Well don't think about it now. We need to figure out what kind of snack to make..."

"Did I hear snack?" Daniel walked in sitting next to Sam as he put his arm around her.

John encircled Lisa's waist. Leaning down to place a kiss on her cheek. She leaned against him, feeling his fierce arousal, *You need to calm that down until later,* laughing in John's mind.

Why? There are plenty of rooms here, sending her vivid pictures.

You need your mind washed out, trying to move away with no luck. "So what should we make?"

"Well I could make Daniel's arm disappear if he doesn't remove it from Sam." Christian answered walking in.

Daniel turned with a smirk. "Didn't you hear you've been replaced."

"Oh really. Sam said that did she. That I was replaced by you." Gliding up to them.

Sam was trying not to laugh, but couldn't help it. Kissing Daniel on the cheek, she hopped off the stool and into Christian's loving embrace, *You are so bad sometimes.*

I did nothing but trying to get the story correct. "I think you've been replaced again."

"Hey!"

"Oh I still love you Daniel." Sam smiled.

"Thank you. See she still loves ME!" Turning back to Lisa. "So what's to eat?"

Laughing, "What does everyone want?" Pouring juice for Sam. "Sam sit back down and drink this while we figure this out." Purposely setting it next to Daniel.

Sam sat back down and Daniel scooted right next to her, putting his arm around her waist just to tic Christian off. He enjoyed pissing him off cause he thought it was funny. "So is everything almost done?" Ignoring Christian's glare.

Nicholas remained expressionless, but laughing to himself over his brothers behavior. "Yes at least what we can do for tonight."

"Good. Let's have some fun. After a snack let's just take a ride." Leaning into Daniel purposely, playfully encouraging him.

Watching Christian, he whispered in Sam's ear, "You know he doesn't like this. Let's keep it up on and off all night. I think its hilarious." Kissing her cheek.

Sam just laughed. She turned to Christian seeing the small anger in his eyes. *Oh honey, he's just having fun. Come here and let me calm you.*

Calm me? Every time I look at you my heart rate goes up, but I will have my own laughs at Daniel expense later.

"Come on let's not fight. Food! What do we want?" Changing the subject.

"Since we're going out for a drive."

"We are Mi Amour?" Rubbing his face in Sam's hair.

"Yes we are. I think we should go get some fries and a shake. So get everyone and let's go." Hopping off the stool.

They took the limo, since it was the only thing big enough to hold everyone. After getting the food, Armond just drove them through back roads. They stopped at a park for a bit. The girls got on the swings for awhile and the guys just watched them and talked about the party. It was cool out tonight with a nice breeze. The moon was out giving enough light to see everything. The crickets and frogs were putting on their nightly melody.

The wind carried the scent of a male feline nearby. Sam's eyes changed to her cheetahs, searching for the other cat. She stopped swinging, making sure everyone was occupied, she slipped into the woods behind the swings. Using the cat's scenes of smell, she followed the male's scent. The cheetah was itching to break free so Sam allowed her, since she was away from everyone now.

Her body began to contort, bones popping starting to reshape, her skin rippled with tan fur, a strange, exhilarating experience every time she shifted. Trotting through the vegetation on the forest floor, the scent became intoxicating. Going from a trot to a full run to find him hardly making a sound moving swiftly through the trees. Loving the wild freedom she felt in the form of her cheetah. She slowed down, feeling the other feline close. Holding completely still she scanned with sight, smell, and hearing. She waiting for him to show, knowing he would any minute now.

Ethan came through the woods on silent paws. He caught her feminine scent first. Coming through some brush he saw her in the distance. She was just as beautiful in cheetah form as she was in human, the moon gave her coat a silky shine he wanted to feel. He slowly walked towards her, afraid he might scare her off, but she remained still as he came up to her sniffing and rubbing her flank with his head. She felt as soft as he imagined, smelled wild , feminine, intoxicating.

Sam remained silent inside her cheetah as they both allowed this male to rub his scent on her. As natural as breathing, in the cheetah world when they are looking for a mate, anyway. He didn't seem a threat, yet she kept her barrier's up and stayed alert. There was something familiar about him like she already knew him intimately. When he came back to face her, his eyes changed, briefly, to those iridescent ones of her mystery man. Sam was so startled she fought her cheetah for control and won. Changing back, she stood her ground as the other cat shifted into the man. "Why are you following me?" Softly asking.

"I had to see you, to make sure you are ok." Amazed at how adapted she was becoming with shifting.

"I am fine and thank you again for your help. I must go." Sam turned to walk back when he caressed her arm in a light touch.

"Please don't go." Electricity went through him to his groin. He ached for her.

Sam looked at his hand on her arm and swears she saw flames leap from him to her. Not wanting to break the contact she placed her other hand on his. "I must. My soul mate will be looking for me." She saw tiny flames in his eyes briefly then they were gone. Not sure if she was just seeing things she remained calm, but called Christian.

Ethan calmed his temper, hoping she didn't see it when she mentioned her soul mate. He understood this, but she was also his partner and tomorrow night would be hell for all of them if she and her mate didn't understand his part in Sam's life. "Until later." Kissing her hand he disappeared as Christian came up to her.

"What is it? Are you alright beautiful?" Christian lovingly asked hugging her.

"Yes, I just wondered into the woods too far and scared myself. Let's head home I'm getting tired." Laying her head on his shoulder while they walked back to the playground.

Christian picked up a male scent on her the beast within roared at him. She was his, no one else's. He fought for control, but a growl escaped his lips.

Sam stopped. Her heart missed a beat then started pounding so hard she thought it would come through her chest. She couldn't deal with his predatory nature tonight it was bad enough she feared it, but more so now after the last time. "What is it? What is wrong Christian?" Knowing what he must have picked up on right after she asked.

"Who was out here with you Sam?" His voice strained.

"I don't know his name. The same man that helped me earlier." Trying to control the quiver in her voice.

"Why?" He bit out.

"He said he just wanted to see if I was ok." Nicholas and Mark appeared.

"Christian calm down there is no need for anger." Nicholas calmly stated.

"Fuck off Nicholas." Venom pouring out of his voice.

"I will take her if you don't calm down. She's scared to death right now." Mark intervened.

"I swear I'll kill you first Mark. Touch her and see." His eyes never left Sam. Cold, dark, ruthless.

"Lucian, Raphael." Nicholas voiced as they appeared and restrained Christian. He fought them.

"No! Please let him go Nicholas. Someone's going to get hurt." Concern in her voice, for all of them.

If we release him now, in this state, he may very well hurt one of us. Let us take him somewhere safe, Nicholas suggested.

After calming herself down enough to think rationally, she realized he was right, but she wanted to try one more thing before they decided to take him. "Ok hold him tight." Seeing the anger in his eyes as her deception.

What are you doing? Nicholas questioned.

Do you trust me?

You know I do. I just don't want you hurt.

Let me try this one thing and if it doesn't work than take him, she watched him nod and step back. She put her palm flat against his chest, then she looked at Nicholas. *Change into your normal form and feed me your power,* he did as she asked.

Sam staggered with all the power, but recovered quickly. "Do you trust me?" Her voice low, husky, sex pouring from it.

"Yes." Trying to control his reaction to her.

"Then look in my eyes." Once he did she held his gaze. Casting a spell in his head to ensure his corporation. "Come to me!" Her voice black magic.

Nicholas was caught. He couldn't look away or stop the compulsion she wove. Her eyes a beautiful green swirling with more power than he'd ever saw. His legs moved at her command, his body not his own, but hers to puppet.

"Sam what are you doing?" Lucian voiced still holding Christian.

"Silence!" Her voice no one would deny. "Don't let him go. Hold tight. He'll get worse." She told them never moving her gaze.

"Sam you are playing with fire I hope you can handle." Mark realized her plan.

"So do I, now give me your power. Remove my clothes and provide a white cloth robe of natural fibers, quickly."

He did as she asked, all the while keeping an eye on Christian. His eyes like fire, teeth and nails had lengthened. A fierce storm came out of nowhere due to his increasing rage. When Mark was done he moved out of her way.

Sam felt all the power in her as she began to glow. Beckoning Nicholas forward, she dug her nails into Christian as Nicholas took possession of her mouth. As their tongues dueled she took Nicholas's strength, draining him. She released him, letting him sit down.

Feeling the brother's grip slipping, Sam turned to Christian, dug her other set of nails into him she pierced his glare with her own hot, feverish gaze and finally took possession of his mouth, mind, and body. Throwing all her power and strength into him. All at once.

The power Christian felt was overwhelming, like a new drug, creating a high so intense he thought he'd never come off it. Next the intense heat hit him like a blow torch, searing all the way to his soul. Finally he felt her, his soul mate. Her light, love, self sacrifice to help him. Her kiss like a craving he would never sate, her body that of an angel, her love never fading. Christian fought the beast, while Sam helped.

His brothers had gone to Nicholas's aid once Mark incased them in a bubble to contain the power until Sam had control. Christian felt even Mark's powers dwindling. He wrapped his arms around Sam giving her his strength so they were both strong. Together they fought the beast as it ravaged Sam again and again. She allowed it while Christian finally was able to leash it.

He lifted her worn out body into his loving embrace knowing she had some how healed every abusive mark so none were left this time. "I love you more than you'll ever know." Wanting to reprimand her, but he'd wait until later.

Mark released them, running to Sam's aid. She reached for his hand, "Is she alright? Are you?"

"Yes, we are both fine. She's just a little weak."

"Let me give her some more energy."

"Your already weak, I feel it. Let's all go to the house and just rest for the night." Waiting for Mark to release her hand. "My idiot brother fine?"

"Yes, Mr. over jealous and I wouldn't piss her off much. She's figuring out her powers quite fast and she can be dangerous at a lot of things." Grinning giving her a wink.

Sam blushed and turned into Christian's chest a little embarrassed at what she did to save Christian. Although he is a good kisser, nothing would ever compare to Christian's kisses.

I'm glad to hear you say that or I'd have to beat him for kissing you, Christian softly whispered in her mind.

No more violence for tonight, she sighed in his head.

Of course Mi Amour. I'll take you home.

Within minutes they were back in the limo. She laid pliant in Christian's lap as they all went back to the mansion for the night. Lisa held her hand all the way back. Right before they pulled in the drive Sam felt finger's lightly caressing her cheek and a whisper in her head, *I'm sorry.*

Please, at least tell me your name.

Ethan. I'll be with you tomorrow night, leaving a light kiss on her neck.

Opening her eyes she caught Lisa's stare, *Sam, Who is he?*

All I know is that his name is Ethan and he helped me. Although I think he has something to do with the ritual. We'll find out. Grandma know.

I'll contact her and let you know.

Good. Have Nicholas with you when you do. In case this Gregory is with her.

I will. He seems very personal to me about you. Yet I don't see him as a threat.

I know.

"Okay you two if your going to talk do it out loud. Not all of us are mind readers or have any powers at all." Shelby teased.

"Your just jealous." Sam smiled.

"As if."

"I'll protect you baby." Daniel implied.

"Yeah, as long as it is in YOUR best interest. I can take care of myself."

"Yeah we all know that." He answered very low.

"I may not have powers, but I do have good hearing. Sam." Shelby looked at her.

Sam caused Daniels drink to spill on his lap. Just to cool him off. "Hey! I thought you loved me Sam."

"I do, but Shelby's my best friend so she comes first. Sorry." Smiling wickedly.

Daniel sent cold fingers up Sam's spine smiling while he did it. So in retaliation she sent a warm breath against his ear causing a sexual reaction he didn't expect. Seeing the shock on his face she got off Christian, put on an arm around Daniel, after telling Christian her intent of course, and seductively whispered, *I can make you do things you'd never think I could do,* looking at Nicholas. *Just ask him,* Daniel looked up at Nicholas and saw him nod.

"How?" He questioned.

"She is controlling her powers fast the closer she is to the ritual the stronger she'll become." Nicholas explained.

Sam sat back down next to Christian. Looking at her, Daniel said, "I know your weakness though."

"As I know yours." Christian plainly stated. No emotion in his voice just fact.

"Which I trust you won't share with her."

"Only if necessary." Running his hands through her silky hair.

Next thing Daniel knows his lap in wet again with ice water. "Sam, what the hell?" Grabbing more napkins to dry himself off.

Trying to stifle a laugh. "I didn't do it I swear." *Lisa?*

What? trying to hide behind John

Daniel looked around the limo, seeing Lisa hiding he questioned her. "Lisa?"

"What?"

"How did you do it?"

Coming into full view, "I guess I got some of Sam's powers when we exchanged blood. I may never be as powerful as Sam, but I will have my own powers soon. We are twins and share almost everything. You threaten her you threaten me and I'm not as nice as she is." Catching Lisa's eyes glowing briefly, then with a blink it was gone.

Armond opened the door to let everyone pile out of the limo. As he closed the door Christian invited him and Maggie to watch movies with them. "Thank you Christian. We both still have things to do, but maybe after we're done."

"Alright, meet us in the TV room in an hour." And with a nod Armond got back in the limo and headed for the garage.

Inside everyone went to change into their comfy night clothes. After Sam did she went to John's room to get Lisa. Knocking softly she heard John swear and Lisa laugh walking to the door. "Yes?"

"Are you busy?" Knowing they were about to be.

"Of course not." Lisa smiled as a growl came from inside the room.

"Walk with me."

"Ok hold on." She ran to John telling him she'd meet him in the TV room, then shut the door behind her.

"Will he be ok?"

"Don't worry about him he'll be fine. What's up?"

"I need you to contact grandma now this is driving me crazy."

"Ok, ok. Have Nicholas meet me in the library its quiet in there. Keep everyone with you. I'll find out."

"Thanks. I love you."

"You too. Hurry." Walking to the library.

Sam turned towards the TV room, *Nicholas?*

"Yes Sam?" He whispered materializing behind her.

Jumping she turned and hit him for scaring her. "That wasn't nice." Catching her breathe. "You trying to give me a heart attack?"

"No, but no more nice than what you did earlier." Grinning at her.

"That was necessary and you know it." Blushing.

"Why are you blushing there is no need, not from me. My reaction to you is due to my tie to Christian, although you are a good kisser."

"Thank you." Becoming uncomfortable, "Lisa needs you in the library she's contacting my grandmother to ask her something for me and I want you there as protection. In case Gregory shows I don't trust him yet."

"Good, I need to ask her something too." Turning towards the library.

Sam stopped him with a touch. He turned to look at her. "Please be nice to her. She's just trying to protect me." Her eyes pleading with him, a slight pout to her luscious lips.

Without thinking, pure reaction only, he pulled her to him and kissed her. Passionately, feverishly no thought but to be with her, in her, an addition.

"Nicholas!" A low warning.

Gaining control, he looked into Sam's shocked eyes. Slowly pulling away, "I'm sorry chere. Lucian take her. I will protect your sister Sam." Turning abruptly he left.

Sam touched her swollen lips, watching Nicholas go as Lucian put his arm around her moving forward. "Are you alright? What the hell was that?"

"I don't know. I asked him to watch Lisa and be nice to my grandma. All I did was touch his arm and then he kissed me."

Lucian stopped just outside the TV room. Turned her to face him. "Sam you can't tell Christian what just happened. He'd go crazy." Watching her shake her head. "We'll figure all this out, ok."

"I need to be alone for a little bit. Can you cover for me?"

"Of course."

"Thank you. I won't be long." Sam slipped past the door unseen and went outside. To be with nature to gather her thoughts.

Nicholas entered the library. It was lit with only candles providing soft light. Lisa sat in front of the fireplace. Turning when she felt his power she pinned him with a glare. "Why did you do that to her? And don't deny it I know you kissed her." Watching him walk over to her.

"I don't know. It was like… I couldn't stop myself."

"Which you couldn't even if you tried." Sarina appeared next to Lisa. "I know you both have questions. First Lisa, Nicholas had no control over his reaction to Sam. Until the ritual she will be a sexual seductress, which is part of her test. Just be careful Nicholas and from what I've seen warn Mark and possibly Daniel, yet I don't see it effecting him as much, but the others too."

"Grandma what about this mystery man, Ethan? Who is he?"

Sighing she looked at both of them. "You both have to promise not to tell Sam or Christian. I mean it or I won't tell you and if you try you'll lose your communication skills until the ritual."

"Fine!" Lisa pouted.

"I promise." Nicholas agreed.

"Ethan is Sam's magical partner. Similar to a soul mate, but for magic." Hearing their reactions she continued. "Ethan will always remain in Sam's life. As with Christian, if Ethan dies so does a part of Sam, a magical part anyway. The ritual is not only to test her magic, but to join them two as partner's for life. Much like a marriage."

"Christian won't allow this."

"He has to Nicholas. This is our tradition. If it isn't done no one will be safe."

"What do you mean?"

"Christian's beast will take over probably and try to kill anyone attracted to Sam. Sam will become more alluring every day. Even more so that every man will want her. The bond will never be complete. Nicholas you have to somehow make Christian understand."

"I don't even understand."

"I can't say anymore, but he must allow whatever will happen at the ritual. Without this, tell him Devin and Victor will win. I must go." Fading away.

"Well what does that mean? I hate it when she speaks in code. This is Sam's area not mine. Now what are we suppose to tell them?" Looking at Nicholas .

"Will she really stop us from speaking?"

"In a heart beat."

"Well I'll have to convince Christian to allow this and you'll have to just tell Sam everything will be ok just do what is asked and complete the ritual."

"Easier said than done and you know it." She continued to watch the flames dance in the fireplace. The color's were beautiful without thinking she went to reach for them, but Nicholas stopped her.

"I don't think that's a good idea." Restraining her hand.

"Thanks I don't know what I was thinking I just wanted to touch them." Still amazed by them.

"Well let's not. We should get back to the others before they wonder where we are." Pulling her to stand they went back to the TV room.

13

Sam looked out over the lake, the water was calm with no breeze now. Sitting on the dock dangling her feet over the water as she decided to practice alone she thought she'd try to locate a person instead of an object. Focusing she was able to see Christian in the TV room laughing at Daniel. He must have paid him back for earlier. John was holding Lisa watching the scene while Daniel was on the floor yet again with a knocked over chair next to him as Lucian and Raphael were just smiling.

Moving from there down the hall she sensed people in the kitchen. Nicholas was helping Christine and Shelby with the popcorn and drinks as Maria and Mike came through the door laughing and telling them what happened to Daniel.

Bringing her focus back to herself on the dock she started having a vision. She saw Devin in a room full of candles, It was extremely cold. The walls stone, the floor dirt, a stairway on the far wall with white sheets. As she drew closer she saw herself laying there. Her feet and hands tied to the ends of it. Only a sheet covering her naked body, blood slowly seeping from her arms and various cuts on her body. She didn't move, her breathing labored.

Turning from the scene she caught movement in the corner a man lay bloody and broken. Moving closer her vision blurred and the scene faded away until she was back in the present.

Tears ran down her face, fire burned in her veins she wouldn't let any of that happen Devin wouldn't win. Ever. Standing up she turned so fast she ran into Mark's solid form. He grabbed her before she fell backward.

"Whoa, what's wrong honey?" Pulling her quivering body into his embrace.

"I had another vision." Hiding her face in his masculine chest.

"Let me see."

Sam merged with Mark and showed him all of it, while she cried in his arms. "I won't let this happen. He'll never have me."

"Its ok we'll all protect you." He just leaned his head on hers, holding her gently wanting to make it so. Knowing is was going to be a long, hard fight for all of them to stop Devin and Victor.

What's wrong my love? Did you have a bad vision?

Rage engulfed her. She pulled out of Mark's embrace and shot flames into the air. *Where are you Devin?*

Close enough to touch you, Unseen hands grabbed her wrist's pulling them to her sides, *Tell everyone to stay away or I'll hurt your sister.*

Sam heard Lisa's distress. She saw Christian and Nicholas coming down to the dock. "Stop them Mark."

"Sam!" Walking towards her.

"No! You all must stay away or he'll hurt Lisa. Please." Sam winced as ice started to form around her wrists.

Mark stopped in front of her as Christian and Nicholas came up. "Sam listen to me. Where is your partner?" Mark asked softly.

"Christian's right next to you." Confused by his question.

"Sam, where is the man that helped you? That's who Mark was talking about." Nicholas explained.

"I don't know where Ethan is, Why?" Her powers draining.

"Call him to you now!" Hearing the urgency in Mark's voice.

She tried, but received the shards of pain she usually got when Devin blocked her path. From behind she felt a body form. Strong, powerful, evil. A shudder went down her.

"Hello my love." Watching the men in front of her John and Daniel came walking up to them with Lisa.

"You can't fight us all Devin." Christian calmly said.

"That is true, but I won't have to. See if you try I'll hurt Lisa and I'm sure Sam would help me stop you just to save her sister." Grinning as he ran his hands up and down her arms. Watching the anger in Christian's eyes increase.

"No Sam! Don't worry about me." Lisa exclaimed.

"Oh Lisa, you know she'll do anything to save you. Won't you Sam."

The wind started up. Lightening formed across the sky, *Sam try not to wince from the pain he can't keep me from you. I'll feed you power. Use it to free yourself, I'm on my way.*

Sam closed her eyes for a second and when she opened them her eyes had a blue glow to them. She greedily absorbed Ethan's power he fed her. The ice on her wrists began to melt freeing her hands.

Waiting patiently for Devin to bring his hands to hers she felt Ethan near, *Don't look for me I'll be near if you need me. Use what you have.*

When Devin reached her wrists he noticed the ice was gone. She interlocked their fingers, pressing her body into his feeling his arousal against her butt. She moved her hips seductively. "You like that? The way my body feels against you?" She asked. Her voice low and husky.

"Yes, more than you know." Looking at Christian, he saw no expression on his face.

"Devin, kiss me. Please. I hunger for you." Her voice haunting.

Daring not to deny her Devin stepped in front of her pulling Sam roughly against him, he tilted her head back slightly as he kissed her. Loving the feel of her, finally able to taste her soft lips, to feel her moving against him voluntarily. Increasing his sexual reaction to her.

While Devin was busy in his own sick fantasy, Sam opened her eyes looking at Christian watching them. Her eyes changed to a bright green, wrapping her arms around Devin to get a better hold on him. She deepened the kiss even more, feeding his fantasy of him and her together.

What is she doing? Christian asked Mark.

The same thing she did to Nicholas for you. She's going to drain his strength.

Will it work?

This time, yes. At least long enough to free herself and Lisa so we can protect them. I feel her partner near by feeding her his power. Just watch.

Sam took that opportunity to strike. She started draining Devin's strength. Building her power she wove a spell to incase them, which broke his hold on Lisa.

John enforced his own protection for Lisa while watching Sam. She began to glow. A dull yellow at first, but quickly increasing to a bright orange. Devin tried to pull away, but Sam was unusually strong holding him with little effort.

Stilling, Devin began to change the air from hot to cold. Increasing the cold to freezing so it would decrease her powers and release her hold. Feeling her falter he pulled away from her lips to see her bright green eyes as her arms still held him in her grasp. "Sam let go. You know I will win and you'll be mine." His voice low and compelling.

Sam felt her power dwindle with the increase of the cold. Devin was trying to use his voice to control her like she did to him. The compulsion was too strong, her grip began to release. Then she felt him, Ethan. He was behind her, solid and warm. "I'm here for only you. Use my heat." He whispered to her.

Sam looked at Devin causing flames to dance up his arms as she stepped away from him backing into Ethan's warm body.

Devin stopped the flames with a thought. "Ethan, what brings you here."

"You have. You threatened my partner and I won't let that happen."

His face twisted with fury. "She is mine! And I will have her."

"The power's didn't bind her magic to you and you can't take it by force." Gently pushing Sam behind him. "Your life had been a long, lonely one. Its time for rest let me help you end it." Compulsion in his low tone.

Fighting the compulsion Devin hit Ethan with lightening. Ethan stumbled a little, but straightened shortly after. A dark stain appeared on the left side of his shirt showing Devin that he hit him as blood dripped from the wound.

Sam's soft cry broke Ethan's spell. Devin went for Ethan. Sam released the in casement so Ethan could maneuver. Grabbing Sam they disappeared right before Devin struck. Reappearing by Christian so he could protect Sam, while he waked back down the dock.

Spinning around Devin sent spears of wood at Ethan from the air, while vines came through the water to the dock winding their way to his feet to hold him. The spears tore through his right arm and leg causing him to hit the dock hard on his left knee before he could provide a shield.

Ethan sent lightening towards Devin, disappearing it missed by a hair, but Nicholas was there when he reappeared, breaking his left arm with one twist. Screaming he struck Nicholas across the face with sharp talons drawing blood. Vines irrupted around Nicholas which formed flowers with poisonous darts that shot into his legs.

Nicholas stood his ground cutting off the excruciating pain he sent a boulder into Devin, driving him into the lake. He waited, but Devin never emerged. No bubbles or movement. The water was still, an eerie silent's.

Sam heard him than, *You think you've won. Let me assure you that you haven't. I know of another who wants you. Using him will help me to distract the others. I will have all of you one way or another,* abruptly leaving her mind her arm's began to bleed again.

Nicholas removed the poison from his body after withering the flowers and vines around him, then he went to Ethan and did the same. "So you are Ethan. Well I'm going to warn you my brother is the jealous type and doesn't share well and if you ever hurt Sam, in anyway I will come after you personally." Attempting to heal him. "I will try to make

Christian understand about the ritual and allow what every you have to do but I can't promise anything."

"I understand and expected resistance on both their parts. This is just part of our tradition I didn't intend for conflict. Bring Sam, she can heal me faster. It was magic that hurt me and magic that can heal." Closing his eyes while he lay waiting for Sam.

Sam kneeled beside him. "Ethan I'm sorry."

Opening his eyes. "You have no reason to be. Devin lost his soul along time ago. I am here to help protect you." Wincing a little as more blood flowed out of him.

"Sam you have to heal him. He said he'd heal faster since it was magic used against him." Nicholas brought her attention back to the main situation.

"Yes of course. Get his shirt off so I can see the damage." As Christian helped Nicholas remove Ethan shirt Sam was shocked that he stayed conscious. There was a golf ball size hole in the left side of his stomach and several smaller one on his right leg and arm.

Placing her hands over his stomach wound she closed her eyes and sent herself into his body. The lightening had torn through muscle almost straight through to his back. Sam started repairing the muscle and cauterizing everything to stop further blood loss. Moving through his body she did the same to his arm and leg, but he had broke his femur too so it took a little longer to repair that.

When she emerged back into her body she was about to provide him with blood, but he stopped her. "No Sam you can't" Weariness to his words.

"Why not? It will help it even more." Concerned for him.

"Because we can't share blood until after the ritual."

"But at this rate you'll be to weak to help perform it. Please Ethan." Tears shown in her eyes.

Seeing his soul mate distressed, even over another male, broke his heart more than caused jealousy. "I can provide for him. If he will accept it."

"Thank you I owe you."

"No, I owe you this for helping Sam yet again." Tearing his wrist he brought it to Ethan's mouth watching him gulp down the ancient blood.

"Christian let me provide for your mate she is weary." Nicholas asked.

"No Nicholas I'll be fine." Not wanting anyone else's, but Christian's blood.

Closing the wound Ethan just laid there exhausted from everything knowing he had to make it home before midnight so he could sleep and prepare for the ritual.

Mark materialized by Sam. Looking down he saw him, the kid he once played with through his childhood now a man and on his back like when he was little. "You haven't changed a bit. Still landing on your back."

Recognizing the smart ass voice of his cousin he flipped him off.

"Yeah, same old Ethan. Come on I'll help you to the house." Lending him a hand to help him up.

"You know him?" Sam and Lisa asked in unison.

"Yes, he's my cousin." Mark replied.

"Although we haven't seen each other in what fifty years?" Ethan confirmed.

"More like seventy five years. Beth was a baby when you moved."

"Your right. How is she?"

"A pain in the ass. She's driving mom crazy cause she won't settle down. Says she hasn't found her mate yet."

"She sound like a firecracker." Laughing remembering the temperamental baby she use to be.

"She is, but she'll be here for Sam's wedding."

"Good It'll be nice to see her again." Walking with Mark back to the house.

"Ok this is just too weird." Lisa said. "What were the odds of that happening? I need a drink. Come on Sam I'll make you one too." Sam blew a kiss to Christian as Lisa dragged her off to the kitchen.

"I have to agree with Lisa that was too bizarre. I think we should keep a watch until we know more about this Ethan." Staring after the girls.

Snapping his fingers, "Hey! That's my woman's ass your watching." Christian stated.

"And a nice one at that."

"Smart ass. Keep your eyes off it." Playfully pushing Nicholas.

"So your Sam's partner. How long have you known and why not contact me about it?" Mark questioned as they took a seat at the kitchen counter.

"I've known of her for awhile, but just set eyes on her this week. I didn't know where you were. We moved a lot so I honestly didn't think to contact you." Waiting for Sam and Lisa.

"Fare enough, but we have a lot of catching up to do. Which we can do tonight."

"Yes we do have a lot to talk about, but I have to get ready for the ritual."

"I'm sure the guys wouldn't mind you staying here we all are." Mark answered.

"That's a great idea Mark, yes please stay Ethan. Then we can all get to know you and you can fill me in on what else I need to do to get ready for the ritual." Sam stated coming into the kitchen with Lisa.

"I don't think that would be a good idea."

"Why not? I could use all the help I can get." Sam looked puzzled.

"To be honest your very attractive and seem to be having an effect on any male close to you."

"Really I hadn't noticed." Looking out the window to watch the moon show on the lake. Their voices faded into background noise, her vision narrowed, and everything went black as she felt herself falling.

She heard her sister yell her name in the distance. Strong arms caught her before she hit the tile. She was being cradled in someone's lap, *Who has me?* unable to come out of the darkness.

I have you Sam don't worry, holing her close to his warm desire shooting through him.

I need blood Ethan, in all the drama I didn't get replenished.

I would love to provide for you, but I can't, not until the ritual. Will you allow Mark. Christian isn't here yet and you can't afford to wait.

This time yes and while he is doing that you can tell me why you can't exchange blood until tomorrow night.

Alright I agree, "Mark she need's blood and said she would allow you to provide." Ethan implied while holding Sam in his lap.

Mark came over moving a chair closer so he could give her blood. Tearing his wrist, he held it to her mouth helping her swallow since she wasn't fully conscious, *Sam, honey is there anything else I can do?*

No Mark, but thank you. I'm starting to feel better, the voice in his head weak.

"She need's to go to bed and rest."

"I know I'll take her. She asked about more info on the ritual. I'll tell her as I carry her to bed." Ethan told Mark and Lisa.

"Ok we'll wait for you here, but just tell her and put her to bed. Nothing more and I mean it Ethan." Mark sternly told him.

"I would never take advantage of her if that's what your implying." Insulted by his accusations.

"Please stop this she wants to go to sleep." Lisa intervened.

Standing up, Ethan carried Sam effortlessly through the kitchen and down the hall. She was very beautiful and glad she was his. He waited his whole life for this ritual, but all their lives would be changed for all time tonight, since it was after one in the morning. Now he would have to stay and prepare here instead. Hopefully Christian wouldn't have a problem with him staying here.

Reaching for the door knob it opened automatically. He looked down to see Sam smiling at him. "Show off. You really should conserve your energy." He sat her down on the bed. "Is there anything else I can do for you before I leave?"

"Could you get my night shirt and bring it here?"

"Sure, where it is?"

"In my drawer in the closet. Go through the bathroom." She watched him go into the bathroom remembering when they first met in there she was naked and now wondered what he looked like that way.

Coming through to the bedroom Sam saw Ethan's eyes go from iridescent to neon blue. "Sam you can't be thinking like that. I'm on the edge of control as it is." Handing her the shirt, then heading for the door. "Good night Sam."

She slammed the door with a thought gliding towards him, "I don't think so." Pinning him against the door. "Stay with me tonight. You still haven't answered my questions." Running her finger's down his neck.

Ethan grabbed her hand bringing it to his lips to kiss. "I can't."

"Why not?" The heat increased as her eyes changed.

"Because your too tempting."

"Then give in, let me see you, feel you." Running her tongue along her lower lip.

That did him in. Covering her mouth with his he lifted her so she straddled him. Ethan walked to the bed and laid Sam down. "You are the sexiest creature I've ever seen." Taking her shirt off so he could suckle her breast.

In the kitchen,"He's been down there too long and he's blocked me. Can you reach Sam?" Asking Lisa as they walked out of the kitchen.

She wasn't able to reach her either. "No she blocked me too. What is going on Mark?"

"I don't know, but I think you should get your grandma."

As they reached the door Sarina appeared. "We can't reach Sam or Ethan and this is the last place they were headed." Lisa informed her reaching to turn the knob. "The door is locked. Sam are you alright? Unlock the door."

They got a growl in return. Lisa saw Christian and the rest coming down the hall. "What's wrong?"

"The door's locked and Ethan's in there with Sam."

"Why?" He growled.

"I gave Sam blood cause she wasn't replenished earlier and Ethan carried her to her room. He was taking too long and we couldn't reach them mentally so we came down here and called Sarina." Mark explained.

"Ethan's in there alone? What time is it?" The urgency in Sarina's voice let them know there was a problem.

"Its after one." Lisa told her, *Grandma what's wrong?*

Letting both Lisa and Nicholas know, *We need to get into the room and separate them. Nicholas take Christian and see if he can put them in separate rooms. Preferably with white candles and lavender in it.*

Why? What is happening? Lisa questioned again.

Because it's the day of the ritual they are unconsciously trying to start it. We can't allow it. Are there any female's of magic other than you here?

No, but Mark mentioned his sister was near.

"Mark contact Beth and have her here a.s.a.p."

"Ok." Contacting her. "She'll be here in two minutes, why?"

"Because only females will be safe going to separate them."

"Why?" Christian growled again losing patients.

"Because of her sexual magnetism towards men, only women can help. Once we get Ethan out you guys put him in a room far from Sam. She must stay in her own room Christian at least until the ritual."

"Sarina, Beth is here." Mark announced.

"Beth how nice to see you." Hugging her.

"You too Sarina. How can I help?"

"I need to separate Sam and Ethan. They haven't done the ritual yet."

"Ok are you ready?" Walking towards the door with her. "Just tell us what to do."

With Sarina's sharp command to unlock, the door flew open and slammed after them. Leaving the guys alone. "Now what?" Mark asked.

"We will split up and find two rooms at opposite ends of the house." Nicholas instructed. "After we need white candles and lavender in them."

"I will stay here and wait for Sam." Christian stated.

"No, you will stay with me until Sarina calls us and don't argue. Now let's go."

❧

Sarina, Beth, and Lisa found Sam crouched in a corner with Ethan in front of her. "Leave us Sarina."

"Ethan you can't do this not now. You have to prepare for the ritual alone. *You* know that. Please come with me." Knowing he wouldn't, she instructed Beth and Lisa to grab Sam when she got Ethan.

"She's mine and I won't leave her now."

"Your not partnered yet, the ritual has to be completed. Come, I will take you where you can prepare for Sam." The command was so strong he was unable to resist.

Ethan walked into Sarina's embrace which was the ok to get Sam, as Sarina disappeared with Ethan. "How could you? You all betrayed me. He's mine!" Sam growled stalking towards her sister.

"Sam its to early for all this you must rest." Jumping out of the way.

"Fuck off Lisa. I'll get him back."

"What about Christian? He loves you."

"I can have them both." Increasing the heat Sam made it hard to breath.

"Sam your not in control right now. If you'd stop and think you'd realize that." Beth tried to calm her.

"Who the hell are you?" Sam's hair crackled around her.

"I'm Beth, Mark's sister." Walking towards her.

Sam leaped back grabbing her sister around the throat to pull her with her. "Go get Ethan or I'll kill her."

"No!"

"Fine!" Lengthening a nail she started to slowly slice her throat open.

Beth wasn't intimidated standing her ground, *Mark get her mate now!*

What's wrong?

She is threatening to kill her sister and all I see in her mind is red fury.

I'll get him, but be careful she is extremely powerful.

"Sam, do you really want to kill her? She is a part of you. Think about it, is a man really worth spilling family blood over?" Beth tried one last time before she would attack her.

Lisa slowly started to cool the room knowing it may be the only way to stop Sam and save herself.

Beth felt the slight change, subtle but evident. She looked at Lisa for confirmation, then added her power. Together they rapidly cooled it so it was icy in there. Beth saw her breath as she felt the door shatter behind her. Turning Christian stalked past her towards Sam and Lisa.

Sam threw Lisa at Christian. Running past him to the door, but when she reached it Nicholas was there. She turned to find another way, but Lucian and Rafael appeared on either side. As Nicholas and Christian moved in she realized she was surrounded. Her anger was immense as flames overtook her body the heat rapidly increased in the room.

Christian took charge instructing everyone of power in the house to simultaneously cool the room Sam was in. It was the only way to stop her since she had lost control and needed to get it back after a long nap.

Mark waked through the door dowsing Sam with water, while the rest made it as cold as possible in there. The flames went out and Sam collapsed on the floor shivering.

Looking at her sister in the distance, "Es tut mir leid, dass. Verzeihen Sie mir bitte mich nie ment, um Sie zu Verletzen." Closing her tearful eyes.

Lisa ran over to her. Holding her hand, " Ich versatile Ihnen. Ich Liebe Sie Sam."

"What did she say Lisa?" Christian questioned.

"She said she was sorry, to forgive her she never ment to hurt me." Looking at her with love. "I told her I forgive and love her."

"What language was that she spoke?"

"Our family native German."

"Why not English?"

"We only speak it when we hurt each other. That's when we know we mean it."

"Sam's room is ready. Christian will you take her?" Sarina announced.

"Of course Sarina." Picking Sam up in his strong arms he held her tight so no one could see her cry. "Oh sweetheart, please stop crying. Your breaking my heart." Walking to the empty rooms above theirs.

He laid her down on the bed. The room was filled with candles and lavender. Sam inhaled, taking in the soothing smell. "I'm sorry I caused all this trouble. I feel so out of control. I just want it all over with so we can get married and take our vacation away from all this." Pushing her hair out of her tear streaked face as she continued to shiver.

"Everything will be all better soon. You just need to rest right now." Helping her change before putting her under the covers to get warm.

There was a soft knock on the door. "Come in." Christian answered.

"I just wanted to leave this for Sam its her favorite meditation tape." Laying it on the night stand she leaned over and kissed her cheek. "I'll see you after your nap. Have a good rest." Shutting the door behind her.

Picking up the tape he put it in the player and pressed play. Immediately he heard ocean waves and a thunderstorm behind it, next a haunting melody began to play with the water. Turning to face Sam, he could feel her relax to the music.

"Can't you stay with me?" Sam pleaded.

"No sweetheart, you must rest alone." Hating this whole thing as much as she did.

"Just until I fall asleep than."

"I see no problem with that." Taking off his shoes he slipped under the covers and held her. Listening to the music they both drifted off to sleep.

14

It was still early morning when Christian woke up. Not wanting to leave her, he slipped out of bed and went to the bathroom. Splashing water on his face he tried to wake up so he could find the strength to leave her in that room while he went to sleep in their room, but he couldn't and got back in bed with her. Holding her against him he thought to hell with it he would never leave her alone again when she was going through something this difficult and with that he drifted back to sleep.

It was early afternoon when Sam finally awoke. Rolling over she found Christian still in bed with her, which brought a smile to her lips. She watched him for a few minutes until he opened his eyes. "Good afternoon."

"Good afternoon beautiful. Are you well rested and better now?" Smiling at her.

"Yes my love. I thought I had to sleep alone?"

"Well I couldn't sleep without you so I'll take the blame." Kissing her, then heading for the bathroom.

She heard him start the shower. Stretching she heard a scratching at the door. With a wave of her hand the door opened and in ran Gabriel. He jumped on the bed and sat in her lap. Sam nuzzled his head with her face, then kissed him, "I missed you." Gabriel meowed in response.

"You want to hop in with me?" Christian yelled.

"Sure, in a minute." Sam answered. "You stay here while I shower then I'll take you down stairs and we'll both get something to eat ok?" Gabriel blinked in response laying his head on the bed.

They showered together omitting from sex until after the ritual tonight even though it was extremely hard to. After, she kept her word and grabbed Gabriel on their way out to get a late lunch.

Lisa was already in the kitchen making BLT's for everyone with Maggie. "Hey its about time you two woke up. Are you hungry?"

"Famished. Those look good." Putting the cat on the floor with some milk.

"Good cause I think we made enough for an army." Smiling at Maggie.

"The way these boys eat I'm worried it won't be enough."

"Oh Maggie, we don't eat that much do we?" Christian playfully questioned.

"You could have fooled me. Go sit, I'll bring it out." Hustling him towards the door. "Now Out!"

"Hey! What about them?" Laughing.

"Women belong in the kitchen. Men don't. OUT!" Pointing to the door.

"Ok, ok I'm going."

"Maggie, do you mind if I steal Lisa for a minute. We'll be right back to help you with the food." Sam asked.

"Of course not. You don't need to ask my permission, but I appreciate the respect."

"Thank you Maggie." Kissing her cheek before leaving.

Walking to the library Lisa asked, "What's up Sam?"

"I need you to do me a big favor which will require Mark's help too. He's on his way."

"Why do I get the impression that I'm not going to like this?"

"Because I think your right and I already don't like this." Mark came strolling in.

With a wave Sam closed and locked the door's, "First put up your strongest barriers I don't need anyone knowing of this."

"Sam." Mark advanced. "What are you thinking of doing?"

"I need to leave for awhile."

"Why? You have the ritual tonight." Concern in Lisa's voice.

"I need space right now, time to think, to gather my thoughts about everything that's been going on lately." Sam pleaded with them.

"But I thought everything was fine now."

"Lisa I haven't been fine for awhile. I just need to think, please help me. You two are the only one's that can. I'll be back before the ritual at midnight."

"Baby, you know I'll do anything for you." Mark embraced her.

Looking over Mark's shoulder, "Lisa?"

"I'll help, but I'm upset that you didn't tell me sooner."

"I'm sorry, but you were so happy." Tears started to fall.

"Your happiness is first."

"See, that's why I didn't tell you."

"Ok girls, let's discuss that later. I sense Christian near." Mark informed them.

"I'll open the doors. Mark do your disappear act and we'll meet in the garage around eight." Sam instructed.

With a nod Mark disappeared. While Lisa and Sam went back to the kitchen to help Maggie with the food. Christian caught them heading for the dinning room. "Where did you two disappear to?"

"Just sister talk. Why?" Sam continued into the room.

"I just wondered." Taking the tray of food from her.

Kissing him she went back for the last tray, but before she could leave the kitchen Christian cornered her. "Are you alright? You seem distant."

"I'm fine just nervous about the ritual that's all." Smiling.

"You'll do fine. Let's eat." Walking with her.

Dinner was the usual talking, laughing, and Daniel on the floor somehow. Christian suggested drinks by the pool to calm everyone's nerves before tonight. They splashed around the pool for awhile, Sam and Lisa sat in the Jacuzzi with John and Christian. At least until Daniel dared them to throw Maria and Christine in the pool. They got up heading for the girls, but took different direction's to get Daniel.

Everyone was laughing, but Lisa moved closer to her sister as Mark got in the Jacuzzi with them. "So how are you going to get away from the guys Sam? You have not only them, but Christian's brothers also watching over you."

"I know, that's where I need both of you. Lisa, you are coming into your power's slowly, but I feel them. I need help blocking them. Plus a distraction so I can have Mark drive me away."

"Okay and how are we to do that?" Lisa questioned.

"Well remember how Nicholas is able to change form? So can we. I need you to change into me for at least 15 minutes. I'll change into you and Mark will go with me to the store for dessert. When he return's change back as you go to the garage carry the bags back like you were always with him."

"Sam I don't have the experience or energy for that. How am I to do that?"

"I'll give you more of my blood to strengthen you for a short time and Mark can show you how to change."

"Sam why tonight of all nights are you doing this?" Mark asked.

"Because I'm scared. I can't breath, please." Close to tears Mark squeezed her thigh in the water to show his understanding.

Sam got out of the water and went back to her room to change. "Do you think she'll be ok?" Lisa inquired. "Should we stop her?"

"No just let her be, this is a trying time for a sorceress and you'll understand soon. Come let's change, I'll show you what to do." Helping her out of the water. Lisa left first telling John she was going to change then look for something for dessert to make. Five minutes later Mark went to change.

Christian went to his room to find Sam. Entering he saw her staring out the window already changed. "Honey?" Walking over to her, "Is everything alright?" Concern in his voice.

"I'm fine, just wanted some quiet, alone time." Not turning around. She stayed merged with Lisa so she would know how to act when she left. "I'll be down in a little while."

"If you need me."

"I'll let you know." Kissing him briefly before he left.

Sam met Lisa in the kitchen ten minutes later. "Ok sis now what?"

Sam pulled out a knife and sliced both their palms. Putting them together she recited a spell to give Lisa enough strength to shift and hold it for the time required. After Sam staggered from the blood loss.

"Sit down. I'll get you some juice. I don't like this Sam. Now your weak. If anything happens you can't protect yourself." Handing her the glass.

"That was her plan so she could appear human." Mark sat next to her. "Are you two ready?"

Drinking the last of the juice Sam nodded and they began to shift. "Can you help me hold this until we are down the road?"

"Yes." Mark answered not liking her weakness.

"Good luck." Kissing her sis.

"You too. See you soon."

Mark got Sam to the car without incident while Lisa, pretending to be Sam, told everyone they went to get stuff for banana splits. Which they bought, for now anyway.

Five miles out Mark asked where to. "Go to Loraine's Bar in White cove my friend Nichole should be working tonight."

"Are you sure you'll be ok?"

"Yes, I use to live there and still have friend's near by if I need them."

He pulled in the parking lot driving to a dark corner he turned off the car. "Sam, you need blood you'll be to weak to be here long." Getting ready to open his wrist for her.

"No! I'll be fine for awhile. If I have need I'll call I promise." She slipped out the door and went inside.

Mark stopped at the store for the supplies to keep up the illusion. Lisa met him in the garage. So far so good, but it wouldn't last long.

"Everything's going as planned?" He asked walking into the house.

"So far, but I think Christian is becoming suspicious."

"Yeah I have a feeling this won't last long. I hope she knows what she's doing."

"Hey babe, need help?" John asked walking into the kitchen.

"Sure." Smiling at him, happy to be herself again.

In the bar Sam sat at the counter, "Hey Sam, what are you doing here?" Nichole greeted her with a smile.

"Just getting away from everything for awhile. Could I get a screwdriver?"

"Sure. Go sit over in that booth and we'll talk."

"Thanks Nichole." Sam went over to a red leather booth. The bar was dark like most. Wood everywhere, dance floor, and a couple pool tables, smoke filled the air. Sam just leaned her head back and closed her eyes for a second.

"Hey good looking."

Oh great she thought, "Listen I'm just here to be alone."

"Samantha, your never alone here."

Opening her eyes she saw a face from her past. "Todd?"

"Hi honey, can I sit with you? Niki said you were here trying to forget your problems." Sliding in next to her.

Sam hugged him. "I just needed to get away for awhile. To have some breathing room."

"Smoke?"

"Thanks." Todd lit the cigarette for her as Nichole brought over their drinks.

"So what's up Sam? Are you getting nerves about the wedding?"

"Your getting married?" Surprising Todd.

"Yes to both questions. My friends are having an engagement party later tonight and I just needed some space for awhile." Taking a drink.

"Have you talked to Christian?"

"No, I can't. He's so happy."

"Well enjoy yourself while you're here then. Come dance with me." Todd held out his hand.

"Go on Sam have some fun while you're here. I have to get back to work. We'll talk later."

Sam took Todd's hand and followed him to the dance floor. "You know I had a big crush on you in school before I moved." Sam said.

"Really? I did too, but I was afraid you didn't. When I finally got up the courage to ask you out that was the night you came to me crying about your parents divorce and moving."

She just smiled, "Sorry, guess it wasn't meant to be, but they did get back together"

"Maybe, maybe not. Just bad timing." He continued with the next slow song. "I'm glad to hear they're back together."

Sam finally relaxed enjoying the dance and conversation, no pressure, no worries. When the song stopped they headed back to the table. Sam stumbled losing her balance.

"Whoa! You ok?"

"Yeah, just got dizzy for a minute." Todd helped her sit.

"Have you ate tonight?"

"I ate around five. I should be fine, why?"

"You didn't eat enough, your sugar level is probably down. I'll get you a burger."

"What are you a doctor or something." Smiling.

"As a matter a fact I am, but I remember you having this problem in school too. Smart ass. Stay here I'll be back."

"Show off."

"I heard that." He yelled.

Sam just laughed, then the room spun so she closed her eyes. When she opened them Todd was there with some nuts and juice. "Here take this for now until the burger's are done."

"Thanks. So you're a doctor. What kind?"

"A family practitioner."

"No wife?"

"Nope."

"Why not your good looking enough. I'd thought women would be banging down your door?"

"He's to damn picky." Nichole interrupted with their burger's. Hearing a crunch she looked down to see a broken glass. "Damn another one broke. At this rate I won't have any glasses left." Picking it up she cut herself. "Shit!"

Sam watched the blood form on Nichole's hand, fascinated at the color and how fast it formed. Nichole saw Sam's eyes change and quickly grabbed a towel to cover her hand. "Sam!"

She looked up trying to focus. "Sorry, I'll be right back." Leaving to go to the bathroom hoping Todd didn't see her eyes change.

It was to late though, Todd saw her eyes. "Is she ok?"

"Yeah, just nerves."

"Don't bull shit me Niki I saw her eyes. What's wrong with her?"

"Just leave it alone you wouldn't understand." With that she went back to the bar. Then to the bathroom to check on Sam.

"Sam? You in here?" Asking quietly.

"Yes."

"Come out here." Watching her come out of the stall, "You don't need the food do you?"

"No I'm sorry. The food only helps a little when I'm this weak."

"Let me help you."

"No! I'll be alright as long as I stay sitting and eat."

"Let's get you out and feed you than, come on." Helping Sam out the door.

Todd was there. "Are you alright?"

"Yes." Smiling.

"Then tell me why your eye's changed when Nichole cut herself?"

"I don't know." Sam was trying to hold her temper.

"Yes, you do." Todd took out a knife and cut his palm. Nichole pushed all them back into the bathroom and locked the door.

"Damn it Todd."

"Tell me Sam. What has happened to you?"

The blood was becoming overwhelming. Her teeth lengthened as she turned from him. "Please Todd cover your cut."

"Why? Tell me, face me Sam."

"Cause if you don't she'll drain you. Now do as she asked." Nicholas appeared behind them. Walking over to Sam, he pulled her to a corner blocking her from view, *Drink sister, I offer freely so you may be strong again,* pulling her to his steady pulse in his neck.

Her teeth sank deep gulping the rich blood to fill her starving body. Strength came back fast making her feel better again. She closed the wound with her tongue. "I'm sorry Nicholas please forgive me."

"I am not the one to apologizes to. Why did you leave?"

"How did you know?"

"I am and always will be your watcher whether Christian is around or not. I followed you, but I must remove your friends memory of all this."

Sam came around Nicholas. "I'm sorry Todd for all of this, but you wouldn't understand." Walking over to him.

"Sam are you ok?" Taking a step back.

"Nichole you can go we'll be out in a minute."

"Alright." Walking over to Sam. "He isn't going to hurt Todd in he?" She whispered.

Smiling Sam said no, so she left Todd with them. "What is going on." Todd questioned. "What are you?"

"I am from an ancient race of people. Sam is bonded to my brother, but for some reason feels the need to finding comfort somewhere else."

"Your Pyrenees." Todd plainly stated.

"How do you know of us?" Nicholas was suspicious.

"Because I've heard the stories of the ancients all my life from my mother."

"And how would your mother know?"

"Because she was one of you."

"Her name."

"Victoria Romanoff. She passed away five year's ago after my father was killed in a car accident. I know she choose to be with him though." Sadness in Todd's voice.

"Was your father human than?"

"Yes, I'm half human and half Pyrenees."

"Then I apologizes for my rudeness. I am Nicholas, leader of the Pyrenees now. I am sorry to hear of Victoria she was well loved among my people. We will morn her loss and yours. Please come back to the mansion with us. We can talk."

Todd looked at Sam. She looked a hundred percent better. "Please come. Let me see your hand." Walking over to Todd. "I won't hurt you now, I'm replenished.."

Putting his hand in hers he instantly felt the heat. Looking down he saw white light coming between their hands. He could feel his hand healing. "How can you do that?" Amazed at her ability.

"I can do a lot of things you don't know about Todd." She smiled wickedly walking out the door.

"She's always like that. Pisses off my brother to no end." Following her.

"Stop her she's in danger." Todd told Nicholas.

"I sense nothing." Scanning, but seeing Todd's eyes glaze over.

"Niki, back door." Sam yelled over the music.

"Through the kitchen. Go."

Sam ran back first with Todd and Nicholas behind her. They ran through the kitchen, out the door, and right into Devin who grabbed Sam around the throat. He wasted no time draining her blood to weaken her fast. "Stop Nicholas or I'll drain her completely."

"I'll kill you first." Venom in his voice. "Let her go Devin."

"Now why would I want to do that, she's mine I told you. Where is your precious twin anyway? I want him to witness my victory."

"Right behind you." Christian said as he sliced deep through Devin's back.

Nicholas made a bold move pulling Sam free before helping his brother with Devin. Mark appeared by Sam. "Drink now!" Thrusting his wrist at her.

Todd watched as Sam's teeth lengthened sinking deep into the stranger's wrist. She fed viciously again regaining her strength. She closed the wound. "You're a prick."

"I love you too Sam. Ready?"

"Yes! Christian, Nicholas stop. My turn." Walking to Devin.

"No Sam, leave now!" Christian instructed.

With a wave of her hand she sent both brother's flying. Just in time for Victor to show up and grab her wrist before she could touch him. "Hello lovely miss me?" Throwing her against the building.

"Not really." Getting up. "You want to spar, Victor?"

"Not now, but soon. Just came to get Devin."

"You'll never make it out of here alive Victor." Christian stated.

"See that's where your wrong." Sending lightening at both brother's and Mark in streams. Keeping them busy he reached Devin. "Combine your power with mine."

"Why?"

"Cause we want the same thing and I'll bring the woman to you for strength. Do it."

Devin did it giving Victor enough power to subdue Sam. He ripped off her amulet and somehow managed to get the protection bracelet off too, which helped Devin. Pulling her to him he sank his teeth into her neck. Draining her almost completely.

"Stop or you'll kill her." Victor reminded him.

"Don't want that do we. Give me a kiss before I leave." Leaning in, but something knocked him away. Victor grabbed Todd and threw him into the building. Knocking him out while Devin took a little more of her soul, then they both disappeared.

Sam shut down. I'm on my way, Lisa confirmed.

Within minutes Lisa was in the back heading for Sam. Raphael was holding her in his arms. Sadness filled his face as he saw Lisa approach. "Say nothing she is in a coma, not dead." Lisa told him quietly trying not to alarm Christian. "Can you take both of us back together through space and time?"

"Yes, Why?"

"It would be dangerous to separate us when she's like this. I'm helping her with her vitals." Lisa explained.

"I will help you with Sam." Christian was at her side. "Are you ready Raphael?"

"Yes, Christian let's go." Answering as all four of them disappeared.

Back at the house, "Whoa, I'm dizzy." Lisa tried to get her bearings.

"That happens for awhile until you get use to it. Sam still does that a lot too." Christian said laying her on the bed.

White candles and incense filled the room as Sarina came through the door with lilies and a garment bag. "Ok, Christian and Raphael out so I can get Sam ready for the ritual."

"Are you crazy? She's in a coma, she needs help Sarina." Appalled at her thinking.

"She is fine Christian, but won't be if we don't continue with the ritual now."

"I don't understand/"

"I'll explain it to you later, right now the ritual must be complete to save her soul."

"Enough said." And with that Christian and Raphael left.

Thank god it was almost time and people already started arriving. They would have to do it as soon as possible Sarina thought sending a message to Gregory to get started.

"Grandma will she really be fine after the ritual?" Lisa asked getting the last of Sam's costume on.

"Yes my child, she should be fine as long as we don't encounter anymore interruptions or problems during the ritual." Smiling at her.

❧

Sam awoke on a beach. The sand was slightly warm. The tide was coming in as the sunset over the horizon. Looking around she realized she was at her grandma's old place so this must be a dream. Getting up she dusted off the sand from the white lace, sleeve dress she had on as the wind blew softly through her blond hair.

In the distances she saw a house. Walking closer she noticed a table was set in the enclosed patio. Two wine glasses half filled, two plates with a lobster tail, baked potato, and veggies, and candle light illuminating the patio while soft music came from within the house.

A figure moved within. Sam didn't know what to do so she walked back towards the water, but before she could reach it she heard her name called from the one person who should have been dead.

"Sam come eat, your food is getting cold." Anthony called to her.

All she could do was stop and stare. He's dead she watched Christian rip out his throat and Lisa incinerate him. Yet he's here alive and well. But its just a dream she thought.

Anthony took her hand and led her back to the table. He pushed in her chair, then took his seat across from her. "Are you alright? You seem confused tonight?"

"Umm..." Is all she could muster.

"This is your biggest night Sam. You should be happy. Soon the ritual will be complete and we will be together forever."

"What! No! This is a dream. Your dead." With her heart in her throat Sam franticly looked for away out, but the scenery started changing.

"No Sam, this is part of your ritual and I am very much alive." He stated pulling her to stand.

"But I watched you burn to ash." Watching the scene as it went from a waterfront patio to a candle lit bedroom. All in dark red and gold tones.

"I did burn, but was reborn." Anthony confirmed.

Something clicked in her racing mind. "Oh my god you're a Phoenix." Color drained from her face at the realization that she'd never be free of him. "But how? Your Pyrenees."

"Yes to both. I'm a quarter sorcerer my dear." Cooling the room to weaken her. "Come sit with me on the bed, time is of the essences."

"No! You are not my bond mate or whatever magical thing Ethan is to me. I won't do anything with you Anthony." Trying to get out of his grasp.

He pulled her to the bed easily since she was weakening at a fast rate. Her struggles were no more than that of a small child's. Then ceased all together as she collapsed in his arms. He laid her gently on the bed and tied her hands and feet to the posts. "I'll be right back Sam. Now I have to get ready for my part." Closing the door behind him.

Tears rolled down her face at the fear of being magically bound to him for all time. He would finally have her and would slowly break her down to serve only him knowing he would make an attempted on anyone's life who got in his way of obtaining and keeping her.

Lisa was getting ready when she felt an overwhelming dread for her sister. She ran down the hall to Sam's room. Busting through the door, her grandmother looked up in surprise, "Something's wrong I feel it." Lisa gasped out.

"Calm down Lisa. Take a couple slow breaths then tell me what's wrong."

She calmed herself enough to speak, "Something is wrong with Sam. Something has happened. I need to get into her dream state she needs help."

"You know you can't. Only Ethan can, to complete the ritual."

"He will die before it is done."

"How do you know this?"

"Sam told me of a vision and I need to see if this is it, cause if it is another will take Ethan's place after his death."

"Bring the other's. We'll find out before we start the ritual."

Lisa wasted no time. Christian, his brothers and friends, Mark, and Ethan surrounded Sam. "Now can I find out?" Lisa impatiently asked.

"Nicholas you are the strongest to anchor Lisa hold her soul while she goes after Sam."

"Of course, Sarina."

"What is going on?" Christian questioned.

"I'm not sure, but something is happening to Sam and I'm going to find out." Lisa explained.

"No!" Christian, John, and Ethan said in unison.

"Its too dangerous for you." Ethan explained. "I will go as it is my right." Ignoring Christian's stare.

"You can't I'm afraid you maybe killed. Besides I've done this before with Sam and Mark." Looking at Christian, "Sorry Christian."

"Its okay Lisa I'm over it. I don't like any of this just be careful." He squeezed her hand in reassurance.

Lisa calmed herself, closed her eyes, and put herself into a trance. Her vision was blurry at first, like when you first wake up. Focusing she saw a dark, candle lit bedroom in shades of red and gold. Making a sweep of the room she noticed one door and no windows. It was very cold in there and seemed to be getting colder by the minute. She saw Sam tied down on the four poster bed knowing she must be extremely weak to be tired up. Cautiously she waked over to her keeping an eye on the door. She leaned down and lightly touched Sam's arm.

"Lisa! What are you doing here? You have to leave before he get's back, Please." Sam whispered anxiously.

"No, I won't leave you like this." Trying to hurry and untie her. "Who did this to you?"

"Anthony, he's alive."

"How? We killed him."

"He's a quarter sorcerer, so his animal is a phoenix."

"And what does that mean?"

"If he's burned to ash he can be reborn and I'll never be rid of him."

"Okay I'm telling everyone everything that is happening. Ethan just said to have you take a little blood and my heat to get enough strength to break fee and I'll help awaken you."

"Alright, but hurry I sense him near." Sam took Lisa's wrist and with a nod of Lisa's head she sank her teeth deep taking just enough to give her temporary strength to get her out of this. As she closed the wound she took her heat also. "Okay Lisa go now. He's almost here and wake me up."

Sam watched Lisa disappear just in time to see Anthony walk through the door in the same place he left her. She watched him approach her, naked, His body looked like a Greek statue so muscularly sculpted that she had to turn her head so she wouldn't fall under his influence like she did all those years ago.

15

Lisa came out of the trance and found herself laying on John, "What happened?"

"Your strength went when you gave Sam your blood and heat." Helping her to sit.

"Oh, well we need to help her wake up and fast before Anthony tries anything."

So everyone merged with Lisa to connect with Sam and helped pull her out of the dream state she was in.

❧

Back in the dream Anthony was lighting incense and some more candles. "Are you comfy Sam?"

"Does it look like I'm comfy? You have me all spread eagle. Of course I'm not comfy you ass." Sam could feel the room temperature rise as she burned through her restraints.

Anthony turned in time to see Sam leap off the bed. "And where do you think your going Sam?" Throwing her into the wall with a wave of his hand, in hopes of knocking her out and taking back control.

Sam slumped against the wall "Wake me up." She whispered.

Walking over to Sam he saw her image fading, "No you don't your mine." He spat angrily, but it was too late. She disappeared as he reached her.

Coming to, Anthony's screams of rage rang in her head. She opened her eyes to see Christian's brown eyes looking down at her. "Are you alright beautiful?" Pushing some hair from her face.

"Now that I'm awake and with you, yes." Smiling at him briefly before pain shot through her, *You are mine Samantha. Always have been and always will be. Now close your eyes and go back to sleep so we can finish this.*

"No!" Fighting the compulsion.

Lisa dug her nails into Sam's arm deep enough to draw blood, but it wasn't working very well. "Don't you listen to him Sam fight it damn it." Slapping her.

Sam swung her head towards her sister. Eye's dark green, heat increasing. "What the hell!"

"Good! Get pissed at me, but don't listen to him. Your not in Florida now. Your not with him. He has no hold over you anymore."

Don't fight me Sam you know we belong together. Come back to me. Remember the sunsets, the long walks on the beach, the smell of the ocean.

The heat stopped, her eyes went back to normal as she began to close them. "Sam No!" Lisa yelled.

"What is he doing to her?" Christian demanded.

"He is trying to take control of her so he can finish the ritual."

"Nicholas merge with me. He will never have her." Christian merged with Sam commanding her to stay awake while Nicholas reinforced it with his own strength.

Sam looked at Christian with love in her eyes. The pain along with Anthony's hold disappeared. "Oh Christian." Holding him as close as she could.

"Sarina we have to finish the ritual now." Ethan told her.

"I know, are you ready? It will have to be done here while your both awake. Anthony is to strong in the dream state to do it there."

"I'm ready let's get started." Ethan took his place by Sam.

"Ok everyone out. I'll start this myself and then they will finish alone." Sarina knew the instant Christian showed his disapproval. "Nicholas, Lisa please, this must be done fast."

"Yes grandma. Come on Christian its okay. Sam will be fine."

"Christian the ritual must be completed let her grandmother do that." Nicholas urged him towards the door.

"Its not Sarina I don't trust." Looking at Ethan.

"Please honey I'll be fine and we'll be together soon." Sam tried to help his uneasiness, even though her own was growing.

He kissed her lovingly on the lips, *If you need me call.*

I will, Smiling at him before he closed the door behind him.

"Sam this is a ritual to bring you and Ethan together magically similar to a marriage, but for magic." Sarina explained.

"Okay, but what is with the sleep dream thing?"

"Usually the ritual is done in a dream like state to make it easier just mind to mind contact instead of physical, but Anthony is getting to strong so it must be done awake."

"I still don't understand, but let's get it done so I can be with Christian again. No offense Ethan."

"None taken Sam. Let's get going Sarina."

"Alright you two I'll recite the words, give you the ritual wine, and finally you two will finish it on your own after I leave."

"How do we do that?" Sam questioned.

"Only you two will know. Its ok, you won't remember any of it." Patting Sam's hand. "Okay Ethan stand on one side and Sam your on the other."

Sarina started reciting the ritual words in their minds, *Life to life, magic to magic, bind Ethan and Samantha together for all time as the magical partner's that the powers have seen. So mote it be,* "Now both of you take a drink from your own glasses then switch. After seal it with a kiss." Glancing at Sam she knew, even though she wasn't keen on the whole kiss she would do it to finish the ritual. She just hoped everything else would go well. As she was leaving she saw them kiss.

As their lips met she felt a strange energy shoot thought her body her sense came alive with sexual wonder for Ethan, ten times stronger then before. She wanted to fight it, feeling it was wrong since Christian was her bond mate, but unable to stop the compulsion she felt.

"Sam its okay to feel this way. Its natural for our people even though we are awake instead of in a dream." Ethan tried to calm her.

"I know. Not sure how I know, but I do I just feel like I'm cheating on Christian if I do this. Can't we just wait until its safe to do this in the dream?" Her anxiety increasing fast.

Sam what's wrong? I'll come to you, hearing Christian in her head.

"Sam you must calm down Christian can't interrupt this when its almost done. Please." Ethan asked sympathetically.

Sam pulled herself together, doing her best to calm her fear, *No Christian. I'll be ok. I'll be with you soon.*

Sam your fear is so strong I can taste it. I will not leave you like this. his words potent.

Honey please, I must complete this even if my emotions are all over. I love you, but let me finish.

Very well, but if he hurts you in anyway.

She sent a smile, then blocked their connection so she could focus completely on Ethan, who was now sitting on the bed shirtless. "Hey that's not fair."

"Come sit next to me." Patting the place next to him on the bed.

She walked over to him, her desire coming alive again and this time she'd let it happen so she could hurry back to Christian. Sitting down on the bed Ethan moved closer and began to massage her neck and shoulders relaxing more with each touch of his fingers.

"I feel you relaxing let me help you more, give yourself to me Sam. Let me release your tension, your fear." He whispered in her ear. His voice black velvet.

She leaned into him closing her eyes she could feel the heat his body was putting off and how aroused he was becoming. He began to kiss her neck softly leaving sparks of electricity in their wake. He rubbed her arms softly, taking her over a little at a time causing her senses to spiral out of control. As purr escaped her lips he turned her to face him.

Looking in her eyes he watched them change to a bright emerald green the feline in him could sense hers going in heat, which aroused him to the point of pain. "You are the most beautiful creature I have ever set my eyes on." Whispering against her lips before kissing them.

She was so soft to the touch, her lips luscious, hair that of golden strands of silk, and she smelled of raspberries. He wanted to feel her skin to skin, taste her sweetness, hear her cries of desire HE was bringing her. He nuzzled her neck taking in her scent while memorizing her body with his hands.

She pressed into his touch. The heat from his hands were scorching which caused her to crave him even more. Black magic she couldn't get away from and at this moment didn't want to. Her teeth and nails lengthened, wanting to tasted him, to experience the spiciness of his blood on her tongue. Lightly she ran her nails down his chest. Hearing his in take of breathe she started kissing right over his steady beating heart. He growled in response right before a horse cry escaped his slips as her teeth sank deep taking in the warm liquid, reveling in its power.

He was blinded by the excruciating passion she brought out of him. He was rock hard with pleasure as she drank. Taking enough for an exchange she closed the wound. Looking up he took possession of her mouth sweeping the inside with his tongue tasting his own blood. He kissed down her throat feeling her rapid beating pulse knowing he caused it he pierced her skin taking her precious blood to complete the exchange and ritual. She was intoxication, he was caught in a vortex of pleasure and pain, he would always crave her. She was his partner and now the ritual was complete. Closing the pin pricks he pulled her with him laying down on the bed they both drifted off to sleep.

Sam awoke to the smell of lavender. Feeling heat from the person next to her she opened her eyes to look at Ethan, but instead Anthony was holding her. The more she struggled the tighter he held her. "Let me go. How did you get here? Where's Ethan?"

"I've always been here and your precious partner is over there." Pointing to the corner Ethan laid in a heap on the floor his body bloody and broken.

"What did you do to him?"

"I just showed him that he was no match for me and that you are mine." Staring into her eyes he held her glare. Slowly he put one sharp talon in a mixture that would help him control and take her over. The mixture absorbed quickly into her blood stream Sam quit fighting instantly. "There that's better now." Releasing his hold on her.

Sam was caught by his eyes, the same ones that made promises of happiness and love, then showed anger and hatred for not doing what was asked of her. His talon cut through her flesh like butter and whatever was on it increased the pain ten fold. She wanted to scream as tears ran down her pain stricken face, but everything was paralyzed. She felt the toxin flowing through her bloodstream doing Anthony's bidding, knowing he did exactly what she foresaw he would. She never should have fallen asleep now he had control of her body and mind while she slept. She tried to call Christian, but the searing pain she received was worse than anything Devin ever did to her, so she ceased all connection.

"Don't worry my pretty everything will be all right. Soon we will be together forever."

How? Sam asked realizing he was the only on she could communicate with without pain.

"You'll see soon don't need you saying anything to anyone. Although if you tried you'd be in agony so I could tell you... Nah, I'll make it a surprise." Leaning forward he took possession of her lips savoring the feel of them. Luscious and sweet to taste, he drew blood with a prick of his teeth. Wanting more and knowing the poison wouldn't attack its creator, he moved down her neck to her voluptuous breast. Reveling in her response to him he ripped off her gown to get a better look at her. The teenager she was back than was all grown up and filled out now. Scrumptious he thought.

Sam tried her best not to respond to him, but her body betrayed her. As he suckled on her breast she became wetter and more needy of him. His hands were everywhere. Caressing her other breast, thighs, and finding her need of him at her core. With the piercing of his teeth a cry was torn from her throat as her body convulsed from the orgasms he was creating in her. She rippled with them as his fingers began to stimulate her clitoris. She hated him more now than ever for causing her involuntary reaction to his sexual assault.

Anthony fed on her for what seemed like hours, stopping every now and then to force his blood in her to replenish her loss. She would buck in response to him, weather it was his fingers, tongue, or his cock that was stimulating her. Her cries were intoxicating causing him to crave more of them with each orgasm until his release.

Finally spent, he laid next to Sam, propped up on one arm looking at her sinuous body all gleaming in the light from their lovemaking. "Your so sensuous I could do this forever. Rest now and I will see you tonight in your dreams again." And with that command Sam was released.

As she closed her eyes in the dream from exhaustion Christian was trying to awaken her in reality. "Sam honey, please wake up. Come on, that's it. Let me see those pretty eyes."

She did her best to open them, but the command was so powerful, fighting it was a battle in its self. "Please Christian just let me sleep a little longer." Weariness in her voice.

"Baby you've slept all night. We had to reschedule the party for tonight at eight." Concern in his voice.

Pushing herself up on the pillow she looked around for Ethan. "Where's Ethan?" Fear began to over take her.

"He's outside with Mark, Why?"

She noticed the bit to his tone. "I was just asking. I'm sorry I slept so long. What time is it?"

"Its just about one. Are you alright? Did you have a bad dream?" Pushing a strand of hair from her face.

The brief touch of his finger tips warmed her. Relieving her fear. "I'll be fine. It was just a dream, even if it was bad." With that last word pain took her breath away as it coursed through her body. She turned her face to look at the floor so Christian wouldn't see the pain in her eyes and she did her best to block him so he wouldn't know, but he did.

"What is it? What is causing you this pain?"

She couldn't respond she just stared off as the pain got worse. Her sister, Mark, Ethan, and Nicholas came through the door questioning her and Christian, but she barely took notice. She couldn't move now, even eye movement brought pain, so she closed her eyes to escape them all. She was so tired mentally and physically.

She started drifting in and out of sleep and eventually the pain receded. Now she knew what Anthony was talking about. He would make her life a living hell and whatever this *"surprise"* was wouldn't be good for anyone. Forcing herself to fully awake she saw Lisa dozing in the chair next to the bed. She quietly got up and went to the bathroom.

Looking in the mirror she saw how awful she looked. Her skin was pale, her eyes were red with dark circles under them, her lips almost white. Sam splashed water on her face trying to freshen up. As she put on make-up to look normal Anthony appeared in the mirror, turning to face him, he wasn't there, she turned back. "This can't be."

"You are seeing me darling. I told you not to tell, but you didn't listen. Don't do it again or something worse will happen."

Tears rolled down her face, "Please stop, I won't tell I promise Anthony."

Seeing her tears satisfied him enough that he wrapped his arms around her waist and kissed her neck. Placing his hand on her womb, "You will only carry my child in here. NO one else's. Do you understand?" He watched her shake her head. "And the answer to the question in your head is yes. My babies only. Now." Pulling the strap of her gown down, "Give me one more taste of you before I leave."

Sam tilted her head unable to resist him anymore. A sigh escaped as he drank. Her will was gone. He now had her and she knew that he was the one to cause her miscarriage. Tears ran down her face at the thought. By the time he finished she was so weak she couldn't support herself. As he disappeared she began to fall.

Lisa had awoke to an empty bed, but saw the light to the bathroom on. Walking towards it she heard voices, but looking in she only saw Sam. Merging she saw what Sam saw and was shocked to see Anthony. Staying quiet he never knew she was there. She heard and saw it all not sure what he was talking about but she would find out soon. The premonition had come true and Anthony would be more dangerous now. She would talk to everyone later, but now she had to take care of Sam.

Not sure how she did it, but she got to Sam right before she hit the floor. "Come on sis its back to bed with you." Using most of her strength to help Sam to bed.

"Oh Lisa, I'm sorry I woke you." Her tears still flowing.

"You didn't, but will you allow me to look at your memories?"

"Why?" Fear clawed at her she couldn't take anymore pain.

Sensing her reluctance she would find another way without her know. "I just wanted to check something I saw with you and Mark, but it can wait."

Relief filled her, calming her down. "Oh yeah later would be good. Where is everyone?"

"Getting everything together for the party. The guys went to town to get more supplies. Some people stayed late last night and we ended up short. The girls are going over everything and making sure it looks good." Wiping her tears.

"What time is it?"

"Almost six-thirty. You think you could eat?"

"Maybe something light."

"Ok I'll send Daniel in to stay with you."

"I'll be fine Lisa." Smiling.

"I'll be back." Closing the door.

Sam got out of bed so she could change. Holding on to the wall she slowly made it to the bathroom, then to the closet. Grabbing black shorts and a tank she headed slowly back to the bed. After she was changed she laid down again waiting for Lisa. What was she going to do now he had tasted her, had sex, and taken her will. She couldn't fight him now and she wasn't sure if anyone could save her anyway. Pondering that she never heard Daniel come in.

Walking in he could tell something wasn't right. The room permeated with uneasiness. Looking around he found Sam laying on the bed all in black with her hair spread around her like a golden halo. He could tell she'd been crying and she looked so pale. He just stared at her for a moment even with her paleness she looked beautiful, haunting. Shocked at his thought he dismissed it and sat down on the bed. "Sam are you awake?"

Opening her eyes she saw Daniel's troubled look, "Yes I'm awake," Smiling while trying to sit up.

Daniel grabbed her arm to help her sit. Her skin was the softest he'd ever felt. Electricity leaped from her to him. Looking in her eye's he was lost, black magic of some kind that he couldn't break. He felt odd like his body wasn't his own.

Kiss him Sam, passionately. Let him feel your need for him, your control over him. Do it now Sam! Hearing Anthony's command in her head she was unable to stop herself. Leaning into him, their lips met. Sweet, passionate, a craving without release.

Daniel pulled her to him as he took possession of the kiss. Wanting more he went under her shirt to cup her full breast. Rubbing the nipple into a hard peak he left her mouth to taste her soft breast. She moaned as he suckled her making his dick even harder unable to help himself he punctured her with his teeth. Her sweetness was like a drug he craved more, but an audio gasp broke the spell right before he was propelled into the wall.

Daniel looked around a little dazed then his eye's met a red fury he often saw only during a fight with enemies. Standing he stood ready to fight. "Christian I'm sorry, I couldn't help myself. It was like she had me under a spell." Trying to explain.

"Christian don't! We must talk."

"Later Lisa." His fury was boiling over at the sight of his friend and his mate.

Jumping between them. "Now!" Her tone stern.

"Fine! But he's not to be alone with her again."

"I'm leaving." Walking out Daniel looked at Sam. She wasn't herself, but wanting her wasn't either.

"Nicholas will watch her while we talk in the hall." Christian stated as Nicholas came walking in.

"I'll be right back Sam." Squeezing her hand as she followed Christian out the door.

"Daniel had no control over his actions in there."

"The hell he didn't. I saw it with my own eye's." The walls were creaking the angrier he got.

"Okay, okay calm down. Listen, when I awoke Sam was in the bathroom talking to someone, but I could really hear or see them until I merged with her." Feeling the tension lightened she continued, "Anthony was talking to her."

"What!" Tension increasing again.

"I think he did something to her, but I'm not sure what. I want to find out first so we know what we're dealing with. Whatever he did she's scared to death and I believe she'd do anything to save us."

"So what do you suggest?"

"You help me find away to look at her memories. Maybe the answer is there. We have to help her even if she doesn't want it."

"I know. I will help and remain with her from now on."

In the bedroom Sam was watching Nicholas. "So am I now a prisoner on my own home?"

"Of course not. We just want to keep you safe." Sitting in the chair next to her.

"I don't need to be watched all the time Nicholas." Getting out of bed.

Grabbing her arm, "Where are you going?"

"To the bathroom unless you want me to make a mess right here?"

"No." Releasing her arm.

Closing the door she quickly searched for a razor and something to use as a vial. She broke a blade from her razor in the shower, then found her saline solution in her overnight bag. Luckily she didn't need it anymore since her eye sight was now perfect thanks to Christian's blood. Dumping out the solution, she wrote a quick note, slit her wrist, and made sure most of the blood got in the bottle before closing the lid. Pain over took her before she could sit down. She screamed before hitting the floor. It was like knives slicing through every inch of her body.

This time she disconnected from the pain trying to control the cheetah that was trying to take over. Nicholas burst through the door as she crouched in the corner. "Nicholas take the things on the counter and leave." Sam growled at him.

"Sam your hurt let me help you." Walking towards her with the stuff.

"No! I'm poisoned." The pain got worse. "Please go. I won't be able to hold control much longer." Watching Christian and Lisa enter.

"Sam!" Pain filled him. That was it he would never leave her until this threat was gone.

Damn it Sam! What did I tell you? Do I need to get you? Anthony's voice was back. "No! I'm sorry." Tears ran free again.

"Honey what are you talking about?" Christian realized she wasn't listening, nor talking to him. "Lisa merge with her."

Merging Lisa heard Anthony in Sam's head. "Anthony is talking to her again."

Call Daniel to you, you can control him mow. If not then let Christian help you. Yes, do that let your mate help you. You will be his destruction.

I would rather die then do anything to hurt Christian or anyone else.

I feel your weakness. You can't hold your control much longer, then I will take over if you won't do as your asked, although you won't go unpunished.

"Sam shut down now!" Lisa commanded adding a strong push so she would.

Within seconds Sam was out and all connection was severed. Christian carried her to the bed. Lisa cleaned her cut and wrapped it with gauze. "She'll have to heal like a human until we can get the poison out." Putting everything in the trash. "Daniel must be watched also until his blood is clean."

"What do you know Lisa?" Christian inquired while covering Sam with the covers.

"Here Lisa, Sam wanted me to take this stuff." Nicholas handed Lisa the blood and note.

She read it. "Is Todd still here?"

"Yes, he's with the girls. Why?" Christian questioned suspiciously.

"Because Sam wants him to have the blood. Have him brought in here please Nicholas. Christian and I will watch over Sam.:"

Nicholas returned with Todd. The shocked look on his face was disconcert. "My god what happened? Why is she so pale? She look's almost dead."

"Enough!" Christian bit out. "I know how my mate looked. You don't need to tell me."

Ignoring Christian, Lisa brought the blood and not to Todd, "Here Sam wanted this given to you, why?"

Reading the note everything became some what clear. "She wants me to analyze the blood. Did she say anything else?"

"She said she was poisoned and refused my help." Nicholas replied.

"Okay you wouldn't have a microscope of anything here by chance would you?" Todd asked the man holding Sam's hand.

"In the lab in the basement why?"

"Because I'm a doctor and obviously Sam wanted me to find out what is in it."

"We can do that by checking her ourselves."

"I know that, but she may think its dangerous. A trap of some kind or she wouldn't have asked for my help. She's very self sufficient you know."

"Yes, I do all to well." Rubbing his thumb across her cheek. Needing physical contact.

"I will show you where it is." Nicholas got up and Todd followed him out the door.

"I don't like him." Just stating his opinion of Todd.

"I know. I don't know much about him, but if he can help. I say let him." Watching the loving way Christian stroked Sam's hair. She was glad he was her mate. He would always take care of her.

"Of course I will and thank you." Never looking up.

"You know that's just rude to read minds without permission."

"Well learn to block it than."

"Ahhh… I'll leave you two alone for now." A little frustrated at his invasion of her thought.

Christian got into bed with Sam, pulled her close, and just laid there listening to the steady rhythm of her heart beat. After awhile he was wondering about the results of the blood so he mentally asked Lisa so he didn't have to leave Sam's side.

Todd has separated the chemicals from her blood and is now working on an antidote.

Can I awaken her?

Only if you can help keep Anthony's intrusion away. He is very strong now and can command her to do his bidding even against her will.

I will protect her. What about Daniel? Can Anthony control him?

Only through Sam, because of the poison running through her blood. As soon as Todd has the antidote we'll give it to both of them. Just have John stay with Daniel for now and I'll be with them soon.

I will Lisa, looking at Sam he softly whispered for her to awaken. Watching her eyes flutter open, his heart jumped at how beautiful they were. "Hello beautiful."

"Mmmm..." Stretching lazily. "Hi."

"How do you feel?" Playing with her hair.

"Hungry let's go get something to eat." Pulling back the covers.

"Are you sure? Do you still hurt?"

"A little, but I need food to help my weakness since you can't provide for me."

"I'm sorry I hate that I can't." Helping her down the hall.

"Its alright food will help." Smiling at him.

She could steal his breath away with that smile. He felt better seeing her up and moving even though he could feel how much pain she was in as he led her to the kitchen. Entering Maggie ran over and held Sam like a mother does her child. Everyone was in there eating dinner since no one wanted to eat in the dinning room. They all asked how Sam was and she did her best to convince them she was fine. Lisa, Nicholas, and Todd joined them shortly after.

"How are you feel?" Lisa looked over her sister with loving concern.

"I'm sore, but I'll be fine. I just need food right now." Grabbing the potatoes and roast beef.

"Have you got an antidote yet?" Asking Todd.

"Unfortunately not. The poison he used was a combination of monk's hood, which is a poison, and tin, which can be used to control a person. Everything I come up with destroys the poison and the cell."

"He obviously studied herbs and poisons." Nicholas stated, *Christian I hate to say this, but what if we drained her and then replenished?*

Christian gave him a severe look. *That would be an absolute last resort,* Hating the idea even though he had already thought of that.

I agree, I'm sorry. We'll find another way my brother, Walking over to Christine to eat dinner.

"Baby, you alright? What's the matter?" Sam asked with care.

Kissing the top of her head, "Its nothing my love just a little disagreement between brothers. Let's eat." Ending the discussion.

After dinner Sam walked around to take a look at everything. Everyone had done a exquisite job. Emerald green and royal blue was everywhere inside and out, little Christmas lights lined the deck and dock areas, lilac scented candles illuminated the inside, and white lilies where placed in various vases. Mike had his band setting up out on the deck. Maggie had made more chicken and veggies while appetizers of meat and cheese were on the opposite end of the deck from the band. She could also smell various pies cooking. Everything was going well which had Sam a little on edge, still worried about Anthony somehow interfering.

"Your worried are needless. I will make sure nothing happens to you again." Christian wrapped his rippled arms around her small waist kissing her cheek softly.

Sam closed her eyes wanting to believe his words, but with a sigh knowing it wasn't for certain. "You know as well as anyone, that as long as I have this poison in me that Daniel and I are both dangerous to all of you." Plain truth in her statement.

Hating that she was right. Turning her to face him he saw the tears in her eyes knowing she was doing her best to hold it together and be strong. "I don't care what is going on, I will never leave you. This you can be sure of and my love grows stronger with every minute we are together." Crushing her against his chest.

His words hit a cord and she couldn't stop crying over his determination to keep her safe. "I love you." She whispered as he held her.

"I love you too sweetheart, always." He held her, never wanting to let go.

With a meow Gabriel vocalized his presents. Sam picked him up and held him in her arms since he was as close to a child as she would get until Anthony was taken care of, then she could start a family with Christian as it was meant to be.

"Don't worry honey. We will start a family when every you want." Reading her thoughts.

"No! Not as long as Anthony is in control." Fear swamping her.

"What is it you are fearing so much? I won't let him hurt our baby."

And with that Sam was overwhelmed with grief and sadness. "Christian, he caused the miscarriage. He said no child but his will grow in me. I can't take that chance again until he's taken care of." She laid her head on his chest knowing he was furious at the truth of their loss.

The rage was fast and swift, moving through him like a freight train. The walls started to creak with the force of the raw energy he was expelling.

"Come let's go outside so you don't destroy the house." Sam pulled him out the sliding glass door in the living room.

"Why didn't you tell me sooner?"

"Because I just found out myself. Please Christian, calm down I feel your pain and I thought it was my fault. That my body wouldn't accept the baby." Feeling the warm breeze from the lake, she felt a little better, but Christian's anger just increased.

"Lisa made sure everything was ok." Trying to relive the fury inside. "I'm sorry Sam, but I'll be damned if I ever let him touch you or our child again. Mine will be here." Placing his hand gently on her stomach. "He will never reproduce. I'll kill him for what he's done."

Sam was in awe at his declaration. She knew she should be upset over his killing statement, but truthfully she wasn't. She knew the only way to be free of Anthony was through his death. " I know baby and I agree with you. You are my mate and your children will be the only ones I birth."

Nicholas came outside, "Is everything alright? I feel your fury Christian." Watching Christian as he held Sam with such gentleness.

"It will be once Anthony is dead. He has committed the ultimate crime against our family Nicholas. He had killed one of us."

"The baby?" Watching his eyes answer. "He will die for killing your child Christian, I promise you that. Justice will be served swift and sure Sam." Placing his hand on Sam's arm.

"Thank you Nicholas, but first we have to get this poison out of me and Daniel or he will use us against you."

Lucian and Raphael joined them. "Nicholas had told us of the iniquity of the crime committed against our family. Anthony will pay the price for it Sam. We will all protect you against him at all costs." Determination in Raphael's eyes.

Warmth enveloped her at their determination to keep her safe. Her love for Christian's brothers was growing at a fast rate. She felt more like a part of their family everyday. Their acceptance of her and Christian's love gave her the strength to continue to fight Anthony's domination over her.

You had better be loving only me not my brothers, trying to be stern, but she heard the humor in his thoughts.

Turning "You know very well what I meant." Smiling at him as Gabriel leapt from her arms to chase a bug.

"All I heard was that you loved my brother's. That is not a good thing when all I want to do is make love to you until dawn. I feel I must compete for your affection." Wickedly smiling at her while he sent her very vivid visions of what he wanted to do to her.

"Christian! You can't show me that right now." Blushing.

"And why is that beautiful?" Drawing her into his warm embrace. Leaning down her whispered, "I could rip off your clothes right now and ravish your body until you begged for release, right here and now. Out in the open for all of nature to see. I would show you how much I love you by making love to you in the one place you feel free."

His voice was pure black magic. Casting a spell to enthrall her senses so all she wanted was him. Touching, tasting, skin to skin. Wanting to feel him inside her, his hands and lips all over her body. The desire for him was so high. "Oh Christian, What are you doing to me?" Closing her eyes as he kissed down her neck. Sensing his craving for all of her, Sam pulled away. Catching her breath, "We can't, it's too dangerous. I won't infect you. That's what he wants.

Wrath surrounded him until all he saw was red. His rage was beyond control the storm he was creating was strong and fierce. Leaves and twigs blew everywhere, the water crashed against the shore, and the wind wiped through the trees so hard Sam thought same of them may actually break..

Nicholas he's out of control. What should I do? I didn't mean to cause this.

Hearing Sam's voice tremble slightly, *Oh chere, this isn't your doing and Christian isn't mad at you. I will help you encase him in a bubble to contain his anger, but you will have to calm him. Do you understand?*

Yes, gently she touched Christian watching as he turned his burning gaze on her. That's when Nicholas helped to encase them both in a protective bubble. The storm outside it disappeared. She breathed a small sigh of relief, but it was short lived as she felt a stir in her mind.

Hello my darling. How wonderful to see him out of control. I think I will have some fun with this, with your help of course, Anthony informed her.

The heat increased ten fold overriding Christian's wrath and bring him back from the beast. " Sam? What is it?" Scanning, but detecting nothing.

I won't help you Anthony. Go to hell. I will fight you every step of the way, her body slowly becoming engulfed in flames.

"Samantha, shut down!" Christian's command extremely strong, but not strong enough.

Oh no you don't, you will do as I ask Sam. You are mine and you will obey my command, small cuts started to appear on her arms, blood slowly formed. Anthony increased her pheromone levels so Christian would be overwhelmed with the sweet coppery smell of her blood. Craving it so much that he had no other choice, but to taste it.

Her screams snapped Christian out of what he was about to do. "Damn it. Anthony leave her alone. I know you can hear me through her. You will never have her and I will kill you for what you've done." Nicholas released the bubble knowing Christian was back in control of himself.

Watching Sam's eyes glaze over, "I already have her. She is lost to you now. She will be my slave and give me enough children to wipe out your lineage. I will be come the leader of the Pyrenees soon enough." And with that he released Sam and was gone from her mind.

As the fire went out she collapsed into Christian's arms. "I'm sorry Christian I'm just not strong enough to fight him anymore."

"Its ok my love. We will fight him together." Cradle her in his lap on the grass.

"I don't think I should stay here as long as he can control me." Her voice strained to get the truth out.

"You aren't going anywhere. I can help you better if you're here than somewhere else. Being alone will only give him more opportunity to get to you and complete his plan, which I can't let happen." He stroked her head as he rocked her until she relaxed.

"Here Sam drink this." Nicholas handed her an awful smelling dark green drink.

"Oh, what is this? It looks gross and smells worse." Hiding her head in Christian's chest.

"Come on chere, it's a very potent protein drink. You need your strength since Christian can't give you his blood. Plus guest are starting to show up, so I suggest you two go get changed."

"Yes dad." Christian said with a smirk.

"Fuck off Christian." Nicholas walked back to the house.

"Was he pissed?" Sam asked as Christian helped her up.

"No, even though he looked and sounded like it." Walking inside together.

16

Looking at his mate outside, as Sarina introduced her and Ethan as partners, he still couldn't believe that he found her after so long. She was everything he could ever hope for and more. His life was in her hands and she's proved to be more than his mate, she was his friend, lover, partner, everything all in one.

"Yes she is and has given hope to the rest of us." Nicholas patted his back. " So have you two decided on a date for the wedding yet?"

"No, too much has been happening to think about it. We'll have one soon though. Don't worry." Smiling at Sam when she glanced his way.

Are you going to come stand by my side or am I to remain with Ethan all evening? I'm sure he wouldn't mind.

Her sultry voice washed over him hardening him instantly with need, *Keep it up beautiful and you will be leaving your party very early. Then Sarina won't be very happy with either of us,* sending her an image of him ripping the skin tight outfit she had on, off and passionately making love to her.

Christian, if you want to play mind games I'm up for the challenge, returning an image of her kneeling while he sat in a chair. Her warm mouth milking him as her hands gently, yet firmly played with is shaft and sac.

Christian stifled a groan as he glided over to her. He took her other arm while Sarina introduce him as her bond mate and future husband. "Keep it up Sam and I will hold you to both images." Whispering in her ear.

"Oh I intend too." Her voice black velvet.

Everyone came by to give their congratulations to all three of them. To Sam, it seemed like hours of congrats, yet it was only half an hour. "I'm glad that's over I need a drink."

"I'll get it. Ethan?" Christian asked politely.

"No, I'm fine thank you." Watching Christian leave. "So are you good tonight? No bad feelings or anything?"

"I'm fine Ethan. I plan on enjoying myself no matter what." Smiling. "How are you?"

"I'm fine, but I sense someone watching us from the corner."

Sam turned to see a man dressed in black with a dark hat and mask watching them. She loved the party except for the costumes cause you never knew who was who. She gently entered his mind to find out it was Todd. Relieved, "Its only Todd he's good. He's an old friend from White Cove. He's half Pyrenees, half human." She explained watching Todd walk over to them.

"Hey Samantha, you look beautiful." Leaning in to kiss her cheek.

"Thank you. Todd this is Ethan. Ethan, Todd."

"Nice to meet you Todd. Sam says you're old friends?" Placing his arm protectively around her waist holding her tightly as she tried to move away.

Ethan, let me go he is no threat.

No! I know nothing of him and I'm sure no one else does either.

I do damn it, causing flames to start up his arm that was around her waist. He quickly put them out without releasing her, which just pissed her off even more, *Mark come get your cousin before I really hurt him.*

What is he doing to you honey? Walking towards her through the crowd.

He won't let me go cause he doesn't know Todd who was saying hi, relief swept through her at the sight of Mark coming towards her.

Pulling her from Ethan's embrace. "Come dance with me Sam. Do you two mind?" Not waiting for an answer.

Out on the dance floor, "Thank you." Wrapping her arms around his neck while he encircled her waist to pull her against him. She felt his arousal through both their clothes. "Mark!"

"What?" Trying to look innocent.

"Why are you so aroused?"

"Sam half the guys in here are that way, especially over you. Your radiant tonight. Ethan has a very protective nature he meant well."

"I'm sure he did, but I'm not one for possessiveness, especially when I already have one overbearing male."

"Honey we are all possessive over you right now and until the danger is gone we will remain that way." Twirling her around.

Sam just bit her tongue on the subject. She knew there was no way to win this argument so she just enjoyed the dance. Another slow song came on, but Sam didn't see Christian anywhere, *Where are you?*

I'm sorry beautiful, I was helping John with the grill. You were enjoying your dance with Mark I didn't want to interrupt and be overbearing.

She sent flames to him showing she wasn't impressed with his humor. Turning to Mark. "Let's go get a drink since my mate forgot." Leading him off the dance floor.

You know I didn't your just mad, trying not to laugh.

She closed her mind to him. "What an ass."

"Who?" Mark asked.

Sam forgot she wasn't alone. "Mark, I'm going to sit on the dock alone if you don't mind." Walking away so Mark couldn't stop her even though she knew he'd watch her along with the others anyway.

She sat on one of the benches on the dock. The moonlight shown on the calm water, the air was warm and fresh, the sounds of frogs and crickets filled the air along with Mike's band. Sam loved the warm summer nights it brought her a measure of peace so the anger washed out of her. Closing her eyes she enjoyed the feathery touch of the wind. She needed the sweet serenity of the night to clear her head and help her continue with the evening in tranquility. Her life had changed so much in the last eight months even though most of the time she was in danger she was glad she met Christian and had new friends. Though she was pissed at him right now.

Sensing someone's hands near her neck she threw her arm's back to catch their wrists, *Don't move Sam.*

Why not Devin? I have more than enough protection. Someone will be here soon, Confidents in her voice.

No Sam, I'm shielding us and blocking all communications, feeling a light note of panic he continued, *First you will release my wrists.*

Slowly she lowered her arms trying to think of a way to contact Christian. Next she felt his hands on her shoulders right next to her neck. "What do you want?" Venom in her tone.

Use only your mind I don't want anyone hearing us and if you attempt to make a scene I will inject you with a paralyzing serum, poking her neck gently with the needles hidden in his sleeves to prove he was serious.

I ask you again what is your business here Devin? I know your not here to congratulate me.

Oh on the contrary I am. I even brought you a gift.

How nice of you. I'm sure its something I don't want.

Now Sam why so mean? Your suppose to be nice and accept all gifts.

Not from you, the air heated, unable to control her emotions. She felt the pricks than he injected her with something that felt cold at first, but turned lava hot as it ran through her system, it overtook her fast, causing every muscle to quit working. She was shock at the feeling of helplessness as she began to fall sideways, but Devin slide next to her to support her body.

Sam you need to learn to control your anger. Don't worry I will help you with that, pushing her golden strands from her face, *You are so beautiful and supple,* he boldly caressed her breast, bring her to a hard peak due to him rubbing his thumb back and forth over it, *I love how you respond.*

I can't help what my body does, but I hate you for it.

Yes that maybe, caressing the other breast, *Yet it happens all the same. I will have you Sam.*

And I will destroy you. They will come soon then what will you do? Disappear like the coward you are.

His anger came fast. He back handed her. Her head violently forced to the right due to the power of the slap, then pain split through her face on both sides. The left side from the slap and the right from hitting the top of the bench. Tears rolled down her face, *Fuck you Devin!*

I intend to very soon Sam.

Your threats are meaningless. I have two other's after me also. One is so much more powerful than you, you spineless dick.

His fury increase with ever word, *Who Sam?* feeling her fighting his compulsion. *Who!* he struck through her barriers so powerfully that she thought her head would explode. Her screams were so loud that Christian looked up from his conversation with John. Only hearing them in his mind he knew something was wrong.

"What is it Christian?" John followed his gaze to the dock, but only saw Sam.

"Something's not right I heard Sam scream, but it was through my mind only not out loud." Walking down the stairs.

"But I only see her. Are you sure she's not asleep. Maybe a nightmare. She has had a lot of stress lately." Trying to keep up with Christian.

"No, I could taste her pain. Something or someone is hurting her." Picking up the pace his heart beating a mile a minute. His mind racing to figure mostly who was causing her pain. It wasn't Anthony, he usually did stuff to her when he could get her alone and Victor was always out in the open about everything. That left Devin. "Sam, are you ok?" Getting closer.

Hearing Christian getting closer, *Stop him Sam or I will put you in a death like coma again and this time you will go with me.*

Fine you prick, waiting for her opportunity to get free.

I will help you with movement and I'll release your voice, but I warn you if you let him know of me I will flash us both away where he can't find you.

Sam concentrated on her heart rate to keep it steady and calm so Devin wouldn't know he was scaring her. That would only make him happy than she'd get pissed and Christian would definitely know than. She did have something else she could try, *I agree not to let him know, but by the way he's stalking this way he already suspects something. So now what do you want me to do?*

Tell him you just fell asleep and had a nightmare.

Yeah right, like he'll believe that.

Her sarcasm was pissing him off. Digging his finger's into her arm, *Fine, you tell him you had a vision. That should work.*

"Sam honey, are you alright? I heard you scream." Watching her cautiously. Something just wasn't right with her.

"Yes, I just had another vision. I'm sorry about the scream I just wasn't expecting it." Smiling a little at him, Her eyes changed briefly. His only clue she could give.

"Tell me about it." Seeing her smile was fake, but afraid to push. Noticing the brief change also.

"I'll tell you later. I just want to sit here for a few more minutes than I'll join you. Alright?" Pleading with her eyes for him to leave.

"Alright Sam, I'll see you in a few than." Turning to walk back.

Puzzled by his actions. John followed Christian leaving Sam alone on the dock, *What the hell was that? Even I could tell something was wrong.*

I know that, but someone has silenced her. She's smart and hopefully can get out of this on her own, the rage building in him was starting to show on the outside knowing he had to calm so whoever had Sam wouldn't know he knew. He slowed his pace while taking slow deep breathes.

So your just going to walk away? appalled that he would just leave her like that.

Stopping at the top of the stairs. *Listen do you honestly think I would do that. I have to do this caused I don't need whoever is holding Sam to know that I know. She already let me know she was in trouble and I think its Devin. Go protect Lisa and just be careful.*

I will. What are you going to do? continuing to the deck.

Not sure yet, but I'll think of something, looking back at Sam. His rage was growing and soon the beast would take over unless he could figure out how to help her. "Where's Daniel?" Asking John.

"He's inside with Shelby, Mark, and Maria. Why?" Figuring Christian had a plan.

"Because I think he maybe able to help Sam."

"How?"

"I'll tell you in a minute." Walking inside to get Daniel.

"John what's going on?" Lisa asked walking over to him.

"Nothing honey why? Has Todd found an antidote yet?" Changing subjects.

"Almost, but we need a little more blood. Don't snowball me John I sense something is wrong so tell me." Causing the flames in the grill to flare up. So John told her.

Feeling Lisa's alarm Sam knew it was now or never since Devin wasn't fully paying attention, *Daniel can you hear me? Feel me, my need for you,* hoping she could still control him.

Yes Sam, I hear you. You have need of me? Where are you? leaving Shelby, Mark, and Maria. Feeling a strong need to get to her.

"Daniel, where are you going?" Christian turned to follow him.

"I need to find Sam." Picking up the pace, the urgency growing stronger.

Realizing Sam must have come up with the same idea. He was going to help her the best he could even if it caused him a little jealousy. Which he knew she would do some how. "Sam is on the deck, hurry."

A little shocked at Christian he stopped. "What? Why are you helping?"

"Because you are the only one that can help Sam right now." Trying to control his anger over the whole situation.

Daniel please hurry, desperation in her sultry voice.

Continuing outside, "I can't help myself Christian. I'm sorry its like a strong compulsion." His legs moving of their own accord.

"Sam is causing your reaction just go with it and hurry. Devin has done something to her and we need to get her out of this quietly." Walking down the stairs with him. "I'll be near, but you'll have to go alone."

"I understand. I'll get her safe." Continuing towards the dock.

Please Daniel. I know you talked to Christian. Devin doesn't know of our connection so think of something quick.

I will don't worry Sam. I don't see him.

He's next to me. I can't move right now so he is holding me up right and controlling almost everything.

"Sam, I need you right now." Walking up to her.

Stop him now Sam! furious that he kept getting interrupted.

Daniel hurry he's going to try something again, merge with me completely and use me if you have to to destroy him.

Damn it Sam! he struck without notice sending lightening Daniel's way. Missing him by a hair.

"Let her go Devin she doesn't belong with you." Continuing his walk towards him. John, Christian, and Mark behind him.

Materializing, "She has always been mine." Pulling her to stand up, "Stop or I will drain her, I mean it." Putting her in front of him exposing her neck.

She felt Anthony than. In her mind moving through her body to access the damage. Relief spread through her mind, *What has her done to you?*

Injected me with a paralyzing drug. I can't move and if anyone tries to come near he threatens to drain me.

Lightening arched across the sky, the thunder was so loud it was like ten bombs going off at once, the clouds opened up into a torrential down pour. Everyone ran inside, except Christian, Mark, John, and Daniel, who remained on the dock. The wind was fierce, blowing through the trees.

Opening his mouth, he clamped down on her neck. His teeth punctured her soft skin shooting pain through her neck. Her breathe caught in her lungs as the pain grew worse. Next thin she knows Devin is ripped away from her by unseen hands and thrown to the end of the dock. Daniel ran over to Sam, picking her up and carrying her to Christian's waiting embrace.

"Christian are you alright? Your anger is fierce." John questioned.

"Its not me this time." Staring down at Sam.

"Its Anthony's anger your experiencing." She answered wearily.

Sam I need you by my side now, hearing Anthony in her head.

I'm so tired. Please let me rest I can't walk yet.

I know Sam, I will help you, but one more thing please. I don't want to force your obedience.

Her anger out weighted her weakness since most of the drug was now out of her body. She grew hot in Christian's arms. "Put me down please I'm being called upon." A bit in her tone.

Letting her feet touch the ground. "By who?"

"Who do you think." Turning to walk down the dock.

Christian captured her arm. "Be careful. I will be monitoring you beautiful."

"I will my love." Kissing him, she moved to where Anthony appeared at the end of the dock.

Devin stood up as Anthony solidified. "Who the hell are you?"

"The one I told you about." Sam answered walking up to him.

Lace your finger's with mine. This is your chance to destroy him. Wipe him out of your life Sam.

Anthony you know I can't. I can't deliberately take a life and you know that. Don't push me or I will leave.

You can try my pet, but I can force your obedience. My blood runs in your veins.

Observing the man and Sam's silence he knew they must be arguing in their minds. "Having problem's with her?" Amused at the situation.

"Not at all she will do as she is told." Stating a fact.

"Yeah alright. Good luck with that one. She does what she wants. She's a defiant little minx."

"She knows her place, but you have hurt her and that is unacceptable. I am the only one who will punish her for her actions, not you." Sending lightening into Devin's body.

Staggering back he caught his balances right before going off the back of the dock. A red stain appeared on his shirt as the searing pain shot through his body. Infuriated at himself for not seeing the retaliation due to his actions. He sent spears of wood towards both of them.

Anthony pushed Sam behind him, deflecting most of the wood. He did get hit in the legs, but refused to give into the pain. Instead he used it to fight Devin sending lightening and wind this time.

Devin put up an invisible wall to stop the lightening and moved forward towards Anthony. He caught movement behind Anthony. Sam was slowly making her way back down the dock. "I don't think so Sam." Appearing in front of her as she began to run. "Going somewhere?" Grabbing her around the throat.

"Yeah away from you." Elbowing him in the gut, then throwing her head back into his. He finally let her go after she stomped on his foot.

Anthony glided up to her, "Finish him Sam."

Aghast at his request. "I can't. Don't make me."

"It's the only way. Do it on your own or I will force you."

"Leave her alone Anthony. Its not in her nature to kill and you know it." Christian was becoming furious with the whole thing.

"You know she must Christian." Keeping his gaze on Devin, who was building power for another attack, while fighting the remainder of the drug he injected into Sam's blood.

Without warning a fireball shot through Anthony's upper chest, right above his hear. He fell back, just as Sam disappeared. He landed on his back with the wind knocked out of him. Looking up, Devin stood over him. "Well it was nice meeting you, but she's mine and you don't fit into my plans." Vines irrupted through the dock circling Anthony's legs and arms to hold him while Devin attempted to finish him off.

"Where is she Devin?" Christian drew his attention.

"How the hell should I know. I thought you did it." Looking back down at Anthony.

She's alright Christian. Todd found an antidote, Lisa informed him.

Relief spread through him at the knowledge that Sam was now safe, *Good, keep her there while I take care of these two. Tell her I'll be with her soon.*

I will. Be careful Christian, loving concern in her thoughts.

Don't worry about me Lisa. See you soon, severing contact so he could focus on the task at hand.

Walking down the dock Christian felt a rush of hot air brush past him. A scent of raspberry followed, *Sam?*

Its ok my love I will take care of Devin.

No beautiful, its not your nature to destroy. Allow me to do this, half way down the dock now.

The water was choppy, a warm wind blew softly through the trees, fireflies encircled the dock. Sam appeared a few yards a head of Christian. Stopping, she turned slightly to glance at him over her shoulder. She was dressed in a flowing sleeveless black silk gown, while her hair cascaded down her back in golden curls. Her eyes now took on the yellow glow of the cheetah in her, as she placed a finger to her lips to stop him from saying anything as she continued down the dock.

Sensing Sam, Anthony kept Devin's attention so she could finish her task. "So am I to assume you won't fight fair?"

"Where's the fun in that?" Striking his left shoulder with a ball of fire.

"You are a coward to fight me like this." Beads of sweat formed on his forehead, yet he refused to give into the pain.

Feeling extreme heat from behind, Devin turned to see Sam gliding towards him. She was breath taking in that black silk gown. He grew hard just thinking of how she would feel beneath him in bed.

"You'll never find out." White light surrounded him incinerating Devin before he could even blink. Looking down at Anthony she withered the vines that held him.

"Sam." Walking up to her, Christian watched her wither the vines with a thought.

Turning her yellow eyes on Christian, "Stay where you are Christian." Kneeling down by Anthony.

"Sam don't!" Hitting an invisible wall. "Damn it Sam. Remove it."

Ignoring him, she placed her hand over Anthony's chest closing her eyes she concentrated on healing him. Her energy flowing into his body repairing bones, muscles, and cauterizing the veins to stop blood loss. Unaware of the time she continued on to his shoulder, then she emerged back into her body so she could set it. "I have to set your shoulder, its dislocated." She informed him.

"Go on darling." Bracing himself for more pain.

Taking a deep breath Sam placed her left hand on the top of his shoulder, then with her right hand she pulled hard then pushed the arm back into socket. Hearing him growl, she felt guilty for causing him more pain. "I'm sorry."

"I'm ok it feels better." Not letting on that it hurt like hell.

Sensing his need for blood Sam leaned into him. Whether a compulsion or not she felt the need to help him heal, *Drink so you may heal,* and with that he sank his teeth onto her soft neck.

The taste of her blood was heavenly. An aphrodisiac of intoxicating sweetness. Flowing through him, he could feel his strength coming back as his starving body soaked up the fresh blood. Sensing her weakness he closed the wound, *Thank you,* he whispered in her mind, *I'll be with you soon,* and with that he disappeared as Christian got through her wall.

The masculine, woodsy scent filled the air around her causing a craving only Christian could sate. Leaning in, the aroma was overwhelming she licked once, twice, then sank deep. The rich liquid quickly flowed through her body instantly giving her strength. Christian's groan increased her desire for him.

Closing the wound she lightly raked her nails down his chest. He stopped her hand, "Sam we can't do this now. We have guests to attend to."

"Well I hope they don't stay long. I want you so bad I can taste it." A little ticked about reminding her of where they were.

Laughing he helped her up. Hand and hand they walked back down the dock to join the party, *I will make it up to you later. I promise,* he told her which brought a smile to her lips.

I will hold you to that promise, a wicked smile touched her lips as he looked down at her with love in his eyes.

"Hey quit all the lovey dovey shit Christian and get your ass up here and help me with the meat." John yelled jokingly.

Joining John, Lisa, Shelby, and Daniel at the grill, "So tell me how Sam disappeared and what the antidote was." Christian inquired.

"Well I'm coming into my powers and discovered that I can flash people from one place to another. It requires a lot of concentration and energy, but grandma says it will get easier with time." Smiling.

"That's great to hear. Will you be like Sam than?"

"Oh no, thank god. No my only power's will be flashing and healing, unless Sam temporarily transfers a power to me. I will train with her though. That way we will both know all of them."

"Does this usually happen with siblings? The training I mean?"

"No, but grandma thought it would be a good idea since we are twins to both learn."

"So what of the antidote? What did Todd use?"

"I had to use Alkanet, which is an antidote for poison." Todd explained as he joined them.

Giving him a hug and kiss, "Thank you, but what about Anthony's influence over me?" Sam asked.

"That will be a little trickier I wanted to get the poison out first. Now I will need someone in magic to help with the rest."

"Well there are plenty of people here who could help."

"I know Sam, but I would prefer someone close to you."

"Sarina or Nicholas could help." Christian suggested.

"Can we discuss it later? I don't think he will be bothering me tonight." Sam said warily.

"Of course, beautiful." Kissing her head.

Gabriel came up to Sam meowing and rubbing his body against her less until she picked him up. She loved him. He brought her tranquility only an animal could bring. She rubbed her face in his glossy fur loving the feel of it.

"Sam some days I think you love that cat more than me." Blaring at the cat.

"Christian stop glaring at him. Of course I love him more."

"You are a mean little thing."

"Keep it up and I'll show you just how mean I can be."

"Come on Sam let's mingle. No fighting tonight. Not even playfully." Lisa pulled her away.

"He started it." With a pout.

"So are you alright for now?" Still concerned for her sister.

"Yes, but his influence is still strong. He said he would be with me soon." Sam saw Lisa raise her hand to her throat. "I don't think he meant tonight, relax. He seems different now."

"Like how?" Walking to one of the tables to sit down.

"I don't quite know how to explain it, but I feel like I can't live without him. If he died he'd take some of me with him. I'd feel empty, lost. I know its not real, but whatever he's done to me has made it feel real. He also seems kind, loving to point. I mean he helped take care of Devine. He was even wounded, which I feel guilty over." A tear rolled down her face.

"Sam!" Getting her attention. "He is controlling your feelings for him. None of it is real. Remember everything you went through, we went through, in Florida."

"Stop it! He's changed he's not like that anymore."

"Ok, ok. Calm down." Seeing Christian glance their way.

Sam?

I'm fine, just a little arguments with Lisa. No biggy, only letting him see what she wanted him too.

"Come on you two Mike's going to play Da 'Butt." Christine grabbed their hands and pulled them to the dance floor that was set up on the grass.

Sam forgot all about the argument with Lisa as the other girls joined them. Dancing set her free to enjoy herself and leave her problems far behind, the music took her away. She was a free spirit with no worries, pain, fear, or men to upset or piss her off. She was with her friends having fun like always. The rest of the evening went great. Mike played a lot of upbeat, fast pace music to keep everyone going. Maggie and Armond were busy with cleaning tables and restocking food. Sam forced them to take a break. While Shelby and Christine cleaned up the tables.

Sam went to the kitchen to bring out more food. The aroma of fresh baked pies filled the air. She pulled out apple and cherry pies, then blueberry and peach cobbler. They smelled delicious as she put them on the counter. She went to pull out the green bean casserole out of the oven and was distracted by a shadow on the wall. Her attention was quickly brought back to the pan as she put it next to the pie, but was too close. Pain was instantaneous as her arm touched the burning hot metal. A hiss escaped her mouth as she ran to the sink to run cold water over it. The water helped, but it was to late, it was starting to blister. She went to the bathroom to put medicine on it and wrapped it with gauze to heal. It would leave a scar though.

Walking back into the kitchen she was caught off guard when Ethan put his hand on her shoulder. She reached a crossed and flipped him onto his back. He landed hard on the kitchen floor. "Jesus Ethan." Helping him to sit.

Catching his breath, "Sorry, just came to see if you needed help." He saw the gauze on her arm. "What did you do?" Retaining her arm.

"I burned it on the damn pie pans I wasn't paying attention." Sitting next to him for a minute.

"So are you having fun now?" Unwrapping the gauze. "Sam, this is a second degree burn." The blister was quite big. The skin under it was bright white while the skin around it was red and awful looking. "What did you put on it?"

"Just aloe that's all we had." The pain was getting worse since it wasn't wrapped to keep pressure on it. "Can I ask you something?"

"Sure anything." Helping her up. "Come on. let's see what else we can find to help the burn." Leading her down the hall.

"Well, I just wondered what your main powers were." Going into the bathroom with him.

Opening the cupboard he disappeared, yet things were still moving inside it. Next spider's started coming out of the cupboard. Sam ran into the bedroom and got on the bed. "Oh I found something else to help you." Walking out of the bathroom he became visible, as the spiders disappeared.

"What the hell was that?" Still looking for spiders.

"My powers, you said you wanted to know what they were." Sitting on the bed with a jar of white cream.

"I get the invisibility, but what's up with the spiders.?" Scooting closer to Ethan.

"They really weren't there, you just thought you saw them like an illusion. Give me your arm so I can put this cream on it." Reaching for Sam.

"What is that?"

"Its Silvadene it helps with severe burns." Applying it to her arm.

His fingers were gentle almost feather like as he applied the cream. It was cool, but helped relieve the pain. Ethan wrapped her wound with gauze telling her to reapply two more times and then it should be all healed with minimal scarring.

❧

Ethan helped her carry out the rest of the food. "These look delicious."

"I know Maggie's peach cobbler is heavenly. Once you try it you'll never like anyone else's." Sam fondly expressed.

"Your really happy here aren't you?"

"Yes, why?" Walking back to the kitchen.

"Just asking. Did anyone tell you how elegant you look tonight?"

"No, not in this dress, but thank you." Becoming a little nerves. She went to the fridge.

You want him don't you? I sense it in you. The feel of his hands on you. Caressing, stroking, delved deep inside your core increasing the fire within.

Ethan knew she closed her eyes as he touched her shoulders. Inhaling her scent he became overwhelmed with such desire. He wanted her with every fiber of his being. Her hands on him, her mouth milking his hard shaft. Just to hear her moan from the pleasure he brought her would send him over the edge. His yearning was alien to him he had never wanted anyone like this before.

A growl broke the spell they were under. Looking at the door they saw Christian casually leaning against the door frame. His piercing eyes missed nothing. "Am I interrupting anything?" His voice calm yet stern.

"No." Ethan answered. "I'll see you after Sam." Kissing her cheek, then walking past Christian.

"How long were you standing there?" Sam asked cautiously.

"Long enough to realize you two were under some kind of spell. Your lucky the ritual is done Sam."

"And why is that?" Already knowing the answer.

"Cause if not I would have ripped Ethan to shreds." Pulling her against him. "Mmmm… you smell so good right now. I could eat you up." He whispered against her neck.

"Just a little longer, then I will gladly let you indulge to your hearts content." Sam whispered back her heart accelerated when he began kissing down her throat. "We should get back before someone comes looking for us." A little breathless.

Christian turned Sam around so her back was against the wall. Lifting her dress, he ran his hand up her thigh. Moving to the inside, he shifted her thong aside so he could caress her sex. Building her hunger, he could feel her craving like it was his own. She was so hot and wet as cream met his every stroke. He wanted nothing more than to taste her right than and there not caring if someone came in or not. He was so painfully hard her needed release soon or he would die.

You won't die my love. I'll make sure of that, but I might if you don't get us somewhere were we can finish. We are beyond waiting.

Crushing her gently against him he moved to the closest bedroom. Laying her on the bed he pushed her dress to her waist. Unable to wait he ripped off her thong tossing the scrap of lace on the floor. He fastened his mouth to her moist channel, her scent brought out the beast. He craved her sweet taste like an addict.

Her hips met every advance of his tongue. She felt out of control. Her clothes were to tight, yet Christian kept up his sexual torture. Taking her higher, beyond any thoughts, giving up all fight for control she merged completely with him. Doing so her senses were over loaded with such strong desire that she dug her nails into his shoulders in an attempted to pull him towards her. She wanted them both naked, skin to skin.

Sensing her longing, he looking up to see she had managed to get her dress off. Seeing her emerald eyes he moved up her, slowly kissing along the way. Her stomach, belly button, each rib, finally her breasts, he took his time with them. Flicking the nipples into peaks, sucking on them until she cried out. His name rang in his head as he towered over her. She moved restlessly beneath him until he pushed through her hot velvet folds with his soft tipped shaft. She was so tight and ready he surged forward fast, hard, possessively.

Sam met every thrust, wild and untamed. Christian rolled over so she could ride him. Controlling the speed she felt free like she could do this forever and never tire. His moans only increased her lust. Both their bodies bathed in sweat. She lowered her head to encircle his nipple with her tongue. Christian moved faster increasing the firestorm that was building inside. Grinding his hips into hers as he surged forward to take them both over the edge to a place of complete ecstasy. Unable to take it anymore Sam screamed her release.

Christian came at the same time. Spilling his seed deep within her. He felt like he shattered into a million pieces. Laying on his chest Sam closed her eyes as the after shocks subsided. He could hear their hearts beating in unison. "Te amo mi amor."

"Y te mi amor." Sam answered.

"We should get back to the party."

"We need a shower first." Getting up she looked around the room. She saw rabbits everywhere and not the cute and cuddly ones. These ones looked crazy almost demonic. "Who's room is this?" Looking at some of the drawings.

"Its Daniels and I know he'll be pissed." Smiling.

Turning she smiled too. "You're a wicked man."

"You have no idea." Running a finger lightly up her arm.

"Stop that." Pulling her arm from his touch. "No more touching!

You stay right there on that bed." Watching him as she backed into the bathroom. Turning she squealed as she felt a rush of air.

Christian solid frame filled the door. "Why?"

"Because your lethal to women looking the way you do. All toned, muscular, and naked." Blushing she walked to the shower.

"Only one woman beautiful, only one." His gaze ran over her sumptuous body. The shower started on its own. Checking the temperature Sam got under the warm spray. It felt so good she decided to take a little longer than necessary knowing Christian would join her. Which he did ten minutes later, unable to stand the brief separation.

The evening went on successfully and the last guest left by two in the morning after which everyone was exhausted and retired for the remainder of the night.

17

Sam got up early the next day. She called up the girls and decided to go to the beach, just a girls day out, even though the guys would eventually find them. Taking the red Corvette, Lisa had Sam put the top down so they could relish in the fresh air. Driving into the parking lot she saw Shelby leaning against her black Monte Carlo talking to Maria while Christine sat in the front seat checking her hair. Looking up, "Hey, took you long enough."

Sam turned off the car. "Well I stopped to get us breakfast." Handing her the bags. Lisa got out with the coffees while Sam grabbed their beach bags and followed them down to the beach. They got a table in the sun. Shelby handed everyone a breakfast sandwich and hash brown while Lisa passed out the coffees. "So how much time do you think we have before they discover we're gone?" Lisa humorously asked.

"Not long that's why we snuck out. I wanted to discuss the wedding." Sam answered.

"Ok, but you haven't even picked an exact date yet." Christine implied.

"Yes I know, that's why you're here. I know Christian wanted to get married soon after the ritual, so I thought maybe we could do it next Saturday. What do you think? I know its not a lot of time, but do you think it could be done?"

"Well it is quite short noticed, but yeah I think it can be done." Shelby answered.

"We have a lot to do in very little time. Can you handle all the stress Sam?" Maria questioned.

"I think so, with all of your help of course."

"Its settled than the wedding will be next Saturday." Lisa responded.

"What about the bachelorette party? No way will Christian allow Sam out of his sight for very long." Christine inquired.

"I'll take care of him. I'll have John do the bachelor party on the same night so he'll be preoccupied with that instead of Sam." Lisa smiled.

"You really think that will work?" Sam knew it wouldn't.

"Its worth a shot. Anyways you deserve one night a way from his possessive ass."

"Lisa!" Sam was shocked at her crudeness.

"What? You know I'm right so don't give me that look Sam. I love him like a brother, but it irks me that he's so possessive over you. I hate to say it, but he's almost as possessive as Anthony was." Lisa felt the heat, knowing she hit a nerve.

"He is nothing like Anthony and you know it. He's kind, loving, and sympathetic. Anthony was cruel, barbaric, monstrous." Attempting to calm down.

"Ok, I get it. Just calm down." Studying Sam's face. She was fighting her emotions, so Lisa placed a calming hand on her.

Lisa's touch relieved the tension she was feeling. The unwanted emotions slipped away leaving a soothing balm in its wake. "I'm sorry. Thank you."

"So where are we going for the bachelorette party and what are we going to do?" Christine excitedly asked.

"Well I figured we'd start at The Pier for dinner." Lisa stated.

"Isn't that expensive?" Maria asked.

"Don't worry about it. Then we'd go to Taon for awhile and end the night at The Lighthouse."

"How long have you been planning this?" Suspiciously looking at her sister.

A wicked gleam in her eye, "Since you told me about the engagement. Shelby was helping too."

Looking at Shelby, "Oh, I see now. You just wait until you get married."

"Like that will ever happen." Sarcasm in her voice. They continued to talk about the party and wedding while they finished breakfast.

The morning sun had warmed the air nicely with a light breeze. They laid out by the water for awhile enjoying the warmth. Sam absorbed it like a sponge, giving her more power. It was a rush like no other, but she understood the responsibilities and the consequence of using it. The birds chirped in the trees around the lake, the bees buzzed by looking for sweet nectar, occasionally scarring one of the beach goers. The water was calm and cool as the smell of pine and flowers surrounded them.

Looking around Sam quietly touched Lisa, *Come with me.*

Getting up she follow Sam into the woods to a small clearing. "What are we doing here?" She whispered.

"I want to practice with you. I feel your powers growing. Come sit across from me."

Sitting Indian style, "Ok so what do you want to do?" Excitement growing in Lisa.

"Let's start with something easy. How about calling the forest animals to you."

"Ok, how?"

"Just close your eyes and concentrate. Imagine the birds, rabbits, squirrels coming out of the woods. Try to connect with them show them a picture of them around us. No fear, just a calm, serene feeling. Let them know we mean them no harm." Sam looked around the clearing as the animals began to emerge from the woods. "Good keep the contact while you open your eyes."

Opening her eyes she was filled with joy at the sight of all the forest creatures around them. A bunny had even hopped in her lap. Petting the rabbit, "I really did this?"

"Yes and with more practice you will have more control of your powers and it will become easier." Sam enjoyed watching her sister's enthusiasm. They practiced for at least half an hour or so before she felt a slight shift of power knowing Christian had arrived so she continued with Lisa.

❧

John watched as Lisa called a bird to her. "She's beautiful." Speaking to no one.

Christian stopped him from interrupting her. "Watch."

He watched as Sam called the winds, forming a tiny tornado of leaves she spun it towards Lisa who took it over. Awed at the simplicity of it he was speechless.

"Amazing isn't it? They are of the earth, this is natural for them. You assumed she could only heal, but Sam will teach her everything she knows and together they will be more powerful, even though Sam is quite powerful alone, together they maybe unstoppable." A warning.

"Why are you being protective? I would never hurt either of them." John stated.

"Just a caution, nothing more. Is she the one?" Christian asked matter effect.

"What?" Caught off guard by the question.

"Your bond mate."

"Yes."

"Don't wait too long to claim her than."

"I thought of doing it in Venice, but its becoming harder to resist and the beast is so close now."

"Than you must do it before. Nicholas had come back with news of the sorcerers gathering. Not sure what they're planning, but it must be why Sarina wants us all together again."

"Why didn't you say something before now?"

"Because they haven't come this far yet. When we go to Venice we will probably run into some of them and I want you to be alert. Claim her now before the wedding. She will be safer than and you can monitor her. Come, I think they've had enough practice for today."

Emerging from the shadows of the woods they walked towards the girls as the animals ran back to safety. "Hey you scared them away." Unconsciously throwing a small branch at them.

It stopped a foot from them, hovered a minute of so, then fell harmlessly to the ground. Christian looked at Sam, who just shrugged. "Lisa, you need to always stay in control and be aware of everything or you could accidentally hurt someone." Smiling at John.

"It wouldn't have hurt them." Brushing herself off.

"True, but just be a where ok?"

"Fine, but they scared off the animals. You just watch yourself." Lisa warned walking past them to the beach.

"What the hell?" John exclaimed.

"Just go after her." Christian said.

"You could have said you were coming out of the woods instead of pissing her off." Sam joked.

"Why? Its fun." Wrapping his arms around her loving how her body fit so perfectly with his.

Laughing they walked back to the beach. "She'll find a way to pay you back you know."

"She can try if it makes her happy.

"And believe me she will." Sam laughed.

Emerging from the woods Christian and Sam could hear Lisa and

John arguing. "Don't touch me. You could have warned me you were coming. You scared them I could feel it."

"I said I was sorry. What else do you want?" John looked pissed and helpless at the same time.

Lisa you need to calm yourself. Your drawing attention to us, Sam informed her, *Take deep calming breathes,* watching her, *Good. John didn't mean to scare them and your very sensitive to animals I'm assuming.*

I'm sorry. I never realize it would effect me like that, "I'm sorry John."

"Its ok honey, we'll make it through this. I'm sure Sam went through a lot of new things too." Winking at Sam.

"I did and still am. Now we can learn together." Putting her arm on Lisa's shoulder. "Let's go swim." Following the other's into the water.

"I told you to watch yourself."

"Shut up." Following Christian to the water.

They spent most of the afternoon at the beach splashing in the water, eating, or laying in the sun. As early evening came Lucian, Nicholas, and Raphael joined them.

Lucian and Raphael had brought steaks and shrimp to grill for dinner along with some salads and Maggie's peach cobbler for dessert. They sat at the picnic table with John, Daniel, and Mark, which Nicholas joined everyone else in the water.

"Your up late today." Christian greeted him.

"I needed some extra sleep, which I advise you get soon." Nicholas replied. "How has the day gone so far?"

"Sam was teaching Lisa some easy magic today. She picks up fast just like Sam. They will both be powerful together."

"And apart?"

"They are still quite powerful, but Sam will always be more than Lisa." Christian explained. "I also told John not to wait much longer to claim Lisa."

"What!" Sam came up to them.

"Good evening chere."

"Hello Nicholas. Now what is this I hear of claiming my sister?" Turning towards Christian.

Can we discuss this later?

"No! Who is to claim her?" She waited with no response. "Christian who is her bond mate? I will find out if I have to invade your mind to do it?"

The heat fluctuated briefly as Sam got her temper under control. "Later." He whispered bluntly.

That was it she would not be shut out like a child by her bond mate. Focusing she drove through his strong barrier cause him some pain, but found the answer she was searching for. "John. Why not tell me? I'm your bond mate, your fiancé."

"Sam..."

"No! Leave me alone for now." Moving farther into the water, then going under and swimming away.

Why did you withhold the information? She asked you, but by doing what you did only caused you pain and her hurt.

"You know you can be annoying sometimes. I was going to tell her, but didn't want her saying anything to Lisa and she was too close and might hear."

"Well why didn't you say so?" Nicholas asked.

"Cause she didn't give me a chance."

"You are both stubborn. Go help John with the grill and I will talk to Sam." Nicholas swam out towards Sam as Christian reached the shore.

Sam was floating on her back with her eyes closed when strong arm's pulled her into a solid chest. The scent was not Christian's but Nicholas. Sighing, "Yes, Nicholas."

"Don't be mad at him he was trying to protect John and Lisa. He would have told you later."

Opening her eyes, "I know, but I'm protective of my sister. He should know that by now." Enjoying Nicholas lightly pulling her through the warm water.

"Damn it Christian." Mumbling under his breath still holding Sam.

Leave him alone. He wasn't doing anything wrong, Sam fumed.

He is holding you to close. Remember I am a jealous man, Christian reminded her.

"Oh my god!" Trying to move.

"Just remain still." Flooding her with warmth.

"Your going to piss him off you know." Laughing as he held her.

"Its good for him sometimes and he wouldn't expect it from me." Leaning down he brushed a kiss on the corner of her mouth.

As the corner of their lips touched she saw her. A young woman mid-twenties, tall and slender with a pale complexion, long bluish-black hair and pale blue eye. She had on a white short sleeve sweater and jeans. She was in Venice walking along the bank at night. The vision faded as Nicholas moved away. "Kiss me again."

"What!"

What!

Hearing them both clearly she had Nicholas carry her out of the water afraid of loosing the vision for all time if he let her go. "I need you to kiss me again. I saw her, but couldn't see where she's going." Sam tried to explain.

"I don't think so." Christian stated walking with them back to the table.

"What did you see? Who is she?" Nicholas inquired.

"Your mate." A statement only. "Take me to the clearing."

Once there, "Both of you merge with me, but Christian please don't touch me. This vision is to help Nicholas and I want to see if I can see more through the kiss. I know you don't like it, just bare with me." She pleaded.

"Very well, but only cause its for Nicholas."

Both merged as Nicholas kissed Sam again. They saw the girl Sam saw. She was on the pier in Venice. It was dark, windy, but not uncomfortably cold. She was alone. Drawn to that spot by an unseen force. Sam blacked out.

Hearing Christian she slowly came back from the darkness. "Sam, you alright?"

"Yeah, I must have blacked out again. Sorry."

"Its ok. You must have over loaded your senses." Christian took her from Nicholas.

"Is she in Venice now?" Nicholas inquired.

"No, but she will arrive while we are there. Hopefully she'll stay at your hotel." Sam answered.

They went back to everyone and ate dinner. Never saying a word about what they saw. Later on they went to The Lighthouse for awhile. It was crowded, but the atmosphere was up beat. Mike and his band were playing tonight. The girls went upstairs to say hi to Tony.

"Wow, I have my own groupies." Tony laughed.

"That's right Tony." Sam kissed his cheek. The other's followed suite.

"So what are you girls up to?" Tony asked.

"Just out for fun. We'll be up during my bachelorette party next week." Sam answered.

"Your getting married? Well congratulations. Who's the lucky guy and when's the wedding?"

"Thank you. His name is Christian. He was the one you were concerned about around Christmas time."

"Oh now I remember. Are you sure.?"

"Yes, I love him so much Tony and he makes me happy."

"Good, that's all that matters. So when is it?"

"Next Saturday." Sam gushed with happiness.

"Wow, that's pretty fast. Your absolutely without a doubt sure that he's the one for you?"

"Yes. You'll come to the wedding won't you?"

"Of course my dear." Hugging her.

"Good. Well we should go. Talk to you later." Turning for the stairs.

"Ok hon., have fun." He yelled after Sam.

They went to the dance floor for awhile. Laughing, dancing, having a good time. Sam danced with Christian to a couple of slow songs. He walked up to her when *Everything I do I do for you* came on. They just started dancing when Ethan cut in. Christian politely let him. *Thank you,* he heard Sam say in his mind. With a nod he walked to a dark corner. Blending with the darkness, he watched her.

"He's very protective isn't he?" Ethan stated.

Smiling up at him, "Yes, but it makes me feel cherished. Will you be at the wedding?"

"If you want me too."

"Yes, I do."

"Than I'll be there."

Just before the song finished Sam felt warmth begin to spread through her. The sensation increased, slightly burning Ethan. "Sam!" She just looked at him unable to speak, *Come to me darling. Say nothing or this of I will take you now. Tell Ethan your sorry about the heat and not sure why it happened. If you understand say yes only through our path.*

I understand and will be out in a minute, "I'm sorry Ethan about the heat. I don't know what happened. Will you excuse me I need some air." Turning to walk away.

Ethan seized her arm. "Sam wait! What is wrong and don't say nothing."

Seeing Christian come out of the shadows Sam placed her palm on Ethan's, "Nothing is wrong I just need some air, please." She said as he let her arm go she seared something into his palm before she left.

Watching her go out the door Christian stopped next to him. "What did you do?"

"Nothing, but something's not right." Looking at his palm he saw nothing but a red burn. Realizing it must be a message for Christian, "Let me see your hand."

"Why?" Looking at him suspiciously.

"Because Sam left a message for you, but I need your palm to read it." Seeing his puzzlement. "Its an ancient way of leaving secret messages and I'm not sure how she knew about it." Taking Christian's palm, Ethan transferred it and found out what was going on.

❧

Outside, Sam walking to the side of The Lighthouse. Anthony materialized behind her. Wrapping his arms around her he increased her sexual desire for him. Leaning down against her neck he whispered, "Thank you for helping me last night. I owe you and intend to pay in full." Kissing down the column of her neck.

Finding the sensitive spot on her neck her legs almost gave out, but

Anthony held her in place. "There's no need." She barely got out the words. Trying, in vain, to control her reaction to him, then he pierced her skin. Her moan was that of pleasure instead of pain. She closed her eyes and gave herself to him. Knowing that no matter what everyone did she would never be free of his influence over her and right now she did want to.

That's right Sam. Only through death will you be rid of me and I'm not that easy to kill. taking her rich blood helped heal him and bring him more strength.

Why do you do this to me?

Because if you look within yourself you would see that you have always felt like this. I'm just bringing those feelings to the surface, hearing Christian coming around that corner, he cloaked them, *Your bond mate is looking for you. Don't worry though he won't find us.*

Powerless to stop him, Sam pleaded with Anthony to let her go, but he refused. He continued to take her blood until her heart skipped a beat, then he closed the wound with a swipe of his tongue.

Christian felt her heart skip. "Damn it Anthony. I know you're here and you have Sam. Show yourself and release her." His rage increasing.

Nicholas appeared next to Christian. "Where is she?" His tone strained.

"I don't know. He's cloaked them, but she's around here somewhere." A storm was starting to take place due to Christian's increasing fury.

Sam you must drink. You are to weak now to survive much longer, Anthony explained, wanting his blood in her veins.

No, I'm to tired. Just let me sleep.

"Christian, I have drained your mate. I know you felt her heart stutter. She is very weak now, but refused my offer of blood. If she doesn't take it now she will die. Do you want that?"

"You know I don't let me replenish..."

"There is no time. I am on the far side of the parking lot now. You'll never make it to her in time. Force her to take it now!"

"Show me."

Materializing at the far side of the lot, Christian could see Sam was in a grave way. She was so pale and limp, lying in Anthony's arms. Lightening struck across the sky as the rain poured down, *Sam honey you must take what he offers. If you choose to leave this world than I have no chose but to follow.*

"You can't do that Christian." Nicholas sternly stated.

John came out with Lisa in his arms. "Force her Christian. She's not thinking straight. I can't loose her, please!" She weakly informed him. Sam's physical state taking its toll on her.

"I will help you." Nicholas said.

Together they forced their will on Sam to take Anthony's blood. It filled her starving cells, bringing back her strength. She tried to pull away, but the three of them were too strong. Anthony gave her enough to survive and continue his hold over her, *My blood will always run in your veins. We will always be connected. Our tie is complete and unbreakable. I leave you for now. See you soon my darling,* laying her on the ground gently.

Christian was by her side within a minute of Anthony leaving. Sighing she snuggled closer to Christian's chest as her carried her back inside. CJ let them use his office to rest in for awhile.

"What has he done?" Christian asked inspecting her.

"He has tied us together for all time. Only through death will it be broken." Feeling ill, "Could you get me a lemonade? I'm not feeling good." Her stomach churned causing bile to go up her throat, but Lisa placed a calming hand on her and the feeling subsided.

Thank you, must have been all the excitement, smiling at her.

Its okay. I don't mind. Let me check and make sure your fine, getting ready to place a hand on her.

Sam stopped her. "You rest. We can do it tomorrow."

"Alright, I am tired." Laying back against John.

"Christian would you..."

"Go take her home we'll be there soon." Watching them leave. "Speaking of tired. I need to rest again, beautiful. Will you be ok? Nicholas will be with you again."

"Yes I'll be fine. It shouldn't be that bad again. What about John? He's always with my sister. Doesn't he need rest too?"

"He get's a little every night while Lisa sleeps, but makes sure he's back before she awakes."

"Why don't you do that?"

"Cause I can't stand the separation. Anyways, John will find that out soon enough."

"But your doing it now."

"Yes and soon, when your ready, you can join me."

"Oh." Curious she asked, "What's it like?"

"Well I never really thought about it. Your not a where of anything. When you sleep, the earth takes care of you, so your body functions cease. The earth wraps itself around you to provide a restful sleep."

"So you are being buried alive."

"So to speak, but it isn't that unpleasant and when you awake you feel rejuvenated."

"Still sounds too much like being buried alive. I'll wait, thank you very much."

"You rest for a bit. Daniel is arguing with Shelby and has blocked me. I want to let them know that we are leaving and that John and Lisa should be home shortly."

"I'll be here. Will they be coming over? The rest of them I mean." Laying back on the couch.

"Only if your up to it. Otherwise I will tell them to come over tomorrow."

"Its fine. I don't mind the company."

"Very well, beautiful. I'll be right back."

18

The next couple of days went by a little slower than Sam had hoped. She missed Christian terribly, even though Nicholas changed to his natural form to help ease her sadness. The girls were trying to get her in the mood for the wedding. They still had a lot left to do and to top it off Lisa kept bugging her about checking her out to make sure she was fine cause she was still a little sick, even though she tried to hide it from Lisa.

"Lisa, I'll let you do it tonight before Christian awakens. I promise."

"I will hold you to it."

"I know you will. Let's get the wedding stuff together." Sam walked with Lisa back to the living room. Everyone was gathered around the coffee table talking about the wedding.

"So what did we missed?" Lisa asked while shoving Maria over on the couch.

"Hey!"

"Well I could have just sat on you."

"You could have just asked me to move."

"Lisa, quit being a bitch."

Lisa just gave Sam a smile and the finger.

"Oh that's cute." Sam gave her a smirk.

"Flowers? What kinds are you wanting and where? My cousin will do it for half off." Shelby interrupted.

"Really?" Seeing her shake her head. "Oh that's great. Thank you."

"Your welcome. So what do you want roses, lilies, orchids, what?"

"Well definitely lilies. Not sure what else." Sam stated.

"Well Sofia lent me her flower arrangement book." Shelby opened it for everyone.

They flipped through it for half an hour. Maggie brought out cut up fruit and dip with ice tea or lemonade to drink. They talked about different flowers and arrangements, what to use for the bouquets, the ceremony, and on the tables at the dinner. Eventually they decided on white lilies for Sam's bouquet while dark red roses would be used for the bridesmaid's bouquets and groomsman's boutonnieres. Tiger lilies would be used for the ceremony and orchids for the tables.

"Well that's one thing down." Lisa said.

"Well we still have food, the cake, and gifts for the bridal party." Sam answered with a sigh.

"I'll take care of the food." Lisa stated.

"I'll order the cake if you know what you want." Christine volunteered.

"I'll go with you to pick out the gifts and Mike's going to play whatever you want at the reception." Maria said.

"For dinner Lisa, I thought maybe prime rid and seafood with salad and veggies. The cake Christine, I thought about a dark chocolate with white icing and red roses. Three tiers if possible and maybe with a fountain, but surprise me I trust you two." Sam implied.

"Come on Sam, Christian will be up soon and I want to check you before he awakens." Lisa reminded her.

"Oh fine. We'll see you for dinner." Following Lisa out of the living room.

"Here, I can check you in this room just lie on the bed." Lisa instructed as she closed the door so no one would interrupt them.

"I said I'm fine." Still doing as Lisa requested.

Lisa lit some candles and incenses, filling the room with a woodsy smell, instantly claming Sam. "Just relax. You want some music?"

"No I'm fine." Sam responded.

Sitting next to her sister, Lisa talked her through a very relaxing meditation which put Sam in a semi-conscious sleep. Before she grabbed her to start the exam, Lisa heard a soft rap on the door. Calming her own thoughts, Lisa was able to see it was Nicholas on the other side. Softly she invited him in. "You can sit on the other side if you want."

"Thank you. May I observe your exam?" Seeing Lisa's hesitation, "I might see something or help with anything Anthony put in her body your not familiar with."

"Very well. Are you ready."

In Sam's body they saw nothing odd. Everything looked normal until they looked at her veins. Tiny blue flax were through out in small quantities. This must have been how Anthony tied them together. When Lisa tried to destroy them with heat they reflected back on her ten fold. The burns appeared on Lisa's arms, but she blocked the pain and continued with the exam.

Nicholas admired her stamina and determination to keep her sister healthy. He knew Lisa must be blocking the pain she was in so he stayed quiet as she continued on her path. As they headed for her reproductive area, to make sure everything was good there too, they both sensed another near by as they drew closer. Cautiously they moved towards the uterus a faint heartbeat was heard. Moving closer still they saw her, very tiny, not more than a three months old, but very strong. Then something strange happened she disappeared, vanished from sight and sense.

Next Lisa and Nicholas heard Sam singing softly, wrapping them along with the baby, in a comforting melody. This soothed the baby, bringing her back into view and putting her to sleep peacefully. Lisa quickly finished up her exam, then emerged, drained and excited all at once. "Here take some of my blood it will help you recover fast." Offering his wrist to her.

"Um… Thank you, really, but no. I'm not like you or Christian or Sam. I'll just get some juice." Smiling uncomfortably at him. "I'll be right back Will you stay with her. She'll stay asleep until I awaken her." Nodding, Lisa left.

Watching Sam, his brain was working out how the baby survived when the other didn't. Why didn't anyone know Sam was pregnant with twins, but lost only one. And how did her subconscious knew, but her conscious mind didn't. Lisa came back a short time later with juice and a ham sandwich.

"Won't that ruin your dinner?" He smirked.

"No! So have you thought of any answers to the questions we are both thinking?" Sitting in the chair by the bed.

"Still thinking. How is it she survived when her twin didn't?"

"She was the stronger one, she has more power." Sam answered.

"I thought she wasn't a where of us." Nicholas asked. Lisa just shrugged. "Alright how did she disappear and no one was aware of her when people examined you?" Directing the question to Sam.

"One of her powers is invisibility, which she is not only invisible to the eyes, but the senses also which is why no one knew I was pregnant."

"Why didn't your conscious mind know you were?"

"Because of everything happening all at once. Between the new powers, being hunted by other's, the wedding, the ritual, and the loss, it over loaded my senses."

"That explains everything now. Will she be safe from Anthony?" Lisa questioned.

"Only with help, she is still fragile like all babies in the first trimester."

"Awaken her now. I will awaken Christian and have him come here. Only than will we tell them what we have found." Leaving to get Christian.

Awakening Sam, Lisa was so happy, but worried. She waited on pins and needle until Christian and Nicholas came through the door.

"Alright I'm here now what is going on?" Pulling Sam on his lap as he held her on the bed.

"You tell them I can't" Lisa told Nicholas.

"You only lost one child. You were pregnant with twins Sam. The stronger one survived and already has one very useful power." He explained.

"What!" they said in unison.

"How can this be?" Sam asked.

"Lisa, you, and Sarina checked her." Christian reminded him.

"Yes, but see the baby's power is invisibility of not only sight, but senses, so that is how we didn't know of her."

"Her? It's a girl?" Seeing Lisa nod her head. "We have a baby girl on the way Christian." Tears glistened her eyes.

Hugging Sam gently. "How did Sam not know she was still pregnant?" Overjoyed at the news.

"She did, well subconsciously anyway. When we examined her to see what Anthony had done we found out how he tied you together."

"How?" Christian's voice stone cold.

"With tiny blue flax. Lisa tried to destroy it, but was burned. Don't worry Sam I'll heal her." Seeing Sam's distress. "Anyway, when we checked your uterus we noticed the heartbeat and saw her briefly before she disappeared. You brought her back with your melody which put her to sleep."

"You can sing? I never heard you sing." Christian stated.

"Not very well."

"She's being modest, she has a very good singing voice. She's just too shy to let anyone hear her." Lisa explained.

"Your voice is beautiful and enthralling chere. You should sing more." Nicholas complimented.

Sam blushed turning into Christian's chest. "Thank you." She muttered.

"Will the tie effect the baby?" Changing the subject for Sam.

"Unfortunately yes, but with help we will make sure nothing happens to her. You have my word." Nicholas formally stated.

"Thank you. Is there away to remove it from Sam's body?"

"All we can do is see if Todd will help us. Maybe between him and Lisa, something can be done."

"Well at least your getting hands on experience Lisa." Sam commented.

"What do you mean?" Christian inquired placing his hand on her belly. Unable to believe his child was growing inside her.

Sam over lapped his hand. Happiness flooded her. "Lisa is going to become a doctor."

"As long as everything goes as planned and I make it through school with no problems." Smiling at Sam.

"Should we tell everyone now or wait?" He asked Sam lovingly.

"We can tell them now we can't hide it and Anthony will know soon. We just need to be alert now."

"Oh Sam, I'm so happy for you two." Lisa gushed hugging her.

"Hey I'm getting squished here." Christian playfully informed them.

They got off of him and went out to tell everyone. Nicholas and Christian followed talking about constructing a nursery in his wing of the house.

❧

It was the night of the bachelorett party. Sam spent her morning making friends with the toilet again. This was getting ridiculous, but at least she wasn't alone. Lisa would bring her lemon water to settle her stomach and the other helped too. Usually by midmorning she felt better and was able to continue on with her day. She was determined to have a great time tonight.

"Sam its almost six why aren't you dressed yet?" Lisa walked to the closet pulling out a cute little red dress. It was silk with one inch straps and a v-neck. It only went to mid-thigh length. Lisa had on the same one, but in orange. Both had shoes to match, same jewelry, and same french twist with spiral curls around their faces.

Putting on the dress, "Why are we dressing alike?" Walking to the floor length mirror by the window.

With Lisa next to her in the mirror, "Because I like looking like twins once in awhile. Like we do now." Placing her hand on Sam's stomach she wanted to see the baby within. "I need you so sing so she won't disappear I want to check her. You know we can't take you to a regular doctor, so I'll be yours through the pregnancy. No one's here but us Sam." Waiting, Sam started the haunting melody to calm the baby for the exam.

Christian was on his way to the to say good-bye to Sam before going to his party. The haunting melody caught him half way down. He was so stunned by it he couldn't move.

Nicholas came up behind him. "That is your mate's voice."

"It is? Its beautiful. Do you know how dangerous she could be?" Unconsciously walking towards the door.

Grabbing his brother. "Yes, I see that now. Go in cautiously, but don't interrupted her." He warned him.

Walking in silently they did their best to block out the mesmerizing melody. Lisa was in her usual trance when she was in a body. Sam was facing the mirror singing with her eyes closed probably staying focused to help Lisa with her task.

Do you think they know how much they look alike now? Nicholas observed staying in the shadows with Christian.

I'm sure they do. What is she doing?

Checking the baby I'm assuming. She can't go to a regular doctor so Lisa had taken over as hers.

They both just watched as Lisa continued with the check. Emerging Sam steadied Lisa helping her to the bed to rest for a bit. "Did you enjoy the show?" Not looking to the shadowed corner.

"Who are you..." Seeing Christian and Nicholas coming out of the shadows. "Nice, now you pissed her off." Trying to stand.

"Nicholas will you help her to the kitchen while I talk to my mate for a minute?"

Inclining his head he helped Lisa out the door. "Yes, my love?" Wrapping his arms around her small waist.

Flames appeared on his arms which he instantly put out still holding her. "Why did you come in here? Lisa was helping me get dressed, then just checking on the baby. I was just singing to calm her had I known you were coming I would have waited on the check up."

"Beautiful, you have such a radiant voice why hide it?"

"Because I don't think its that good. Anyway I don't like being the center of attention." Blushing at his compliment.

"Well I would love to hear you sing again sometime. When you are more comfortable will you sing for me?"

"I'll think about it. So where are you guys going tonight?" Changing the subject as they walked down the hall.

"I don't really know. They said it's a surprise. Why? Where are going?"

"First we are going to The Pier for dinner. I guess Lisa is taking care of the bill for that."

"Wow, that's an expensive place how nice of her. So where else?"

"I guess after that we are going to Taon for awhile, then we may end up at The Lighthouse." Getting excited about a night out with the girls.

"Where it Taon? I've never heard of it." Christian asked relaying everything to his twin.

"Its an upscale club in Bradford. I heard its really nice."

"Well have a nice time sweetheart. Are you going to drink at all? I don't think its good for the baby."

"Probably not. Did your brother get everything you told him?"

"Yes, my little minx. I'm just watching out for you and our baby."

"I know." Going into the kitchen she kissed Christian good-bye, then she watched them leave in the vet.

"Damn it I wanted us to take the vet." Lisa commented pouting.

"Armond offered to take us all in the limo that way everyone could drink and get home safely." Sam explained.

They had seafood dinners and drinks except for Sam of course. They got to Taon around nine. It was a very nice place with it was an Asian theme. The outside was dark brick with a red door, the inside was dark except for the small light like candles that illuminated it. Music filled the air along with smoke. There were booths all along the walls on the first floor. Going upstairs they had a little cubby that you could use for privacy with sheer black curtains. Turning right you could follow the hall to the dance floor which you had to walk through to get to the bar.

If you turned left it took you to a private dance floor and bar which was a little quieter. The girls decided to go right it was a night for fun. Christine went up to the DJ to see if he would play Da `Butt for Sam's party, which he did, after making Sam come up there by him to announce her bachelorett party. Sam threatened to get Christine back for it.

Sam and Shelby were sitting at the bar when the bartender brought them some drinks. "This is from the guy at the end of the bar."

"Wow, tell him thanks." Shelby said.

"Yes, tell him thanks, but I can't have alcohol I'm pregnant." Sam explained.

"Alright." Walking back to the end of the bar to tell him thanks for them.

"So how are you feeling anyways?" Shelby asked taking a sip of her drink.

"I'm dong fine still a little sick in the morning."

"What would you like to drink?" the bartender asked. "Its on the house." Smiling at Sam.

"A virgin strawberry daiquiri please." Smiling back.

As he left, "Sam!"

"What?"

"You flirt." Shelby laughed.

"He's cute and I get a free drink."

"Oh my god you guys, I just met the cutest guy. Come with me I want to introduce you to him." Christine grabbed their arms.

"Sam's waiting for her drink." Shelby halted her.

"Its ok. You go, I'll catch up." Sam watched Shelby leave with Christine.

"Here you go honey." The bartender handed her the drink with a smile.

"Thanks." Taking a sip.

"May I sit here?" A sexy southern voice asked.

Looking up she was caught by a pair of golden eyes, like cat's eyes. A quick glance showed her a man about six-three, muscular and very tan with short sandy blond hair. "Um…sure, go ahead."

"Thank you. So you are the bachelorette?"

"Yes, I'm Sam."

"Well hi Sam, I'm David."

"Nice to meet you."

"The pleasure is all mine. Are you enjoying yourself this evening?" Taking a swig of beer.

"Yes its been nice to just go out with my friends." Looking around, "So are you here alone?"

"No, I believe one of your friends is introducing one of mine." Pointing to Christine.

"Oh jeez sorry she gets like that sometimes."

"Its ok, Nathan seems to be soaking up the attention. So will you be here later?"

A strange shimmer caught her eye from around him. "Yeah for a little while anyway. Why do you ask?" Dismissing the odd feeling.

"I would like a dance with you, if you don't mind, before you leave." Charmingly suggesting.

"Sure, that would be nice." Smiling at him.

"'Til later than." Kissing the back of her hand, he moved fluidly through the crowd to his friend.

Sam was astonished at his old world mannerism. "Miss?"

Breaking the spell, she looked at the bartender. "Yes?"

"I know its none of my business, but I'd watch out for guys like him. They come off all suave at first, but end up being monsters. If you know what I mean."

The bartender was a nice looking man. Not exactly hot, but nice to look at. At six foot he could probably hold his own. His dark brown hair was in a ponytail and had light blue eyes. Any woman wouldn't mind being his girlfriend. "What's your name?"

"Joe."

"I know what you mean Joe and thanks for the warning."

"Your welcome. Have fun tonight and if there's any trouble let me or the bouncer's in the tuxes know."

"Alright I will, I'll be back for another drink later."

"See you than and all your drinks are on the house for your party."

Sam waved at Joe and joined her friends. They all were having a good time. Meeting new people, trying new drinks, and learning some new dance moves. Time slipped by as the night went on and Sam was feeling weak again. Needing food she went to the bar to see if they served any food. Unfortunately not, but Joe gave her some nuts and a big glass of juice to hold her over for a while at least.

Are you alright beautiful? I feel your weakness, Christian's loving voice slipped into her mind.

I will be alright. I'm eating some nuts and drinking juice right now, she affectionately answered.

You need more than food while your pregnant. You will need to feed more than just once or twice a week. Is Beth with you?

I'm not sure, looking around, *Oh wait she's with Maria and Nichole. Why?*

She will supply you with enough to get by until I see you later.

No, I'll be fine.

Sam don't argue with me on this.

"Hi Sam, come with me to the restroom." Beth said taking her hand.

Damn it, Christian! Just wait until I see you again.

I can't wait mi amor. Te amo.

I love you too, going into the restroom with Beth.

She walked Sam into the handicap stall while Maria and Lisa kept everyone else out. "Here drink so you maybe strong again." Offering her wrist.

"I've never done this without help." Sam admitted.

"Its not that hard. Think of the sweet smell of blood. Of how it feels going through your body. The power it gives you once the blood touches your tongue for the first time."

Sam envisioned it, smelling the sweet musk of Christian's blood. The warmth and strength it brought as it filled her starving cells. Her incisors lengthened at the thought as she took Beth's wrist puncturing her skin, taking just enough to feel herself again. With a swipe of her tongue the holes closed up as if they were never there. "Thank you for both."

"Your welcome, but why didn't Christian or any of the other's for that matter, show you how to do it without their help?"

"I guess because it took me time to get use to the idea. Then I always took from Christian with help."

"Is he the jealous type?"

"Yes, why do you ask?"

"Figures, he probably never showed you because than you wouldn't need him to feed. Take it from me, these guys can be worse than humans man with their jealousies and possessiveness. Don't let them rule you and teach your daughter the same thing. You don't need them, you're your own person."

"See Sam she's sounds like mom." Lisa commented.

"Yeah I guess I have been letting Christian run everything, but its hard when I also have his brother's, your brother, and cousin always around." Washing her hands.

"Well Mark's just a dumb ass most of the time and I haven't seen Ethan in forever, but welcome to the family anyway. Let's go enjoy the rest of the night." Beth linked her arm with Sam's and out the door they went.

The music was loud, yet inviting so they headed to the stage to dance. Beth was a surprisingly good dancer and accepted by all their friends. Not that Beth really cared about that anyways. Sam went back to the bar to rest and get another virgin daiquiri. She talked to Joe for awhile, learning he was a mechanic by day and here at night. He didn't mind it though he was single and liked it that way. She sat watching her friends dance. When a slow song came on they joined her at the bar. She was engrossed in conversation when that southern voice invaded the talk.

"Excuse me, but may I have this dance?" Extending his hand.

"Of course I would love to David." Ignoring the stares, Sam took his hand.

Pulling her into his strong embrace she caught a whiff of his California for Men, which she loved. His arms were like bands of steel unbreakable if she wished to leave, but he held her gently like a lover would. "Where are you from? Your southern accent tells me that much." She asked.

Bending down slightly he whispered. "I'm from Louisiana. New Orleans area. Mmm... you smell of vanilla and raspberries."

"Thank you. Why are you here?"

"Just visiting friends. You are very attractive Sam." Pulling her against his hard body.

"And I'm getting married tomorrow."

He pulled back and caught her eyes with his, yet continued to dance them to a dark corner. "I know, I was only stating a fact." Pulling her into the darkness. "You are the hottest thing here and every guy has been eyeing you all night, but I was the only one who had the guts to ask you for a dance." Distracting her enough to corner her.

"Really? I hadn't noticed." Realizing where they were. "Why are we not on the dance floor?" Her heart rate increasing.

Lifting her chin he held her gaze as he mentally told her, *Love is but a flower waiting to be plucked. Take care of it and it will bloom forever, but neglected it and it will die,* He watched Sam go limp in his arms. He turned so no one could see what he was about to do. Drifting towards her neck his teeth lengthened to pierce her soft flesh. A soft moan escaped her mouth causing him to grow harder as he took enough to continue there connection and had her take enough for an exchange. He knew she would figure out who he really was, but for now he would have his fun, *Awaken my love and remember none of this moment.*

Sam opened her eyes a little dizzy. David was holding her up. "What happened?"

"You fainted, are you alright?" Concern in his voice.

"I think so." A bit confused.

"Come on Sam we'll sit in one of the privacy booths and get you a drink." Leading her to one of the booths in the hall away from her friends.

Sitting down Sam leaned her head back against the cushion. The waitress came by, "Could I just gat an orange juice?"

"Make that two." David added. After the waitress left he had her lay her head on his shoulder to make her more comfortable. "Tell me about yourself."

"What do you want to know?" Tiredness showing in her voice.

"Anything you wish to share." Trying to calm her uneasiness that was radiating off her.

"Well I'm getting married to a wonderful man named Christian. Both our families are here so I've been a bit overwhelmed with everything."

"Well a wedding can be a stressful and exciting time. Its almost over with just keep that in mind. So how long have you been with your fiancé?"

"Since December." the waitress brought their drinks. "Thank you."

"That's not a lot of time is it.?"

"No, but its like we were meant to be together." Thinking of Christian.

"So have you always lived here?"

"No I lived in Florida for a few years. I loved it there."

"Then why did you leave?'

"I had to due to some personal problems."

"I understand. New subject." Smiling at her.

Sam where are you? Lisa's voice frantic in mind. "I should get back to my friends. My sister is looking for me."

"How do you know?" Figuring Lisa had been mentally calling her.

"I just do." Scooting towards the end of the booth.

"Let me help you." Getting out to help Sam up. "Don't forget your juice."

"Thanks." Leaning on David as they walked. "Listen we are going to go to The Lighthouse later, in White cove, do you want to meet there? It's a fun place and I guess I'm going to sing for the first time in public. I could use all the support I can get."

"I'll be there than." Walking up to Sam's friends.

"Great we'll see you at The Lighthouse." Christine answered.

"Let's go get my sister some food right now." Lisa stated eyeing David.

"I'll walk you out Sam." Still supporting her.

"Ok let's go." They left the club with David and Nathan.

Armond was waiting in the limo. Getting out he noticed a strange man holding Sam. He ran to her side, "I'll take it from here." Opening the door for her.

"Thank you David for your help." Stepping into the limo.

Sam stop, David said in her head. She stopped and turned towards him.

For some reason she wanted to take one last look at him before getting in the limo. His eyes glowed briefly. Maybe it was the moonlight hitting them, but she felt like she was falling into them. He leaned in to whisper, "One more dance tonight." Then kissed her cheek releasing her to Lisa. She watched him and Nathan go back inside and noted what a fine ass he had. She wondered if he looked that good naked, probably. Turning red she went to the front of the limo.

Its ok to look, but don't allow another kiss. I'm just cautioning you, we're suppose to see the boys at The Lighthouse, so watch yourself, Lisa warned her.

"Where to now girls?" Armond asked.

"Sam need to eat so find us a restaurant." Lisa answered.

"So where's he from?" Shelby inquired.

"Who?" Sam questioned.

"The guy who was too close to you."

"His name is David and he's from New Orleans. He's here visiting his friend Nathan. You know the guy Christine was with that I didn't get to meet."

"Just be careful I don't like something about him." Shelby cautioned her.

"Why? I think he's very nice and seems sincere enough."

"A perfect southern gentleman." Lisa stated looking at Sam.

Its not Anthony I would know, getting pissed for no reason.

"Ok girls we're here." Armond interrupted, turning off the limo.

Helping them out Lisa asked him to join them. He agreed, escorting Sam inside as her bodyguard. "Do you need to feed?"

Startled by his question Sam just stared at him. "Sorry Armond, that just caught me off guard. No I'll be fine, Thank you though."

"I just wanted to make the offer. If you needed I could provide." Sitting next to her.

"Thank you again, but I'm alright." They eat quickly, then left for The Lighthouse.

CJ was outside when they arrived. Helping the girls out of the limo he stopped Sam, "Everything is ready for you hon. When did you want to sing?" He whispered.

"In a half hour."

"Alright sweetie, have fun."

They went in saying hi to Tony before dancing. Life was good. She was getting married and had a baby on the way, and was the happiest she'd ever been. Although tomorrow she'd probably be tired from everything. After a couple of song she sat down and watched everyone else. Sensing him she looked towards the stairs. Seeing David she thought black suited him.

Be careful little brother, we are on their turf now. If Christian shows up he will know who we are and confront us, Victor told him.

I'm not afraid of him, Sam is already mine. I'm just trying to get her to see it that way. Keep the other's busy for me, walking towards Sam.

Dumb Ass, walking towards the girls.

"Hi Sam, taking a break?" Sitting next to her.

"Yeah, just getting tired. Where's Nathan?"

"He went to look for Christine." The music changed to a slow song. "Come dance with me."

"David I'm tired."

"I will hold you, come my love." Lowering his voice an octave to control his power over her, knowing she would know who he really was.

"Anthony!" Shocked, but having no control over her body she let him lead her to the corner of the dance floor.

In his arm's she felt different. Her pulse quickened, but not of fear. She wanted him so bad to feel his muscles ripple around her as he held her, caressed her. The thought of his mouth kissing every corner of her body, bring her to orgasm with the flick of his tongue.

Reading her thoughts made him swell instantly. He could make her thoughts come true tonight and he intended to, but for now he would only do it in her mind, *It is alright my darling no one but you knows who I really am. Just lay your head on my shoulder, close your eyes, and let me make all your fantasies come true,* slowly twirling her into a dark corner of the dance floor.

Christian's going to kill you, becoming more tired.

"Shh my lover, I'm not worried about that right now. Let's just dance and enjoy ourselves." Feeling her body heat warming him made him want to make love to her right than and there.

Feeling the invasion in her mind Sam just let the images flow in, unable to stop them anyways. She saw herself in a dark red teddy waiting for Anthony on a white fur rug in front of a roaring fire. Looking around she saw nothing but rock, like she was in some kind of cave, but with rooms in it.

The door opened, Anthony emerged out of the darkness in only a pair of black silk pants. His eyes looked her over like she was the feast. Unable to take her eye's off him he moved forwards kneeling in front of her, she watched his muscles ripple at the movement. Electricity went through her at the sight making her hot and wet.

He laid her down on the rug, after taking off the teddy he ran his hands over her skin feeling her quiver under his touch. Her lips beckoned for a kiss which he gave. She tasted sweet leaving her mouth he travel down her throat, stopping at the fast beating pulse. Unable to resisted he sank his teeth into her, her blood even sweeter still. With a swipe of his tongue he stopped the blood, but left his mark.

He moved down her chest kissing every inch of her. Her response only excited him more. He flicked her nipples into hard peaks, sucking on them as she moaned in pleasure. Inch by slow inch he neared his ultimate goal of ecstasy.

Her body was not her own. His touch scorched her, his lips drove her crazy as he assaulted her senses beyond rational thinking. Powerless to control the primal craving she felt for him she raked his back with her nails drawing blood. As the warmth of his mouth closed around her core she lost all control. His tongue probed her relentlessly bringing Sam to exquisite pleasure over and over again.

Anthony looked down at Sam her body bathed in sweat. She looked so gorgeous lying in the fire light all wet for him. He stood up to take his pants off, but she was already there doing it for him. Kneeling, Sam looked up at him as she took the length of him in her mouth. He moaned throwing his head back. She rubbed his tip with her tongue while continuing the suction knowing exactly what he wanted Sam cupped his sac, gently squeezing, which brought Anthony more pleasure.

Even though he wanted to cum in her mouth he decided against it, for now anyways. Helping her to stand he pushed her against the wall. Lifting her, Sam wrapped her legs around his waist as he impaled her with his hard shaft. Building the friction between them they exploded together flying so high they'd never come down. Collapsing on the floor they were both breathless. Anthony just held her as their heart rates went down.

Bringing Sam back to reality she looked up at him speechless. "I can make you feel like that every time."

Shaking her head, "No, no this isn't what I want." Turning to leave he grabbed her arm.

"Samantha you belong at my side, not with Christian." Trying to control the glamour and his anger.

"Never." Ripping out of his grasp.

You can't run from me Sam. My blood is in your veins and I will always know where you are, watching her go to the drink station.

Fuck you Anthony! I will stand by Christian and watch him kill you, her anger causing the room to heat up.

He was on her in an instant, pulling her to a dark corner before anyone saw. "Listen to me my little tigress, you mention one damn word of me to anyone and not only will you disappear, but so will your precious daughter." Feeling the air cool again he knew he had her attention. "Good. We have an understanding than?"

"Yes." Sam bit out between clenched teeth.

"Good girl." Kissing her cheek. "You will be nice to me. Now let's go join your friends." Taking her back to the drink station, *Acted normal,* Anthony warned her.

"Sam its time." CJ took her hand. Relieved to be away from Anthony she relaxed a little.

She was still nerves about being on stage singing in front of an actual audience. Tony introduced her and announced she'd be singing *My heart will go on* by Celine Dion. Everyone applauded, but she didn't see the one person she was singing for, *Where is he?* Questioning her sister.

I don't know, but someone's getting their ass kicked. Hold on, Lisa ran to the window facing the parking lot, *Where the hell are you?* Sending the query to John.

We just pulled up. Damn!

Well hurry, she getting ready to sing tight now. He still doesn't know?

No, we are on the stairs now.

Ok, Lisa ran on stage. "They are on the stairs now." She whispered.

Sam nodded to Tony to start the music. As the first note hit the air she had everyone's attention including Christian, who had stopped at the top of the stairs. John pushed him to the side so they could get through.

"She's singing in public." Stunted at Sam's boldness.

Lisa came running up to them. "Its for you Christian. Her gift to you. She is singing only to you."

It took a minute for Lisa's words to sink in. "She's doing this for me? Why?"

"Because she's a giving person and she wants too. This is her love for you ."

She was beautiful. Her body, voice, love, everything about her. He blocked everything out. It was only him looking at her on stage. She was sing to only him. This was one of the most precious gifts anyone had ever given him and he will treasure it always.

When she was done Christian escorted her off the stage, then his brother's flanked her between them. "She even has her own body guards everyone so be careful not to get too close. She'll be wed tomorrow anyways. Sorry guys your too late." Tony told everyone as Sam waved at him.

"That was the best gift anyone had ever given me. Thank you." Kissing her passionately.

"Hey, wait until tomorrow the rest of us want to congratulate her too, man." John interrupted.

"You have a lovely voice chere." Nicholas complimented.

"Yes, who knew you could sing like that." Mark added.

"Well thank you everyone, but I need a drink before I fall down. The reality of what I just did is finally hitting me." Leaning on Christian.

"I think your pregnancy is hitting you and you need to feed again." Christian pointed out.

Mmm and are you going to feed me, my love? Sam voice black velvet.

"Samantha!"

"What? I didn't say anything." A wicked smile crossed her lips.

You are a wicked woman, nuzzling her neck.

I can show you how wicked if you like.

I think I'll take you up on that offer later tonight, pulling her closer.

"Both of you stop it right now." Lisa reprimanded.

"Why are you yelling at them they didn't do anything?" Shelby questioned.

"Not yet, they didn't." Nicholas glared at them.

"What we do is our business. We are getting married tomorrow and already have a baby on the way so we can't do much about that now can we?" Christian replied throwing it back in their face.

Sam grabbed Lisa's hand during the small spat. "Ouch Sam, what the hell?" Holding her burnt hand.

"Ethan, will you take Lisa to get a drink."

"But I don't..."

"Please!"

"Sure Sam." Taking Lisa towards the drink station they veered to a dark corner. "Let me see your hand."

"I can heal it myself."

"Damn it Lisa quit being stubborn and let me see it Sam sent you a message." Grabbing her hand again.

"How? I don't see anything but a burn." Looking at it.

"Look closer, see how the line looks a little different?" Ethan explained.

"I see it now." Reading the message. "That's not good. We need to tell Christian."

"Tell him mentally Anthony must be here somewhere." Looking around as he followed Lisa back to Sam.

Christian, Anthony is here and has threatened Sam and the baby, his eyes flared at her. Lisa laid a calming hand on him. *Stay in control. Ethan is telling everyone else, but only through their minds. Don't talk to Sam about this he's monitoring her, threatening to take her if anyone finds out. For now just be calm we will figure something out. Go feed her.*

"Let's take a walk Sam." Helping her up. "How is our baby doing?" Touching her tummy.

"She is asleep. Everything will be just fine. No trouble with the wedding?"

"Never. Everything will be taken care of by tomorrow. Come here and let me take care of you." Sitting on a booth by the back stairs where no one could see them.

Sam leaned close to his neck. Breathing in his scent, she let her senses over take her, teeth lengthened as she pierced his skin. The rich blood flowed down her throat, making her feel better. She heard Christian let out a quiet moan. Taking enough for her and the baby she closed the wound.

"Oh Mi Amour, you did it without help."

"Beth showed me how. Let's go back to everyone."

When they returned, Lisa mentally told Christian her plan of how to find Anthony and take care of him once and for all. He didn't like it at all, but knew it was the only way to flush him out. So he kissed Sam, then took Lisa's hand and went out on the dance floor. He hated leaving her all alone, but hopefully Anthony would go to her, which he did within a few minutes of their departure.

"Are you ready Sam?" Anthony asked.

Glaring at him, "Ready for what?"

"To spend the night with me. I will bring you so much passion you'll be begging for release. Let's go before Christian comes back."

One last look at Lisa and Christian Sam calmed. "Let's go, Christian is pissing me off anyways."

"What is he doing honey?" Taking her hand.

"Just look at how close he's holding my sister. That's not right." Pretending to get pissed.

Leaving the dance area, Sam left Lisa a very faint trail to follow, knowing they were up to something. Going outside the air was warm, calming. The baby was getting upset, but Sam did her best to calm her. Reassuring her that daddy and aunt Lisa would be here soon to help. "So now what?" Stopping him from waking to give Christian time to catch up.

"My car is over there. We'll go to my place."

"What about Victor? How will he get home? I don't want to leave him here."

"So you figured that out too and your still compassionate. Lucky for you Victor."

"Yes, how sweet." Appearing next to Sam seizing her wrist.

"Let go Victor." Sam struggled, but his hold was unbreakable. "Anthony?"

Taking her other wrist, *Sam be still it won't hurt, I promise,* watching her calm down Anthony brought her wrist to his lips. Piercing her flesh he felt the warm liquid flowing into him. He saw Victor flow suit.

They were slowly draining her getting colder by the minute. Sam would have fell if it wasn't for both of them holding her up. A warmth and power swept through her to give her enough strength to break free from their grasp.

Blood trickled down her hands. "Back off, I'm not a sheep you use for whatever or whoever you want." The heat was scorching.

"Sam you are mine and I will do what I want with you." Anthony advanced towards her.

"The hell you will!" Christian's voice venomous.

Turning, Anthony and Victor saw Christian, his brothers, his friends, and Lisa approaching fast. Instantly he had Sam by the throat, a long talon at her carotid. "One more step and I'll slice her." Anthony threatened.

Lisa winked and Sam stepped into the talon causing blood to pool. Lisa flashed to her side, hand and hand the wind picked up, lightening arched a cross the sky. Sam abruptly grabbed and twisted his arm away from her hearing the bones break. Stepping back, Sam sent a ball of energy at Anthony. Lisa did the same to Victor. They both were thrown thirty feet.

Getting up they moved forward sending energy back at the girls throwing them into the wall of the building. "So you guys are such cowards that you'd let your women fight us?"

"No, I'm just letting them have some fun kicking your asses before we destroy you." Assisting them to stand, *Go on beautiful just don't overdo it.*

Giving a wicked grin Sam move towards Anthony building her powers. With Lisa moving with her, the energy was almost to much to control. Fire formed in her palm. Growing, she threw it at Victor, then Anthony. Lisa hurled lightening bolts at them.

Anthony was hit several times. Unable to miss both attacks, he started to cool the air around them. Sam's power only weakened briefly before she was at full strength again. Victor caused venomous roots to erupted out of the ground at their feet injecting poison into the girls. Next he flew at Lisa knocking her down. He went for her neck, ruthlessly penetrating it, but instead of taking, he injected her with a paralyzing poison. Not much made it in before he was hurling through the air into a car with John was on him in an instant.

Anthony on the other hand, regained control of Sam with the brief interruption. Walking to her he sealed them in an invisible, impenetrable box. "Well darling what a predicament you are in now. Christian will now watch as I kill the child inside." Grabbing her hair savagely, pulling her head back.

"You can go to hell! I won't allow you to lay a hand on my baby." Anger overriding fear.

"You little bitch, first you break my wrist and now you think you can get away from me? I don't think so, not this time." Piercing her neck.

Sam gripped his arm drawing the warmth from his body into hers. The more blood he took though the harder it became so she began a soft melody inserting a spell to stop his feverish intake. Within seconds he stopped mesmerized by her voice he could do nothing, but obey it. She commanded him to wither the roots and remove the box. After he did as she requested she sent him after Victor. Her voice faltered a few feet from the car, which broke her spell as she collapsed on the ground.

Christian had Anthony by the throat watching him fight for air. Intent on choking him to death he missed Anthony swiping his leg which released his hold Anthony sent shards of wood at Christian. Some of the wood found their target, but it didn't stop him. He kept coming at Anthony determined to kill him once and for all.

Lisa we have to destroy them or we will never be free, Sam informed her.

And how are we to do that with the boys in the way?

Take them out of the equation. Together we are quite powerful if we combine our powers.

How do you know this? going to Sam

I know through Christian's memories, making an effort to stand.

Both John and Christian were too busy with Anthony and Victor to notice the girls approach. One minute they were fighting and the next they were thrown from Anthony and Victor. Landing hard on the ground, some invisible force was holding them there. All they could do was watch the girls go to their enemies.

Nicholas go stop them, Christian bit out.

Just watch they will be fine, Confidence in his voice.

If they're not...

Watch!

Together their power's were very strong, but draining to hold John and Christian plus fight these two. Sam sent bolts of lightening towards their feet while Lisa brought up several tornados that formed around Anthony and Victor. Vines came through the ground in an attempt to hold them and rain came down in sheets to camouflage the scene.Sam started a binding spell to stop them from hurting anyone else. Lisa did a protection spell for them knowing if the binding spelling didn't work they would retaliate.

Your spells are weak darling, sending pain to Sam.

Trying to catch her breath from the pain. "Air and water hear my plea. Freeze these two and let them be."

"Sam stop!" Anthony commanded.

But she kept going. "Transport them to another place. Where we will no longer see their face."

Samantha remember that my blood runs not only in you, but the child's too.

"A place of ice and snow. Where no one would ever go." Walking over to Anthony she pulled him to her, *One last exchange,* sinking her teeth into his neck.

"What is she doing Nicholas?" Christian's anger growing at the inability to help her.

Be still brother, she is doing one last exchange so she can monitor him until his death.

Closing the pin pricks she licked his blood from her lips, but didn't move fast enough. His hand encircled her wrist pulling her to him, he took her blood to finish the exchange knowing she wasn't planning on it.

Trying to keep focus she finished the spell. "Keep them lost for a time." Ripping her wrist from his mouth, she jumped back. "Until they've learned to be kind." And with that Anthony and Victor disappeared.

Lisa released John and Christian as Nicholas picked up Sam bringing her to Christian. He sealed her wound, then checked her and the baby over briefly. "They will both be fine although the baby is frightened. Maybe mom could sing a calming melody. I think that would calm all our nerves." Nicholas smiled.

"I think you just want to hear that beautiful voice again." Christian held her closer.

"Christian, not so tight your squishing the baby."

"Sorry my love, I just never want to let you go again. That was way to close."

"Where did you send them?" Raphael inquired.

"Antarctica. They should stay frozen for at least a century, unless something happens." Lisa answered.

"Either way, I will know if he is near and Lisa, if they do get free before that, watch yourself. Victor took your blood and can find you anywhere now." Sam informed her.

"She will always be protected I'll make sure of that." John declared in front of all of them.

"Oh? And what are you proclaiming?" Christian innocently asked already knowing the answer.

Turning to Lisa, John handed her a black velvet box. She looked at him then at Sam who nodded for her to open it. When she did it revealed a necklace in the shape of a heart. Diamonds outlined the heart, the center was left open so a heart shaped ruby could dangle in the middle. Lisa's eyes welled up with tears at such a wonderful gift. "Lisa, I'm asking, in front of our friend's, will you stay by my side and be my bond mate?" Holding his breath for the answer.

"Yes, yes I'll be your bond mate. Whatever that is." Hugging him overjoyed with emotions.

"The perfect ending to a scary evening." Smiling at her sister, *Would you like me to explain the bonding to you?* Laying her head against Christian's chest.

"Sam don't interfere in their bonding." He whispered.

Tell me later without his possessive ass around. Lisa smiled.

She loved her sister so much, even when she was moody. Everyone went back inside for a bit. They split up for the remainder of the night afterwards. All the guys stayed at the mansion and the girls stayed at Sam and Lisa's. Oh yes, their dad was overjoyed with that one.

19

The guys only slept a few hours, especially Christian, who spent the rest of the night mentally talking to Sam. He couldn't wait to see her in her wedding dress. He was so nerves yet won't let anyone know it.

You can't hide it from me, Nicholas came walking into his room.

"Screw off." Going into the bathroom.

"Everything will be fine. Now hurry up I'm hungry and we still have to pick up Sam's wedding gift."

Christian came out of the closet in jeans and a tee shirt to find Nicholas holding Gabriel. "What the hell. That cat only let Sam hold him."

"Maybe if you were nicer to him." Putting him on the bed.

Christian ignored them both walking out of the room. "Did John make it home yet?"

"You mean he never came back last night?"

"No, he took Lisa somewhere special."

"Are they?"

"Yes, they are bonded now. Lisa is content with it and doesn't want a wedding."

"So I will have two honeymooner's, so to speak, staying at my hotel. I'll make sure they have a suite also. So where are we eating?"

"Not sure. Daniels and John were suppose to pick it." Heading for the living room.

❧

"Where is your sister?" Sam's mom questioned suspiciously.

"She left early this morning with grandma to make sure everything was ready for the wedding, they will meet us for brunch. We should leave now since our hair and nail appointment is in two hours." Hustling her out the door with the other girls.

Lisa and grandma were both at O'Malley's when they arrived, sitting in the back. Half way through their brunch Sam felt warmth. Looking up she saw Christian in the door way watching her. She would have gone to him, but was boxed in by her mom and grandma.

He walked over to her with the guys behind him. "Hello Beautiful."

"Hi babe. I'd kiss you, but I'm being held prisoner." *Lisa help me, I need to feed and mom and grandma don't know about the baby yet.*

After convincing her mom to allow the guys to eat with them, they all seemed excited about this evening. Christian took care of Sam and the baby. She didn't want to leave, but soon they would be together always. He walked her to the car. "I miss you."

"Me too." Holding on to him.

He bent down giving her a very sensual kiss. "I will see you later Mi Amour."

Sam smiled as he closed the door. She was so beside herself with happiness. Her wedding day was here and there was only five hours left. The baby decided to do gymnastics right than which sent pain through her.

"Are you alright?" Lisa asked with concern.

"She's gong to be a gymnast. I think my excitement is rubbing off on her." Answering as they pulled into the salon.

"Well calm her down or mom will find out before you guys tell everyone tonight."

"Are you telling mom about you and John?"

"Not yet. I will after you tell her about the baby."

"Your being a pain in the ass. Are you all packed?"

"Yes, are you?"

"Pretty much. We leave at three in the morning." Walking in with Lisa, *Are you ok?*

Yes, it was a strange experience, but I'll adjust.

I'm glad. Your handling this better than I did.

I know. Enough talk lets get ready, saying hi to the others inside.

Lucian found Christian pacing the room. "Nerves?"

"No, I'm waiting for John to get his ass back here with the bouteniers. Where the hell is he, its almost five?"

"I'm here just calm down, jeez." Handing Christian a boutiner, then Lucian.

"Its his wedding day he's just nerves." Raphael came waltzing in.

"I'm not nerves." Getting pissed.

Christian are you alright?

Yes beautiful. Are you almost ready?

Of course. I'll see you in a few, sending him a mental kiss.

"Okay guys just back off." Nicholas came through the door with Daniel. "She looks absolutely gorgeous Christian."

"That is not helping. I just want this over so I can be with her." Continuing his pacing.

"Hey its time for us to go up front." Mike announced. So they all went to the alter.

"Oh honey, you look so beautiful" Sam's mother cried.

"Mom stop crying or you'll ruin your make-up." Lisa handed her a tissue.

"Its time Sam." Mark popped his head in.

"You look beautiful, Sam." Ethan commented escorting her to her dad.

"Thank you." Smiling.

The music started as Lisa and John came down the aisle first. Followed by Shelby and Daniel, Lucian and Christian, and Raphael and Maria. Christian didn't pay much attention to anyone else once he saw Sam and her dad in the entrance way. Watching her walk down the aisle was breathtaking. She was breathtaking. There was a golden glow to her and it had nothing to do with the pregnancy.

As her dad put her hand in Christian's, he gave her a kiss. "I know you'll take care of her. I love you baby."

"I can't begin to describe how you look. Your breathtaking." Christian whispered.

"Thank you. You look extremely handsome yourself."

The ceremony was lovely. They said their vows, then Mike played *I Swear* as Sam and Christian lit the unity candle. Sam's mom cried during the whole thing. After signing the license, pictures were taken by the water as the sun was setting. Finally at the reception Sam and Christian announced the pregnancy, which caused her mom to start crying again. Their life together would always be new and exciting experience.